SOAR

Tiffany Noelle Chacon

WRITE HORSE
Publishing

Contents

For my Dad, who always cheered me on from the sidelines. If everyone had a dad like you, the world would be a better place.

OFF COURSE:

A Prequel Novella

Scan the QR code or go to the link below to download the FREE prequel novella for the Equestrian Dreams series.

tinyurl.com/offcoursebook

THE SOAR PLAYLIST:

Scan the QR code or go
to the link below to listen
to some of the songs
mentioned in the book.

http://tinyurl.com/
soartheplaylist

Glossary of Horse Terms

Broken line—two or more show jumping obstacles jumped in succession that are not in a straight line

Cavalettis—low, adjustable horizontal poles used in training to develop a horse's rhythm, balance, and coordination. They can be set at various heights and distances apart to challenge and improve the horse's jumping technique.

Colic—severe abdominal pain which can be life-threatening depending on the cause and severity. Colic is the number one killer of horses.

Clean—to jump over an obstacle without knocking it down. A "clean" round in a show jumping competition means that you completed the round without any faults.

Chip in—to add an extra stride or half-stride before going over an obstacle

Crossrail—a type of jump in which two poles are set in an "X" shape, with the center lower than the ends. It's often used as an introductory jump for young or inexperienced horses and riders to encourage straightness and centered jumping.

Fetlock—a part of a horse's leg, above and behind the hoof

Forelock—the top foremost part of a horse's mane, essentially its "bangs"

Gelding—a male horse that has been castrated/neutered

Girth—a piece of tack that goes under the horse's belly to keep the saddle in place

Grand Prix—the highest level of competition for show jumping, with obstacle heights of up to five foot three inches

Gymnastics—A series of obstacles set to improve the horse and rider's technique, rhythm, and flexibility. In show jumping, gymnastics are used to train horses to navigate courses with precision and agility.

Hack/flat—to exercise a horse without jumping them

In-and-out—two show jumping obstacles back-to-back with only one or two strides in between

Jump-off—the second, shorter round in a show jumping competition. The riders who went "clean" in the first round can advance to the jump off. The fastest, clean time wins the event.

Leg up—a technique used to help a rider mount a horse. Another person assists by cupping their hands to boost the rider's leg, enabling them to swing over into the saddle with ease.

Liverpool—a jump obstacle that includes a pool of water beneath the fence

Oxer—a show jumping obstacle made of two (or more) poles spread a distance from each other to give the jump width

Rollback—a tight turn from one jump to another

School—to exercise or warm up a horse

Stall—the place in a barn where a horse lives; an individual enclosure for the horse.

Standards—the part of a show jumping obstacle that holds the poles in place. Can be plain or decorative.

Tack—the equipment used to ride a horse. Consists of saddle, bridle, etc. Also a verb—"to tack up" means to put your tack or equipment on your horse.

Triple combination—three show jumping obstacles back-to-back-to-back with only one or two strides in between

Vertical—a show jumping obstacle with poles on top of one another to give it height without the spread or width

WEC—the World Equestrian Center, a premier equestrian venue. In this book, WEC refers to the location in Ocala, Florida.

WEF—the Winter Equestrian Festival, a series of horse shows from January to April in Wellington, Florida.

Bridle Buzz ✔ · Follow
Wellington, FL

293 likes

Bridle Buzz It's been a fabulous WEF season, my lovelies!! You'll want to check back in as we round into the Olympic season. Yes, you heard that right.
Oh, we know. The 2024 Olympics are almost two years away, but in the show world, we have to prove our mettle for way more than just one competition! Most other Olympic sports have clear-cut events that either qualify them or disqualify them from going to the Olympics. But not this one! We like to keep people on their toes - or rather, on their hooves!
Show jumpers who want to go to the Olympics will have to compete in many high level events in order to make the long list - that's a list of show jumpers who are being considered for the team - before they can be chosen. Olympic hopefuls will have to compete at a variety of locations (local and international) and five-star Grand Prix wins will be most heavily weighted. Who has what it takes?! Find updates here at Bridle Buzz. XOXO ... more

View all 12 comments

Parker Lowes I'm so confused about how people make it onto the Olympic team.
Jay Wyatt @Parker Lowes - you're not the only one. I think USEF *likes* to make it confusing...

Add a comment...

4 hours ago

1

It's a Wonderful Life

Mila

We're in this magical dance, between horse and rider. Communicating, but without words. It's a squeeze of a finger, the slight press of a heel—indiscernible to the average person. But to Cyrus and me, it's a world of meaning, as we canter around the arena, crossing the center of the ring and changing directions. With the tiniest of movements, I ask him for a flying lead change, and Cyrus obliges in the blink of an eye.

We fly around the ring, momentarily lifting off the ground, before returning back to earth.

We are magic. We are flight. We are glorious.

It's my day off, which means I'm in Wellington to ride my Grand Prix horse, Cyrus. We're training at Zen Elite, my show jumping barn, in the outdoor sand arena. I have a lesson with my trainer, Trina, and we're working on gymnastics. She's set up the Winkler gymnastics—a set of five jumps in a row. The first two jumps and the last two jumps are bounces—not even one stride in between—and the middle jump is a large oxer with only one stride before and after. The gymnastics require us to take off and land in quick succession. The exercise is meant to improve Cyrus's agility, to keep his front end engaged.

We canter around the turn, striding through the gymnastic. We bounce through the combination, Cyrus finding the rhythm easily. Our connection is a silent symphony, where each movement is a note played in perfect harmony.

"Nice, Mila," Trina calls out. "Keep the connection with his mouth, let him know you're there."

On the next round, Trina instructs, "Keep his pace. He thinks he can slack off now that he's done it before. Use your voice to keep him moving."

I click to Cyrus, pressing my calves just a touch into his side, regaining our momentum. "Very good," Trina encourages.

Each time we go around, Trina raises the middle oxer higher and higher until we're jumping heights as big as the standard itself. "Amazing. Great ride," Trina says when we wrap up. I let Cyrus have the reins, and he stretches out his long, dappled gray neck.

"I'm so proud of you, Mila." She pushes her sunglasses up, perching them on top of her blonde hair. "You've grown so much as a rider these past few years. I know you always hoped to be here. But now you're actually here. You've arrived, my friend." She gives me a rare, full smile. She's referring, of course, to my journey from terrified rider, after my sister's accident, when I was gripped by fear, to the confident Grand Prix rider that I am now. I shake my head. Sometimes I can hardly believe it. But when I look back at my journey—and my sister Anya's—I know everything happened exactly as it was supposed to. And Trina was such a pivotal part of my transformation. She believed in me when I couldn't even believe in myself. My transformation into a Grand Prix rider felt a bit like emerging from a chrysalis, where there was once doubt, now wings of confidence unfurled so I could soar.

"And you," Trina says, turning to my horse. "You're such a good boy, Cy Cy," Trina says in a sing-song voice, scratching Cyrus's neck. I laugh at Trina sweet-talking my horse—it's no secret that she prefers the company of our four-footed friends to, well, pretty much anything else. Normally, Trina's pretty tight-lipped with her praise, but not with Cyrus, or any other horse for that matter. But since Trina rides Cyrus a couple times a week, because I can't always get up to Wellington during the work week, they have a stronger bond than most. She's currently waxing poetic about how handsome and strong he is. My gelding snorts in response, as if he knows the praise he's due.

We both laugh, and I pat Cyrus's neck, sticky with sweat. Trina walks beside me as I cool down Cyrus, and we catch up, discussing the latest at The ViaTech Center for Equine-Assisted Therapy, the facility I opened with my sister, Anya, and my now-husband, Alex, a couple years ago. What began as a dream—in response to my sister's spinal cord injury and the depression that followed after she was paralyzed—has evolved into a massive enterprise. We now employ two full-time therapists, rotate through more than twenty volunteers weekly, and we're actively looking for a full-time barn manager to take care of our twenty horses. My sister's boyfriend, Luke, is our lead therapist, and once Alex gets through his licensure in May of next year, he'll be a therapist at the Center as well.

I tell her about how we've started working with a group of military veterans with PTSD and anxiety, and how amazing it is to get a front-row seat to see the way the horses help them re-build their trust and emotional resilience. The vets come in broken and emotionally wounded, and watching them recover a part of themselves has been incredible.

"Horses are better than people at pretty much everything, it's not surprising that they make better therapists than humans do," she says. "How's married life?"

I can't help the smile that breaks loose. I'm *married*. It's still surreal sometimes that for the past six months I've been able to call Alex my husband. We had a slightly non-traditional engagement—it was one-week long—so that we could keep Alex from getting deported. It worked, and he was granted residency. It'll be a long road to full citizenship, but the scary stuff is officially behind us. Thank God.

"Wonderful. Amazing." I sigh, knowing I sound like a dreamy teenager. "Alex is perfect." I glance down at Trina. "I want this for you too, Trina. One day...hopefully soon."

Trina scoffs, shoving her hands into the pockets of her riding pants.

"You deserve to be happy," I tell her.

"I am happy," she says quickly. Too quickly, I think. "I have Leo." Referring, of course, to her Grand Prix horse.

I lean down and run a hand down Cyrus's neck. "Don't tell Cy, but this isn't all there is, you know."

"Maybe for you," Trina says, with a touch of defensiveness. "But really, Mila, I'm good."

I nod, letting it go for now. But I know Trina. She keeps her heart of gold locked down with her sky-high walls, but one day, someone's going to discover just how amazing she is. And he'll obliterate those walls.

A couple hours later, I get home to the cozy two-bedroom house where Alex and I live on the grounds of the Center. We affectionately refer to the house as the Cottage, and the carriage lights and flower boxes overflowing with marigolds that Alex planted still bring a smile to my face.

Alex is still at his internship—he's almost done with his hours to become a fully licensed therapist—so I shower and pour myself a bowl of cereal, scrolling through the Center's Instagram feed. A few years ago, before Anya's accident, I did quite a bit of work on Instagram—horse-related companies sent me products that I would review or promote—so I was the natural choice for running the Center's social media accounts, in addition to functioning as the Center's business manager. I'm doing a series right now where I'm highlighting the various horses in the barn, sharing their quirks and backgrounds.

I upload a picture of Rainbow—a gray mare with a white mane that we've dyed the colors of the—you guessed it—rainbow. We originally did it because we thought it'd be a hit with our younger clientele, which it certainly is, but the biggest reactions we get are from the over-sixty crew. They are *quite* enthusiastic about Rainbow's dye job.

I hear the door and Alex comes into the Cottage, slipping off his shoes at the front door and padding into the kitchen in his socked feet. I cringe when I realize that I walked all the way to the bedroom with my dirty boots on, without a second thought about it. Oh well, the Roomba will get the dirt. My grandma's wedding gift to us has definitely proved its usefulness.

Alex bends down to kiss me, his day-old scruff tickling my cheek. I still get butterflies when I see him, with his lanky yet muscular frame and dark hair and eyes, which perfectly offset his olive skin. "Hello, Mila Kozak."

"Uh uh."

"Dang it," he says, bumping his forehead gently against mine. "I did it again."

"I'll give you another chance." I smile up at him, his dark eyes dancing.

"Good evening, *Mrs. Caballero.*"

I stand up on tiptoe and wrap my arms around his neck. "Hello, husband." His lips meet mine and I realize I've missed him, and it's only been a few hours since we parted ways this morning. How does that happen? How do you become so knitted together with someone that you can barely stand to be away from them for *hours*? I shudder when I think about the fact that I could've been separated from him for much longer if we hadn't gotten married and he'd been deported.

"You've showered," he says, a little sadly. "That's too bad."

"I was so gross, it's ridiculously hot today." I lean back onto my heels, then catch the look in Alex's eyes. "Oh." His hands go to my waist, his thumb brushing just underneath the hem of my shirt. "Well, I was just thinking I could *totally* use another shower."

Alex laughs and then surprises me by sweeping me up into his arms. I squeal as I hold tight to his neck, laughter bubbling up from the deepest part of me. He nuzzles my cheek, breathing me in as he holds me against his chest. "I missed you, wife."

"You were only gone for five hours," I tell him, even though I was just thinking the same thing.

"It was about four hours and fifty-five minutes too long," he says with a perfect-for-me smile.

"It's a good thing we don't have any plans the rest of the night."

"Oh, I have plans," he says coyly as he marches me toward the shower, both of us laughing as I hold on to my husband and thank my lucky stars he's mine.

After we shower, Alex is putting away laundry while I start a new load. "How do you even fold these?" Alex asks, holding up a tank top of mine. "It's like this was made for a doll and not a real human being. Does this even fit you?" He marches over to the washing machine in the hallway and holds up the tank top to my torso. "I don't understand this."

"It stretches, look." I grab the tank top, showing how it stretches to fit me. "But I don't usually fold them, I just throw them in a drawer."

Alex gives me a horrified look—he's the quintessential neat freak who has a very specific way of folding all of his clothes. He doesn't even throw his boxers into a drawer—they're all rolled carefully in a line in a little container in his drawer.

"Trust me, Alex. You do not need to waste your time in folding these."

His lips bunch thoughtfully, like he is not at all convinced of what I'm saying. He heads back to the room, and I'm fully prepared for my tank tops to be color coordinated and folded carefully in their own part of my drawer when I come back to the room.

When we're done with the laundry, Alex asks, "Did you eat already?"

I head to the couch, flopping onto it with a sigh. "I had a bowl of cereal."

He stares at me as if cereal doesn't constitute a meal—a point on which we differ.

"Hey, I have an idea," he says. "What if we pick a couple nights of the week where we each cook? We don't have to cook every night, we can scrounge up sandwiches or *cereal*," he says it with mock contempt. "But we could get into the practice of making dinner here, together even. Or we could take turns? What do you think?"

"Yeah, I like that." I especially like the part where *Alex* might be cooking more regularly—he's a very good cook. Me, not so much. But what are TikTok and YouTube for other than to help me become a Master Chef, right?

We chat through our schedule for the rest of the week, and decide that Mondays will be Mila Mondays, where I cook something, Wednesdays will be for Alex to cook, and Saturdays we'll cook together. Thursdays we typically have dinner with his mom, and Fridays will be for date night. Tuesdays and Sundays we'll scrounge or eat leftovers. Or, in my case, cereal.

The food plan has left me hungry again, so I eat some toast while Alex reheats some leftovers and we settle in to watch a show. I doze off at the end and wake up to Alex picking me off the couch to carry me to bed. As my head hits the pillow, I think, *What a wonderful life.*

2

Miss Independent

Trina

For the first time in my adult life, I am in control of my destiny. There are no boyfriends holding me back or dictating my every move. And the mourning period for those guys is long over—I'm a free and independent woman. Heck, Kelly Clarkson could've written that Miss Independent song about *me*. But, wait, doesn't she fall in love and lose her independence in that song? I shake my head. It's not a very aptly named song, then, is it? I suppose I'm the "before" picture of that song—and that's exactly where I want to stay.

I've got an incredible job at Zen Elite teaching riding students. I've got my beloved Chevy Silverado, which only took me a decade to be able to afford. And, the cherry on top of the ice cream sundae that is my life, I finally—*finally*—have another Grand Prix horse to ride.

This is no small matter. Since my first Grand Prix horse, Blue Thunder, took me to the top of the show jumping circuit, I haven't been able to find another like him. That's not to say I haven't tried—oh, I've tried—but disaster always ensues when I try too hard. I learned that lesson the hard way.

My most recent disaster ended when my bank account bottomed out. Since my riding instructor budget couldn't handle a full-fledged Grand Prix horse on its own, I decided to take matters into my own hands. I purchased a young horse from Argentina—an Argentinian Thoroughbred mixed with Dutch Warmblood. He had a powerful, broad back and legs for days. He was smart, motivated, and energetic. The horse could jump a mile high and gallop at top speeds for hours. He was incredible—my dream horse. That is, until he was transported to the States.

It's not uncommon for horses to get sick during transport. In fact, out of 100 horses transported commercially, eleven percent of them will contract pneumonia. Want to guess whose horse landed in that eleven percent statistic? That's right. This girl's.

Pneumonia's not a death sentence by any means. But Onyx—that's what I named my Argentina dreamboat—developed complications. And those complications led to scar tissue in his lungs. Which led to coughing fits every time he got above a trot. Which led to bleeding lungs. Yeah, not ideal for an athlete.

So I did what any self-respecting horse woman would do: I spent every dime I had on trying to get Onyx well.

Did it work?

No.

Onyx is now a full-time pasture horse out in Okeechobee. *C'est la vie*, am I right?

I had all but given up. Resigned myself that I would have to be content to watch my students ride in Grand Prixs but not ever be able to afford it myself. Until Caterina came into my life. She's one of my student's moms—a bona fide horse person herself, though she's a dressage rider and not a show jumper. She obviously thinks I'm crazy—as all dressage people seem to think of show jumpers—but her daughter has the need for speed and height like I do, so I've taken her under my wing. Apparently Caterina has more money than Oprah and likes to live her life like it's her own personal Christmas special. *Heeeeerrrrre's a horse for you! And you! And you!*

I happened to be in the way when she was feeling particularly benevolent one day and am now a (very) partial owner of a gloriously gorgeous Grand Prix horse, Leonidas. She paid full price for my bundle of joy, which means she's out a quarter million dollars and, as long as good ole Leo stays healthy, I'm set for the next few years of top-level competition.

Oh, and did I mention that the summer Olympics are coming up in less than two years? I've got as good a chance as anyone to make that team with Leo on my side and Caterina funding the whole shebang. Five-star competitions, here we come.

To say that I love Leo is like saying the sun is a star—it's totally true, but it just doesn't do it justice. I remember hearing one time about maternal-fetal microchimerism—where a baby's cells enter a mother's body and stay there. If some part of the mother's body is damaged, the fetal cells will rush to help it heal. I'm not going to lie, when I heard about that, I teared up. Not because I ever want to be a mom, but because this is what being a horse rider feels like to me. That this horse is becoming part of me, and he's healing me from the inside out. All by being a part of my life. That's what Leo means to me.

For the first time in forever, I'm letting myself *hope*. And I know, I know. Hope is a dangerous thing. But I'm jumping feetfirst into an Olympic-sized pool of it, manifesting the heck out of my Olympic dream.

So even when my feet are about to fall off after walking twenty thousand steps from a zillion lessons at Zen Elite, I ride. I train. I skip the cake pop at Starbucks and opt for a green smoothie at home. I take ice baths and gulp down supplements that are bigger than any horse pills I've ever seen. I ignore the ache in my knees that tell me I'm not a spring chicken anymore. Since when did being in your thirties mean you weren't young anymore? But bones don't lie. And mine *hurt*.

Lately, I've decided to take a note from racetrack riders and show up to ride Leo in the predawn hours. Today when I show up to the barn, I'm greeted by Leo's low rumble as he pricks his ears at me. He hasn't eaten breakfast yet, so I bring a bag of carrots—organic, of course—and offer him a handful while I tack him up.

I bring my Bluetooth speaker out to the grass arena and play music from my favorite playlist while I ride. Sure, I could use headphones—but then Leo wouldn't get to enjoy it too. We start with Straylight Run's "Existentialism on Prom Night," one of my absolute favorite songs. I really do believe there are moments when the world revolves around us, like the song suggests. In this moment, there is nothing else but me and Leo, Leo and me, keeping this delicate balance of turning the whole world with each hoof step. As we trot figure eights and leg yield from one side of the arena to the other, the song crescendos. Lead singer John Nolan is singing his heart out, raw and unhindered in a way I want to be. In my mind, I change the lyrics slightly: Ride like you think no one's watching.

So I do. I ride my heart out, each stride connecting me and Leo more and more.

I've just finished my third lesson of the day and I'm walking into the barn when someone pulls up in a red Maserati. I internally groan—hoping it's not one of my student's dads coming to complain about how calloused their hands are or some other trifling issue. I scan my brain to think if any of my students have fallen off recently, and can't think of anyone in recent weeks, but you never know. For whatever reason, moms seem to "get it"—they understand the horse obsession, the hard work and the sacrifice it takes in this sport. But dads...dads are difficult. Especially the rich ones. As a rule, I make a point to stay away from guys—been there, done that, don't want the t-shirt thank you very much. So when a man gets out of the Maserati looking too put together for the barn—with his perfect pompadour and thousand-dollar sunglasses—I hide in the feed room between lessons.

I'm measuring out tonight's feed—only four hours too early—when one of my student workers, Ellie, finds me and closes the door behind her.

"Trina? There's some GQ guy looking for you." I laugh at Ellie's assessment. There's a reason I hired her—she's a hard worker, horse obsessed, and tells it like it is.

"You can tell him I'm busy," I say, not looking up from measuring the super expensive Platinum Performance GI into Leo's feed bucket. "You could give him my number if he insists."

"Oh, okay—"

"I can wait," a male voice calls from the other side of the feed room door. I release the scoop into the supplement tub and glance up at the ceiling. Why, God, *why*? I take a deep breath, trying to summon all of my patience for whatever Mr. GQ wants from me. No one shows up in a Maserati if they don't expect something from someone. And that someone is usually me.

I wipe my hands on my riding pants—my favorite pair of Ariat's TriFactor breeches with their cooling technology, perfect for Florida—and open the door.

Of course Mr. GQ takes off his sunglasses to reveal pale gray eyes that could slice through your heart, if you let them. He's clean shaven, not a hair out of place, with light-colored slacks that don't have a single wrinkle in them. His shoes look vaguely expensive in that 'I'm-not-trying-too-hard' kind of way that still costs hundreds of dollars. I've never been very impressed with civilian clothes—but show up in a pair of Tucci boots, and I'm here for it. That being said, Mr. GQ is rocking this look. He's lithe and lean, channeling British soccer player vibes—without the accent. More's the pity. At the first flutter of attraction, I think of Jess from New Girl: *Shut it down.*

"Yes?" I say, exuding a bit of annoyance to cover up the fact that I'd stared far too long at this guy. Ellie must sense the tension radiating off of me because she scurries out of the feed room and back into the barn breezeway, disappearing into one of the stalls where I'm sure she's listening.

"Miss Powers? I'm Grayson. Grayson J. Sterling," he says, as if I should know who he is, and then he extends his hand. I take it, still waiting for him to make clear why he's here. Grayson J. Sterling? Sounds like a lawyer. I notice a stack of papers in his other hand. Am

I being sued? "You don't know who I am, do you?" he asks, his mouth tilting into a smile that threatens to wedge into my heart like a dart, but I swat that thing away before it gets too close. *Shut it down*, I remind myself.

Guys like this were one of many reasons why I dropped out of high school. Rich, too handsome for their own good, and super smart—they'd mock me mercilessly for my difficulties in school because of my dyslexia. If I can help it, I usually don't get within a ten-mile radius of people like Grayson J. Sterling.

I stand on the lip of the feed room door, pressing an arm against the door jamb in a way that I hope looks like a power pose. Even with the added height of the feed room, I'm still a little shorter than Grayson—we're barely eye level. It's not that he's particularly tall, it's more than I'm particularly short.

"Am I supposed to?"

"I thought Cate would've told you..." He spreads his hands apologetically, the papers in his other hand fluttering with the motion.

My mind is racing, thinking, *Cate, Cate, Cate*, but I'm coming up short. "Cate who?"

"Caterina," he clarifies. "Our daughter, DeDe, takes lessons here?"

"Did something happen?" I know Leo is fine, I just rode him this morning, so that means this must be about DeDe, which makes my stomach coil in fear. I don't get attached to a lot of my students, but DeDe worked her way into my heart like few can. Her parents strapped her with the name Demetria—far too cumbersome of a name for an unsuspecting infant if you ask me—but everyone calls her DeDe for short.

"Well, yes. Caterina and I have divorced." He says the word like he's still getting used to it.

Why Caterina would feel like she has to inform me of her personal life, I have no idea. We're business partners, not buddies. And I haven't exactly positioned myself as a beacon screaming, *Come tell me all your problems!* It's just not my style. I realize Mr. GQ—I mean, Grayson—is waiting for me to say something. Should I say 'I'm sorry'? Instead, not wanting to invite more discussion since I clearly don't trust myself with this man, I just say, "Okay."

He's still staring at me, waiting for *something*, I'm not sure what, and I'm losing my already-thin patience—and resolve. "I'm late for a lesson," I tell him, looking down at my Rolex, a token from a Grand Prix win with Blue Thunder. I walk past him, unfortunately too close because I catch a whiff of his scent—warm and spicy, drawing me in when I really should be running away.

Before I can lose my mind, Mr. GQ opens his too-perfect mouth and says the worst words I can imagine, "I'm here to tell you," he hesitates, his hand going to his neck, rubbing for a moment before continuing, "After the divorce—Leonidas is mine now."

3

(S)He Will Be Mine

Trina

"Excuse me?" My voice sounds shrill, even to my ears, but this is about as zen as it gets right now. Grayson's words resound in my head like a clanging cymbal, *Leonidas is mine now. Mine now. Mine. Now.*

"I wanted to discuss the future of Leonidas's career—"

"Wait a second," I say, holding up my hand. My mind trips momentarily on his phrasing of 'Leonidas's career'—I'm conveniently missing from that phrase. "Are you telling me that you 'won' Leo in some sort of twisted custody battle between you and Caterina? And no one thought to inform me of this?"

"I'm sorry Cate failed to mention this to you." He seems almost apologetic, but quickly moves on, holding out the paperwork he's holding. "I've done an analysis on Leonidas's performance over the past year since Caterina purchased him, and it seems he's vastly underperforming."

I take the papers and give them a cursory glance. There's a table with wins and losses—as if Leonidas were a race car instead of a living, breathing being. I don't find my name anywhere on the papers.

My hands start to shake. *What if this man is here to take Leo away from me?*

The papers fall from my hands, fluttering to the barn floor, splaying out between Grayson and me. I want to run away, to grab Leo and never see this Grayson guy ever again. Instead, I swallow the dread trying to claw its way out of my chest. "Sorry," I mumble as I step out of the feed room door, squatting to pick them up. I take a deep breath, attempting to steady myself.

Grayson crouches, picking up the papers alongside me. I glance at each page, but the words blur before me, the anxiety only making my dyslexia worse. "Here," I say, handing the papers back to Grayson as we stand.

"Those are for you," he says. "When can we discuss these figures? I have a plan for optimizing performance."

I gape at him, feeling like a dog he just kicked. I try to remind myself that he's in *my* realm—this is my kingdom, and he's the intruder—no matter how he's making me feel right now. I take another deep breath and square my shoulders. "I have students waiting for a lesson right now. Why don't you email me to set up an appointment?" I fish a business card out of my phone case and hand it to him, wishing the card was far more crisp than the dingy one that's been in my wallet for a year. "I will warn you that my schedule is packed and the best times are usually before seven AM"

He gives a singular nod. "Tomorrow, then? Six AM?"

"Sure."

"No time to waste," he says, placing my card carefully into his wallet—I bet he doesn't have even a stray receipt in there. "If we want Leonidas to compete in the Games."

"Indeed," I say because it sounds like something one should say to the likes of Mr. GQ with his performance charts. "See you then."

I turn on my heel and stalk down the barn breezeway, flush with heat and anger. How in the world did *I* get caught in a custody battle? With the likes of Mr. GQ himself as the "winner"? I shudder to think what kind of lawyer Grayson J. Sterling could afford. Probably someone who drinks the blood of opposing counsel for breakfast.

I don't know this guy from Adam, and I suppose it's possible he's actually a nice guy. A nice guy who divorced his wife and took her prize Grand Prix horse from her.

What in the name of Linkin Park just happened?

Ugh.

There's no way this guy is a nice guy. And now I'm business partners with him? With only ten percent equity in Leo, it's a stretch to even call it a partnership. I hurry out of the barn, trying to get as far from Grayson J. Sterling as possible before the tears come.

After all of my lessons are done, the horses are fed, and everyone's cleared out, I find myself in Leo's stall, running my hands over his legs. I do this obsessively, checking for any swelling or heat, but today my inspection is extra thorough. It's almost like every press of my hands on his body is declaring him as mine.

Mine, mine, mine.

Hands trickling down his hocks, over his cannon bone, then gently pressing into his tendons at the back of his leg. I run a thumb over his fetlock and pastern, feeling the comforting firmness of his skin and bone, healthy muscles, no swelling.

Relief rocks through me, even as panic hides underneath the swells of comfort. He's healthy, but he's not completely mine. And even though he's no less mine than he was this morning, he feels twice as far from being totally mine.

My connection with Leo is the anchor in my storm-tossed life, grounding me when waves of uncertainty threaten to sweep me away. But now that my anchor is being threatened, I don't know what will hold me together if I lose him.

Once I'm content that he doesn't have an ounce of swelling in his entire body, I slump into the shavings at the corner of his stall, watching him nibble his hay. His lips lazily pluck at the strands of alfalfa, an extra-rich and nutrient-dense hay. I try to give Leo the best of the best, and Caterina has made that possible. I wonder if her husband—*ex*-husband—will have the same priorities.

I try calling Caterina, but the call goes to voicemail. I'm sure she's been preoccupied with her divorce, but this whole thing with Grayson has me feeling like I am galloping towards a jump, and someone ripped the horse out from under me—I'm in free fall, unsure of where I'll land.

Caterina was relatively hands-off with Leo's maintenance, which made our partnership thus far very easy for me. But the idea of sharing a horse with someone terrifies me, especially after what happened the last time...

I shake my head, trying to rid myself of thoughts of Victor and Blue Thunder. An ache in my chest forms, and I attempt to rub it away with the heel of my palm. I've tried to replace the throb of those losses with emptiness, bitterness even, but every once in a while I remember. I remember how good it was for so long—how Victor and I made such an incredible team. How glorious it was when Blue and I rose to the top of the Grand Prix circuit in Wellington. How much hope, love, and sheer thrills there were.

Until there wasn't.

Horses have always been my safe place—the answers to all the questions I didn't even know how to ask. My life was heading down the drain at fifteen years old, a sad dyslexic girl who could barely read and who was failing out of school. It wasn't until I stumbled on a barn near us that I discovered I had worth. Here. At the barn, I am a whole person—the only place in the world I've ever felt that.

Of course, Victor made me believe I was whole with him, but that ended up being an illusion.

No, this right here, this horse sturdy and steadfast in front of me, is the only real assurance I have in this life. And I won't let Grayson J. Sterling take it away from me.

I sit in Leo's stall until it grows dark. The bay gelding nuzzles me curiously then returns to shifting through the shavings for more hay. I finally get up, joints creaking as I stand.

"G'night, Leo," I say, wanting so badly to say *My Leo*, but I don't. I can't get my hopes up again. It's too dangerous.

4

Burn, Burn

Trina

As I drive to my apartment that night, I call my brother Tripp. I know, I know. It's *so* adorable that we're Tripp and Trina. In actuality, my brother's name is Charles James III, but we've always called him Tripp. Despite the similarities in our names, we could not be more different. And yet we're still close.

"How's it going broski?"

In the background, children are screaming, a dog is barking, and Tripp is speaking to someone other than me. He's saying something about 'not lighting your sister on fire.' Y'know, trivial things.

I bite my lip, almost regretting the call. Here I thought I'd unload on my brother—but he's got his own set of issues. Plus, it's not like he can buy Leo from Grayson.

"Hey sis," he sighs into the phone. "I swear, it's less stressful at work than it is here." Which is saying a lot because Tripp is a trauma surgeon.

Yeah, I know, I *really* got the brains of the family.

"Well, your patients aren't exactly talking back to you or lighting people on fire," I say.

"Thank God for that," he says with a caustic laugh. "Let me just step outside, hold on." As Tripp steps into his backyard, the chaotic background noise falls away. "Much better. So, how's my favorite retsis?" he asks, calling me by his nickname for me. Tripp started calling me 'sister' spelled backward when I first started writing words backward in grade school. It wasn't until years later that we found out I had dyslexia—and Tripp was the one who pieced it together. Our parents were far too busy to make the connection themselves, and I slipped under my teachers' radars in packed public school classes. For a long time, retsis was his secret nickname for me, and even after the dyslexia diagnosis, it stuck around.

I sigh, debating what to even tell him. "I found out that Leo's owner got divorced, and her sleazebag husband now owns him."

"Ouch. Sorry, that sucks."

I tell him all about Grayson's performance charts—which I combed through in the privacy of my office when I had plenty of time to decode the tiny font. By the time I get to the end of my tirade, I've pulled into my apartment complex. I park, leaning my head against the steering wheel, sighing. "I just wish I could buy Leo straight up."

There's a silence on the other line, until Tripp says, "I wish I could help." His words are tight, like they hurt as they come out of him.

"Oh, Tripp, I know. I'm not asking anything—"

"I know."

"I'm just telling you what's going on."

"Sorry, I'm not trying to make it about me—"

"You're not, you're totally not. Anyway, it's going to work out," I say, not at all believing it. "Tell me what's going on with you."

Tripp goes on to detail a horrific surgery he performed yesterday that involved a guy's arm that got caught in his tree stump grinder. Unlike Tripp's wife, Rosalie, I can stomach the gore that Tripp has to go through on a regular basis, so he often vents to me.

By the time I force my tired body out of my truck and into my apartment, Tripp's kids are apparently about to burn down the house, so we say our goodbyes and I go inside. I eat my dinner by myself, listening to one of my favorite horsey podcasts, *Adulting with Horses*. But today I'm too distracted to pay much attention as I try not to think about the sad state of my life—and Tripp's.

Growing up, both of our parents worked at least two jobs each to make ends meet. We weren't ever poor per se, but our parents made just enough money for Tripp to not be eligible for any kind of free money for college, while simultaneously not being able to receive any support from our parents. When Tripp didn't get into medical school his first go-around, he went back to graduate school for a master's degree in biology, then reapplied. He met his wife in grad school, who went on to get her PhD (in *poetry*) at an insanely expensive private school. Between the two of them, they managed to rack up close to a million dollars in debt by the time Tripp was a practicing doctor.

Yes, it's as ridiculous as it sounds.

Sure, he makes a crap-ton of money now, but between their McMansion payments and Rosalie's Tesla, the kids' private school tuitions and the mounting credit card debt from Rosalie's shopping addiction, it's not looking super promising that he'll be in the black anytime soon. I learned the hard way to never bring up Rosalie needing help with her outrageous spending habits. They won't even confront the addiction. I hate seeing Tripp so burdened, but he's relentlessly defensive of his wife. Needless to say, I don't visit very often, though we do talk on the phone a few times a week.

I'd be lying if I said watching my brother and his wife's difficulties didn't contribute to my own feelings about marriage and relationships. The ball and chain analogy has never felt truer than when I look at Tripp and Rosalie. And then given my own experiences with men...yeah, no thanks.

5

Perfect Illusion

Mila

Being the only married couple in your friend group has some downsides to it, not the least of which is there's no one to get advice from. Sure, I could talk to my mom. Or even Mrs. Caballero. But that feels a little too close to home. Literally.

So I do what any self-respecting Gen-Z wife would do: I go to the Internet. I search for recipes, cleaning hacks, bedroom tips, and all the things I would've never imagined I needed to work on. Now my Instagram feed is flooded with these perfectly made-up women with utterly clean houses and healthy, delicious dinners made with vegetables grown in their backyards—all done without a hair out of place.

In the back of my mind, I'm perfectly aware of the realities behind these posts. So I know that the rest of their house might be a mess, but they just cleaned the areas where they were shooting. Or the meal might look amazing, but it tastes terrible. No one can be picture-perfect all the time. But the more I scroll, the more inadequate I feel.

How can they possibly get all of this done in one day? Do they wake up at four in the morning to do their hair and makeup? I just can't possibly keep up with that. I think this over and over again as I save recipes, pin cleaning hacks, and plan Instagram-worthy dates. After just fifteen minutes of scrolling, I'm more exhausted than if I rode in a Grand Prix.

Add to the fact that Alex is a seriously Instagrammable husband. Forget #ManCrush-Monday—this guy crushes EVERY DAY. His meals are delicious, he never lets a dish sit in the sink, and after a full workday he still has the energy to scrub the shower until it gleams. I mean, way to make me look bad, *husband*. I want to tell him to take it down a notch—or five—but I'm also benefiting greatly from his crushability. Crushingness? Crushament?

Ugh, whatever.

One of my favorite things about the Center is talking to the parents of our adolescent clients. It's inspiring and encouraging to see progress in the kids themselves, but it's the parents who come in here with a heavy burden—weighed down by their child's disability, or depression, or whatever diagnosis brought them here. Unfortunately, equine therapy is usually a last resort for a lot of people instead of a first line of defense, so by the time our clients get here, they're at the end of their rope.

Watching the life return to parents' eyes when they see their children beating depression and anxiety, or learning new skills, or simply being accepted for who they are, it's amazing.

I'm standing at a turnout paddock with one of our client's moms, Gaelissa, as we watch her daughter, Nevaeh, interacting with Rainbow. Nevaeh is on the spectrum, and her parents brought her because she showed interest in horses—and basically nothing else—but they didn't expect the benefits their daughter would receive from equine-assisted therapy. "She's like a completely different person," Gaelissa tells me, flipping her dark braids behind her shoulder. The tiny golden hair cuffs wrapped around some of her braids glint in the sun. "She's talking more, having less tantrums. I keep holding my breath, waiting for those behaviors to come roaring back to life, but they haven't yet."

Nevaeh, who's wearing a bright pink shirt turned inside out so that the seams aren't rubbing against her skin, reaches out to her mom, asking for a treat for Rainbow. "Use your words, sweetheart."

"Treat?" Neveah says, her word clear and vibrant. Gaelissa smiles, tears in her eyes, as she hands her daughter a horse treat.

I give her instructions on how to feed Rainbow—flat palm, steady hand. Neveah shrieks with delight as Rainbow gobbles the treat from her hand. Rainbow responds by nibbling at Neveah's hair. Neveah giggles, swatting Rainbow away. The mare lifts her head, snorting into the air, before returning to Neveah's hand for more treats.

"I just wish more parents knew about this," Gaelissa says as she runs her fingers through Rainbow's colorful mane. "There's so many other people like me at their wit's end, you know?"

"You have friends with kids on the spectrum?"

"Well, I wouldn't necessarily call us friends, but I have acquaintances with kids on the spectrum. Honestly, we're all just too overwhelmed with our own situations to be real friends to each other."

I turn toward Gaelissa, leaning my shoulder against the white paddock fence. "What if we had a support group? Here at the Center? Time for the parents to meet with one of our therapists while we work with the kids with the horses?"

Gaelissa's eyes light up. "That sounds amazing."

"If I set it up, will you spread the word?"

Gaelissa nods as she hands her daughter another treat, which Neveah promptly stuffs up Rainbow's nose. We quickly take it out, but not fast enough to keep the mare from sneezing—right in Neveah's face. Luckily, Neveah thinks this is a funny game instead of being totally grossed out by the horse snot that's now covering her shirt.

The next afternoon, I'm in my office. Anya, Alex, and I share office space—Alex's desk is in the far corner, with my desk and Anya's connected back-to-back, much to my sister's chagrin. Between the three of us, I'm by far the messiest. I've got used Starbucks cups and papers scattered across my desk, multiple (very full) desk organizers crowd the desktop along with several framed pictures, one of the walkie-talkies we use to communicate around the Center, and various little tchotchkes. My laptop barely fits between all of the clutter. Anya is constantly pushing my stuff back so it doesn't cross the line onto her desk. She has two framed pictures—one that I gave her and one that Luke gave her—along with a fancy mug warmer and a cute paper tray. Alex's desk is immaculate, without so much as a speck of dust on its surface.

Today, I'm alone in the office while Anya and Alex are meeting with clients and getting lunch. I'm emailing with a reporter at the Sun Sentinel that wants to do a piece about the Center. When I'm done setting up an interview time, I get an email from Alex with a link to an article titled '21 Ways to Be a Perfect Wife.' The body of the email says, "I saw this and thought this was cute and funny." I open the article, skimming through it. It starts out simple enough, but the more I scroll, the more overwhelmed I get.

1. Make the bed every morning.

2. Greet him with a kiss.

3. Make him delicious, nutritious meals that he loves.

4. Keep a tidy, clean home that smells amazing.

And so on. I can't even make it to the end of the article—number seven ("Keep track of appointments, important dates, and other household maintenance items") makes me throw my hands up in the air. "Guess I'll never be a perfect wife," I mutter. I can barely keep track of my own important dates—and that's with a shared Google calendar between me, Alex, and Anya who both remind me of things like doctor's appointments or oil changes.

I look back at Alex's email. *Thought this was funny*, he'd said. What is funny about this? Maybe he thinks it's funny because I could not be farther from a 'perfect wife.' More like 'ha-ha, funny-not-funny' kind of humor.

I'm still steaming about it when Alex comes back into the office thirty minutes later with lunch. I ask him, "What's with the article you sent me?"

"Oh you saw that? I thought it was funny."

"Why? Because I'm a terrible wife?" I inject some halfhearted humor into my voice, but it still sounds bitter.

Alex frowns at me. "No, because you're the best wife."

I gape at him, wondering how he could possibly think an article consisting of things like 'dress up regularly' and 'keep him guessing in the bedroom' could possibly be related to Alex saying I'm the best wife.

Alex, being the literal perfect husband, senses that his joke has not landed with me. He swoops in and pulls me into his arms. "Aww, Mila, c'mon, it wasn't serious. It was just the en—"

"Loose horse," Anya's voice crackles over our walkie-talkies. "Mila, Alex, anyone...All hands on deck."

Alex presses a kiss to my forehead, and we quickly exit the office, all talk of the 'funny' article forgotten.

Momentarily.

6

Control

Trina

I'm on my way to the barn at five fifteen the next morning. My head feels fuzzy, like I'm walking underwater—sleep was elusive last night, with bizarre dreams about Victor and Grayson swapping faces. The black tea I guzzled this morning hasn't kicked in yet and I drive to the barn on autopilot.

Despite my zombie status this morning, I don't mind being here so early—the barn in the early morning is so peaceful. Horses living uninterrupted by human interaction, dozing quietly. There's a smattering of stamping hooves and snorting horses, the sweet ambient noises of barn life. The quiet settles into my chest so that I feel slightly more calm for my meeting with Grayson.

There's a coolness to the early morning November air that hints of nicer days to come. In most parts of the country, it's firmly autumn weather, but in Florida, we're still stuck in summer, usually until Thanksgiving rolls around.

As I flat Leo, the dewy morning drapes us in a thin layer of moisture. We ride to a playlist of Motion City Soundtrack and Taking Back Sunday. I let myself forget, momentarily, about Grayson J. Sterling and his stack of condemning papers.

Once Leo's cooled down and back in his stall, I head to the feed room. The earthy scent of hay and the fragrant smell of molasses from the sweet feed fill the room. I measure out the horses' feed, the cascade of grain into the buckets is met with soft nickers from the horses. The sounds fill my aching heart, and I imagine it's what a mom might feel when her baby giggles.

By the time Grayson pulls up a half hour later, I'm considerably more zen. But the moment he climbs out of his Maserati, anxiety swaps places with the fleeting peace. The man looks like he just walked out of a photo shoot for *Modern Luxury Palm Beach* with his tailored button down and slacks, the sleeves rolled up his tanned forearms. His dress shoes are a deep burgundy, paired with a matching leather wristband for his Cartier watch. His Tom Ford glasses are folded at the deep V of his button down.

Good grief, *who is this guy?* I glance down at my worn riding pants, faded polo shirt, and scuffed boots. I'm hearkened back to my high school days, where I frequently missed fashion memos everyone else seemed to be privy to.

I take a deep breath, reminding myself that my horse doesn't care about what I'm wearing. That's all that matters.

"Mr. Sterling," I say, nodding in greeting. He walks straight through the little mud puddles dotting the ground, and I grimace thinking about his fancy leather shoes. But he doesn't seem to care—probably because he's so rich he can just throw those shoes out without batting an eye.

Grayson starts talking before we're even seated in my office, which is really just a not-so-glorified tack room. My desk is on one side of the room, and the other side is overflow storage for various tack and equipment. When I first started working here, I hung some pictures on the wall, but they're dingy and faded now. I've never really been bothered by it...until this moment.

"I assume you've had a chance to look over the performance charts and my recommendations?"

I nod, already feeling triggered by this man's commanding demeanor.

"I've already taken the liberty of registering Leonidas for the Saut Hermès in France, the CHIO in Aachen in July and the Longines in Rome—"

I hold out a hand. "Mr. Sterling, with all due respect, those are decisions we should discuss together—"

He blinks at me, almost confused. "We are discussing them. Right now."

"*Before* you register. Making international flights with a horse is not as simple as hopping in first class. There's risk of illness or injury." I try to swallow down my images of my Argentinian dreamboat—head hung low in the stall, lungs audibly struggling for breath. I shudder at the memory.

"I see. My consultant didn't mention that."

"Consultant?" I hold back a scoff, just barely.

"When I ran Ironmans, I often used a consultant, with great efficacy. So I hired a show jumping consultant. He informed me how important performance in international competitions is in the selection of the Olympic team."

I didn't even realize there was such a thing as show jumping consultants—or Ironman consultants for that matter. "That may be true," I say. "But we have plenty of five-star Grand Prixs right here in Wellington with plenty of International power with zero risk of travel injury. We should choose our international travel carefully. Leo needs to stay healthy in order to compete."

"That's the other thing I wanted to discuss with you. His feed and supplements. Cate gave me a breakdown of what he eats. The fat content is lacking..."

And on it goes for two more hours, with Grayson J. Sterling—who has never even touched a horse—telling me how to run my business. How to train my horse. Correction: *his* horse. For two hours, we bicker. On some points, I go toe to toe with him. At others, I capitulate. The whole time trying to remind myself that I need to work with this guy for the next year and a half (at least) while we aim for the Olympic team.

At the end of our meeting, I just don't know if I'll make it that long.

A few days later, Grayson shows up for DeDe's lesson holding a rather thick book. "I didn't know if you had this already," he says, handing it to me. "I've been chatting with an equine vet at Cornell, do you know Kayla Miller? Anyway, she recommended this." I glance down, thankful that the title is in a font I can easily read. It's called *Sport Horse Soundness and Performance: training advice for dressage, show jumping and event horses from champion riders, equine scientists and vets.* "I started reading it and thought we could talk about it next week."

Awesome. So not only does Grayson J. Sterling think I need a whole truckload of help taking care of my horse, he also name-drops Cornell vets and expects me to read this in a week so we can have a fun little book club together?

Yeah, right.

"Thanks," I say, because what else can I say? *Oh, actually, I'm dyslexic so I don't typically read if I can help it at all because my overburdened parents didn't catch my condition until it was basically too late for me and so now I just listen to podcasts and watch YouTube videos?*

Right. So he can go laugh about his new idiot rider with his Cornell-grad buddy? No, thanks.

DeDe runs into the barn, holding a bag of treats that's almost bigger than she is. "Look what I got!" she says, swinging the bag.

"Those look delicious," I tell her with a smile.

She gives me a skeptical look, glancing at the bag and then back to me. "I got these for Leo," she says, and then hesitantly holds the bag up to me. "But you could have one if you want."

I laugh, shaking my head. "That's okay, Leo needs them more than I do."

She looks relieved, like she really thought I'd gobble up the bag if given half a chance. "Save some for Persephone!" I call after her as she skips down the hall to Leo's stall. Persephone is DeDe's mare, named after the goddess Demeter's daughter by Zeus. I'm not quite sure why this family is so obsessed with Greek mythology, but I suppose it seems fitting for someone who drives a Maserati to name their daughter and her horse after Greek goddesses.

During DeDe's lesson, Grayson is practically hanging over the fence, watching like a hawk. I'm on edge, my brain going in about fifteen different directions as I struggle to focus on the lesson.

I set up some cavalettis for DeDe and her horse while she trots around the ring. I'm so distracted I have to re-walk the strides between the poles to make sure I got the distances right.

Why do I even care what this guy thinks of me?

Oh yeah, because he's my new partner. My new partner who thinks I'm underperforming.

And to make it to the top, I need him to foot the bill—a *massive* bill—and I need him to believe in me.

A rider who can't even read that well? Yeah, not super compelling.

After the cavalettis I set up a simple crossrail course for DeDe to go through. She's competing this weekend for the first time and, let me tell you, she's stoked. The girl's been talking about nothing else for weeks.

DeDe rides through the course several times, with me raising the jumps until they're a little over eighteen inches—the height she'll be competing in this weekend.

She has a bad habit of letting go of her reins momentarily while she adjusts them—releasing the rein as she moves her hand down the leather straps. It's a small movement, but a risky one. So today I have quarters that I give her to hold on to as she rides to make her extra conscious of the movement. She can move the reins in one hand with the help of the other hand, keeping a hold of the reins—and the quarter in each hand—the whole time. She only drops them once the entire lesson—a vast improvement from last time.

On our last practice course, I raise the jumps one more hole so that they're a solid twenty inches—practically monstrous for a six-year-old. But not DeDe, the girl has nerves of steel and thirst for speed. God love her. Persephone grazes one of the jumps in the first line, and the rail topples, but the rest of the course is flawless.

"You are so ready for this weekend!" I cheer to DeDe as she walks her mare to cool her down.

As we walk out of the practice ring, Grayson asks, "Shouldn't she do it again if she knocked the pole down?"

What is this guy's deal? Not only is he undermining my authority as the trainer, but he's sowing seeds of doubt in his daughter when she really needs to be going into her first show feeling confident.

I clench my jaw, certain I'm going to grind the tops of my teeth off. "Her ride was very good, that last line was a perfect note to end on."

"I just thought—"

"Mr. Sterling, why don't you let me be the trainer, and you can just be DeDe's dad? How's that sound?" I applaud myself for restraining my tone—it doesn't come out nearly as acerbic as I want it to—but Grayson gets the idea.

He presses his lips together, giving me a quick nod. I let the two of them walk back to the barn together with Persephone while I stay back to work off my frustrations, resetting a new course for my lessons tomorrow.

That night, when we're at Kickback Tavern—our favorite post-ride haunt—I'm seething. After two beers, I'm venting to Ellie and Ryan, one of my other students, about the audacity of Grayson telling me what to do when he literally knows nothing about horses. I don't tell them about the book, especially since they don't know about my dyslexia, but I rehash our meeting, with his pages and pages of recommendations, his casual references to his Ironman days, and his comment about DeDe riding the course again since she had a rail. I mean, *come on*.

"What a jerk," Ellie says as she gnaws on one of Kickback's famous wings.

"People like that in their Maserati's and hundred-thousand watches think they own anywhere they go," Ryan says. It's a little ironic coming from Ryan, whose dad is a named partner at a massive law firm with his own fair share of luxury vehicles and fancy watches. But Ryan seems to be pushing against the man, with his salt-of-the-earth vibes driving around a Ford F.150 with an American flag emblazoned on the back window. I'm pretty sure he's studying construction management at Florida Atlantic University, despite his father's constant whining.

"Seriously, like who owns a car like that unless they're trying to compensate for something?" I say between sips of beer.

We snicker like immature teenagers, bashing everything about Grayson from his pompadour to his impractical shoes. As good as it feels to vent, it doesn't change anything and when I go to my apartment that night by myself, I'm reminded that for better or worse, I'm chained to Grayson if I want to pursue my Olympic dream. And something about positioning my students against him feels wrong.

It doesn't stop me from raking him over the proverbial coals for his pompous performance charts. But the aftertaste of the conversation is like my favorite IPA, leaving my mouth dry and bitter.

7

Girl on Fire

Mila

It's been a couple weeks since Alex sent me the Haha-Perfect-Wife email. I'd (mostly) forgotten about it. Until I went to search for something in my inbox and stumbled on his email.

Today, instead of feeling defensive, I feel resolved. Sure, I realize I can never be perfect, but I sure can try.

It makes me think of that quote, "We cannot become what we want by remaining what we are." Alex is the most important person in the world to me, and he deserves the absolute best I can give.

So I decide I'm going to work my way through this list, doing each and every one of these items as often as I can.

The good news is that numbers one and two on the list—make our bed and greet him with a kiss—are easy peasy. Number three? Make him delicious, nutritious meals that he loves...Not so much. I am *not* a cook.

But, I won't remain what I am. I can evolve. I can change. I can become the perfect wife.

Starting with Mila Mondays—my day to cook. Which, to be honest, I'd kind of forgotten about since we'd decided on that a few weeks ago. I frown, trying to think if Alex had been cooking on Wednesdays like we'd said...And yes, of course he has.

I groan, feeling another wave of shame as I think about how far I am from being a "perfect" wife.

I understand why Alex laughed at the article—it's *hilarious* how bad I am at this. So hilarious, in fact, that tears are pressing against my eyelids.

But no, I won't allow it. I straighten, take a deep breath, and steel myself.

Today is the day I will cook.

While I grocery shop, I FaceTime my best friend, Monica. She's living in New York City right now at her big-girl job at Goldman Sachs. She's crushing it up there, and I'm so proud of her. Alex and I are planning to visit her during our first Christmas together—it's a little non-traditional, but we wanted to see snow, and I really miss Monica.

While I walk through the aisles of Publix, toggling between Monica and my grocery list, throwing things haphazardly into my cart, Monica is being her typical self. Which is to say, she's being *loud*. I'm telling her about my new goal of getting through this perfect wife list, and she's cackling over the speaker.

"Chica, don't act a clown," Monica says. She's in her bathroom, applying makeup as we talk. She's currently doing a double-winged graphic liner, with one line in classic black and a second line in metallic silver. "You don't need to be perfect. All men really need is food and—"

I cover the speaker, knowing *exactly* what Monica is going to say. "Monica!" A mom with her two sons walks past me, and I give them a sheepish smile. Maybe FaceTiming in Publix with Monica isn't the best idea, but I have so little free time these days, I'm making do with what I have.

"Alex deserves the best, Mon," I tell her as I throw a can of black beans into the cart.

"He already has the best, babe." She purses her lips, tilting her head from side to side in the mirror as she examines her eye liner. It's a good thing double-winged graphic liner isn't on my perfect wife list—I'd totally fail on that one. "He didn't marry you because you're a good cook. He married you for *you*."

"Uh huh." I flip back to my grocery list, checking off the broth and wine needed for the risotto. I can't find arborio rice, so I just grab a bag of regular rice. How different can they be? "Why can't he have both, though, you know?"

"If you want to kill yourself being Helen Housewife, that's fine. Just remember what I said, the key to a man's heart is—"

"*I know*." I cup my hand under the speaker and whisper. "Monica, I'm in *public*."

"Touchy, touchy," she says, smacking her lips with her cloud lipstick—whatever *that* is. I glance down at my own barn-appropriate wardrobe, sighing. I've really gone downhill since Monica left for New York.

"I gotta run," I tell her, not willing to risk any more explicit comments from her while I'm in the grocery store.

"Well, good luck with the risotto. You're going to need it!" she cackles again as I hang up the phone, hoping and praying I don't need *that* much luck.

I check out, and the number at the cash register is astounding to me. I glance back over my items—I didn't get *that* much—but it's still way outside of the weekly budget for groceries that Alex set. And this is just one meal. I cringe as I pull out the emergency credit card my dad gave me.

I mean, it *is* an emergency...we have to eat, right? I know my dad wouldn't mind, so I swipe the card, load up my groceries, and head home.

I am freaking wife of the year over here. I've got an Instant Pot dish cooking, I've vacuumed the whole cottage, and now I'm working on these vegan brownie bites that are Luke's favorite recipe. It's a bit strange—black beans with cocoa powder and dates, but Luke swears by it. I've got my AirPods in and I'm listening to my go-to equestrian podcast. I'm feeling like I'm on top of the world. I'm totally crushing this wife thing. Is there a woman crush Wednesday hashtag? It's Monday, but still. I'd totally be trending.

When Alex comes home, I stand on tiptoe and give him a heartfelt kiss. Number two, check. But when he says, "What's that smell?" and it's not with a positive inflection, my heart drops. He quickly walks over to the Instant Pot and unplugs it, but not before I see that it says "food burn." He flips the release valve, and a billow of steam pours out.

"You didn't hear it beeping?" he asks, and even though his tone is kind, I feel defensive.

"I guess I didn't hear it with my headphones in," I mumble. I want to show him all the other good things I did—the flawless vacuum lines in the carpet or the folded laundry—but now the wind has whooshed right out of my sails. I decide to at least give him one of the brownie bites plucked from the fridge. "Want to try one? It's Luke's recipe."

"Hm." Alex says, and I'm watching his expression closely, so that's why I notice him trying to cover up something.

"What's wrong with it?" There's panic swelling in my chest. Can I really screw this up? I didn't even have to bake anything. They're literally "no-bake" bites. Even a monkey could do it.

But when I take a bite, I know instantly they're no good.

"What *is* that?" I scrunch my nose, trying to figure out what went wrong. "Could the beans have gone bad?"

I open the trash and fish out one of the bean cans. I check the expiration date, but it's still a few years away. Alex comes up behind me, staring at the can in my hand. A moment later, he's laughing. "Mila."

"What?"

"Look." He puts his thumb under the label. Where it says "*with diced jalapenos.*"

"Ugh." I throw the can back in the trash with a bit too much force. I screwed up the brownie bites—apparently I'm more worthless than a monkey.

Maybe Alex should've married a monkey.

The steam has released all the way from the Instant Pot, so I open the lid and check the risotto. A two-inch layer of the risotto is burned (perhaps permanently) to the bottom of the pot, but the rice at the top is still crunchy. Inedible. I slam the lid down and throw my hands up. "I give up."

I trudge to the couch and throw myself into the throw pillows (that I had so carefully lined up an hour ago). So much for #WomanCrushWednesday.

8

New Shoes

Irina

Ah, horse show weekend.

In most parts of the world, people are preparing for things like Thanksgiving and Christmas. Here in Wellington, we're preparing for the best season ever—and it's not a holiday season. It's WEF season.

Slowly, the town of Wellington starts to swell—with riders, trainers, and their horses flocking in from the north, escaping the cold and snow to enter into Florida's prime weather season.

I'll be the first to admit that Florida is *miserable* in the summer—hotter than Venus with humidity that fogs your windows and mosquitoes that nest in every blade of St. Augustine grass. Daily thunderstorms—and I *do* mean daily—with a healthy dose of hurricane and tropical storm watches. It's a lot.

But the winter? Oh, wintertime in Florida is *glorious*. Blue skies, sunshine, and temperatures that make you feel happy just for existing. Everything about a Florida winter makes you want to seize the day.

Except for this day.

This day has only just begun, but it already sucks. First, I get an email from Grayson saying that he and DeDe will be showing up first thing to help me with Leo—whatever *that* means—and to watch my class this morning.

I showed up at Wellington International at six AM, only to find that Leo had thrown a shoe. Not a terribly big deal, except for the fact that I can't get ahold of the on-site farrier—and my usual farrier is at the hospital, his wife is in labor.

Of course.

An hour and a half later, when I should be walking my course, I'm Googling farriers all over the tri-county area. And that's when Grayson shows up looking even more glorious than a Florida winter. He's wearing this white, short-brimmed hat that absolutely shouldn't work, but totally does. It contrasts nicely with his tanned skin, the beginnings of a five o'clock shadow dusting his chin and—oh no, I'm cataloging his facial hair?

No, no, no.

"Miss Trina!" DeDe runs in front of her dad, her French braid bouncing behind her. She wraps me up in a hug, with her skinny little arms around my waist.

"Morning, DeDe." I give her a rare hug—none of my other students would ever think to hug me, but DeDe always does. "I think someone special might be competing today for the first time, but I just can't remember who." I smile down at her, and she bounces on her toes.

"Me! Me!"

Despite the shoeing disaster, I laugh. DeDe's excitement is infectious. And even though she's unfortunately joined to Grayson J. Sterling, she holds my affection like no one else can. Not for the first time, I wonder how someone as sweet as DeDe came from someone like Grayson. Caterina is generous, but she's not exactly what I'd call 'sweet.'

"Morning, Trina." Grayson, wearing another pair of designer sunglasses I've never seen before, holds out a tray of Starbucks drinks. "I didn't know what to get you, so we grabbed a couple different options. Black tea, green tea, herbal mint tea, hot chocolate."

"How nice," I say, examining the labels on the drinks. "Thank you."

"DeDe said you weren't a coffee drinker, so we picked alternatives."

I squeeze DeDe's shoulder. "You are very observant for a seven-year-old," I tell her.

"I'm only six!"

"What? No way. I don't believe you." I grab the green tea and then hand Grayson my phone. "Leo threw a shoe, and I can't get a hold of a farrier. Can you find one on this list and get him here ASAP? I have to go walk the course if there's a chance of us competing today."

"Oh," he glances down at my phone, then back at me. "Sure. Yeah. No problem."

You want to be an active partner? I think. *Now's your chance. Let's see if you'll step up when it matters, Grayson J. Sterling.*

I walk to the International Arena, sipping the green tea on my way. It's quite good, which for whatever reason makes me feel even more flustered. All I want is a silent partner—not one who's going to show up with four different kinds of drinks looking so painfully handsome.

I walk the course—twice, because the first time I was still kind of fuming about Grayson for no good reason. I keep an eye out for Mila, so we can walk together, but she's not here yet. And of course I left my phone with Grayson so I have no way of getting ahold of her. I should've thought this through before storming off, but it feels like my brain is not fully functional when Grayson is around.

On the second go-around I run into Evangeline Rutherford.

I wish I could say I'm way too old to have an archnemesis, but that would be a lie. The reality is, I didn't choose Eva as mine, she chose me. Eva Rutherford's family is so rich they could use hundred-dollar bills as shavings in their horses' stalls and not even blink an eye. They have a hand in every major industry you could think of, from hotels to restaurants to construction. Someone even said her dad is on the board of SpaceX. Evangeline has never worked a day in her life—she's got a barn full of ready-made horses and whole team of employees to do her bidding. She spends her days riding, working with her personal trainer, and playing pickleball in her spare time.

I try to scoot away before she can see me, but she manages to intercept me at the in-gate. "Katrina," she calls out in a lilting accent that isn't true to her heritage. She was born and raised in West Palm Beach and yet she talks with a voice tinged with a British accent. It's ridiculous. Also, she insists on calling me Katrina even though it's not my name. "I've heard so much from Pierre about Leo! He saw you at WEC while I was in Bhutan. I can't wait to see him go today."

I give her a tight smile and a quick nod. Her boyfriend, Pierre, is also a trainer. He seems like a decent guy, so I have no idea what he sees in Eva.

"I know you've tried your hardest to turn pumpkins into prizes with all your little pet projects. I admire how resourceful you are, but I'm happy you've joined the big leagues with the rest of us."

Outrage rises in my throat like bile. I want to spit on her fancy, custom-made Vogel boots. I glance down and notice that she has rose gold spur rests on the sides of her boots, and it takes everything within me not to roll my eyes. Who has the time, money, and inclination to get rose gold spur rests on their custom-made boots?

Apparently, Eva Rutherford does.

Eva's got five—FIVE—Grand Prix horses trained by pillars in the show jumping world like the Beerbaums, Eric Lamaze, and Rodrigo Pessoa.

I wish I could think of a sufficiently snarky comment in this moment, but I can't. Whoever divvied out abilities at birth left me sorely empty-handed when it comes to thinking on my feet. Tonight, I'll come up with fifteen amazing clapbacks, but right now my brain is emptier than a hay bag after a long trip.

"Gotta run, Eva," I say, figuring a brush-off is the best I've got right now. "Always a pleasure."

I turn on my heel and hightail it to the Mogavero where the children's jumpers are walking their course. I still haven't seen Mila, but once I get done with the children's jumpers, I'll go back to the barn and find her. I meet with two of my students at the in-gate and we go over their course. I desperately want to get back to the barn to check on Leo's status, but I've got to get these girls in the ring, so I school them and send them in back-to-back before I head to the temporary barns where Leo and Grayson are.

I'm praying that Leo has his shoe on by the time I arrive, that I can tack him up and still make it early in the order of go. When I finally get to the barn, Leo's in the tack stall and he's all ready to go. One of the grooms, Luna, has even done his mane in the button braids that I love. DeDe's standing near Leo's rump, brushing out his tail.

"You did it, then?" I ask Grayson with a smile.

"The farrier just left," he says.

"He's got his shoe…?" I glance down at Leo's feet, noticing something strange.

Stomach sinking to my feet, I turn toward Grayson. "Grayson, *explain*."

"Well…" He puts his hands into his pockets and rocks back on his heels. Something about his demeanor reminds me of a nervous kid about to give a presentation in class.

"Well, what?"

"Well, we took all his shoes off."

"I can clearly see that," I say, trying to keep the tremble of anger out of my voice for DeDe's sake, even if Grayson deserves it. "The question is *why*?"

"The only farrier who answered my calls, well, he had some really progressive ideas about horses not wearing shoes." Grayson must sense that I am a ticking time bomb, so he leads me outside of the temporary barns, away from prying eyes. "The research supports it, Trina. Going barefoot seems like the right move." His apprehension seems to drop away, and he starts talking animatedly. "We did a fair amount of reading while we waited for you to come back. I'll send you the articles. This is the right move for an athlete, think about the improved traction and proprioception..."

I gape at him, unable to form words for a few long seconds as he goes on, saying things that I'm barely comprehending.

"Where is this farrier?" I say, interrupting his monologue. "We need to get him back here and have him put the shoes back on my—" I cut myself off, clearing my throat before I can say '*my* horse.' "We need shoes on Leo. Right now."

He rubs his neck, grimacing. "He's not that kind of farrier..."

"I don't understand."

"He doesn't put shoes *on*. He takes them *off*."

I'd never really understood the phrase 'murderous look' until right this moment—because I am sure that the way I'm looking at Grayson in this moment conveys my deepest desire to see him turn to ash right before my eyes.

I want to scream and wail, to point a finger at every single person in the barn and ask them what they were thinking allowing this idiot of a man to take the shoes off of my horse right before we compete. I want to stab a finger into Grayson's chest, to tell him, *Let's add this moment to* your *performance chart, why don't we*?! Instead, I take a deep breath, dragging my fingers through my hair.

"Mr. Sterling," I say. "I understand that this 'farrier' was very convincing, but this is a *huge* decision, to make a horse go barefoot in a major competition." I hold up a hand when Grayson opens his mouth to argue. "Please just listen for a minute. *This* is not the time to make that kind of decision—Leo isn't used to jumping without shoes. It's likely that he hasn't been without shoes since he was two years old. Imagine if you'd worn your shoes since you were a little kid and took them off for the first time now as an adult, what do you think that would feel like? And then, what if you took your shoes off and then immediately ran a marathon?"

He presses his lips together into a tight line, and then nods. "I see." He looks back at the temporary barn, where Leo stands barefoot. "Let's table this conversation until next week, then."

"Yes, let's," I say, barely masking the sarcasm in my voice. And then, with tears in my eyes, I stalk to the show office to scratch me and Leo from the class.

9

Speed Me Up

Mila

It's a perfect horse show weekend—just cool enough where wearing a jacket is bearable, sunny without it being scorching, and well, it's a horse show. So that means it's perfect no matter the circumstances.

Except for the fact that I'm here to walk the course and I can't find Trina. I call and text her with no response, so I decide to walk by myself. I feel vulnerable, exposed. As if everyone can see I'm here without my trainer. It's stupid, I know. No one's thinking about me, they're all just worried about themselves. But it's strange to be here without Trina, and to not know *why* she isn't here with me is disconcerting.

I send Alex to the barn to check if she's there while I sit in the stands to watch the first few riders. I get a text from Alex saying that there's been some drama with Leo and his shoes. I text back, asking if she's still able to school me.

Alex: *No one knows where she is right now. She left her phone here. Luna thinks she might be at the Mogavero. I'll go check there, but if we can't find her, I'll set a jump for you. You can do this, even without Trina.*

I clench my jaw, steeling myself against tears. I don't want to do this without Trina. I've never done this without Trina, and I never *want* to do this without her. Panic presses against my ribcage, making it hard to breathe. I force myself to practice my deep breathing techniques from my therapist, and then when I'm a bit calmer, I work on some visualization exercises. By the end of it, I'm slightly calmer, but still upset with Trina.

Twenty minutes later, Alex arrives with Cyrus. "She's coming," he tells me. "She had to scratch the class. Apparently all of Leo's shoes are off. Some drama with the new owner."

I nod but choose to focus my energy on warming up Cyrus. He's agitated—clearly picking up on my off-kilter energy. The longer we warm up, the more I'm able to shed the bad feelings. It's as if they slough off of me as we canter through the warm-up arena. When Trina shows up, apologetic yet still distracted, I tell her, "It's okay."

They're calling my name at the in-gate, and Trina sends Alex over to push me back in the order. She raises the warm-up fence higher and higher—quicker than usual—but Cyrus and I are laser focused now.

By the time we're in the arena, all of the emotions that had been swirling in me for the past hour have given way to a calm alertness. I'm ready to prove to myself—and everyone else—that I can rise above anxiety and messed up plans and whatever else life throws my way.

We fly around the course—it's a speed class, our specialty. Cyrus gets 'gymnastical,' as Trina calls it, with his twists and turns over the ridiculous rollbacks I'm pushing him into. With every challenge I throw his way, he meets it—and more. This is our home turf, and we are claiming this course as ours.

As we gallop through the triple combination—notorious for its difficulty and for many dropped rails in this class—we press through it in perfect rhythm. I press my heels into his side, urging him forward to the next obstacle: the sprawling water jump.

Wind in my face, thundering hooves beneath me. We are winning this thing.

We fly over the water, Cyrus stretching out like he's Superman himself.

When we tear through the timers at the end of the course, a cheer goes up from the spectators.

"That's our class leader, ladies and gentlemen," the announcer says. "With only three left to ride, Mila Caballero and Cyrus Van Der Bergh hold the time to beat."

I give Cyrus the reins, throwing my arms around his neck and patting his shoulders. "Good boy, Cy." When we reach the in-gate, Cyrus reaches his head back to receive his obligatory mint—I always keep a stash in my pocket while I'm competing. His ears perk at the sound of the wrapper, and as I lean down, his lips nibble the candy from my gloved hand before I can even get it completely unwrapped. Alex laughs, sticking his fingers in the horse's mouth to get the wrapper out.

Trina and I discuss the ride, but she keeps it brief—probably because it was impeccable. I notice she's quick to head back to the barn, not hanging back to chat about life or anything else.

Keenan Wilder, who's on the USEF Olympic selection committee, is standing at the in-gate. "Great ride, Mila," he says with a smile.

"Oh my gosh," I whisper to Alex after I dismount and we're walking Cyrus out of the warm-up ring. "Do you know who that is?"

"A guy checking out my hot wife?" Alex grumbles as he glances over his shoulder at Keenan.

"No!" I elbow him in the side. Alex always thinks everyone is checking me out. It's hilarious and endearing at the same time. "That's Keenan Wilder, who works for USEF and he's part of the committee that selects people for the US show jumping team."

"Why do *you* know who he is?"

"USEF did this thing about him on their Instagram page." I stop walking, grasping Alex's arm and shaking him. "Alex, the *Olympics.*"

"Wow." Alex has a slightly dazed expression, like he's trying to wrap his mind around the Olympics.

Cyrus puts his head between Alex and me, like he wants to be part of the conversation. I loop my arm around Cyrus's nose, kissing his face. I'm getting a little ahead of myself—okay, *a lot* ahead of myself—when I whisper into the soft skin of his nose, "We're going to the Olympics, buddy."

10

Silent Lucidity

Trina

An hour after Mila's ride, the show farrier magically appears out of thin air and replaces Leo's shoes. Of course he's thirty minutes too late for me to actually make it to my class—not that it mattered, I scratched anyway. But what's the point of having a farrier on the show grounds if he's not even going to be *on* the show grounds when you need him? I'm pretty sure the scent of whiskey billowing around him explains his absence well enough.

Grayson wisely makes himself scarce until DeDe's class—a small jumper class affectionately called the 'puddle jumpers.' I try to remove ShoeGate from my mind as I school DeDe, but the whole drama left me smarting. Why couldn't he just *apologize*? I roll my eyes as I set up a jump for DeDe, thinking, *Typical man*.

I finish helping DeDe warm up, and then we stand at the in-gate to watch a few riders in front of her. I point out a couple sticky points in the course but try not to overwhelm her with too much feedback. "Just have fun," I tell her with a comforting pat to her boot.

When DeDe enters the ring, Grayson, who's standing at the fence to the left of the in-gate, calls out, "Looking good, Demetria Sterling!"

Something about him voicing support for his daughter—in such a public and affectionate way—fills my heart with a sudden longing I haven't had for a while. To be supported like that. I no longer crave that from my parents—not really—but to have someone on the sidelines cheering for me like that? Not *Grayson*, but anyone, really. The desire pings around in my chest until I settle it down, focusing on DeDe as the buzzer sounds in the arena.

"More leg!" I click loudly to try to get Persephone moving as they approach the first fence. They jump in seemingly slow motion, moving around the course in a way that looks like a hunter class more than a jumper one, but at least they go clean.

At the end of DeDe's ride, I clap, but Grayson whoops and cheers for his daughter, a proud smile on his face as he watches her exit the arena.

"That was fantastic, DeDe!" He claps her on the leg.

"You rocked that, girl," I tell her, smiling at the glee emanating from her. "Grayson, why don't you let us debrief for a moment and then you can walk DeDe back to the barn?"

"Oh, right, sure thing." Grayson backs up a few steps while I talk with DeDe about the ride—how to get more momentum through the turns and give her horse the support she needs. She takes it all in, a little sponge soaking up everything with a smile on her face the entire time.

Once I send her back to the barn with Grayson, I watch the two of them walking side-by-side with Persephone. DeDe seems to be animatedly telling her dad about the course, and Grayson is listening with rapt attention.

I sigh, running my hands through my hair. Grayson Sterling may have ruined my class with Leo today, but one thing is for certain: he's a good dad.

On my way home, I call Caterina again. After ShoeGate—and not that I'd ever admit it, even to myself, Grayson's increasing attractiveness—I'm resolved to try to find a way out of this partnership.

She's been dodging my calls for weeks, but today, she picks up. "Trina," she says, guilt etching her words. "I'm so sorry I haven't had a chance to talk."

"It's okay," I say, even though I don't think it's okay. "You've had a lot going on."

She sighs deeply, the sound blurring the line. "It's true. Sergei and I just got back from Lake Como, celebrating the divorce. It just wasn't as nice as I remember, and we missed the foliage."

My mouth literally falls open, and I move the phone away from my ear, staring at it. I regret letting her off the hook even one modicum. *Celebrating the divorce?* I've been over here dealing with Grayson's printed accusations of my deficits as a rider and trainer, managing to stay (somewhat) poised through ShoeGate, and Caterina is bemoaning the lack of foliage in Italy?

My fingers itch to hang up on this lady that a few weeks ago I'd considered a friend. I almost laugh at myself. Apparently, I need higher standards for what I consider 'friendship.'

"Caterina, I need your help." I cut her off as she's telling me about a winery they visited.

"Sure, what do you need?"

"I need you to buy back Leo from Grayson."

Laughter fills the call, and my cheeks heat from Caterina's response. This is not at all the conversation I'd hoped it would be.

"I shouldn't laugh," she says, at least somewhat self-aware. "We were married eight years, I understand *exactly* what you're dealing with."

I grunt in response, unable to manage anything more. I want to tell her that being married to Grayson couldn't be worse than being his business partner, but something tells me that's not going to win her over.

"Here's the thing, I'd love to help, but Grayson's lawyers made it very clear. The horse realm belongs to him."

"I don't understand."

"Who knows why Grayson does what he does, honestly. He probably just wanted to stick it to me. But, no, I can't buy Leo back."

I'm silent. Brooding would be an accurate term. Why do I have to live in a world with *people*? Horses are just *so* much better.

"I have someone in mind, though," she says hesitantly. "He might be able to—"

"Yes. Whoever it is, yes." Anyone would be better than Grayson at this point. "As long as they're willing to be a distant partner. A silent one."

"I wasn't a silent partner," she says coyly.

"You weren't annoying."

Caterina snorts. "Grayson's getting to you, isn't he? He can be a little overbearing when he gets focused. Must be the Aspergers in him."

I scrunch my nose, glad that Caterina can't see me. "C'mon, Grayson doesn't have Aspergers."

"Oh you know him so well now, don't you?" she says in a syrupy sweet voice that makes me cringe. "No, he's not on the spectrum, at least I don't think. But the man develops deep, intense, focused interests and no one—not even a meteor crashing to earth—can get him to come off it."

"I see."

"Anyway, Trin, I'm going to run but I'll check in with my friend to see if he'd be interested in you and Leo."

"A silent partner," I reiterate.

"You got it. Gotta run. *Ciao*!"

I roll my eyes and hang up the phone, hoping I'm not making a huge mistake.

396 likes

Bridle Buzz It was an exciting weekend for the ESP Holiday & Horses show! Congrats to Louis Pluss and Tamlin for winning the $226,000 Holiday & Horses CSI4* Grand Prix on Sunday.
So many equestrians were looking dapper this weekend. Whitney Rubles competed in a custom Vogel boots and a show-stopping (pun totally intended) teal jacket by Karisma Equestrian.
Congrats to Mila Caballero and Cyrus Van Der Bergh for winning the $39,000 Score at the Top 1.45m Speed class. Mila sported a gorgeous bordeaux colored jacket which contrasted nicely with her pristine white breeches.
Her trainer and fellow Grand Prix rider, Trina Powers, was unfortunately looking harried and distracted this weekend. She was not seen competing on her sponsored horse, Leonidas. A shame.
If you'd like to get your own Karisma Equestrian jacket in teal (or a variety of other show stopping colors!) use code BRIDLEBUZZ20 for a discount!
Comment below, if you could have a show jacket in any color, what color would it be?? ... more

View all 25 comments

Debbie Poole black.
Erica Dawes oh my gosh I love the teal!!!!! I want it I want it I want it!!!!

 Add a comment...

2 hours ago

11

Ctrl+Alt+Del

Trina

Next week, when I'm untacking Leo after our morning ride and Ellie is readying a lesson horse for one of our students, she's chattering on and on about the 'billionaire.' It takes me a moment to realize she's talking about *Grayson*.

"Is he actually a billionaire?" I ask, unbuckling Leo's girth and letting it swing to the other side of him.

She shrugs. "I overheard Caterina telling someone over the phone that he sold his company for like three billion dollars. I don't think she was hyperbolizing."

"Wow." It's making more sense—his high standards, his ridiculous wardrobe, the whole shebang.

"He's pretty hot," Ellie says as she sprays down the horse with fly spray, the mist giving off a citronella smell that most people dislike, but I don't. "For an old guy."

I snort and roll my eyes. From a completely objective perspective, Grayson *is* attractive—and not just for an 'old guy.' If I had to guess, he's probably only late-thirties or *maybe* early-forties. Which, if that's true, makes *me* old in Ellie's book, too. I try not to groan. Sure, Grayson is easy on the eyes, but I tell myself he'd be much more appealing to me if he'd shown up in a truck with barn-appropriate attire.

And if he didn't all of a sudden own my horse. And then subsequently take off all my horse's shoes right before we were supposed to compete.

I mean, who *does* that?

"I just wish there was a way to permanently repel that guy. He's like a splinter I can't remove," I grumble under my breath. Ellie gives me a meaningful look, but I shrug it off.

I can't tell if I'm angry at the guy because he's Leo's owner, or if it's the fact that he's the first guy since Victor that's made me feel any sort of attraction. His gorgeous face flashes in my mind, those stormy gray eyes gazing steadily at me, and I have to quell the nausea building in me. More than any other time in my life, I need to stay focused on Leo and our training. It's the Olympics or bust for us. If this is going to work, Grayson needs to stay in his place—far from me.

It's clear Grayson J. Sterling hasn't come to the same conclusion as I have about his place. Because here he is, bright and early on a Tuesday morning. I'm still getting out of my Silverado when I see his flashy car pull down the barn driveway. I sigh as I run my hand through my hair, working through a few knots that I didn't bother with before I left my apartment.

I try not to do a double take as Grayson gets out of his Maserati. How is it even possible that the guy is somehow more attractive today than last time I saw him? He clearly just got out of the shower and today his hair isn't styled back, but it's falling in his eyes like a young Leo DiCaprio. Back before he got that weird look in his eyes, when he was still boyish and charming.

Oh my gosh.

Stop it, Trina.

I press a hand to my stomach, steeling myself for this super hot guy who—oh yeah—*owns my most valuable possession.*

Get it together, I tell myself. "You're here early," I say, in a tone that *some* might call *unwelcoming*. Not me, but some people.

"DeDe wanted to come before school," Grayson says, gesturing to his daughter, who's still getting out of the Maserati. I notice a bag of McDonald's breakfast at her feet. My icy interior softens—just a tad—when I catch sight of DeDe's thick blonde braids.

"Look, I'm sorry about the shoeing fiasco," he says as he holds out a Venti Starbucks drink as an offering. "I spoke with my consultant, and he said it was a high risk move. Not at all the GTO move I thought it was."

I almost roll my eyes. *I'm so glad your consultant and I agree,* I want to say, but don't. "Thanks, I appreciate it."

"Look, I want to support you, to be involved in all of this," he says, waving a hand to encompass the barn. "It's important to DeDe. And it's important to me."

I glance over his shoulder at DeDe, who's still getting her shoes on. An idea forms as I watch her reach into the middle console and grab a bag of mints for the horses.

If he wants to be involved, I'll give him involved. "Why don't you come back tomorrow when DeDe's in school and I'll get Ellie to show you the ropes? You can get a real insider's view on what horse care is all about."

He'll run away from the barn screaming after one day of mucking stalls and picking hooves. Maybe he'll return custody of Leo to Caterina, or maybe he'll just leave me in peace to do what I like with the horse.

And, as an added bonus, my heart—or what Victor left of it—will be safe from Mr. GQ and his billion-dollar smile.

"Sure, that would be great," he says, showing off the aforementioned smile. And, to top it all off, there's a dimple on his cheek that I'd never noticed before—probably because he hasn't been doing that much smiling around me. Can someone please tell me why a glorified hole in Grayson's face looks *good*?

Ugh.

I'm about to turn away, to get started with exercising Leo, when he opens his mouth again. "I hope it's okay, but I scheduled for a friend to come to the barn today, to talk with you about this new type of PEMF treatment for Leo." He glances at his *very expensive* Patek Philippe watch that could buy at least three stellar Child/Adult jumpers. "He'll be here at nine." I narrow my eyes at this guy, attempting to remind myself that I need to be nice to him because he owns ninety percent of my horse. "I'm assuming you're well acquainted with PEMF?"

I know a cursory amount about PEMF, but it's never been in the budget for me to learn much about it. I don't even know what it stands for. I hate how his question makes me feel stupid, inadequate even. "Sure, I know about PEMF," I say as casually as I can manage. "I gotta run, trying to get on Leo before my first lesson arrives."

I stalk away from him, hiding in my office while I Google 'PEMF for horses.' I typically use my Read Aloud extension to read articles to me, but with Grayson in the barn, I don't want him to know what I'm reading. I have another extension on my Chrome browser called OpenDyslexic, which makes the fonts easier to read, but I still prefer to listen when I can. I find that Pulsed Electromagnetic Field therapy is used on horses for increased circulation, rapid healing, pain management, and overall better performance. It kind of sounds miraculous. I can't afford to buy any PEMF machines (I don't even know if they're called machines) but if Grayson wants to foot the bill, who am I to stop him?

When I head back into the barn aisle, I find Grayson loitering next to Leo's stall as DeDe feeds him treats. "Hey DeDe, I've got an open slot if you want an extra lesson today before school, my treat."

DeDe squeals, clapping her hands. "Can I, Daddy?"

Grayson glances my way, his steely gray eyes leveling me, giving me a small nod. "Of course, sweetheart."

Later that night, I find that I'm the owner of a brand-new, top-of-the-line PEMF device not only for Leo, but for me too. I put the device in the corner of my apartment, laying the mat on the carpet, but not turning it on.

I tell myself I should be happy—this is an insanely expensive piece of equipment that's meant to help me and Leo. But instead, I feel hesitant. Suspicious.

Not of the equipment, but of Grayson. What kind of person does this? And why does this feel different than Caterina's generosity?

Let's be real, I *do* know why—Grayson's a man, and an attractive one at that. It triggers so many reminders of Victor—how he controlled me with his money, his smarts, and his business prowess. I've only just started working my way out of the pit that Victor left me in, and I don't want to let a new man dig me another one. So my only response is to push as far away from Grayson as possible.

All I know is that I better find a way to scare Grayson away from the barn, or else I'm in a world of trouble.

12

Coffee Shop Soundtrack

Mila

My birthday is in a couple weeks, and I can already feel tension coming off of Alex in waves. I promise I never *meant* to be high maintenance about my birthday—but for some reason, Alex feels like he has to do this big production for my birthday or else I'll be disappointed. I'm going to blame my ex-boyfriend, Michael, for setting unrealistic standards. However, as I go through my perfect wife list, I'm pretty sure one of the items *should* be: "Don't be high maintenance." So after a fitful night of sleep for Alex, I decide to do something positively low maintenance.

I may be a failure in the kitchen, but I've become quite adept at making Cuban coffee. I wake early and make Alex and I a pair of *café con leches* with sweetened condensed milk, the brand that Mrs. Caballero always buys, *La Lechera*. "I'm canceling my birthday," I declare as Alex and I huddle around our mugs.

If he were a lesser human being, my husband might scoff at me or roll his eyes, but instead, he glances thoughtfully at me over his coffee cup. "Tell me more," Alex says in his gentle therapist voice. (Side note: I may never be a perfect wife, but goodness gracious, Alex is already a perfect husband. How can I possibly compete with this guy?)

I sit across from him at our tiny dining table with my own cup of coffee that's more cream and sugar than actual coffee. "I just want a break from celebrating this year." I realize that if I tell him that I'm trying to give *him* a break from stressing about my birthday, that's only going to stress him out more. So I try to come up with a reason that doesn't involve him. "It just doesn't feel right to celebrate in some kind of extravagant way when there's so many people in the world who don't get nice birthdays, you know?"

There's skepticism in the gentle furrow of Alex's dark brows. I know my excuse is a stretch—like trying to do six strides in a ten stride line—but what's Alex going to do, call me out on my lack of altruism? It's just not in his nature. "So, is this an indefinite thing, like you think it's somehow wrong to celebrate all birthdays?"

Well, he's got me there. The obvious flaw in my very shaky excuse. I *love* my birthday—every holiday, really—and I want to celebrate it to its fullest potential every single year. Except for this year, so I can give Alex a break. Next year, he can come back to it, refreshed and with a clean slate. I mean, you can only go up if you didn't even celebrate the year before, right?

But for now, I need to sell this. I lift my chin, steeling my resolve. "Maybe."

So strong, Mila. So *resolved.*

Alex takes a long sip of coffee, his eyes never leaving mine. He's waiting for me to elaborate, so I scramble. "I saw this thing the other day on Instagram that talked about how much money is spent on the average kid's birthday and how much it would cost to feed a child in Africa and how it's, like, half of what we spend on birthdays."

"I see." Alex sets his mug down, his tired eyes searching mine. "So when we have kids, you don't want to have birthday parties for them?"

"Well, no, I-I don't know," I sigh. "Let's cross that bridge when we get there." An idea springs to mind like manna from heaven. "But for this year I was thinking we could donate whatever we would spend on my birthday toward some kind of charity for kids."

Alex hums, nodding. "Okay," he says simply.

"Okay?" I'm honestly surprised he's agreeing to this so easily. Maybe he *wants* to be off the hook?

"Yeah, if that's what you want." He shrugs. "I'm not going to force you to celebrate your birthday. Pick a charity and we'll donate to it."

I force a smile, reminding myself that this is exactly what I wanted. "Sounds good. Thanks, Alex."

He stands, kissing the top of my head before draining his mug and washing it in the sink. The man never leaves a dish in the sink.

I sigh, feeling mixed emotions. This is what I wanted...right?

13

(S)He Works Hard For the Money

Trina

The next day, when Grayson shows up, he's at least dressed in practical clothes—jeans, sneakers, a t-shirt, and a hat. My heart was hoping he'd look frumpier this way, but my head is telling me (objectively) he looks just as good. Maybe better.

He's early enough to watch my ride with Leo—this time without the accompaniment of my music, since I'm not sure how Grayson would feel about my Story of the Year and All Time Low riding playlist.

When we're back in the barn, with Leo tucked away after a bath, Grayson claps his hands, rubbing them together. "Alright, boss," he says. "Put me to work. Where do I start?"

I wave Ellie over. "She's going to be showing you the nitty-gritty of horse care. You sure you're ready for this?" I ask Grayson, hoping he'll take the out.

"Not getting rid of me that easily," he says with a quick grin.

I hand him off to Ellie and get ready for my lessons. I can't help but chuckle because I know he won't be smiling for long.

At the end of the day, I walk through the (very clean) barn, checking in on our horses—stalls cleaned to perfection, horses groomed without a hair out of place, there's not so much as a stray shaving in the breeze way.

Wow. I grin, feeling smug about my work-study program for our resident billionaire hottie. Ellie really put Grayson to work today.

I find the two of them huddled in the tack room with the first aid kit.

"Everything okay?" I ask, eyeing them. Grayson's palm is splayed out in front of Ellie and she's applying ointment to it.

"Just some blisters from the pitchfork," Grayson says.

I get a closer look and— "Holy moly, those are some blisters, Grayson." I can't help but gape at them because even though as a horse person I've had frequent blisters, these are another level. His palm is mottled with massive, open blisters—some the size of quarters, a couple bleeding and oozing. "Why didn't you stop?"

He shrugs, but then sucks air through his teeth as Ellie accidentally hits a blister too hard while putting on a bandage. "Sorry," she says, and before she can finish, I take the bandage from her.

"I'll finish up," I tell her.

Before she leaves the room, she says, "Good job today, Mr. Grayson."

"Thanks for showing me the ropes, Ellie. You're a good teacher, I appreciate it."

Ellie ducks her head in a nod and then exits the tack room as my heart sinks. Ellie's supposed to be on my side, not his. Then I chastise myself for the juvenile thought. I'm a grown adult, even if sometimes my head doesn't quite remember that.

I wrap Grayson's hand in silence, our breathing the only sound in the room. And suddenly I feel far too aware of how close I am to Grayson, how oddly intimate this is, to be caring for his wounds. I should've let Ellie finish.

"You didn't have to do this to your hands, Grayson," I say when I can't stand the thoughts whirling around in my brain—which for some reason have to do with what Grayson's breath would feel like on my cheek, on my lips...*no*. It needs to stop.

He gives me a look that I swear seems to say, *Do you really believe that*? And then he says, "I finish what I start, Trina."

His words seem loaded, and I'm not even sure how to interpret them. I stare a little too long into his eyes, which initially seemed gray but now I'm seeing flecks of green and gold in there. I force myself to refocus on my task. "Well, thanks, then." I finish wrapping his hand and take a big step back, my heart racing with the need for space from this guy.

He salutes me with his bandaged hand. "See you tomorrow."

"Wait, Grayson," I say. "You did so much today, you don't need to come back tomorrow."

He shrugs, a small grin playing on his face. "I need something to do while DeDe's in school." He gives me a little wave, sweaty hair falling in his face.

He leaves the tack room and I sigh, falling back on the paneled-wood wall. My plan of scaring Grayson is totally blowing up in my face—because not only did Grayson not get scared away, but he managed to impress me at the same time.

And that is *not* okay.

14

Confident

Mila

Today, I'm focusing my attention on number nine on my list: invest in what he cares about. And what does Alex care about more than his mom? Nothing.

After we got married, Alex's mom moved in with a friend she met at church, getting free rent in exchange for helping to care for the friend's aging mother a few times a week. Alex has mentioned that she wants to work, but between her immigration status still being in limbo, the fact that she doesn't speak English very well, and her health challenges with her epilepsy, she doesn't have a lot of options. So I decide: I'm going to find Mrs. Caballero a job.

The simplest option would be if she did something at the Center. So I pick her up on a Thursday afternoon and bring her to the barn.

We're about five seconds into a grooming lesson when I realize Mrs. Caballero is *terrified* of horses. As in, it'll take at least six months of therapy to help her overcome her fears. And then another six months of training for her to be helpful around the barn.

How did I not know this about my mother-in-law?

So, I pivot.

Maybe she can't help with the hands-on horse care, but surely she could feed the horses. Except, the moment we enter the feed room, she starts sneezing uncontrollably.

I quickly usher her out of the room, wondering how it's possible that she lived in a barn for years if she's allergic to something in the feed room.

"Are you allergic to hay?" I ask her in Spanish.

"No, it's the molasses."

Molasses? What person is allergic to molasses? But sure enough, horse feed is coated with molasses, and the scent of it fills the feed room.

It makes sense to me now why Alex didn't have Mrs. Caballero working at the Center—or at Zen Elite when he worked there.

I bring her back to the Cottage to find some Claritin for her.

Guess I can't check number nine off my list today. The only jobs I can think of would require her to speak English, so I help her download an app on her phone to help her improve her English. In the meantime, I'll need to think of something else.

I'm back in Wellington for my lesson with Trina. Even though it was supposed to be my day off, two of our volunteers didn't show up this morning so I had to fill in for them while calling others to see if they could come in last minute. I barely make it on time to Zen, and once we start our lesson, it's clear Trina's distracted, distant. I've never seen Trina like this before—she was out of it at the horse show last weekend, and now she's hardly responsive when I ask her questions. She keeps glancing at the barn, where a red Maserati sits like a flashing beacon in the parking lot.

I know she's got a lot on her plate, but it's disappointing to drive over an hour up here to not get her full attention. After the lesson, I ask, "Hey, are you doing okay?"

I wait for her to confess, to tell me what's really going on, but she doesn't give me anything. "Oh, you know, same old, same old."

I can't help the hurt that splinters within me at her response.

We're having dinner with my family tonight. As usual, my dad is grilling us on the goings-on at the Center—which is all well and good, especially considering that his company, ViaTech, is our primary financial backer. But tonight, I can tell Anya and Alex are being worn down by my dad's questions.

"Hey, you know something cool happened last weekend," I say, and then I tell my family about the brief interaction with Keenan Wilder, and what that could possibly mean for me.

"So this man, this Keenan Wilder," my dad says the name like it's in a foreign language. "He's in charge of who goes to the Olympics?"

"Well, he's part of a committee who determines who goes."

"Do you think that's a possibility? The Olympics?" He directs the question at Alex, and I don't know if I should be offended—ahem, woman power—or encouraged because my dad hasn't always held a lot of respect for Alex.

"With Mila? Anything is possible." Alex winks at me across the table, and I warm at the sight. Alex has always believed in me, even when I was too scared to compete.

The conversation quickly evolves into all of the things I should do in order to make it onto the Olympic team. "You should do some cross-training," Anya says.

"We can get you a personal trainer," my dad says, as if I have time in my schedule to cross-train.

"It could be a good idea to move Cyrus closer," my mom says. "What about that other trainer who's local? James something?"

"Jimmy Torano," Anya says.

My entire family goes round and round, suggesting—or sometimes demanding—various improvements for me to make in order to make it to the Olympics. Changes to my diet, equipment, and routine.

As excited as I was to tell them about Keenan's (probably offhanded) comment, now I'm regretting it. Because I can't add a single thing to my already-full plate.

On the drive home, Alex and I discuss some of the things my family suggested, and I say, "I think I might want to bring Cyrus closer to us, so I can ride him more. I'm worried Trina will be hurt, but she's been really distracted lately."

Alex hums, nodding thoughtfully. "Trina's pragmatic, she'll understand."

I sigh. "That's probably true." But it still doesn't make me feel better—I love being at Zen, and I love Trina. Getting lessons is my quality time with her, although it's felt much less *quality* the past few weeks.

The next morning, I call Trina, telling her that I'm considering moving Cyrus to Jimmy Torano's barn, which is only fifteen minutes from the Center. "I just want to be able to ride him more as we get into the WEF season," I tell her, though for some reason I don't elaborate on my Olympic hopes. "I'll probably take lessons with him during the week but I'd still like for you to train me at the shows."

"Makes sense," Trina says. "I'll miss riding Cyrus for you, though." My stomach sinks—Trina is going to miss my horse, but not me? Guess I know where our friendship stands. Not that I'm surprised, Trina couldn't even open up about what's bothering her. And something is clearly bothering her.

"I'm sure he'll miss you too." I decide to try one more time to see if Trina will tell me what's wrong. "Is everything okay, Trin? You've just seemed...distracted."

"Oh, you know, there's just always a lot to do to prepare for WEF. And this new owner is a pain in the you-know-what. Anyway, I gotta go. Lesson's about to start. Talk soon."

And just like that, Trina's gone. So much for trying to get her to open up. Trina clammed up faster than a turtle hiding in his shell. I sigh, tossing my phone onto my unmade bed. I know friendships go through different seasons—so maybe this isn't a season where Trina and I will be super close, but it still hurts.

And what stings the most is the fact that Trina doesn't even seem to notice.

It's Mila Monday again, and I'm wandering around the aisles of Publix again, looking for inspiration for dinner. Something I can *actually* make in under an hour. I mean, how do people do this every night? I'm only cooking once a week and it's destroying me. I can't wrap my mind around the idea that there are people out there who make dinner every single night.

It makes me feel pathetic.

I text my mom and ask her: *How did you manage to make us dinner every night while working full-time??*

I'm utterly unprepared for this monumental task.

It's a good thing I don't have any kids yet. I'm on the slow track for wife/mother growth. Is there a course for people like me with delayed life skills? I mean, what are they teaching in school these days? Sure, I can perform complex financial analysis, but if you asked me what the internal temperature of a cooked chicken should be I'd be completely stumped.

I wander over to the seafood section, eyeing the not-so-appetizing shrimp. Is that really what it looks like uncooked? I grimace at the container of dead, gray sea creatures. I can't believe I eat those things. I definitely can't cook them—I'm not sure I'll ever eat them again, now that I know what they really look like.

My phone dings, and I see that my mom laughed at my text and then said: *Just get something pre-cooked.*

"Huh." I guess that's how my mom did it: she doesn't overcomplicate or overthink things.

I search for the 'pre-cooked' section—I'll give you a hint: there's not one. But eventually I stumble on some of Kevin's paleo meals, with pre-cooked chicken. I scan the ingredients for the Thai coconut curry chicken and put it in my basket. I grab a pre-cooked packet of rice—been there, done that, with regular rice and I almost ruined my pot—and a bag of frozen peas that says "steam in the bag!" That seems foolproof, right?

I hurry home, preparing the already-cooked meal. With the extra time I have, I tidy up the living room, light some candles, and set the table with our nice plates. I make sure to hide the box for the chicken at the bottom of the trash bag.

Once Alex gets home, I greet him with a big kiss—check—and hurry him into the kitchen for a healthy and (hopefully) delicious meal—check, check. "Wow, babe, this looks amazing," Alex says as he sits at the table. "The candles are a nice touch."

I preen under his praise. Sure, I'm not qualifying for #WomanCrushWednesday, but this also isn't a Pinterest fail like the rest of my attempts. We chitchat about our days, but I'm anxious to see Alex's reaction to the food. I hold my breath as he takes a bite. "Oh man, this is good," Alex says with a full mouth. "What's in this?"

I start listing off the ingredients from the back of the box, ticking them off my fingers. "Coconut milk, curry, vinegar, lime juice, tapioca starch—"

"Tapioca starch?" Alex's eyes are wide. "I've never even heard of that before."

"Oh," I laugh nervously. "You know, it's the starch of...tapioca."

"Well, yeah, but why not just use corn starch?"

"It's not as...good?" I say.

He shrugs, like what I'm saying makes sense. "Yeah, that's true. I mean, corn is so genetically modified I guess tapioca must be better."

"Exactly." I nod confidently. But the guilt starts building in my chest, constricting me so that it's hard to swallow.

"Did you just get it at Publix?"

"Yep." I really hope they have tapioca starch at Publix. I mean, I suppose it's true that it came from Publix...Ugh, what is with the twenty questions? Can't he just let me have a simple meal without grilling me on it? I don't know how much of this I can take.

"I really like this," Alex says as he takes another bite. And the sincere look on his face slices right through me.

Ugh.

I sigh, slumping down in my chair. "I didn't make it," I confess. "I mean, I sort of made it? I just heated it up. It's pre-cooked. I didn't find the tapioca starch and stuff, it's just in the box."

"Okay?" Alex says, gazing at me as if he's waiting for me to say more. When I don't, he says, "I still like it."

"You're not disappointed?"

"Why would I be?" Alex's gaze is warm and soft. It's a look I'm completely undeserving of. He reaches across the table and takes my hand. "Mila, it's a delicious meal that you prepared. Who cares if you cooked it from scratch or not?"

"I guess I care," I say. "And I kind of thought you would too."

Alex puts my palm against his face. "*Mi tesoro*," he says, calling me by my favorite nickname. *My treasure*. "All I care about is being with you and you being happy. If you cooking from scratch makes you happy, then do it. If not, stick a frozen pizza in the oven. It doesn't make one iota of difference to me."

Tears fill my eyes, and I fight against them as Alex presses a kiss into the center of my palm. "If you hate cooking, I can be in charge of cooking, and you can do something I hate, like dishes. We're a team, Mila."

I sit up. "I can totally do dishes," I say. "I'll crush the dishes."

Alex laughs, his eyes dancing at my enthusiasm. "So, it's settled. No more cooking for you, no more dishes for me."

He smiles at me, and I smile back, but in the back of my mind there's a voice telling me we shouldn't have to make this compromise. I should be able to do it all.

Hot Garbage

Trina

Grayson is nothing if not consistent. For the fifth day in a row, he's showed up first thing in the morning. It seems like he's trying to get here in time to watch me ride Leo—probably to assess his new venture and my worthiness as well. I do my best to tune him out, but his piercing eyes are difficult to ignore. To make things worse, he's showed up a few times in the middle of my ride, while I'm blasting The Starting Line like I'm stuck in high school. He didn't say anything, but I could feel the judgment from beneath his rotation of designer sunglasses.

Then, once I'm done riding, he goes to work on whatever tasks Ellie or the grooms put him up to. After the blister fiasco, I've given him a break from mucking stalls, but he's cleaned all of our tack—no small feat—washed all our bandages, untangled them and rewrapped them; fixed some of the automatic waterers; repainted some boards we replaced last year; and can now groom and tack up any horse without help.

Next I'll have them teach him how to screw in studs to the horses' shoes for when we compete on grass arenas. That's always a task no one wants.

DeDe begs me to give Grayson riding lessons—and how can I say no to her?—so now I'm giving Grayson lessons on Wednesday mornings. I was hoping he'd be one of those hopeless cases that would never be able to figure out how to trot on the correct diagonal, but since this is *the* Grayson J. Sterling we're talking about, he's a natural—in addition to being Ironman of the Century or whatever.

One afternoon between lessons, I hear him on the phone. He's behind the barn in one of the tranquility gardens but from my office, I can still hear his muffled voice. I lean into the window as he says, "No, I know, Dad. I'm trying, but it's hard. I've been at the barn every day this week." He sighs and then says, "I can't tell if she's any good." My eyes fly wide open as I realize he's talking about *me*. "No, I know. She's really sensitive though, I'm not sure how much I can...Right, right. The horse is fantastic, it's just, she's, you know."

Fire is flooding my veins—she's *what*? What is Grayson saying to his dad about me? He can't tell if I'm any good? He's been watching me ride all week! I force myself away from the window, pacing my office.

Anger is radiating down my limbs, and I itch to *do* something. I want to run out there and grab his latest release iPhone and throw it to the ground. Then I'll stomp on it for good measure.

I cover my face with my hands, groaning into them.

You know what, it doesn't matter if he can't tell if I'm good or not—his opinion doesn't matter! He doesn't know a thing about horses. I tell myself this again and again, trying to convince my bleeding heart.

And then there's the fact that Mila is picking a new trainer, which only makes this sting that much worse. Not only am I losing a weekly student, but time with one of my best friends. Not that I could tell Mila that and make her feel guilty—she's got to do what's right for her and Cyrus.

Still, it hurts nonetheless. It's one thing for Grayson to not know if I'm any good—but if Grayson *and* Mila are convinced that I'm a trash horsewoman, then the odds are not in my favor.

My stomach churns with frustration and pity. If I'm not a fantastic horsewoman, then what am I? If I don't have this, I have nothing. I press the palm of my hand into my stomach, attempting to quell the nausea rising there. Tears sting the edges of my eyes, but I don't let them fall. I won't.

Grayson gets off the phone with his dad, and I rush back to my desk, acting like I wasn't eavesdropping in case anyone walks in. But the conversation stays with me, anger simmering just below my skin each time I see Grayson.

What does he know? I tell myself.

Why does his opinion even matter?

It's been so long since I felt like I had to prove myself in the horse world. I worked my way to the top with Blue, and I've gotten the respect I earned with my students and other riders. Why, all of a sudden, do I feel so thrown off course by this know-it-all who doesn't actually know a thing? And Mila moving her horse to a closer barn? It has nothing to do with me, I tell myself. It's just a convenience thing.

It's Grayson who's messing up my head.

Grayson, who doesn't know I overheard his conversation, is still trying to play Mr. Nice Guy after the ShoeGate incident. And he keeps showing up, day in and day out, doing work around the barn and being involved in DeDe's lessons. He even set jumps for me yesterday, which would've been nice if it hadn't been, well, *Grayson*.

I'm still seething as evening rolls around, when we're all getting ready to head out to karaoke for Mila's birthday. Or, rather, her 'non-birthday,' as Alex is calling it. I'm ready to blow off some steam and be away from Grayson when he calls out, "See you there!" I gape at him as he walks to his red-hot Maserati. Then, I wheel on Ellie.

"Who invited him?"

Ellie, wide-eyed, points at Ryan.

I throw my hands out. "What the heck, man?"

"He overheard us talking! What was I supposed to say?"

"Ugh." I run my fingers through my sweaty hair, tugging my ponytail out.

"He's been really nice all week long," Ellie says. "He's done everything we've come up with—and I mean *everything*—no complaints, and he's done it really well too."

I suddenly feel defensive, like I need to keep Ellie and Ryan on my side. I know I shouldn't, but I tell them about the conversation I overheard with Grayson talking to his dad.

"Oh no he didn't," Ellie says.

"That's hot garbage," Ryan says.

"It is, right?" I find myself needing their reassurance, even though I'm a grown woman, even though I *know* I'm a good rider and don't need anyone's approval.

...Right?

Ryan and Ellie are quick to back me up, to tell me how amazing I am and how much Grayson sucks, but their words are hollow. I know I need to believe in myself and that's the only thing that's going to make me feel better.

Easier said than done though.

16

A Very Merry Unbirthday to You

Mila

It's my birthday.

Last week, Alex clarified expectations for today. "You're *sure* you don't want to celebrate your birthday?" he asked.

"Positive," I said. "In fact, I'll be upset with you if you do *anything* for my birthday."

So I should be fully ready for today—to receive nothing. And yet, my heart still drops when I wake up and there are no balloons, no flowers, no gifts anywhere.

Alex greets me with a kiss. "Happy cancelled birthday, wife," he says as he hands me my coffee. I wait for something more—an explanation of what we'll do today, or a promise of more to come, but there's nothing.

I know, *I know.* I wanted this. But I guess a part of me thought Alex wouldn't really listen.

I should be glad he listened, that he respects me enough to take me at my word. And, really, this is my way of loving him—of not being high maintenance. That's my mantra today: *I will not be high maintenance for the sake of my husband.*

So I keep my head high as we walk together to the Center, without so much as a hope of a birthday card or anything else. Except, I am a little disappointed when there's nothing on my desk—not a stitch of birthday thoughtfulness.

It's as if my birthday really did get cancelled.

I try not to think of it as I answer emails and reply to comments on our social media accounts. When we have our morning huddle with our staff and volunteers, I wait for Alex to stop the meeting to tell everyone it's my birthday. I mentally practice my surprised face when they break out a cake—or at the very least stick a candle on one of the muffins we always have available in the lounge.

But it never happens.

After our meeting, I head into the barn to teach some of our newer volunteers how to groom and tack up a horse, and then take pictures for our social media pages. By lunch time, there's not one shred of evidence that it's my birthday.

I head back to the office, where I find Alex at his desk. "So," I say, as casually as I can muster. "What's the plan for the day?" Okay, I'll be honest, my delivery isn't casual at all. It's pointed. *Very* pointed.

Alex pushes his chair away from his desk, turning to face me. "Nothing out of the ordinary that I can think of. Why?"

He's testing me. I know he is. The look on his face is so calm, so unassuming. And I just know it's all a sham. Surely in one second, people will leap into the office, yelling, "Surprise!!" and Alex will tell me about an extravagant birthday plan. I narrow my eyes, but Alex's peaceful exterior doesn't shift one bit. "I just wondered if you had planned something special for today."

"Why would I have done that?" Alex says, leaning forward so that his elbows are resting on his knees. His dark eyes are steady on mine. "Since my wife told me she wanted to cancel her birthday."

I throw up my hands, unable to continue this charade. "Well, I didn't think you'd actually listen to me!"

"So let me repeat back to you what I'm hearing—"

I point a finger at him. "Oh no, don't you pull your little therapist tactics on me."

"Mila." He says it so calmly it makes me want to scream.

"*Alex.*"

"What I understood from what you told me is that you did not want me to do anything for your birthday. In fact, you said you'd be very upset with me if I *didn't* listen to you. You said you wanted to cancel your birthday—*indefinitely* if I'm remembering correctly." He takes a deep breath, folding his hands together. "I donated a healthy amount to a children's charity in Africa on behalf of your 'cancelled' birthday."

"Because that's what I *wanted*."

"But now you're upset because I followed what you said?"

"I just didn't think you'd actually listen to me when I said something so ridiculous." Okay, I *know* I'm sounding like a crazy person right now—but why in the world would Alex agree to something as insane as me cancelling my birthday? I know I was trying to be selfless, but apparently I'm not *that* selfless. Alex should know better.

He raises a brow. "So do you want me to uncancel your birthday?"

"No!" I'm already halfway through the day with no gifts or special plans—if he does something now, I'll know he's just reacting to my reaction. It won't be sincere, and I won't be able to really be happy about it.

"Okay," he says slowly. "I understand completely."

And I'm one hundred percent sure he doesn't understand—because I'm not sure *I* understand myself.

Alex stands up, leaning over to press a kiss onto the top of my head. "I love you," he says, but the way he says it, I'm certain what he means is, *You're crazier than a mare in heat.*

And I don't disagree.

An hour later, Anya and Luke roll in. "Happy birthday, *sestra*," Anya says in that melancholy way of hers.

Luke, who's the yin to her yang, practically bellows out a "happy birthday"—and then hands me a folded up ribbon. I open it up and it's a hot pink sash that says 'It's My Birthday!' Anya offers me a Venti Starbucks drink. "It's your favorite," she says.

"Practically a whole bottle of syrup in there." Luke scrunches his nose in a disapproving way, though I can tell he's being playful about it.

"Thanks you guys," I say, putting the sash over my head. "You shouldn't have." Except, I'm secretly really, really glad they did. "I told you though that I don't want anyone spending money for me on my birthday."

I notice a pointed look from Alex to Luke and Anya, who speak at the same time: "Someone donated it." "They gave it to us for free."

I raise an eyebrow. "Someone donated it or it was free? Which one?"

Anya sits up straighter. "Someone donated the birthday sash to the Center for us to use for clients on their birthdays."

"And I had stars available at Starbucks, so it was free," Luke says.

I narrow my eyes at Luke. "*You* had enough stars at Starbucks for a free drink?" Luke is notorious for being a stickler about his health and wellbeing—he'd never drink a froufrou coffee drink.

"I buy so much Starbucks for Anya these days, I'm practically a shareholder."

"Uh huh."

"It's true," Anya says. "And he buys them for Katie Jo too."

"That's right," Luke nods. "I buy expensive, sugar-coffee for Katie Jo. All the time."

I hide my smile behind my Starbucks cup, knowing they're not telling the truth, but I'll let it pass. It's my birthday.

"On a completely unrelated note," Anya says. "We're going to karaoke tonight with Trina and some people from Zen. You know, if you and Alex want to come."

"No pressure," Luke says. "It's just a chill thing."

"I'd love to," I say, glancing at Alex. He hasn't said anything else about my birthday since our quasi-fight.

"It's your day," he says. "Whatever you want to do, I'm game."

17

U Can't Touch This

Trina

I wasn't planning on it, but I take a longer time than usual getting ready for karaoke. It has nothing at all to do with Grayson being there. At least, that's what I tell myself. I'm not putting *that* much effort into my appearance—I don't even wash my hair. I just pull it up into a tight topknot and swipe a little mascara on. And some lip tint. And maybe a little blush too.

Again, *nothing* to do with Grayson and how attractive he is. I mean, he's still infuriating. After the hit to my ego, I just want to feel good about myself.

On the way, I pick up a cake from a local bakery for Mila's birthday.

Non-birthday. I remind myself.

By the time I get to karaoke, Grayson's there, and he's already ingratiated himself with some of the kids. I feel possessive of them, and a little hurt that they're so readily accepting him as one of our own. I settle myself in a seat as far away from Grayson as possible, and yet I can still feel the tug of his gravity.

Ellie and Ryan come to sit on either side of me. Ellie jostles me with her elbow, leaning into me as she whispers, "We got you, boss. Don't worry."

"We'll defend your honor," Ryan says, winking at me. "To the *death*," he draws out the word dramatically. Ellie reaches across me and fist bumps Ryan, and I kind of feel like I've missed some inside joke.

"Great," I say with a chuckle. "I'll let you know when it's time to duel."

Across the table, Grayson's got the kids laughing over some story he's telling about an Ironman he did in Hawaii, and I feel a sudden pang of loneliness. I wish Mila and Alex were here already. I'd even settle for Anya in all her sulking glory. I am grateful for Ryan and Ellie, of course, but the age gap between us is more stark than with Mila and Alex. They just had to go and get married and live happily ever after. Which leaves me as this expendable third wheel that you feel pity for.

Ugh.

I order a glass of wine and attempt to join the conversation, but every reference Grayson makes to *college* or something he *read* or this *important person* he knows—it feels like a personal affront to me. It's dumb, I know. But it's like Grayson's this archetype of every know-it-all from high school who made me feel stupid and unworthy. Worse than that, he reminds me of Victor—not that he looks like Victor at all, but the way he talks and laughs and connects with people. Victor made me feel inadequate, and that's part of the reason why I deferred to his judgment—which was wrong—instead of trusting my gut. I won't let that happen again. Even if Grayson is handsome and charming and smart and hardworking.

Finally, Mila, Alex, Anya, and Luke show up. Mila and Anya are dressed like they're ready for the runway—making me feel starkly inadequate in my jeans and black tank top, even with the last-minute addition of some poorly applied makeup. Mila's wearing a bright pink sash that says 'It's My Birthday,' which makes me chuckle—I knew Mila's insistence on us not celebrating her birthday was a bunch of baloney. I don't know the reasoning behind it, but I'm sure it has something to do with some misconception on her part about Alex.

We all greet each other, exchanging hugs and Spanish-style cheek kisses. I'm not affectionate like this with anyone, but Alex and Mila have a way of demanding that of me, in the nicest way possible. And I give it to them willingly. I guess.

"Isn't this karaoke thing below you?" I bump Alex with my shoulder. "I mean, do you even sing *mainstream* songs?" I ask him, teasing Alex for his love of indie artists.

"I don't know, Trina, do *you* know any songs that don't sound whiny," he sings the last word in a warbling voice that's a pretty good imitation of Simple Plan.

I smile, wanting to wrap my arms around both Alex and Mila, to tell them how much I miss having them around more often. I'm happy for them, of course, but it still feels like something's missing. I don't say anything, or hug them, but I know that they know how I feel. I don't need to gush about it.

We present Mila with the cake I got her, lighting candles and singing to her—"happy *non*-birthday" like a bunch of weirdos—while there's a break between karaoke songs.

"You guys," Mila says. "I told you I didn't want you spending money on me for my birthday."

"They gave it to me for free," I lie. "Some kind of special going on at the bakery."

"They gave you a free birthday cake that says 'Happy Birthday Mila'?"

"A happy coincidence," I say as Mila rolls her eyes playfully. It's silly that we're all going along with this charade, but if Alex wants to do it, so be it.

When Mila, Ryan, Luke, and Ellie go up to put their names on the karaoke list, I surprise myself and go with them. Luke and Mila decide to do a Shania Twain song together, cackling about their choice. It's a good thing these two can team up, as their much more reserved counterparts keep their seats warm. Ryan writes down his name, waggling his eyebrows at Ellie and me as he heads back to his seat.

Ellie and I are the last to look over the song list, perusing it for something that speaks to us. We finally pick a song, snickering at the meaning behind it. Back at the table, I polish off my glass of wine, needing the liquid courage to do what I'm about to do.

For Luke and Mila's turn, since they don't have a wheelchair-accessible ramp onto the stage—something I never would have paid attention to before Anya's accident—they move the mics down onto the floor for them. The immediately recognizable synthetic riffs of Shania Twain's "Man! I Feel Like A Woman!" reverberate through the bar. When Luke starts singing the first verse, the crowd goes nuts—they're hooting and hollering. Alex has his hand over his mouth, smothering a smile, while Anya's rolling her eyes so hard I'm afraid she'll strain a muscle. But by the chorus, when Mila joins in, Anya's laughing along with the rest of the table. Luke's singing at the top of his lungs about "the best thing about being a woman," as he shimmies his broad—and very manly—shoulders.

When they finish, our table erupts with cheers, as Mila and Luke bow and wave.

"What a ham," I remark to Anya as Luke tips his cowboy hat to the crowd before wheeling back to the table.

Mila plops herself in Alex's lap, kissing him. Luke rolls between Anya and me, winking at his girlfriend. "That was for you, sugar."

Anya rolls her eyes again and says, "You were pitchy."

Luke chuckles before pressing a kiss to Anya's cheek. I avert my eyes, feeling less like a third wheel and more like the spare tire you forget is below your trunk.

Ryan takes the stage, giving Mila and Luke a run for their money with MC Hammer's "U Can't Touch This," with a gratuitous amount of hip thrusts.

When it's mine and Ellie's turn, my nerves are humming as if someone just strummed them like an electric guitar. Ellie and I go up on stage and the first piano notes of Carly Simon's "You're So Vain" ring out through the bar. I'm immediately regretting this decision, but Ellie's strutting around the stage, so I follow her lead. After Grayson's outfit at the horse show a few weeks ago, the hat line feels very on-the-nose and I refuse to look his way as we sing.

By the second verse, I've found my confidence, and together Ellie and I are yell-singing into the mic and the crowd is singing along. Thoughts of Victor flit through my mind as the song continues, and I wish I could scream this in his smug, handsome face.

I really did feel like my dreams with Victor were clouds in my coffee—and I hope my Olympic dreams don't end up that way too.

We finish the song and the crowd cheers. I'm surprised when Grayson takes the stage two songs later. "I was originally going to do a different song," Grayson says into the mic, "but this one seemed fitting for the occasion."

He starts singing a song that sounds vaguely familiar—like maybe I've heard it on the radio recently. The verse is talking about how it doesn't matter to him if you have money or if you're young or old, but then the chorus really gets to me as he's singing about how he'll be kind, *could you be kind to me?*

I rear back in my seat, my hand clutching my wine glass so hard, I might break it.

The song feels very pointed. I don't know whether to feel chastened, humiliated, or defensive. I just sit in my seat, getting pummeled by these lyrics and by the man singing them. I can't quite figure out where to land my emotions, so when Grayson steps off the stage, I escape to sit at the bar.

Did we just sing karaoke songs at each other? Or am I reading into that?

I shake my head. I know I need to get it together, to just grow up and act like an adult with Grayson. We're business partners, whether I like it or not.

As I'm sitting at the bar, I feel someone come up beside me. They're quite close—too close, really—and for a moment I think it's Grayson, until I turn and realize it's a stranger. A man with dark hair and thick brows. His coloring reminds me so much of Victor that I jerk back when I see him.

"Can I buy you a drink?" he asks in a thick accent.

Chills run through me, and I feel like I'm seeing a ghost. I stare at him for a few long seconds, trying to convince my brain that this isn't Victor. Victor's long gone and far away. "I've already had a drink, thanks."

The man leans in close so that I can smell the wine on his breath. "So does that mean you're ready to get out of here?"

I scramble off of my stool, a strange flood of emotions weaving through me that have very little to do with this drunk man in front of me, and a lot to do with Victor. I'm backing away from the bar when the man grabs my wrist. I'm twisting away when someone else comes up behind me.

"That's enough of that." It's Grayson, breaking the hold the man has on my arm. I stumble away from the Victor lookalike and watch as Grayson goes into full alpha mode.

He's got the guy by the shoulder, keeping him pinned to the bar. Grayson gets into the man's face and says, "When someone says no, it means no."

"Hey man, we were just talking."

Grayson glances at me, an eyebrow raised as if to ask, *Did you want to be talking to this guy?* I give a small shake of my head.

"When you touch someone who doesn't want to be touched," Grayson says with fire in his eyes, "that's a violation, plain and simple."

Then, he waves down a bartender telling them, "He's had too much. Can you take care of it?" He takes a bill out of his wallet and leaves it on the counter.

Then, he turns to me, putting an arm around my shoulder as he guides me out of the bar and into the cool night. "You okay?"

"Yeah, I'm good," I try to say it casually, like it didn't bother me, but my words falter. I clear my throat to cover the break in my words and then say, "Thanks for that. I appreciate it." Another day, another time, I'd remind Grayson of my ability to take care of myself, but that man's appearance really shook me.

I needed saving.

Do I wish it were someone—anyone—other than Grayson? Yes.

Am I still grateful? Absolutely.

Grayson squeezes my shoulder and then lets his arm drop away. I forgot how good it felt to be held by someone—even if that someone is Grayson J. Sterling. He did protect me back there, and the way he did it...wow. I think that's the definition of what the kids are calling 'boss status.' He'd probably do that for anyone, but it still felt good to be cared for in that way.

He takes a deep breath, blowing it out slowly. "It's a haunting reality, raising a daughter in a world with creeps like that."

"I can imagine." Grayson's quick reaction makes a lot of sense from that perspective—as a dad of a daughter, he's more in tune than the average guy with this kind of stuff.

"Want me to drive you home?" he asks, pointing a thumb at his car. I feel bad leaving Mila's birthday get-together early, especially without saying good-bye, but I also can't imagine going back in there right now. Grayson seems to sense that intuitively, which makes me a little uncomfortable.

"That's alright, I'm fine to drive. Besides, I'm sure I'd get horse girl all over your seats."

He tilts his head back, laughing. "After this week of barn chores, there's a ton of horse *something* all over my car. Horse girl would be a significant upgrade."

I crack a smile at this and he winks at me. Which feels a lot like we're...friends. Or at the very least acquaintances who are nice to each other. I think of his karaoke song and feel a wave of shame. Despite his delivery, Grayson has tried hard to be kind to me, and I can try harder to do the same for him.

Easier said than done.

"You look lovely tonight, by the way," he says, and my stupid heart flips traitorously. Why does a complement from Grayson of all people do this to me? It's not like I really care about what he thinks. He doesn't say it in a lecherous way or even with surprise—this isn't a "wow, look at how the horse girl cleaned up!"—he says it matter-of-factly. And definitely platonically.

"Thanks," I manage to mumble. "You do too," I say automatically.

Grayson gives me a cheeky smile as heat rushes to my face when I realize what I just said. "I look lovely?"

I roll my eyes, forcing myself to act more chill than I feel. "You know what I mean." We've reached Grayson's car, and he leans on the trunk.

"I can't say that I do," he says, crossing his arms. "Care to elaborate?" Is he *flirting* with me? There's no way.

Right? We're *barely* friends.

"No, thanks," I say breezily, suddenly needing distance from Grayson. "Have a good night." I step away from him, throwing back a small wave.

He ducks his head in a nod, a small smile playing on his lips. "You too, Trina."

What in the name of the Red Hot Chili Peppers just happened? Did Grayson and I just *banter*? I never thought I'd see the day we got along, much less have a playful back-and-forth like that. I can't help but smile to myself as I walk toward my Chevy.

I'm a few steps away when I hear him say, "What the—"

"Everything okay?" I call out, turning back to him. He's crouched by his car, examining the paint on the side, which at first strikes me as insanely vain until I realize: someone keyed his car.

Yikes. Who would key Grayson's car?

Unless…

I think about Ellie and Ryan's reaction to my venting about Grayson earlier, and the little inside joke they had when I first got to the bar.

Blood drains from my face, and I'm pretty sure every red blood cell in my body has pooled in my feet because I just realized what Ellie and Ryan were fist bumping about. I cover my mouth with my hands.

"Oh my gosh, Grayson. I'm so sorry."

"It's not your fault."

Oh but it is. I should tell him, but then what would I say? *I overheard you talking on the phone, and you insulted me as a rider, and I told my students because I'm a total professional, and now they're exacting revenge on my behalf…*

I've really screwed this up. For a moment there, I felt like Grayson and I had moved past some sort of invisible barrier that I had put up. Perhaps we were even on our way to being friends. Or at the very least cordial partners. And then I had to go and mess things up.

18

Happy, Happy Birthday

Mila

After we get back from karaoke, as I'm about to drift off to sleep, Alex snuggles up behind me, nuzzling my neck.

"Alex?" His breath rustles the hair around my neck, making me shiver.

"Hm?" His chest rumbles at the noise, the vibrations warm against my back.

"I don't want to cancel my birthday forever."

Even in the darkness, I can feel Alex smile. "I know, *mi amor*." He moves my hair aside with the tip of his nose, pressing a kiss onto my neck. "Your mom booked a spa day for the girls tomorrow, and then we're going night kayaking around Miami."

"That sounds wonderful." I smile, turning my head in my pillow to hide it. Alex's hands wrap around my waist, pulling me flush against his chest.

"Completely unrelated to your birthday," he says.

"I'm sure."

"Totally a coincidence that it was booked for this weekend."

"I believe it." I turn over, tucking my head between his shoulder and neck. "Thank you, Alex." I breathe in his clean scent, fresh from the shower.

"You're welcome, Mila." He shifts backward, tilting my head up with his fingers. "Happy birthday, *mi tesoro*."

19

I Write Sins Not Tragedies

Trina

I manage to avoid Grayson as much as humanly possible the following week—which is really freaking hard because Grayson has made himself insanely available in the barn. The guy is more ubiquitous than a Starbucks on a busy street.

To his credit, he never brings up his keyed car. He seems as happy as ever. But it doesn't stop me from worrying about it. What if he somehow connects it back to me? How would I ever begin to pay for the paint job on a Maserati? The thought makes my stomach shrivel within me. I don't even ask Ellie or Ryan if they had any hands in it, though they seem really chummy with Grayson. Maybe they're covering up their guilt with friendliness.

Whatever, to each her own.

Though he doesn't bring up the keyed car, Grayson certainly finds ways to bring up every single suggestion he can possibly think of to improve the efficiency and flow of the barn. Everything from the order of stall cleaning to where the manure should be dropped to the layout of the tack room. And he has articles and research for me to read on every subject known to man. Grayson may be one of three people in the world who has read the fifty-page analysis of manure management out of Penn State's College of Agricultural Sciences, and, naturally, he wants to foist that riveting reading material on me.

I'm on my last straw by the end of the week—literally, because Grayson has implemented a new system for sweeping after feed times so there is not a stray piece of hay anywhere.

I'm in my office making the lesson schedule for the following week when *he* comes in, sweaty and yet still as attractive as ever. How does he do that? If I get sweaty and dirty, I look like an extra in *The Walking Dead*. When *Grayson* gets dirty, he looks like he's in a photo shoot for Wrangler.

To make matters worse, Mila and Alex picked up Cyrus today and took him to Jimmy Torano's barn. I hugged them and pretended like this didn't feel like a hot knife to the back—I'm more mature than that—but my chest is aching with the sting of the move.

To top it all off, I'm on the second day of a period straight from the underworld, as if my uterus is torturing me alive for not impregnating it. Why does this have to happen once a month and not, say, *never*? I'd even be okay with having a really awful period once a year for a whole month just to have a break the rest of the time.

I'll admit (begrudgingly) that this is affecting my interactions with everyone today—especially our billionaire stable hand with his stupid dimples.

"Horses are fed," he says, wiping his hands on his jeans that are getting more worn every day. "DeDe and I are going to head out, but I wanted to give you this first." He places a supplement bottle on my desk. I glance up, holding back a groan as I prepare myself for yet another meddling moment with Grayson. Does he not realize that I have existed without his assistance—perfectly well thank you very much—for thirty-one years?

"I overheard you telling Luna about your knee hurting and I thought this might help. It's a proprietary blend of type two collagen, Boswellia, hyaluronic acid, MSM, and some other things—you can read about it here," he takes a folded up paper from his back pocket and puts it next to the bottle. The words he's saying don't quite compute in my mind, and when I try to read the bottle, the font used by the manufacturer swims in my sight. This doesn't happen to me often, but every once in a while a certain font triggers my dyslexia and I simply can't comprehend the words. It's flustering on so many levels, and when I put the bottle back on the desk, it's a little too forcefully. Why does this man seem so insistent on giving me things to *read*?

"Thanks," I say, my jaw tense, the word hardly sounding like a thanks. I just want Grayson to leave. I feel so exposed in these moments, and with people like Grayson—clearly highly educated and intelligent—I'm always on edge that he'll somehow figure out my secret. Can he tell I can't read the bottle? It feels so obvious to me, like I've tattooed 'dyslexia' on my forehead. "I can buy my own supplements, you know."

Grayson seems taken aback, and he opens his mouth to say something, then shuts it. I can't quite meet his eyes because I just feel embarrassed, defenseless. Eventually he says, "I know you can, Trina. I didn't buy this, I just had it because a doctor friend of mine makes these."

I clench my teeth—as if I needed another reminder of how important, well-connected, and intelligent Grayson is. I feel defensive suddenly. Why does he even want to be at the barn? Why isn't he off with his *important* doctor friends instead of slumming it with me? It's as if Grayson has decided I'm *so* needy that he's going to be my personal genie, fixing things I didn't need him to fix.

"I asked him to make a version of this for Leo—he's doing some research to see about the equine crossover benefits, but from what I've read online, it could be really helpful."

At this, my eyes dart to his. I know I'm glowering, but I can't help it. Why does this feel like an assault on my capabilities? I can research the best supplements for Leo—I *do* research them, and I spend every spare cent of my income on them. I tell myself I should be happy that Grayson is willing to do this for Leo, at least it won't come out of my measly paycheck.

I'm so in my head about this that I don't even respond to Grayson. I'm shocked when he says, "What is with you? I'm trying to do a nice thing and you're acting like I'm a monster." His tone is gentle, but his words are not.

I stare back at him, surprised at his bluntness. I make a conscious effort to soften the scowl that I'm sure had settled on my face just moments before. "It just...gets under my skin," I say. If he's being honest, I suppose I will be too.

He leans his hands on my desk, gazing down at me, eyebrows furrowed. "Me being nice to you?"

He really is so clueless, and I scoff. "You making decisions about my horse."

"I'm not trying to—"

I stand up, mirroring his pose so that it looks like we're in a standoff. "No, Grayson, I get you're not trying to, but you show up here like you own the place, wanting to change every system I put in place—"

"I'm mucking the stalls, that's not exactly acting like I own the place." He throws his hands open, waving out the door toward the stalls.

"It's triggering, okay?" I say a little louder than I meant, but I can't stop now. "I've had men—a man—put me in compromising situations with my horse, where he held the purse strings and I felt like I had to go along with it, and it ruined my horse and...it almost ruined me." The emotion in my chest is rising, threatening to strangle me. And I don't realize I'm practically in Grayson's face, shouting at him as if he were Victor. I don't notice the tears until one trickles down my cheek. I breathe in sharply, swiping at the tear as I take a step back. "I'm sorry—"

"Don't be." Grayson's face softens, and he steps around the desk, wrapping his hands around my arm. His gray eyes are skating back and forth over mine, like they're trying to read me, trying to consume the thoughts in my head. "I'm sorry that happened to you."

I shrug. "It's over."

"It doesn't seem like it's over, not in your head anyway." He says it softly, like a secret.

I nod, trying—and failing—not to sniffle like a child. "It feels fresh sometimes, even though it was years ago."

"Wounds are like that."

Grayson's hands drop from my arms, and even though I didn't want them there, as soon as they're gone I miss their warmth. "Look, I'm sorry that I've overstepped some bounds here. I've never done this before. I'm trying to be helpful, but I can understand the dynamics here are tense. I'll try to be more thoughtful."

I'm staring down at the ground, absorbing his words. He crouches to meet my eye, and I lift my gaze to his. His eyes are soft and sweet, inviting me closer. "Can you do something for me?" he asks softly.

My mouth feels dry and sticky, and I have to try extra hard to say, "Sure?"

"Just, communicate. Be straight with me, and I'll do the same for you. We can have a good partnership, you know."

His eyes linger on mine, and it's like I've been caught in a tow line—Grayson is reeling me in, and I'm helpless to resist.

I clear my throat, realizing Grayson is waiting for me to respond. *Way to go, Trin. Instead of proving my intelligence and worth to this guy, I'm staring at him like an empty-headed oaf.* "Right, yes," I say. "I can do that."

Before Grayson and his stupid sincerity can tug me back in, I make an excuse to head out. "I've got an appointment to get to."

"See you tomorrow," he says.

"Oh, actually," I pause at the door, hand on the frame. "You can take tomorrow off. You know, Mondays are usually our rest day."

He raises a skeptical brow. "Well, who takes care of the horses?"

"Well, I'll be here, and some of the grooms, but we—"

"I'll be here then, too."

"Grayson—" I sigh, reminding myself to keep it professional. "Mr. Sterling, that's not really necessary."

"I know," he says with a quick nod and twinkling eyes. "See you tomorrow, Trina."

I nod before darting to the safety of my truck, breathing hard. My brain is skittering through our interaction—from the way that Grayson's eyes took me in, to the gentleness of his touch when I told him, vaguely, about Victor. I still feel the heat from his hand on my arm, like a brand. I rub my hands up and down my arms, trying to shake the sensation.

And why, oh, why, does my name sound so good coming from him?

I try to remind myself that Grayson is a smarmy businessman who capitalized on his divorce to take his wife's Grand Prix pet project. He's overbearing and meddlesome.

But as I drive away from the barn, there's a distinctly sinking feeling in my chest. Because my suspicions all along have been confirmed: not only is Grayson ridiculously attractive, but behind all that billionaire businessman bluster, he's proving to be a really nice guy.

Bridle Buzz · Follow
Wellington, FL

1,529 likes

Bridle Buzz Hello lovelies!! We're back for another WEF season! Make sure to tune in for all the Wellington show news, style tips, and of course the insider scoop on all things WEF!! Comment below and let me know how excited you are for the WEF season! ... more

View all 27 comments

Ignatio Diaz I hate WEF. I'm going to WEC this year instead. The show grounds are nicer and the people are nicer.

Orlando Gelatino @Ignatio Diaz - why are you even commenting on this WEF-related post? If you love WEC so much, go find a WEC post to comment on.

Ignatio Diaz @Orlando Gelatino - aaaaand this is why I'm going to WEC.

 Add a comment...

6 hours ago

20

Crossfire

Trina

After the Christmas holidays—where I had a blissful break from Grayson J. Sterling—I endure another week of our billionaire babe at the barn. It feels so much worse after my confession about Victor—not that I told him any specifics, but still, I feel more vulnerable than ever now that Grayson knows I let a man take advantage of me and my horse. It makes me feel weak and stupid.

And I hate feeling stupid.

During our first weekend at WEF in early January, Grayson shows up with a Venti green tea, wearing clothes worthy of a timeworn groom. Does it make him look any less attractive?

Of course not.

He keeps himself busy, helping Luna and the other grooms tack up horses. He passes out water bottles and Larabars to my students, reminding them to hydrate and wishing them luck with his blinding smile. DeDe's not even here this weekend—she's off on some vacation with her mom—and yet he's still here.

Grayson insists on making things as difficult as possible for me.

Somehow, in the span of only a few weeks, he's made himself invaluable in the barn, ingratiating himself to everyone—horse and rider alike. It's awful. I just want him to go away.

When he turns his megawatt smile on me, I'm about to wither away. Does he understand that he's wielding that thing like a weapon? How much more can I take? I really don't know.

"I'm going to walk my course," I announce to no one and everyone at the same time. I'll be there early, but I'm ready to get away from Grayson's overpowering handsomeness.

"Where are you in the order?" Grayson asks. "I could bring Leo down."

"Luna's got him," I assure him.

"Want me to save you a practice jump?"

I almost groan. The guy has been to *one* horse show and he's already an expert. And not in a not-actually-useful way—he's downright helpful.

Ugh.

"Oh, sure," I say after glancing around the makeshift barn, waiting for someone else to volunteer to set a jump for me. No one else pipes up. Which leaves me and Grayson together. Wonderful.

Mila and I walk the course together, and then I send her to the stands to watch a few riders while I go school Leo. I'm early in the order, and Mila is later, so I'll ride first then come back to help her with her ride.

I find Grayson holding Leo in the warm-up arena. Something about the image makes my heart leap most unhelpfully in my chest. What is going on with me, anyway? Grayson and I are *business* partners. So he's handsome, so what? That kind of thing doesn't usually have an effect on me. If he were less helpful, less present, this whole thing would be much more palatable.

Once I reach Leo, I spend an inordinate amount of time adjusting my tack—which was put on perfectly, by the way—while I wait for someone other than Grayson to show up to give me a leg up.

No one comes to my rescue.

I dare a glance at Grayson's sunkissed face. "Do you, um, know how to give a leg up?"

"I've seen a few," he says. "You're tiny, though, so it shouldn't be too difficult." For some reason, my face flushes when he calls me 'tiny.' I should be offended, right? I'm a grown, thirty-one-year-old woman—adjectives to describe small children shouldn't be so thrilling to me. Yet when I think of the curves that I struggle to fit into my skintight breeches, I'm wholeheartedly flattered.

I'm about to turn and hold out my leg for him to give me a boost when he stops me. "Oh, wait, here." He reaches out for the chin strap on my helmet, his fingers brushing my skin as he tightens the strap. "Can't have your helmet coming off, can we? No TBIs on my watch."

I chuckle nervously, all the while staring at his lips—which are unfortunately the only thing in my line of sight. He's standing so close, I can smell the subtle hint of his morning coffee still clinging to him—a white chocolate mocha with an extra shot of espresso. I've seen his order on the occasions he's brought me Starbucks. Grayson is fastidious to a fault in most things, from his diet—which would give Luke's a run for its money—to his appearance, but the white mocha seems to be his one nod to normalcy.

I'm getting antsy as Grayson's fingers continue to graze my skin underneath my chin. "Hold still, one sec," Grayson says, chiding me like I'm his six-year-old daughter. "There, much better."

I nod, words escaping me, and silently turn and offer my leg. He grips under my ankle, his fingers firm yet somehow gentle. I almost miss the cue to jump up because I'm so focused on his hand on my leg.

I warm up Leo, willing myself into distraction. But it's really hard when Grayson's the one setting up my jump—and smiling his stupidly attractive grin every time we go over it. It's wonderful and horrible at the same time.

I'm not allowed to do this—no one should be able to distract me. It's an Olympic year! I give myself a pep talk as I wheel Leo into a rollback to our final warm-up vertical.

We walk to the in-gate, where I watch the rider in front of me, not at all aware of Grayson's presence beside me. I definitely did not notice the way his biceps peeked out of his shirt when he folded his arms. Nope. I didn't. *Stop, Trin. He's attractive, yes, you've decided this before, but that doesn't mean anything to you. Get your head in the game and ride!*

As I'm about to ride into the arena, none other than Eva Rutherford approaches. She stands way too close to Grayson, her shoulder grazing his arm—not that I'm paying close attention. I heel Leo into a trot and try my best to ignore Eva's tittering as Grayson makes a joke to her.

Fire sparks in my chest, igniting a jealousy that shouldn't be there. I chastise myself as I quickly go through the course in my mind before the buzzer goes off. I have nothing to be jealous about.

We canter to the first jump, a vertical with purple accents and faux brick jump standards. We take the outside turn to a massive oxer, but Leo's momentum isn't what it should be, and he grazes the back rail. It falls with a disappointing thud. I click to him, urging him to pick up the pace as we head into a five stride line. At the last second, he chips in and we add a sixth stride to the line. He tries his darnedest to get over the fence, but his knees knock into the top rail, sending it to the ground.

My stomach clenches, feeling like I've wasted this ride. I have half a mind to pull up Leo so as not to waste his legs on the rest of this course. But I think about what I tell my students: that we learn valuable lessons from even the worst rounds.

I just wish *I* didn't have to learn this lesson.

I take a long route to the triple combination, using the space to gain speed and confidence. We sail into the triple, and all of the gymnastic work we do really pays off because we hit each stride perfectly, soaring out of the final jump in impeccable rhythm. We salvage the rest of our ride, with Leo not even blinking at a funky Swedish oxer and a sturdy brick wall.

When the course is finished, the announcer declares our faults—eight jumping and six on the time. I loosen my reins, patting Leo on the neck. This pathetic excuse for a ride wasn't his fault.

There's one thing that is abundantly clear to me: I cannot work with Grayson J. Sterling. He is absolutely a distraction I can't handle.

He needs to go. ASAP.

21

TikTok Made Me Do It

Mila

I may be failing at the wife list, but I'm crushing this WEF season. It's as if all of the years of practice—as well as the time I've invested in my mental health—are overflowing into this epic showing as a competitor and horsewoman. Cyrus and I absolutely dominated the five-star Grand Prix.

I only wish the same could be said for Trina. During her ride today, she was distracted and disconnected from her horse. Technically, we're competitors, but I'd rather we rise through the ranks together. I have this (probably unrealistic) dream of the both of us making the Olympic team, taking on Paris together.

But lately, Trina's been so out of it, I'm genuinely concerned about her. And despite my best attempts, she's not letting me in about what's going on.

However, I think I might have an idea...

I was standing on the bridge overlooking the International Arena when I saw Grayson bringing Leo to the warm-up arena for Trina. I didn't think anything of it, until he adjusted her helmet strap for her. And the look in her eyes was unlike anything I've ever seen on Trina's face.

And I realized: she likes Grayson.

Or, at the very least, she's attracted to him.

And if I know Trina, it's freaking her out worse than if her horse got stolen.

I tuck that revelation into my pocket, resolving to find an opportunity to help Trina in whatever way I can. Even if she won't want my help, this is what friends do, right?

A few days later, I'm working on item number five of the perfect wife list: *surprise him*. Lately, Alex has enjoyed following these indie artists on TikTok. I don't even know what genre this music is—pop rock? Hip-hop? I don't even know. But I've been searching for a concert by one of his favorite artists—Nic D, GRAHAM, or Connor Price—but apparently these guys aren't big on concerts. The few I've found are already sold out, or really far away.

I'm one click away from messaging these guys to beg them to come to Miami when I see something interesting. There's a course available from GRAHAM that teaches people how to produce music. I click through the description of the course, which covers everything from basic equipment, software instruction, legal and financial considerations, and how to market and make a business out of indie music production.

It's a risk, getting something like this for Alex without discussing it with him. He's not one to put himself out there—he wouldn't even sing karaoke with me on my birthday without a lot of prodding, even though he has a nice voice. But when I look at his favorite artist, GRAHAM, I know there's a place for Alex somewhere in the indie music scene that he loves so much. Alex told me that GRAHAM started out behind the scenes as a producer for other artists, and now he's making music with millions of listeners. He's sweet, a little nerdy, and only has eyes for one girl—just like Alex—and the more I peruse GRAHAM's page, I decide it's worth the risk.

A few days later, after I've purchased the basic equipment recommended in the course—thanks to my emergency credit card—I sneak back to the Cottage while Alex is busy at the Center and set up a mini studio area for him in the corner of our spare bedroom. It's a simple setup, with a computer, microphone with a pop filter, a good pair of closed-back headphones, and a MIDI controller and keyboard. I pull up the course on the computer and then head back to the Center to get Alex.

"Hey, I need your help with something," I say to him as I pop my head into our office. He follows me back to the Cottage, asking if I broke the toaster oven—again. I grimace. I *did* break the toaster oven again this morning, but we'll come back to that later.

I drag him into the spare bedroom. "Ta-da!" I present his little workstation to him.

"What's this?" he says with a small smile.

"I know how much you've enjoyed following these Indie artists and seeing their creative process, so I decided to get you a course about how you could do it yourself." I clasp my hands together, suddenly feeling nervous—I spent a lot of money on this stuff...what if Alex doesn't like it? What if he likes it but he's upset that I spent so much money? What will he say when he finds out my dad has actually paid for it all? "I got the basic equipment they said to get," I wave a hand at the music station. "But, um, if you don't like it or don't want to—"

Alex pulls me into a crushing hug. "I love it," he says.

"Really?"

He nods. "I never would've thought to do this for myself, but I really love this idea. I'd love to learn more about the process of making music."

A week later, Alex has been working on his music course nonstop. It's made it easier for me to leave the house to ride Cyrus—which has been almost daily now that he's at Jimmy's barn. I've felt guilty dipping out on Alex so often, but now that he has his own project to work on, I don't feel as bad.

One evening when I get home, Alex meets me in the living room with his headphones around his neck. "This is a good look on you," I tell him as I greet him with a kiss.

"Thanks," he says with a mischievous smile. "Want to do something with me?"

"Uh oh."

"It'll be fun."

He pulls me into the spare room—which is now a studio, with equipment and musical instruments I didn't know we owned strewn across the bed in a manner that's very un-Alex-like. I give a little laugh, thinking I've created a monster. Alex sits me in his lap, showing me an TikTok video of GRAHAM and his wife making a song together—she gives him a melody, a word to work with, and a drumbeat, and they look very adorable in the process.

"Let's try this together," Alex says.

I shrug. "How hard can it be?"

"Alright, give me a sec," Alex shifts me onto one knee so he can access his computer and other equipment. "Okay, give me a melody."

I think for a second. "Doo doo doo," I say in a pitchy, sing-song voice.

Alex laughs. "Okay," he says, drawing the word out. "Guess we're making a kids' song," he teases.

"That's obviously what I was going for."

"Alright, let's try something else. How about a beat?"

I press my lips together, attempting to make some kind of beatbox soundalike, but apparently my mouth doesn't work like that. Sound comes out, but not anything close to a beat, along with a gratuitous amount of spit.

I glance over at Alex, who's staring at me wide-eyed, until he bursts into laughter. "That was so bad," he says, wiping tears out of the corner of his eyes.

"Let me try again." But no matter how many times I try, my mouth just simply will *not* beatbox. I wonder if it's one of those genetic things, like tongue rolling or ear wiggling. Alex, of course, is getting a kick out of my repeated failed attempts. Also, he's going to need a tissue to wipe up all the spit around his equipment...

"It's actually a little surprising," he says, compressing his lips to keep his laughter in. "You're good at everything."

I scoff. "I'm not good at everything." I've had plenty of proof of that lately.

"It's true," Alex says, a laugh escaping. "You're *terrible* at this."

I sigh, finally giving up on the beatboxing. I guess I can check number five off the list...I certainly surprised him, didn't I?

22

The Devil Wears a Suit and Tie

Trina

Next week, once she's back from vacation, I call Caterina to follow up with her about finding someone to purchase Leo.

"Please, Caterina, I need your help." I hate the sound of my own whine in my ears, but it can't be helped. Caterina needs to know how desperate I am. Of course, I won't tell her the particular source of desperation, but I'm desperate nonetheless.

"Antonio seemed interested when I spoke with him. Let me see if he can come to the show this weekend and meet you there."

"That would be amazing! Thank you, Caterina."

We hang up, and a few minutes later, I get a text from her saying that Antonio can come for my early afternoon class on Sunday and we can talk after.

I respond with a GIF that shows a girl blowing a kiss. She replies with a winking kissy face, and I scrunch my nose.

I should feel relieved, so why does it feel like I just got in bed with the devil?

It's Sunday after my class. The horse show has wrapped up, and I've managed to have minimal thoughts about Grayson's lips. This mostly has to do with the fact that I've kept busy, sent him on errands on the other end of the show grounds, and helped students that I don't even teach. It's finally time for me to meet up with Caterina and Antonio.

We meet at the Tiki Hut next to the International Arena. Antonio looks to be in his late-fifties or early-sixties. He has a full head of salt and pepper hair, stylishly tousled, with dark rim glasses on his round face. I'll be honest, I'm relieved when Antonio isn't remotely attractive—sure, he's nicely dressed in his Polo shirt and slacks, but he's old (for me) and rotund. I shake his hand, feeling hopeful that this arrangement might work.

But then, I feel Antonio's eyes rake over me, lingering on my ample hips, and meandering their way to my eyes.

What in the name of Jimmy Eat World is happening? My skin crawls at his greedy gaze.

Caterina seems completely unaware of his ogling, and we all sit down and order lunch. Antonio narrows his eyes when I order a burger—it's not my go-to option, but I'm starved after a full show day. I try to brush it all off—the leering gaze, the evident opinion on my food choice. My view of Antonio softens somewhat when he shows me pictures of his grandkids. Someone who adores his grandkids so much can't be all that bad, right?

I remind myself that Antonio is going to be a silent partner. I'll only need to see him every once in a while. Unlike *some other partner* who just won't go away, even in my dreams.

Yep, you read that right.

Ugh.

"Here's the deal, Antonio," I say, folding my hands and lean forward on the table. "Me and Leo—"

"Leo, that's the horse?" Antonio asks, even though we've said that at least twice.

"Yes," I say patiently. "Me and Leo are on track for the Olympics." This is a slight fib—there's not even a long list yet, but what Antonio doesn't know won't hurt him. "I'm looking for a silent partner who can back our progress. The current owner is lacking in the *silent* department."

Antonio throws his head back and laughs a booming sound that vibrates through the space. "I hear you loud and clear," he says when he's done laughing. "Let's talk numbers."

I tell him what Leo will cost, including feed, vet bills, and general upkeep.

The reality is there's not much money to be made on one horse—they cost a lot, win big pots only occasionally, and as I can attest, they get hurt and you can lose your investment easily. But Caterina seems to understand that this isn't about money to

Antonio, it's about status. "Show jumpers are the new racehorse," Caterina says. "It's the ultimate status symbol. And a potential Olympic gold, that's luxury you can't buy easily."

We talk for a while longer, and eventually Antonio says, "If you can convince the current owner to sell to me, I'm in."

We shake hands, and I leave Caterina and Antonio to their drinks, anxious to get away from here. I should feel grateful to be one step closer to exiting Grayson's gravity, but instead I feel...slimy.

23

One Promise Too Late

Trina

After my conversation with Antonio, I feel like I'm cheating on Grayson. I do something unthinkable and avoid the barn on Monday. I call Luna to tell her I'm not feeling well and give her instructions that she absolutely doesn't need, but it makes me feel better. I just can't face Grayson yet.

So I lounge around the house, listening to my podcasts, doing some yoga, meal prepping my food for the week. I even attempt to take a nice, relaxing bath—but I can only stay in for two minutes because *what the heck do you do in a bath?* My bath isn't really big enough to completely sink into it, so my neck is at a weird angle, my knees are poking out of the water, and I'm either too hot or too cold depending on how much of my body is protruding from the soapy water. I'm about ninety seconds into my "relaxing" bath experience before I decide baths just aren't for me.

When I get out, I check the time—it's only eleven o'clock in the morning. What am I supposed to do for the rest of the day?

This day off business is a waste of time.

So I do what any self-respecting horse woman would do: I change my clothes and head to the barn.

And since I can't catch a break to save my life, He-Who-Shall-Not-Be-Named is the first face I see when I stroll in.

"Hey," Grayson says, setting down the massive orange wheelbarrow he's carting through the barn. It looks like Grayson's been busy: a pitchfork balances atop a mound of horse manure and shavings, and he's covered in sweat. He lifts his shirt to wipe his face, and I have to school my eyes away from the flash of skin.

I will not check out Grayson Sterling. I will not check out…

Dang it. I just checked out Grayson Sterling. "Hey," I say, my voice far too loud, compensating for the guilt thrumming through my chest.

"Luna said you weren't feeling well."

"Yeah, guess I was just tired from the weekend. I attempted to have a relaxing morning."

He lifts an eyebrow. "Attempted?"

I sigh, throwing my hands up in defeat. "Yeah, I guess relaxing just isn't in my DNA."

Grayson chuckles, his gray eyes dancing.

Do they always dance? Or is it just for me?

I point a finger at him. "Don't you dare mock me, Grayson Sterling. I see you busying yourself around the barn. You're as much of a workaholic as I am."

An unreadable look flashes across Grayson's face. "Guilty as charged," he says, and though his tone is friendly, there's something about his words that make me feel like I've offended him somehow.

"Anyway, don't let me keep you," I say, waving a hand at the wheelbarrow, and then I rush to my office, closing the door behind me and leaning against it.

How am I supposed to tell Grayson about Antonio? Why does it feel like I'm betraying Grayson? Grayson—the ridiculously attractive and smart billionaire businessman who stole my horse from his ex-wife in some kind of weird power move. I have to remind myself of that fact. Because it certainly doesn't fit with the Grayson in the worn jeans and killer abs—*yes, I noticed them, who wouldn't?!*—who's cleaning stalls and endearing himself to everyone in the barn. Including me.

How do I let him go?

But I suppose the better question is—how could I keep living with him by my side? Because there's one thing I'm certain of: if I spend much more time with Grayson Sterling, he will be my undoing.

I vowed that I would never let a man get between me, my horse and my dreams ever again. And just because Grayson is sort of cute and kind of nice doesn't mean I should suddenly change my tune.

I open my office door with shaking hands. "Hey Grayson," I call out. "Can I talk to you for a second?"

"It's not personal," I tell him after I've told him about Antonio. Though who am I kidding, it absolutely is personal.

Grayson gives a little grimace that tells me he sees through my lie. "DeDe's going to be devastated."

"I know, I'm sorry. The deal he's giving me..."

"I can match it. Beat it. Whatever it takes." The steely glint in his eyes reminds me that Grayson is a businessman. His newly calloused hands and affable smile don't change that.

I shake my head. "He's agreeing to be more...hands-off."

"Ah." He pinches the bridge of his nose with his fingers. "So it *is* personal."

"It's not about you, it's about me."

He lets out a caustic laugh. "Sounds like you're breaking up with me."

"I have to do what's best for Leo." *And me.*

He narrows his eyes at me, leaning forward so that his elbows are resting on my desk. "You know that I'm majority owner. If I wanted to buy you out, find a different rider, or take his shoes off again, I can. I read the contract."

All of the breath leaves my lungs, like I just got punched in the gut. "You wouldn't," I whisper, my voice strangled by pure fear.

Grayson sighs, running a hand over his face. "No, I wouldn't." He fidgets in his chair, looking around the room at everything but me. "I'm apparently not the kind of guy to impose when I'm not wanted. Despite everything, I know when to bow out."

Something about his words feel way bigger than just this moment—like maybe he's referring to his marriage? I have no idea, but every second I sit in Grayson's presence feels more and more like I just downed a jug of rotten milk. The nausea and unease of what I've done, what I'm doing, is swirling uncomfortably within me.

"Grayson—"

He shakes his head. "I'll find a new place for me and DeDe, you won't have to bother anymore with us." He pushes back from the desk. "I get it. If that's what you want."

DeDe. How could I not have considered how this would affect her? I rub my chest, as the stabbing sensation of my overwhelming selfishness hits me. Tears fill my eyes as I watch Grayson stalk out of my office.

He shuts the door behind him, closing the chapter of our partnership.

I should be relieved that getting rid of Grayson was so simple—but it wasn't easy.

For so long, I've viewed Grayson as a thorn in my side. Something I couldn't get rid of. Now that he's leaving, the thorn is removed, but I'm bleeding out.

And I don't know if I'll be able to face myself at the end of this.

24

Cake by the Ocean

Mila

Things at the Center are so busy. Yes, we're all ecstatic that things are booming, but it's that kind of thrill where you're not sure how to manage it all. On top of that, since we haven't been able to find a barn manager, I'm essentially acting manager, making sure that the horses are fed and watered daily with a good exercise rotation so that they're not too fresh for our clients, and I'm staying on top of the worming, shoeing, vaccination schedules, and about a million other things that are constantly falling through the cracks. Most days, I wake up before the sun so I can ride a few of the horses before my actual job starts. I manage to fit in a personal training session during my lunch breaks a couple times a week, and then after the Center closes for the day, I head to ride Cyrus. It seems like there's always something new to implement in our training schedule—this week, I'm trying to incorporate a stretching routine with him every day along with our new low-level laser therapy to aid in his muscle recovery. By the end of the day, my head is spinning and my body is exhausted.

But if this is what it takes to be an Olympian, I'm all in.

My best friend, Monica, has tried FaceTiming me three times this week and I've missed her each time. I haven't had a chance to catch up with her since visiting her in NYC for Christmas which was—I glance down at my phone to check the date—wow, way too long ago. Where has the time gone?

But she'll be moving back home soon, and we'll be able to spend more time together then.

There's this constant pressure following me around, like a niggling reminder in the back of my mind that is telling me I have too much to do, and I'm failing on every account.

Today is the first day of our support group meeting for parents with kids on the spectrum. One of our therapists, Tamara, is getting ready to meet in the lounge with them while Alex and another therapist, JoAnne, take the kids to groom the horses. That is, until Luke rolls up to me. "We've got a problem," he says.

"What is it?"

"Our Vet group is about to meet, but there's a bunch of moms congregating in the lounge who say they've got a support group meeting there?"

Oh no. My hand goes to my forehead. I double-booked the lounge, thinking that the 'Vet' marked in the calendar was for a visit from a Veterinarian for the horses. Not our weekly Veterans group. How did I mess that up?

And of course, as I'm mentally scrambling for a solution, Anya rolls up to witness my failure. "What's going on with the traffic jam in the lounge?"

I groan, telling her about my mix-up, feeling like an amateur in front of Luke and Anya.

"Can you take the Vets to the tranquility garden?" Anya suggests to Luke.

"Sure thing, boss," he says as he tips his cowboy hat.

"Problem solved," Anya says, nodding decisively.

"Sorry, you guys," I mumble as they both roll away from me, but I'm not even sure they hear me.

It's a Tuesday night and I'm at the Cottage preparing for a monthly online meet and greet on our Facebook page for people who are interested in learning more about the Center. The event is about to start in fifteen minutes, when someone knocks on the door.

"Anya?"

My sister's high-tech Scewo wheelchair takes up the doorframe, a Publix bag in her lap. "We're watching LIB and having Jeni's." Love is Blind—AKA, LIB—is our sisterly tradition where we bond over judging people who are naive enough to believe they can fall in love on reality television. "We're overdue, and you've been super lame with me about eating sweets lately. You need to loosen up."

"As nice as that sounds, I've got that meet and greet—"

"Luke's doing it. You need a break."

"Oh." I glance at my computer screen, sitting on my kitchen table. "Is this because of the support group mix-up? I'm getting benched?"

"Don't be ridiculous. You're a founder, you can't get *benched*."

I narrow my eyes at her, wondering at the truth of her words.

"Don't fight me on this, *sestra*. You won't win," my sister says with her classic eyebrow raise over her bright blue eyes.

I laugh as Anya hands me one of three cartons of Jeni's ice cream she has in her lap. My favorite flavor, Blackout Chocolate Cake. "Fine, fine," I say, though it's not like I would've put up much of a fight. I can't say no to Jeni's...or my sister.

I grab a throw blanket for Anya and a pair of spoons for us. Anya sets herself up next to the couch, and I stretch across it, turning on our favorite show.

"How are you and Alex doing?" Anya asks between bites of ice cream.

"Good, fine, you know," I say.

"I don't know, that's why I'm asking."

I sigh, deciding to tell Anya about the perfect wife article that I'm working my way through. At this point, I've got the first ten items on a note on my phone—I was originally planning on putting all twenty-one in my phone, but that felt overwhelming. So I decided to start with the top ten.

It's going swell.

"Mila, that's the dumbest thing I've ever heard."

I rear back, defensiveness pushing up inside of me like steel walls. Also, what does it say that both Monica and Anya agree on this point? The two of them could not be more different, and yet they agree here. Against me. "I'm just trying to be a good wife."

"No, you're trying to be a *perfect* wife." She gives me a pointed stare. "But you're going about it the wrong way. Alex doesn't honestly care about all that stuff."

"Then why did he send it to me?"

"Did you ask him?"

"Yeah, and he said—" I stop, trying to remember what Alex said. "I don't remember what he said. All I remember is that he said it was cute and funny."

"Look, Mila, I've never been married before, and I'm not exactly a relationship guru—"

"No, you're not."

"But, what I do know is this: Alex loves you. I don't know why he sent you that stupid article, but I guarantee it wasn't so you could kill yourself doing all this stuff. Besides, aren't you trying to focus on qualifying for the Olympics?"

"The two things are not mutually exclusive."

"Whatever," Anya says with her signature eye roll. "All I know is that you're focusing on the wrong things."

I grit my teeth, returning my focus to the TV show. Even though a part of me thinks Anya may be right, there's an even bigger part of me that wants to prove my perfectionist sister wrong. Surely *she* would be able to check every item off the perfect wife list, plus make it to the Olympics, all while learning to knit and getting her PhD in literally anything. Her reaction makes me want to prove her wrong—that I can do it all, even if she thinks it's dumb.

25

Existentialism on Prom Night

Trina

Two nights later, I'm fidgeting in front of my apartment complex, waiting for Grayson to pick me up. We'd texted about the details of the sale meeting, and he'd requested to drive me. I can't imagine why he'd want to be in such close proximity with me while I'm in the middle of yanking Leo out from under him, but I felt like I couldn't say no to his last request.

I purposely dressed as casual as I'd allow myself—I don't care what Grayson thinks of how I look, I told myself. I did, however, spray on one singular spritz of perfume since we'll be trapped in his tight little car. I wouldn't want to smell bad now, would I? That's just a regular human reaction—to want to smell good to the driver in your car—not at all based on attraction.

When Grayson's Maserati whips into the parking lot, I nearly fall over when I hear the song clearly blasting from within. He turns it off as I step into the car, but before he can even greet me, I turn the radio back on. Sure enough, the song I'd thought I'd heard comes on: Straylight Run's "Existentialism on Prom Night."

"You know this song?" I stare at him with narrowed eyes like I'd just caught him listening to something condemning instead of my favorite song in the whole world.

He gives me a quick glance, and then looks out the window, his hands shifting (nervously?) on the steering wheel. "I don't just know this song, I *love* this song."

I fall back against my seat, the soft leather enveloping me like a warm hug. I blankly put on my seatbelt, telling myself that sharing a favorite song isn't a reason to like someone.

When we pull up to the Polo club a few short minutes later, Grayson puts the car in park and turns to me. "You sure you want to do this?"

Again, I don't have the words to convince him—or myself—that this is the right move. I simply nod, and he gives me a quick nod back. Gazing into his eyes, I don't find any of the hurt that was so prevalent on Monday when I first told him about Antonio's offer. Did he forgive me? Or is he just that good at masking his feelings?

We get out of the car and walk to the Stallion Restaurant at the Polo club. Grayson's back in his typical billionaire with a capital-B outfit—dress shirt rolled to his forearm, revealing a fancy watch that matches his fancy shoes and fancy belt. Now that I've seen him for a few months in regular clothes, it almost looks like he's a different person. Someone...untouchable.

A gust of cold air blasts us as we walk inside. The hostess escorts us to our table—we're there before Antonio, so I make a show of spending a long time looking at the menu, even though I know exactly what I want. I can feel Grayson's eyes on me even from behind the safety of the menu.

When Antonio arrives, I'm relieved.

Until I'm not.

Despite it only being six o'clock in the evening, Antonio is very clearly drunk. And very, very handsy. When I stand to shake his hand, he instead pulls me into a hug, placing his hands a little too low on my back for comfort. Antonio situates himself rather close to me, and every time he tells me something, he has to touch my hand or my knee below the table. I've scooted my chair—as discreetly as possible—further each time, but the man is relentless.

Antonio orders champagne, a charcuterie board starter, and charred octopus for the table. "We're celebrating," he tells the waitress, with a squeeze of my knee. I jerk my leg away, and when I glance across the table, I can tell Grayson noticed the movement.

He is *livid*. I've never seen him so mad—even when my students' ruined his paint job. Even when I "broke up" with him a couple days ago. His lips are pinched in a thin line, his jaw clenching and unclenching. His normally light gray eyes are as dark as the ocean before a storm.

Grayson and I snack on the charcuterie board as Antonio yaps on and on about how much money he has—he's currently telling us about a deal he just wrapped with an "undisclosed" actor whose name rhymes with Fohnny Tee Lones. When Antonio smacks his hands on the table, laughing at his own joke, neither of us join in.

I can tell Grayson is trying to catch my eye across the table, as if he's questioning the same thing I am—is this guy really better than Grayson? It's an easy answer—no way, Coldplay. But how can I possibly turn it around right now? I'm trying to think through my options, but Antonio's loud braw is so overpowering, it's hard to think.

When the waitress comes back, I'm about to order the black truffle risotto, when Antonio jumps in and orders the salmon for me.

"Actually, I'll have the risotto," I say through clenched teeth.

Antonio waves a hand. "She doesn't know what she wants," he says to the waitress, then looks over at me with a wink. "Have to keep that figure trim if we're going to win the gold, hm?"

All of the indignation I'd been feeling up till now comes to a boiling point. I stand, shoving my chair back so hard, it falls over. "You have absolutely no say over what I do or don't do with my *figure*," I bite out.

"Is that so?" Antonio says with an amused twist of his fish-like mouth. "Because this check would say otherwise." He pulls a check out of his wallet, and I don't even see the numbers because my eyes are blurring with fury.

"Can I see that?" Grayson says, plucking the check from Antonio's chubby hands. He glances at it, and then up at me, his eyes conveying just as much anger as I feel—maybe even more. "You want this?" he asks me. I shake my head decisively. "Good," he says. "Me either."

Then he does the most satisfying thing I've ever seen anyone do for me: he holds the check up in front of Antonio's face and rips it in half. Then he rips it again, and again, until there's a tiny mound of shredded paper sprinkling Antonio's charred octopus.

"Fine," Antonio says, pushing back from the table. "If that's what you want." He looks over at me, his gaze roughly moving up and down my body in a way that makes me cringe. "It was too much money for an overgrown dog anyway."

That's when I snap. I close the distance between myself and Antonio, reach my hand back, and with every ounce of force I've honed over thousands of hours on horseback, I slap him.

I don't care how much money you have—no one gets to insult my horse like that.

His glasses clatter to the floor and his hand grasps his cheek, a howl of outrage emitting from his jowls. Before Antonio can make a move, Grayson throws a wad of cash on the table that could pay my grocery bill for a month. With one hand, he grabs the bottle of champagne and two of the glasses, twining them through his fingers. Then he skirts the table and takes my hand. "Let's get out of here," he says. "Apparently, they'll let just anyone in here these days." He gives Antonio a look that could wither a live oak, and then leads me out of the dining room.

Antonio's finally found his voice and he's shouting at us, but I don't hear what he's saying. All I'm attuned to is Grayson's hand in mine, his firm fingers enveloping mine.

We head out a side entrance that I didn't even know about, which spits us out onto the golf course green. I wait for someone to chase us down, to kick me out of here for slapping Antonio, or at the very least tell us we can't take the alcohol from the dining room. But no one does. Then I remind myself I'm with Grayson J. Sterling—they all probably think he owns this place. And maybe he does.

There's something comforting about Grayson's hand swallowing mine, and I start to feel anxious about the moment he'll pull away. The sun has set over the golf course, and the further we get from the Stallion Restaurant, the more the darkness pulls us into the night. I take a deep breath, feeling free and almost giddy.

Grayson surprises me by collapsing onto the grass, leaning against a hill on the course. My hand feels suddenly cold where his was a moment ago. But when he pats the grass beside him, I sit down, much closer than I ever would've done an hour ago.

"I think we should celebrate," he says, undoing the foil on the champagne. "That guy was a creep of the highest order, and you dodged a bullet." He presses both thumbs against the cork, and pops the bottle, bubbly liquid fizzing onto the grass. He pours us each a glass.

"To dodging a bullet," he says. We clink glasses, and I down the champagne in one sip, the fizz burning my throat and flushing my brain with something akin to bravery. I set the glass down and then lay back on the grass, sighing. The sky is clouded with dark gray haze, the edges of the clouds glowing with the dregs of the sun. My arm tingles as Grayson lays back next to me, his shoulder brushing against mine.

I turn my head to look at him. "Thanks for saving me back there," I say. "I didn't...deserve that. But I'm grateful nonetheless." He turns to look at me and our faces are so close, I can feel his breath splaying across my cheeks. It's not the worst feeling in the world.

"You're welcome," he says, and I wait for him to gloat or ask me what I was thinking choosing a guy like Antonio, but he doesn't. He simply gazes at me—slightly longer than is strictly polite—and then settles his head back on the grass, staring up at the sky.

We lay in a comfortable silence that I find both surprising and unnerving. When did I become comfortable with Grayson J. Sterling? How does a guy like this—with his billions in the bank and his flashy red Maserati—sneak past my defenses?

Not that he's gotten by all of my defenses. Oh no, this girl has *layers*.

After a few minutes, Grayson refills our glasses. "Guess you're stuck with me," he says with a smile that looks almost apologetic.

"It's alright, you're not that bad."

Grayson chuckles into his glass as he takes a sip. "I'm looking better and better compared to Antonio, aren't I?"

I laugh, the champagne releasing a more carefree side of me. "He's doing wonders for your image."

"Should I send him a thank-you gift? Maybe some sort of fruit basket?"

"Oh! Yes. A basket of road apples would be perfect."

Grayson's brow furrows. "Road apples?"

I smile. "Horse poop."

"Ah. Perfect." He smiles back at me. "Although I was thinking we could get some of those charred octopus for him. Maybe wait a week and then send it to him. Rotten like his heart."

I scrunch my nose at the thought of week-old octopus arriving in the mail. "Don't forget a side of risotto."

"Road apples, week-old charred octopus, and risotto. Forget the Olympics. We should start a gift basket company."

I laugh again, the warmth and freedom of the sound surprising even me. I'm laughing with Grayson Sterling. No big deal. We can do this, right? I mean, we're business partners, and we're turning into friends. I think.

We're cracking up so much that we don't even notice the security guard approaching until he's towering over us.

"Sir? Ma'am? You know that you can't have an open container unless you're inside the restaurant."

Grayson stands, and I follow his lead. He assesses the security guard, then gives him his signature smile. It's not even directed at me and I feel charmed. I think I've had too much champagne. "Hey there, Joe," he says, reading the man's name tag. "We were just about to leave. You want the rest of this?" He hands Joe the half-empty champagne bottle. "I think it's like a three-hundred-dollar bottle." Grayson shrugs like holding a three-hundred-dollar bottle of champagne is no big deal. "Anyway, enjoy!"

He takes my hand—again—and we walk toward the parking lot. Once we're safely in Grayson's car, I glance back at the security guard. "Look," I nudge Grayson so he can see what I see: Joe taking a swig out of the champagne bottle.

We crack up as Grayson peels out of the parking lot. "Glad it's not going to waste," he says. "Hate to see good champagne go down the drain."

"Every sip is like the cost of one riding lesson."

Grayson leans toward the middle console, nudging me with his shoulder. "Maybe it's time to raise your prices. You're worth it."

I flush, looking out the window, marveling at how the evening has changed course. We've gone from something like enemies to co-conspirators in the span of one night—and based on the electricity mingling between us, perhaps something a little more.

Yep, I've definitely had too much champagne.

26

Untold Story

Trina

Since we skipped dinner, we eventually find ourselves at a little Mexican food truck. We order burritos and then sit in Grayson's Maserati to eat—something I'm shocked by. If you surveyed a hundred guys with Maseratis, I'm pretty sure one hundred out of one hundred would *not* let you eat in their precious car.

A few weeks ago, this would have felt far too familiar, far too dangerous. But right now, sitting here with Grayson, listening to Motion City Soundtrack as we eat our burritos, salsa dripping down our chins—this feels somehow *right*.

"I need to tell you something," I say. "You know how your car got keyed?"

"Uh, yeah?"

"I'm pretty sure I'm responsible."

He looks at me with wide eyes, his burrito suspended halfway to his mouth. "You keyed my car?" His tone of voice isn't harsh or mean, only incredulous.

I shake my head quickly. "I think it might have been some of my students."

"So why do you say you're responsible?"

"Well..."

"Did you tell them to key my car?"

"No, but I think they might have wanted to because of the things I said about you."

"What could you have possibly said about me that would make someone want to key my car?"

"Well, you weren't exactly the chillest person when we met. You had all those charts and ways I wasn't measuring up—"

"Is that what you thought about my tables?"

"Grayson, what other conclusion could I possibly have drawn from that other than I wasn't measuring up in your mind?"

"It wasn't about you, it was more about how to optimize Leo—"

I shake my head. "Me and Leo are inseparable. You criticize him, you criticize me. That's just how it works."

"I see," he says genuinely, like he actually does see what I'm saying.

"It's not only that, though." I grimace. "I heard you on the phone that day, you were right outside my office talking to someone on the phone. You were saying that the horse is good but you can't tell if I'm any good. It just, I dunno, pissed me off. I vented to some of my students about it—which I know is very unprofessional, and I'm so sorry—but it was the same night your car got keyed." I fix my eyes on my lap, feeling the weight of shame wash over me. "I'll pay for the damage, of course."

Grayson stares out the window, eyes roving back and forth like he's thinking. It scares the tar out of me, and I'm regretting my confession immediately. What if he kicks me out of the car right now and I have to hitchhike home? Or, worse yet, he decides to buy me out and find another rider for Leo? "Grayson, I'm so sorry—"

"I'm trying to remember who I was talking to that day or what about. But Trina, I've never said anything disparaging about your skill to anyone. Because I genuinely think you're an amazing horsewoman."

"Oh." Well, now I feel like an even bigger idiot than ever.

"But, Trina, you're not responsible for the keying."

"If I hadn't—"

Grayson shakes his head. "It wasn't your students. They had video footage of this guy keying the car that night, but it wasn't anyone from the barn."

"Well, that's a relief," I say with an awkward chuckle. "Still, I shouldn't have said anything to the students about you. That was wrong. I'm sorry."

"I agree, but I accept your apology."

"Thank you," I say with a small smile. "I'm sorry, too, about your car."

He shrugs. "It's okay, I actually hate this car."

I laugh, thinking he's joking. "Oh wait, you're serious."

"Yeah, I was actually going to trade it in before it got keyed. But now I'm waiting for the custom paint to come in so they can fix it before I sell it."

"Why would you buy a car you don't like?"

"I didn't. Cate got it for me."

Ah. That makes sense. Something about this realization makes me that much more ashamed of how I judged Grayson. I assessed his character based on his outward appearance—the fancy car, expensive watches, and careful hairstyle. Come to find out, those things don't define him at all.

Go figure.

"I'm sorry for trying to cut you out," I blurt, because apparently my brain thinks this magical Maserati is akin to a confessional booth. "I-I'm scared. I told you a little about Victor—" I think about how to describe Victor to Grayson. A long-term boyfriend? A business partner? Whatever phrase I come up with, it doesn't quite encapsulate what our relationship was like. "He was the owner of my first Grand Prix horse, Blue. And...my boyfriend." I look down at my burrito, toying with the wrapper. "He really screwed me over, and it's honestly messed with my head a lot."

Grayson takes a massive bite of his food, nodding. "I get it," he says with a full mouth. I bite back a laugh, because I've never seen Grayson so...casual. So undone. I really like this laid-back, almost messy Grayson. When he finishes his bite, he says, "I think I might've been a little overbearing since I came here," he gives me an apologetic look that tugs at my nonexistent heart strings. At least, I *thought* they were nonexistent until Grayson showed up. "I might've gone a little overboard."

"You think?" I say, not even bothering to hold back the sarcasm.

"So, is that why you wanted to find another owner?" Grayson asks, his voice tinged in something akin to vulnerability. "Because I was overbearing?"

I sigh, leaning my head back on the seat. I can't be one hundred percent honest with Grayson—I'm not even sure I can be one hundred percent honest with myself—but I can choose to tell him something close to the truth. "Yes? But also, I've just had a bad experience in the past with Victor and the horse that we owned together. I can see now that you were just trying to be helpful, but it felt really triggering for me."

"I'm sorry, Trina. I can be a bit more hands-off—if that's what you want. I'll still come around with DeDe, but I don't have to stick my nose in places you don't want me to." He wipes his mouth with a napkin, folding it into perfect fourths and then tucking it in with the burrito trash. Okay, so 'undone' Grayson is still...Grayson. "We need like a code word or something if I'm being too overbearing."

I give him a sideways glance to see if he's pulling my leg, but he's totally serious—in that cheerful-Grayson way of his. I'm grateful—and relieved—he isn't forcing me to linger on the Victor bit too much. "Like what?"

"It has to be something we don't say a lot." He drums his fingers on the steering wheel, thinking. "Carburetor?"

A laugh bubbles out of me. "Carburetor? I don't know if I've ever said that word in my life."

"Well, there you go, it's perfect then," he says with a smile. I take another bite of my burrito, which has long since gone cold. But even at room temperature, a burrito is still a burrito—and today I'm letting myself take a break from my very stringent diet. Which means this burrito tastes like heaven.

"What about something that fits with the situation a little better? A big, overbearing animal or something," I say between bites. "Grizzly bear? No. Panda! Panda!"

"Pandas are overbearing?"

"Well, they're *bears*."

"I suppose that's true. Just not sure I appreciate the comparison. You think I'm like a panda? I'd prefer grizzly."

"Grayson, you are a lot of things, but you are *not* a grizzly."

He scoffs. "What are you talking about? I can be aggressive and loud. Sometimes."

At this point, I'm laughing hysterically thinking about Grayson as a Panda bear—all curled up in a tree somewhere eating bamboo. "I've never heard you be loud or aggressive." Even in tense situations—like at the bar with that creep, or when we've argued—Grayson maintains a serene intensity.

He bares his teeth and growls in a very ungrizzly bear way, which only serves to further fuel my laughter. "Stop, stop," I say, wiping tears from my eyes. "We're going with panda, I can't unsee it now."

He slumps into his seat, pretending to be upset. "I don't want to be a panda," he mock grumbles. "I want to be a grizzly bear."

"You're too cute to be a grizzly bear."

He scoffs again. "Oh but I can be a panda?" Then, he gets a sly look, turning to me with a raised eyebrow and a smirk. "You think I'm cute."

"Psh, you wish."

"You just said it."

"I mean, yes, in a general, anyone-with-eyes-can-see kind of way."

"You have eyes."

This prompts me to roll the aforementioned body part, but my heart is racing at this point because it feels like I just revealed my cards far too early. "Don't let it go to your head, mister. Now, back to the code word: if you're being over*bear*ing, I'll call you a panda."

He sighs dramatically and says, "If you must."

"Hey, just think of it as extra motivation to *not* be a panda." I give him my best smirk, and I can't help the warmth flowing through me when he flashes his smile at me.

We're driving back to my apartment, listening to Rise Against's "Swing Life Away," as I work up the courage to ask him the question I've wondered since I first met him.

"Why Leo?" I finally ask.

"I'm sorry?" Grayson glances over at me, clearly confused.

"Of all the things you could have chosen in the divorce, why choose Leo?"

Grayson's eyebrows raise, and I'm afraid I've stepped over all the goodwill we've built up in the past few hours. "I'm sorry, I shouldn't have asked."

"No, it's okay." He reaches over and turns down the music to conversation-level. We're sitting at a pointless red light—there's literally no other cars on the road right now. "I just thought, I don't know, that it would be obvious."

"Revenge?"

Grayson barks out a laugh, but when I don't join him, he says, "Oh, you're serious?" He grips the steering wheel with both hands, rotating them around the leather. "Yikes, Trina, good to know what you think of me." He looks more vulnerable now than I've ever seen him, and I want so badly to reach out a hand, to comfort him, but I don't.

"I'm sorry, I shouldn't have assumed."

He nods, his eyes flicking to the dashboard, and then around the car, like he can't quite find a place to land. "I was a workaholic, you know. With my research, my business. I poured everything into it, like I couldn't rest until I'd gotten the device right where I wanted it. I needed it." He sighs, running a hand down his face. "It wasn't until last year when I realized it would never be perfect. I finally took a step back only to find that my wonderful little family had fallen apart while I'd had my head stuck in the research." He fiddles with a leather piece on his key ring, still not looking me in the eye, like he's too embarrassed to admit all that he's saying. "I really tried to save my marriage, but Cate was just too far gone. I had no idea she'd moved on. Not that I blame her, I should've been there—" He cuts himself off, shaking his head, like he's had this conversation with himself a million times over. "But with Demetria, I knew I had to do whatever it took. I sold my business and decided I'd do whatever DeDe wanted to do." He shrugs, almost bashfully. "And you know how much she loves the horses, loves Leo in particular. I haven't told anyone this, but it's the only thing I asked for in the divorce. I gave Caterina everything else. God knows I didn't have to, but I did. For DeDe."

I finally reach across the middle console and place a tentative hand on his arm. "You're a good dad, Grayson."

He finally meets my eyes, a sadness dwelling there that's beyond anything I could imagine. "Not yet," he says. "But I will be."

Somehow, Grayson and I end up driving around Wellington, blasting music with the windows down. We tear down back streets, the wind whipping through the car, and I'm regretting any bad thoughts I've had about this car ever.

"Oh, I've been saving this one for you," Grayson says, as he thumbs through his Spotify. I just about choke on my spit when I register what he just said—Grayson's saved a song for *me*? "I know you like to listen to music when you ride, and it seems like we have similar tastes."

Then I really do choke on my spit. I'm sputtering and coughing as Grayson pounds on my back, all while I digest the fact that Grayson and I do seem to have similar tastes in music. Which is just...baffling. How could we have *anything* in common? And yet, I find that I don't mind having something in common with him.

"You okay?" he asks. I nod and give him a thumbs up. "Alright, good. You ready for a song to blow your mind?" He waggles his eyebrows at me and I can't help but smile.

"Hit it."

Grayson had me pegged right, because not only do I love the raucous electric guitar and drums, but the lyrics speak directly to my ambition in the show jumping ring. The first line of the song rocks me to my core because of how much it resonates: *Don't wanna live as an untold story/Rather go out in a blaze of glory.*

And I'm a sucker for a song that cuts out the instrumentation and has the singers singing a capella in a choir-like sound. When the song ends, I immediately reach forward and repeat it, turning the volume even higher as The Strut's "Could Have Been Me" plays again. Grayson only smiles at me. Pretty soon, we're singing at the top of our lungs, "I can't hear you, I won't fear you!"

I'm trying to remember the last time I felt so good, so free. It's different than how I feel when I'm riding Leo—not necessarily better, just different. But somehow the feeling remains: I feel free.

27

Sugar, We're Going Down

Trina

After talking for hours last night, today is the first full day of a true partnership with Grayson. We're committed to communication and balance. I can tell it took a lot of restraint on Grayson's part to not create a flowchart for our communication dynamics.

I didn't tell him why, but I told him he wasn't allowed to print anything out for me, send me any articles, or bring me books to read. "You can send me videos, podcasts, or summarize books you've read," I told him. "But I have enough on my plate as it is right now."

Grayson surprisingly agreed to this without any probing.

Today, we're meeting to discuss our show plans moving forward. There's an easiness between us that hasn't been present before, and I feel more relaxed than ever around him.

"So, what do we need to do to make this Olympic dream happen?" Grayson asks, clapping his hands and rubbing them together like a mad scientist.

"As you know, we need to hit up as many five-star Grand Prixs as possible," I tell him. "Preferably, in multiple locations. It's not enough to prove that we can compete in Wellington—we have to show we can hang with the big guys anywhere in the world, but I'd prefer to keep international travel to a minimum." When he frowns at me, I sigh and tell him, "I had a horse permanently injured after international travel."

"Say no more," he says with an understanding nod.

Grayson's typing on his phone and then says, "There's Longines in Miami in April, and then maybe we could spend some time up North during the summer—Traverse City and then head to the Hampton Classic in August."

"Sounds nice, escape the Florida heat." He hands me his phone and I pretend to look through the FEI show jumping calendar—I know it by heart already, and Grayson doesn't have any reason to have dyslexia settings uploaded to his phone. "We could head up to Maryland for the Washington International Horse Show in October. And of course we'll have our fair share of five-star options here in Wellington."

"I wouldn't mind going to WEC in Ocala at some point, DeDe went last year with you and Cate, I'll never hear the end of it." He says it with a smile on his face that melts my hardened heart a little more. The guy may be overzealous, but he loves his daughter. And like the good book says, love covers a multitude of sins.

"That's music to my ears," I tell him. "I love WEC. Too bad they don't have any five-stars."

"Not yet," he says with a pointed look, as if he knows something he can't share.

As we continue to discuss our calendar for the year, I'm beginning to open up to the idea that partnering with Grayson won't be all too bad. It'll be fantastic, as long as I can manage to stifle my attraction.

In the coming weeks, my days take on a predictable shape. In my mind, each part of my day is divided up into a ring—similar to the Olympic rings. The early morning is my 'beat my body' ring—I start the day on the BEMER, making sure to get my achy knees, then I meet up with a personal trainer at five thirty and work on cross-training. It seems like every day my trainer pushes me harder and harder, until I think I can't do it anymore. But that's when the willpower kicks in, adrenaline takes over, and I surprise myself with what I can do.

It's an amazing feeling.

The second ring is my Leo ring. After my workout and breakfast, I head to the barn and exercise him. We have a regular schedule, with dressage training on Tuesdays and Thursdays to keep him supple, gymnastics on Wednesdays, and if we're not competing over the weekend, we ride a big course on Saturdays. Ellie and the other students have fun crafting the hardest possible course they can come up with each week. We end our sessions with carrot stretches and the BEMER blanket.

The third ring is my job ring—giving lessons and exercising client's horses. Because, you know, you need money to live and all that jazz.

The fourth ring is my relationships—chatting with Tripp on the phone, going out for a barn dinner or hanging with friends. This is admittedly the smallest ring, the one I have the least capacity for. I'm trying my best to keep it in the routine, but it feels like there's something always trying to squeeze it out. I can't think of the last time I've seen Mila outside of a horse show.

The fifth ring is self-care when I go home. I listen to my favorite podcasts, do some yoga and meditation, and go to bed. Some nights I watch a show, but most days I'm just too tired to keep my eyes open.

Every day, there's an undercurrent of electricity connecting each of the rings, reminding me of my *why*. I want this Olympic dream with every cell in my body, and it's as if my blood is humming with it: *I want this. I want this.*

So, even though I'm exhausted and my knees hurt and I have to see Grayson's stupidly handsome face most days, I get up. I beat my body into submission, and then I sacrifice it on the altar of my horse, my barn, my dreams.

Because I want this.

It's a Wednesday morning and I've just finished stretching Leo while I put the BEMER blanket on him when Grayson shows up. He's a little late today—normally he makes it in time to see me work with Leo, but today he's sporting a mischievous grin that makes my stomach drop to my toes.

"Oh no," I say. "What did you do now?" Ever since our close encounter with Antonio, the tenor of my relationship with Grayson has evolved. It's almost like we're friends, with a healthy dose of sarcasm running through most of our interactions. Some people might call it a defense mechanism. Not *me* per se, but some people.

"I got you something." But the way he says it, it sounds like this is going to cost me something. Not in dollars, but in willpower. I pat Leo on his rump, locking up his stall and then I follow Grayson to my office. Splayed out on my desk are brochures and more print outs. I mean, what is *with* this guy and print outs? Is he in love with his printer? With research articles? Give me a break.

And yet the gesture feels different today than it would have a few weeks ago. I still don't want to read any of this stuff, but I'm starting to trust Grayson's intention. It doesn't mean I won't give him a hard time, though.

I pick up a brightly colored brochure with a picture of a woman in a bathing suit dipping herself into some kind of tank. "What is this?"

"It's a cold-water therapy tub. I used a similar one when training for my Ironmans—" I notice how Ironmans is plural, which makes me think Grayson really is as crazy as I initially thought. "Except the one I got you is even more state-of-the-art. It has a chiller, which means it'll keep the ice water cold on its own..."

I hold up a hand, stopping him. "So let me get this straight, you got me a barrel full of ice water? That you want me to, what? Take a little dip so I can get my daily dose of frostbite?"

Grayson chuckles, but his enthusiasm doesn't let up. "Cold water therapy is proven to reduce inflammation, increase blood flow and muscle recovery time. Speaking from experience, it also improves psychological fortitude—"

"Meaning it's ridiculously hard to stay *in* the tub."

"It's also been shown to improve mood," Grayson says with a very pointed—yet playful—look.

I scoff. "I'll let you guess what freezing my tush off is going to do for my mood."

"I promise I won't stick around for it," he says with a laugh. As if I'd voluntarily dunk myself in a bucket of ice in a swimsuit in front of Grayson.

"I mean how much is this thing?" I flip through the brochure looking for numbers until I zero in on one that feels completely absurd considering this is a bucket of ice water. "Grayson!"

He looks at me with mock innocence, and I smack his arm with the brochure. "This is way too much."

"A worthy investment for an Olympic athlete."

"Grayson, this feels like a very *panda* thing to do. First, you printed stuff out, which is a no-go, remember? Second, you didn't even ask me about this before you spent five thousand dollars—" I choke on the words.

"You're right, I'm sorry. I should've asked you about it first. And I'm sorry about all the print outs, I got excited." I'm thrown off by his quick apology and his earnest gaze. For a moment, I see a young Grayson giving his poor mother a run for her money. Who could say no to those gray eyes? All of a sudden, I'm actually considering voluntarily freezing myself to death all because of Grayson's ridiculous face.

"When does it come in?" I say with a resigned—and maybe a touch dramatic—sigh.

"Tomorrow night, to your apartment." He glances around the office. "Didn't think you'd want to do the cold plunge in here."

"I don't want to do the cold plunge anywhere," I mumble under my breath. But then I turn to him, and say, "Thanks, Grayson. This is quite...nice."

"You're welcome," he says with a nod.

"Can't say I'm looking forward to it, but I'm interested in the benefits," I say in an attempt to choose my words carefully.

Grayson chuckles. "Oh, it's brutal. Nothing to look forward to here."

I glare at him.

"Except the benefits, of course," he says with a cheeky smile. "Is six o'clock okay for the drop off?"

"Sure."

"*I'm* looking forward to it," he says. I laugh, throwing the brochure at his head before walking out for my first lesson of the day.

At five fifty-five the next evening, I'm pacing my apartment, waiting for Grayson to show up with this cold-plunge tub. Grayson Sterling is going to be in my apartment, and it's safe to say I'm freaking out. I'm not quite sure why, but I am.

It is what it is, people.

I've showered and changed into fresh clothes since coming home from the barn. My apartment is perpetually tidy—it's just me living here—but I've straightened it even more, adjusting the throw pillows and picture frames. At five fifty-seven, I sniff the apartment, wondering if it still smells like the salmon I made yesterday.

Oh, *no*.

I run to my kitchen, grabbing a lighter and a candle. A moment later, the candle's moonlit walk scent—whatever *that* means—is wafting through my living room. Much better.

Except the candle being lit feels…romantic, doesn't it? That's definitely not the vibe I'm going for with Grayson coming over, so I quickly blow it out. But now my apartment smells like blown out candle. So I run to my back sliding glass door, opening it as I wave my hands through the living room trying to diffuse the smell.

When Grayson knocks at my door a moment later, I'm really beginning to wonder if I'm not a crazy person.

I open the door, plastering on a smile that probably is more Joker-ish than Julia Roberts.

(Maybe I *am* a crazy person?)

"Hey, Grayson," I say breezily. At least, I hope I sound breezy. Am I breezy? Easy, breezy, Trina. That's me. Ha.

Grayson has changed out of his barn clothes and is sporting a pair of fitted black jeans, a casual but expensive looking t-shirt, and white high top Converse.

Huh.

Not exactly an outfit I thought would be in Mr. GQ's closet, but I don't hate it.

The rep for the cold-plunge barrel sets it up on my patio, and we fill it with water from the patio hose. He goes through a few steps of how to get the chiller to work, recommendations and so on, but I'm not one hundred percent paying attention because I'm pretty sure there's no way I'm using this thing regularly. Even if Grayson did pay way too much for it. Hey, if he wants to come over and use it he can.

Actually, scratch that. I don't need Grayson hanging out in his swim trunks on my patio.

What feels like hours later, the rep finally leaves and it's just Grayson and me alone on my patio. He claps his hands together. "Ready?"

"For…" *you to leave?* Yes, yes I am.

"To take your first plunge."

"With you here? Absolutely not." Also, the temperature gage on the chiller says forty-five degrees. So, I'll pass.

"Oh come on, I'll be a good support. I've done this before and can coach you through it."

The look in his eyes tells me Grayson is not going to let this go. I sigh. "Fine. What should I wear?"

"You got a wetsuit?"

I give him a glance that should answer his question.

"I'm kidding. Sort of. A swimsuit is fine."

"Great. Awesome. Fantastic. I'll go...change."

A few minutes later, I'm in my bathing suit, a towel tight around me. I may or may not have spent a solid five minutes examining every flaw visible on my body before scowling at my reflection and stalking back out onto the patio.

"Okay, the key is to just commit," Grayson tells me. "Don't go slowly, it'll only make it more painful. Submerge yourself as quickly as possible. We'll start with one minute and then you can work your way up from there."

"Okay." One minute. How hard can one minute be? I climb up the steps, hovering over the lip of the barrel, still holding my towel tight against me.

"Want me to count you down?"

I nod, though I really don't want him to.

"One...two..." he stops. "You know you can't bring your towel in there, right?"

I sigh, letting the towel drop as I close my eyes so as not to gage Grayson's reaction to my half-naked body.

"Alright. One, two, three, go!"

In one quick motion, I grip the edge of the barrel and lower myself into the water. The instant my skin touches the cold, I suck in my breath.

All I feel is regret. The cold slices through me as the nerve-torturing needles of ice water prick every inch of my skin. I'm cold in places I've never even thought of before.

Grayson's talking to me, but I can't even comprehend what he's saying because all I can think is that I'm going to die. My breaths are coming in weird spurts—like my lungs are too cold to breathe properly.

I immediately start shivering, my teeth chattering. "Grayson," I grumble because that's the only thing that I can think to say right now. Grayson. This is his fault. His stupid idea. Then I realize that talking warms me up—at least as much as my body is capable of being warmed at the moment. "Grayson!" I shout, and it feels good, so I keep going. "I hate this! I hate this. I will never ever do this again. I can't believe I let you convince me to do this."

Grayson laughs, the corners of his eyes crinkling as he does. "You've got thirty seconds left."

"Thirty seconds? I've been in here for only thirty seconds?"

"You're doing great."

"I'm doing terrible. I've never felt so horrible in my entire life." I shudder, clenching my teeth together as I groan. It's like my body is warring against itself—do I give in to the cold and just *die*? Or do I fight to warm myself up? By the way the shivers have stopped, I think my body is giving in. I'll be dead by the time I'm supposed to get out.

"Fifteen more seconds."

"Agh!" I cry out because I'm seriously not sure I can last fifteen more seconds. In any other situation, fifteen seconds would feel like a short amount of time. Maybe if I was trapped underneath a car it would feel like a long time. Or if an alligator had his jaws on my knee.

All comparable situations to what I'm experiencing now.

"Five, four, three, two, one. You did it!"

"Grayson?"

"Yeah?"

"I can't move. My body has stopped working." I glance around at the barrel. "Also, how am I supposed to get out of here? This thing is taller than I am." It's not taller than me, but I'm feeling dramatic (can you tell?) and if I'm being honest, a little mad at Grayson for putting me in here. And *a lot* mad at myself for agreeing to it.

Grayson reaches into the barrel, taking out my hand. He rubs my fingers, his thumbs pressing into my palms. His hands move up my forearm, squeezing it so I can feel again. He takes my other hand and does the same on that side.

The entire time I'm watching, speechless. I can't remember the last time another person has touched me like this—literally rubbing life back into me.

"There, how's that?"

I mumble something incoherent, which makes Grayson laugh. "There should be a step at the bottom of the barrel, on the right side, do you feel that? Yep, there we go."

I start to rise out of the cold-plunge, which only makes the sensation worse - the cold water doesn't sting quite as much when I'm not moving. But I force my limbs—that are essentially glorified ice blocks at this point—to lift me out of the barrel, balancing on the lip before coming down on the step stool on the other side. Once I'm out, Grayson wraps my towel around me. Then he's hugging me to his side, rubbing his arms down my back and across my shoulders. "You did it," he says. "See? It wasn't so bad, was it?"

"It was horrible," I mumble into his chest. I resist the urge to burrow there—I know the desire is only because I want to be warm and Grayson's is the only warm body around. But I stand stock straight, allowing him to warm me with his hands.

And I feel nothing.

Zero.

Zip.

Nada.

"You'll feel better after you shower," he says.

"I may never feel my toes again. Toes are really necessary for life, you know."

He laughs again, and I realize how much Grayson has laughed with me since we came to this truce. It's not too bad.

And the way his hands are moving all across my back, strong and steady and WARM. It's fantastic. I let myself lean just a little into him, like a moth to flame, seeking heat and warmth and light. I let my eyes flutter closed.

This is nice.

Really nice.

He smells so good too. Like the top of a mountain—how do you bottle-up a mountain? I'm not sure, but Grayson's managed to do it. And I like it.

My eyes fly open. Nope.

Nope, nope, nope.

"I'm going to shower now," I say, extricating myself from his warmth.

"Not too hot though, don't want to undo the effects of the cold plunge."

I glare at him on my way into my apartment, but my icy gaze does nothing for my rapidly warming feelings for Grayson J. Sterling.

28

Gonna Buy Me a Dog

Mila

I'm going over our monthly budget when Matthew Craig—Luke's brother and Monica's boyfriend—pokes his head into the office. "Got a minute to chat?" he drawls.

"Sure," I say, though I really don't. I'm so far behind in life that if I had a magic button to pause time while I got caught up, it would still take me five hundred years to get my ever-growing to-do list done.

Matthew walks into my office and leans against Anya's desk, like one hundred percent the cowboy that he is, with his Stetson hat, worn jeans, and alligator skin cowboy boots.

"I'm going to propose to Monica," he says, and I can't help it, my jaw drops. Monica and Matthew have only been together a few months. My mind flits to Anya, who's been with Luke three times longer than Monica's been with Matthew. I know she wants to marry Luke, but I also know Anya wants to take her time. How will she feel about this?

"Wow. That-that's incredible. Congratulations." I smile at Matthew, who's as calm as ever as he gazes down on me.

"I know it's soon, but dating for a long time before you get married is a dumb modern social construct."

"Very true." Monica will love that she's bucking the system with her cowboy fiancé. "So, what do you need help with?"

Matthew's lips tilt into a ghost of a smile—the best I'm going to get from him—as he walks across the room and drops into Alex's seat. "Can you help me brainstorm?"

An hour later, my brain is officially squeezed dry of any and all proposal ideas. I'm not even sure what we decided on—the trail ride at sunset? The movie theater takeover? Or the far more elaborate indoor snowball fight with the rented snow machines with the sign that says, 'you won my heart, can I win your hand?'

Once Matthew leaves, I lean my head on my desk, no longer able to focus on budgets. I know I need to leave soon for my lesson on Cyrus, but I decide I'll close my eyes for just a minute...

What feels like a moment later, I'm being scooped up into someone's arms—definitely Alex's, I can tell by his sandalwood scent. I can't quite open my eyes, but I manage to murmur, "I'm going to ride Cyrus."

"It's past nine o'clock, *mi tesoro*. You can ride him tomorrow."

I groan, leaning my body into his chest. I'm wide awake now as I realize I somehow managed to botch my ride time with Cyrus—it's the one thing I'm supposed to be excelling at, and I can't even manage to do that right.

I let Alex carry me to bed, but I lay awake wondering, if I can't even be good at this, what am I good at?

Today, I'm working on a creative gift idea for Alex's birthday. The problem is, Alex isn't easy to shop for. I've searched through all of the Amazon gift finder suggestions, as well as the Pinterest lists for 'fabulous gifts for your guy.' Alex just isn't the kind of person to appreciate an engraved flask or a beard maintenance kit.

When I drop into Luke's office for suggestions, he gives me an amused smile. "There's really only one thing I can think of that will be met with one hundred percent satisfaction."

He gives me a sheepish grin, and I can tell where this is going... "What is it, Luke?" I say warily.

"Well, what is the *unique* item you possess with exclusive control over its supply? The one where you dictate the timing and regularity of its distribution?" He raises a brow at me before taking a sip from his mug.

"Ugh," I say, throwing up my hands. "But I want to give him something. Like an actual item."

"Here's the thing: you can get him anything in the world, but there's nothing that's going to come close to you."

"We'll see about that." I narrow my eyes at him. "You're lucky I'm not like Anya or I'd write you up for impropriety."

He raises his hands in a gesture of innocence. "You asked, I answered honestly."

I roll my eyes. "Whatever."

But as I go to leave, Luke says, "Hey Mila?"

"Yeah?"

"When Anya and I tie the knot, and she ever asks you this question about me...you know what to say."

Now that Monica is back in South Florida—dating Matthew and working for Luke at his wheelchair company, Wheelz—she stops by the Center on a regular basis. I wish I could say it *wasn't* because I'm really bad about returning her text messages and setting up hang out time with her but...it's totally because of that.

Today I'm working on the exercise schedule for our horses while Anya sits across from me doing something horrible with our insurance when Monica waltzes in, looking like she does not belong in a barn. Her dark brown hair is pulled into a sleek yet elaborate topknot that would take me approximately a bajillion years to do. She settles herself into Alex's empty chair—he's at his internship right now—and proceeds to touch everything on his desk. Which, since this is Alex and his desk is immaculate, it's not much. But still, I know it would irk him.

"Hey," I say to get her to stop. "Any ideas for Alex's birthday?"

"I've got just the thing," she says as she rummages in her purse. I have a lot of experience with Monica's purses, and she could literally pull out *anything* and I wouldn't be surprised. "Ta-da!" She shoots something at me, a little black blur that hits my chest and lands on my lap. "*Feliz cumpleaños*, Alex."

I hold up the piece of fabric that is less like underwear and more like...*string*.

"Do you just walk around with a thong in your purse?" Anya grumbles.

"Doesn't everyone?" Monica says with a wink.

I glance between Anya and Monica, knowing that my sister can only tolerate so much of my best friend. I grab Monica's hand, tugging her toward the door. "Come run errands with me," I say, even though I absolutely do not have time to do this. "Help me find something to give to Alex."

"We could get you a bow, you could wrap yourself—"

"Monica!"

"What? *Es perfecto.*"

I roll my eyes, channeling my inner Anya. "Something else, c'mon."

Monica and I walk around the Shops at Pembroke Gardens, with no luck. As we're heading home we pass a sign that says: *Jack Russell Puppies Call 954-555-9623*

"That's it!" I shout. I U-turn so that Monica can take a picture of the sign. While we hop on I-75, I call the number.

An hour later, I'm the proud owner of the most adorable little puppy in the world. He's white with reddish-brown spots. His face is mostly brown with a white-tipped nose and a narrow white stripe down the middle of his face. Alex is going to adore him.

Together, Monica, the new puppy, and I head to PetSmart and stock up on everything we'll need. He's the most enthusiastic, snuggliest puppy ever. His little wet nose pumps against my cheek as we walk around the store. I laugh as his puppy breath washes over me, his tiny little teeth nipping at my nose.

But holy cow, owning a dog is *expensive*. So I swipe my dad's credit card—feeling a little less guilty this time around because this really does feel like an emergency. I can't bring this dog home without food, now can I?

Monica and I pick up celebratory Starbucks on the way home, along with a puppuccino for the dog. Once we're back at the Center, Monica heads home while I sneak back to the Cottage. I set the puppy up with food and water and a cushy dog bed beside the couch. After running around the house like a madman, he falls asleep on the dog bed. I sneak out to get a little more work done in the office before surprising Alex with his perfect gift.

29

Dog Days Are Over

Mila

An hour later, I tug Alex away from his computer. "I have a surprise for you."

"Oh yeah?" his eyebrows raise suggestively, and I think about what Luke told me.

"Not that," I say with a swipe at his chest. I guess Luke and Monica weren't totally off in their assumptions about what Alex would like...

"But...later?"

I laugh. "Sure, later." I keep pulling at him until we reach the Cottage door. "Are you ready?"

He nods, laid back as always.

But when I open the door, it's not to reveal a cute little puppy asleep on a dog bed.

As I wave my arm like Vanna White, I show off...pure chaos. Couch cushions are ripped to shreds, their stuffing dots our living room like fallen snow. A pungent odor greets us, and there's brown wheel tracks systematically laid out across our carpet that look like our Roomba encountered..."Oh, no."

"Mila, what happened?"

I turn to Alex, putting my hands on his chest. "I got you a dog. A really, really cute dog but..." I glance behind me, biting my lip. "This is not how I left him." I laugh nervously. "I'll take care of it. Here," I hand him my keys and shove him out the door.

"Mila..." He shoves his foot in the crack of the door so I can't close it all the way.

"It's fine, Alex." I push at the door without any effect.

"It's not fine, I'm not leaving you to clean this up by yourself."

"But I want you to."

"Can I at least see the dog?"

I sigh, opening the door. "Fine."

Alex walks through the door, both of us navigating the war zone of our living room on tiptoe. There are puddles of dog pee with Roomba tracks through them, and much worse than that is the brown tracks crisscrossing the carpet where the Roomba intercepted the dog poop. "I see lots of evidence of a dog, but, where *is* the dog?" Alex asks. He whistles, the sound echoing off the walls. But there's no response from the puppy.

We check under the couch and entertainment center, but he's nowhere to be found. We hurry into our room, where we find the puppy curled into the blankets of our bed. He's got pieces of white fuzz stuck to his coat from the couch cushions, but he's sleeping peacefully.

"He is adorable," Alex says, putting an arm around me and kissing my temple. "Thank you for my gift."

I whirl on him, a hand on my hip. "Are you joking?" I whisper-yell, so as not to wake up the dog.

"I mean, he's a puppy. Puppies make messes. I get it. But the fact that you thought of me and got me something so adorable is really sweet."

I snort. "Puppies make messes? Are you kidding me? It's a freaking war zone out there!" Tears well in my eyes. "I'm just failing in every way possible."

"Mila," Alex says as he pulls me against his chest. I burrow my head against him and let the tears come. As I let go, the words start tumbling out of me as I tell Alex about all I've tried to do the past couple weeks. "I was trying to do all those things from the article, but I just keep failing one after the other after the other. I don't think I'm wife material, Alex. You deserve better than this."

I sob against his chest, as Alex holds me, running his hand over my hair. He's saying all kinds of things to me—in English and Spanish—that I know are meant to be reassuring, but I can't hear them through the screaming of my failures in my head. Finally, he leans back, his hands cupping my face, his thumbs catching my tears, swiping them gently off my cheeks. "Mila, when I said 'for better or worse,' I meant it. We're in this together, forever. No matter what."

"Yeah, but I thought the 'better' would outweigh the 'worse.'" I sniffle. "Or at least be even. I'm a total wreck, Alex."

He laughs, a genuine, chest-filling laugh. I smack his chest. "Don't laugh at me."

"I'm not laughing at you, I'm laughing *with* you."

"I'm not laughing!"

"Well, you should be."

"Why's that, exactly?"

"Because, *mi tesoro*, it's funny to think that you are defining being a good wife by these arbitrary standards. What about what I think? What about what's important to me? I don't care if you cook for me or buy me a perfect gift. You are enough for me, just as you are. And, look, even though you think this is a disaster, you know what I see?"

"A pathetic woman?"

Alex shakes his head, a small smile playing on his lips. He pulls out his phone, opening a note. It's titled 'Ways I know Mila Loves Me.' "Look at this, Mila." He hands it to me, and I read off:

The way she kisses me.

The smile on her face when I come home.

How she sends me funny Instagram posts that show me she's thinking of me.

Her texts throughout the day, even when we're sitting side by side in the office.

How she loves my mom.

The list goes on and on. When I'm done reading, I glance up at Alex, fresh tears brimming my eyes. "I do love you."

"Yes, you do." He brushes his lips against mine. "And that's all that matters to me."

"But why did you send me that whole article about being a perfect wife?"

When he frowns, clearly unable to place the article he sent me months ago, I pull it up on my phone, showing him. "Oh, I remember this." He scrolls down the article. "This is what you've been trying to do?"

"Yeah, I've been trying to go through this list—but I can't even get past number nine—"

Alex starts laughing again. "So, are you telling me you never read the end of this article?"

"I couldn't get that far!"

"Mila, the ending is the whole point." He hands the phone back to me. "Read it."

I scroll past all the numbers I've yet to check off, all the way to the ending that I never read because I couldn't get that far.

Number twenty-one: none of these things really matter. Just show up every day and give him your heart. That's all he really needs from you.

This is the part where I should be happy, or relieved, or hug and kiss Alex because all he wants is my heart. But right now, I'm mad. "Are you freaking kidding me?" I whisper-shout. "I did all of this and all you really wanted me to see is *this*? I can't believe—"

Alex cuts me off with a kiss. "I love you, Mila Kozak."

"You did it again."

"Dang it. Mila Caballero."

"I love you too, Alex. I'm sorry I've made our lives such a disaster recently."

"Mila, you're not a disaster. You're a joy. Do you know how boring my life was before you? You are my light, you are my life." He glances over at the puppy asleep in my bed. "Do you cause more messes? Yes, yes you do. But I wouldn't have it any other way. This is exactly how I want my life to be."

"Are you sure?"

"A thousand times, yes. Will you let me prove it to you?" he says, edging me closer to the bed.

I laugh, pressing up on tiptoe to kiss him once more. "I think we should probably clean up first."

He sighs. "You're probably right."

"You still love me though? Even though I make a mess more often than not?"

"Yes, my beautiful mess." He kisses me from forehead to cheek.

"What should we name the dog? Assuming, of course, you want to keep him."

Alex looks behind him at the dog asleep between the covers. "We're definitely keeping him. How could we possibly get rid of something that cute?"

"Uh, because he's a mess?"

Alex looks at me, eyebrows raised. "Did we just learn nothing?"

I laugh, burrowing into my husband's arms. "Fine, let's keep him."

"Why don't we name him Chance? That seems to suit him."

"Like he gets a second chance?"

"As a reminder that when you love someone, they get unlimited chances."

"Aww." I nuzzle my nose against his. "You already love him?"

"I wasn't talking about the dog, you goof."

I grip his shirt and tug him closer to me, "I know," I say, before pressing my lips against his.

30

Somethin' 'Bout a Truck

Trina

In the weeks after Grayson rescued me from Antonio, we fall into a comfortable rhythm of business partners who are also friends. I let myself enjoy the benefits of having Grayson on my side, while also actively pushing away any attraction I may or may not have. I let myself talk and laugh with Grayson, but never flirt or touch in any unnecessary ways.

I am a professional.

But somehow Grayson manages to worm his way into my dreams, which sometimes makes things awkward for me when I see him in the barn the next morning.

Stupid, attractive, helpful man.

Couldn't he just be ugly? It would be so much easier to work with him.

We make it work, though. Or rather, *I* make it work. Grayson's given no indication that he reciprocates my attraction, a fact that I remind myself of constantly. Not that it would make a difference in my interactions with him—I'm not having any relationship with any man right now, period. Add to that fact that Grayson is a businessman and it's a double no from me. I'm not going through that again.

But, we make a truly stellar team and decent friends.

Leo and I are starting to gain traction as well. We win the CDD Wealth five-star Grand Prix in Wellington and then head to the Live Oak International where we land in the top three. Grayson and DeDe have started to act as my unofficial—and unpaid—grooms.

They set fences for me, tack up Leo, and DeDe is even learning how to do Leo's button braids from Luna.

Grayson has paid for a consultation with a super fancy doctor who prescribed me all these supplements to keep me healthy. I'll admit, my knees are a little less achy than normal and I feel stronger than I have in years.

Maybe, just maybe, I should've listened to Grayson a long time ago.

It's a Wednesday afternoon and I haven't seen Grayson yet today. It's not that I need to see him, it's just that he's usually here first thing in the morning after he drops DeDe at school—and sometimes before that if Caterina has her. He also typically takes a lesson on Wednesdays.

Not that I miss him—though he has become quite a helpful staple around the barn.

That's why I'm wondering where he is...because of his usefulness. Not his achingly beautiful smile or his perceptive, lovely eyes or the way his lean muscles pull taut under his shirt when he mucks a stall. Nope, none of those things have any bearing on me wondering where Grayson is.

That's what I'm going with, anyway.

(Don't judge me.)

So when a truck pulls down the barn driveway at four o'clock, I glance up anxiously, shielding my eyes so I can see who's driving. It's a silver Toyota Tundra, so I know it's not Grayson, but still I look.

Except, it *is* Grayson. I can just make out the shape of his face, with his slicked back hair and fancy sunglasses.

I shake my head, chastising myself, because I'm certain I'm just seeing what I want to see. Grayson has only ever driven a Maserati—if he had a truck I would've seen it by now.

I finish my lesson with Ellie and then we walk together to the barn. Grayson is there at the front of the barn, looking like a puppy with a new toy. "Want to see my truck?" he says with a big smile.

I'll be honest, I'm relieved it really was Grayson in the truck and not my eyes playing tricks on me.

"Uh, sure." I try to act nonchalant, when really it feels like a whole host of annoying fluttering insects have taken up residence in my chest. *Grayson's here*. And no matter what my brain says, my heart missed this man.

After not seeing him for one whole morning.

Ugh.

What is *wrong* with me? It's like I want to sabotage our working relationship. Nuke it with stupid attraction and, dare I say it, *feelings*. Friendly feelings though. Nothing more than friendly.

Grayson leads me to the silver Toyota Tundra that seems to match his eyes. If Grayson had a tail, it would be wagging right now. *Hard*.

I'll admit, despite it being a Toyota—a brand that should stay in its lane with its reliable sedans—there's a sportiness to it that I haven't seen in other Tundras. It's sporting a huge grille at the front and sleek rims on the massive tires.

Grayson opens the passenger door. "M'lady," he says, gesturing with his hand for me to hop into the cab. I climb in and he shuts the door, jogging around the front of the truck. When he's ensconced in the cab with me, he starts spouting off stats and showcasing different features—the fourteen-inch infotainment screen, the 'Hey Toyota' virtual assistant that feels redundant with Siri at your beck and call, and, get this, a hybrid engine.

"Hold up," I say. "This *truck* has a hybrid engine?"

Grayson nods, eyes lighting up, and I start to laugh. Like, hysterically.

"Gray, this is not a truck," I tell him, wiping tears from the corner of my eyes. "This is a confused SUV with a bed strapped to the back."

He scoffs, leaning over the middle console. "Hey, I'll have you know that's a six-and-a-half-foot bed back there."

I roll my eyes playfully. "What's the towing capacity on this cutie? Two thousand?"

"*Twelve thousand*, thank you very much." There's a teasing glint in his eyes, and despite myself, I lean forward too so that we're face-to-face.

"Oohhh," I exclaim, my tone dripping in sarcasm.

"What's your Chevy's towing capacity?" He's so close, I can feel his breath on my left cheek when he talks. His scent is filling the cab. Despite the new car smell, it's Grayson that's taking over this space. Like a crisp breeze with an undertone of pine and evergreen.

"Sixteen thousand." I smirk, my eyebrows raising.

"You must be so proud."

"Well, I know how to pick 'em, that's for sure."

"I guess that remains to be seen." His eyes are searching mine, and it feels like there's a double meaning in his statement that I can't quite latch onto.

"I guess so." I pull back, leaning into the leather seat to get some distance from Grayson and his intoxicating scent. "We'll see how your overgrown SUV performs, Gray. You want to drive Leo to Longines this weekend?"

"With you driving shotgun?"

I shrug. "Sure. I'll have to witness this 'twelve-thousand-pound towing capacity' first-hand," I say, putting air quotes around the towing capacity.

"It's a date, then." He gives me a wink. "*Chevy.*"

And holy Thrice, those stupid winged creatures taking up residence in my chest break loose, wreaking havoc on my heart. Did Grayson Sterling just give me a nickname? And then wink at me?

Heaven help me.

31

Always Running Behind

Mila

I've avoided talking about my wife list—and the dog incident—with Anya since she told me it was dumb. And...she was right. But she doesn't need to know that—or else she'll be even more insufferable than usual.

When she rolls into the office after lunch on Thursday, I can tell she's going to talk to me about something. My defenses go up—way up—and I try to prepare myself for whatever Anya's going to say.

"We need a barn manager," she says, as if I don't already know that. And yet, her declaration still rubs at a raw spot—that I'm not doing a good enough job managing the Center. "This volunteer rotation we have going just isn't cutting it. People cancel or don't show up, horses don't get ridden and the nighttime feeding schedule is wonky on the days when you and Alex aren't here."

"I'm doing the best I can." Not to mention that with Alex preparing for his National Clinical Mental Health Counseling Examination next week in order to become licensed, I've picked up some of his responsibilities, too.

And I've been ordering out dinner a lot.

On my dad's credit card.

"I know, but you can't keep doing two full-time jobs," she says, even though I'm pretty sure Anya juggles at least three jobs at the Center. "I was thinking of Matthew Craig."

"Matthew...as in, Monica's boyfriend?"

Anya rolls her eyes. "Matthew as in Luke's brother."

"If you two are going to be sisters-in-law, you'll have to get over whatever you have against Monica." I raise my brows, smirking at her. Anya pales at my reminder that she's probably going to be related to Monica one day. I feel like I should tell her that Matthew's going to propose, but I also don't want to betray his trust—the knowledge sits like a brick in my stomach.

"Don't remind me," she grumbles.

"I'll arrange an interview with Matthew, see what he thinks." I sigh, rubbing my fingers over my eyes. "I honestly don't know when I'd fit that in though. I have to schedule in time to shower these days," I laugh, though it's partially true. "I'm wondering if this is even worth it, trying for the Olympics. It's draining every ounce of energy and time I have. But it feels like this is the thing I'm best at, like I owe it to myself to keep pursuing this Olympic dream." The words come out before I can catch them, and I didn't realize I'd been feeling that way until I said it out loud. "If I'm not the best at this, I'm not the best at anything."

Anya studies me, and it's as if she can see through to all the ways I've been failing the past few months. She can probably even tell I'm not super consistent in taking my birth control. I take it *most* days—that still counts, right? "Don't try to go to the Olympics because you're trying to fill a hole in your life. You're enough just as you are. Besides, you're the best at things other than show jumping."

I want to snort, to say, *Yeah, right.* This is *Anya* talking. She graduated summa cum laude from Stanford while running the Center. I can trust that I'm enough for Alex—he's gaga about me—but that doesn't mean everyone else in my life is going to be so gracious with my shortcomings.

"You don't believe me, do you?"

"Well it's hard to believe you when you're constantly criticizing me."

"When have I criticized you?"

"Just now, when you talked to me about finding a barn manager—and then with the support group, and when you had Luke take my meet and greet—"

"That's not criticism, Mila. I'm just trying to help you." Anya's piercing blue eyes make me feel like I'm a child getting scolded. "You're doing a great job, *sestra*, but you've got a lot on your plate, so I'm just trying to give you support."

"Well if I were better at-at, you know, *life*, I wouldn't need help." And I wouldn't need to prove my worth by going to the Olympics.

Anya scoffs. "Everyone needs help."

"You're managing your job just fine without help." I raise an eyebrow, challenging her.

"I'm not trying to go to the Olympics *or* figuring out how to be a wife."

I groan, covering my head with my hands. Before getting married, I didn't realize that you had to 'figure out' how to be a wife—I thought it would just happen. Or maybe I'm the only one in the world with this adjustment problem.

"But, remember Milochka, I've spent *years* learning to be dependent on people. It's a horrible feeling, but at some point everyone experiences dependence." Anya rolls closer, holding her hand out to me across the desk. I reluctantly take it. "What I'm learning is this: instead of begrudging the fact that we need help, let's choose to be grateful that we have people in our life who love us enough to be there." She squeezes my hand, leveling her gaze at me, but this time her eyes are warm.

I squeeze back. "You're right," I say. "I need help, and I'm grateful you're here for me."

"And don't beat yourself up about Alex cooking more or something silly like that."

I bite my lip, feeling so transparent—how can my sister see so clearly what's bothering me, even when I'm trying to hide it? I suppose I should be grateful that someone knows me that well and loves me that much. I sigh. "I just feel bad that he has to pick up so much of my slack sometimes."

"But that's what a good relationship is all about—you'll do the same for him in a busy season. It'll come, don't worry. Besides, you do so much for Alex. Think of how much he's changed these past few years—he's blossomed into everything he's meant to be. Without you, he wouldn't be a therapist or making music or anything like that. That's because of you, Mila. That's what love does, it helps us become the best versions of ourselves—the truest versions. And you've done that for Alex, and will continue doing that for him, because you love him. That's what love's about, not who does the dishes or cooks."

"You're right," I say, tears pressing on the edges of my eyes.

"Well, obviously." Anya scoffs, flipping her hair behind her shoulder. "I mean, when am I *wrong*?"

I laugh, rolling my eyes.

That evening, with Anya's words of wisdom swirling around my mind, we head to Alex's mom's house for dinner. She's made us picadillo—a ground beef hash with raisins, capers, olives, and tomatoes—along with rice, tostones, and her famous guava cheesecake. I'm always tempted to skip to dessert when she makes her guava cheesecake, but the picadillo smells so good, with its pungent blend of savory and sweet, I decide I can wait for dessert.

"Oh my gosh," I say after my first bite, the meat is perfectly tender—how does she manage to do that every time? "*Esto está tan bueno*, Mama," I tell her. She smiles at my praise, and then tells me that she made a platter for us to take home. Any other day, I might feel insecure that Alex's mom thinks I need so much help with my wifely duties—but today, I'm just grateful for her help.

"This is enough to feed an army," I say when I see the massive platter she made. An idea begins to form, and I glance over at Alex. "Do you think your mom would consider cooking for the Center?"

"You mean for a special occasion?" Alex asks.

"I was actually thinking we could do it for a regular lunch time, to feed clients, volunteers, and staff." I start to talk faster as I get more excited about my idea. "We could get a little food truck for her. People would pay a premium for this food, it's really good. And she loves doing it."

Alex looks over at his mom. "I'm just concerned about her health, being on her feet for so long."

"She could set her own hours, only do lunch, or do it a few times a week to start. If she's not feeling well, no biggie, people can go get food somewhere else. But it could be regular income for her."

"I want to do it," Mrs. Caballero says, pronouncing each word in perfect English. "*Esto es perfecto para mí.*"

I smile, taking her hand in mine. "It *is* perfect for you," I say, feeling relieved that we came up with something she can do that fits her so well.

Alex leans over, wraps an arm around me, presses his lips against my temple, and whispers in my ear, "Thank you for loving me and my mom."

It's a Monday morning when I get the call from the NetJets Team USA Show Jumping's Chef D'Equipe, Anne Kursinski, asking that I join the team to represent the USA at the FEI Longines Nation's Cup Qualifier in San Juan Capistrano in California. She also mentions Trina will be on the team.

I stand in my kitchen, holding my cream-with-coffee, and do a little happy dance, spilling coffee over the edge of my mug. After I tell Alex the good news, we dance in the living room to Nic D's "Milkshake," hands in the air as we celebrate. I laugh when Alex sings along to the lyric, "I'd say 'Bless You' but it looks like God already did," giving me a flirtatious once-over as he sings.

After we've thoroughly celebrated, I call Trina. "Hey! Looks like we're heading to San Juan Capistrano," I say, still smiling.

"Exciting, huh? Congrats, Mila."

"You too. Honestly, I'm excited to hang out. I feel like it's been forever since we've had time to just chill together."

I wait for her to say something like, *Me too, I've missed you!* But she never does. "It'll be great," she says instead. "Grayson said he'd get a place for us to stay all together."

"Wow, that would be so fun."

"Yep."

The conversation stalls, and disappointment pools in my stomach. "Okay, well, I guess I'll see you then," I say. We give brief goodbyes and I hang up, wondering if Trina and I will ever get back to normal.

32

The Artist in the Ambulance

Trina

We're driving down to the Longines Global Champions Tour in Miami Beach, Grayson with his beloved new Tundra pulling Zen Elite's horse trailer. Since DeDe's with Caterina this weekend, it's just the two of us for this three-day event. Grayson's looking smug as we drive away from the barn. "Surprised that your precious truck can carry such a heavy load?" I tease him.

He tilts his head toward me, giving me a cheeky half-smile. "I'm confident in this baby's ability." He rubs his hands over the steering wheel, and I laugh thinking how ironic it is that he treasures this truck more than his old Maserati.

And why does that make me admire him that much more?

I clear my throat, forcing my thoughts to something other than Grayson. "I'm slacking on my DJ duties," I say, connecting my phone to his aux port and pulling up a playlist that I know Grayson will appreciate.

When Thrice's "The Artist in the Ambulance" comes on, Grayson turns up the sound. "I thought you'd like this song," I say above the music.

"I love how raw and real Dustin is," he says as if he and the lead singer, Dustin Kensrue, are best buds. And who knows, maybe they are. Grayson's got so much money he could hire Dustin to follow him around, creating a soundtrack of his life. "There's an almost unpolished element to this record that resonates with me."

It's not the first time I've noticed that Grayson values genuineness—being *real*. I wonder if it's a reaction to being married to Caterina, whom I would describe as sleek and precise—gorgeous to be sure, but highly curated. Genuine and real might not come to mind if you met her.

I guess I'm not the only one who creates new and important values based on bad experiences with an ex. In a strange way, it makes me feel closer to Grayson. Like I understand him a little better, and I think, in some small way, he understands me too.

"I listened to this song a lot," Grayson says. "When Cate and I split."

I nod, but don't say anything—sensing that there's more to this story. He's quiet for a moment, and then continues, "It kind of feels like our divorce was that car accident that he's singing about. It was as if I were looking at my life wondering what do I have to show except the promises I never kept?" He shakes his head, his jaw tense. "I couldn't really get a second chance with Cate, but with DeDe...that line about 'I hope I'll never let you down'—it's like that's my anthem to her. Empty words are not enough, 'rhetoric can't raise the dead,' you know?"

I nod. "I do know."

"This song is a reminder to me that people can change—I can change."

I surprise myself by saying, "You *have* changed." He glances over at me, skepticism plain in his eyes. "I mean, I didn't know you before, but I do know one thing: you say you weren't present in her life, and now you are. You can't go backwards, all you can do is move forward. And you are."

He presses his lips together, his whole body tense. I reach a hand across the console and place it on his arm. "You're a great dad, Gray."

He sighs, relaxing under my touch. "Thanks, Trin." His skin feels good under my palm—warm, inviting. I could run my fingers over his wrist, tracing each knuckle, feeling the soft skin under his wrist.

Instead, I let my hand linger on his forearm for one heartbeat, two, three, and then pull it away, tucking it under my leg where it can't play with fire anymore.

We arrive at the event that is, quite literally, situated on the beach. The sand arena stretches across the Miami Beach with the Atlantic Ocean glittering in the sun not twenty feet away.

I wonder if they used beach sand for the arena or if they had to bring in other sand as they leveled the arena.

We meet my brother, Tripp, ringside at the VIP Global Champions lounge area, where Grayson purchased a table for us. He's in town for a conference and came to watch me today. "Retsis!" Tripp scoops me up in his arms, squeezing me against his chest. I grumble—affectionately—as I squirm away from him. I keep myself an arm's length away from him—who knows if he'll whip out the big brother noogie. You'd think that a trauma surgeon who's closing in on thirty-five years old would be too mature to give his adult sister a noogie, but you'd be wrong.

As my brother reaches his knuckles out for my head, I swat his hand away. "Tripp," I say with enough sternness in my voice to make him try again. This time, I grab his fist and twist his arm around his back until he says, "Okay, okay!" I loosen my grip, and he holds his fingers up, wiggling them. "Can't harm the money makers," he says with a cocky grin.

I roll my eyes, moving to the side so that Grayson and Tripp can meet each other. "Grayson, this is my very mature brother that some lousy institution decided to award a medical doctorate."

Tripp sobers up, clearly not realizing that Grayson was with me, and reaches a hand out to shake Grayson's. "Tripp Powers, nice to meet you."

"Grayson Sterling, likewise. What kind of medicine do you practice?"

"I'm a trauma surgeon. But wait, are you—" Tripp shakes his head, a bashful grin on his face. "You're Dr. Grayson Sterling. I went to your talk at the Global Congress of Surgical Innovations. The advancements you've made with AI..."

Tripp continues to talk as the ground beneath me bottoms out. Grayson's a *doctor*?

"Trina, I can't believe you didn't tell me that Dr. Sterling is your horse's owner."

"I...didn't know he was famous." Or that he was a doctor. All this time I thought he was a sleazy businessman, not a world-renowned doctor. I'm not sure which is worse.

"Not famous," Grayson says.

"Dude, stop," my brother says, all of a sudden sounding like a frat guy instead of an MD. "Trin, Grayson's like *the man*. His name is basically synonymous with AI surgical innovations."

"AI, as in, artificial intelligence?" I ask.

Grayson nods. "We've spent the last ten years working on prosthetic limbs with artificial intelligence integrated into the prostheses. The AI learns their movements and is able to predict patterns of behavior so that it could function like a regular limb."

"Wow," I say, trying—and failing—not to be swamped by all the big words he just threw at me. "That's amazing." What's even more amazing is that he gave it all up to spend more time with his daughter. I shake my head, feeling suddenly overwhelmed by this new revelation about who Grayson is.

"I'm going to get us some drinks," Tripp says, slapping Grayson on the back like an old friend before heading off to the bar.

I feel thrown off—like an earthquake just knocked me off my feet. I plop down onto a chair at the table and Grayson settles next to me as we gaze out at the sand arena, the ocean behind it. I'm still trying to piece together what I know of Grayson with this newfound version of him. "I thought you were a businessman."

Grayson laughs. "Don't let my actual business partner hear that. He'd laugh you all the way to Hong Kong."

Huh. That's not at all what I expected. Ever since Grayson waltzed into my barn with his spreadsheets and consultants, I'd thought of him a certain way. But now...now I don't know what to think. "If you were making so many advancements, why sell the company? Why stop?"

Grayson shoves his hands in his pockets, shrugging. "It's like I said in the car, none of that is worth it if I don't have anyone to enjoy life with. Like, if I can slap a new hand on ten thousand strangers but I'm not there for my daughter at her first horse show, what does that mean about who I am?" He glances over at Tripp, who's walking back to the table, juggling a handful of beers. "I just didn't want to sacrifice my daughter at the altar of my ambitions. Love is more important than advancement. People are more important than research."

"But...you help people with your research."

"That's true," he nods thoughtfully. "But *which* people I help is up to me. I hope it's not selfish that I chose Demetria."

Tripp comes up then, handing us a round of drinks. I let myself drift into the background of their conversation as I try to fit together this new version of *Dr.* Grayson J. Sterling.

33

Champagne Supernova

Trina

Showing right on Miami Beach is unlike anything I've experienced before. There are yachts dotting the shoreline, parasailors hovering in the sky, and high-rise condos lining the beach behind us. Leo is fresh, dancing a jig in the warm-up arena as Luna and Grayson set a fence.

By the time we head into the arena, Leo's worked through some of his anxiety, but not nearly enough. He charges at every single fence, and I'm holding him back as much as I possibly can, but we tear around the course nonetheless.

He's getting gymnastical as we fly over an oxer with colorful stacked macaron cookies on the jump standards. I feel his body twist beneath me, his hind end shifting sideways so he can avoid hitting the fence. I hold my breath until we clear the obstacle, Leo refusing to lose steam.

I sit back, collecting him as we gallop to a solid fence made to look like a bridge. It has tiny faux bricks on the top of the jump, and we barely graze one of them off. The crowd 'ahhs' but I keep pace with Leo as we canter to the last line: an ascending oxer then three short strides to an in-and-out. Leo's breath is coming in short spurts as we get right to the base of the oxer, soaring over it. At the final combination, I lift my hands just a touch, giving him the support he needs to get through the two stride. We get through it, zipping through the timers.

Despite his maniacal showing, Leo is still full of energy. He prances sideways as I pull him up, taking my time getting out of the ring so he can get more accustomed to it for our next ride tomorrow.

Leo is considerably calmer on the second day of the show. We have a solid ride, if a bit slow. We end with no jumping faults, but a few on the time. It's hot today and I spend extra time walking Leo to cool him down and make sure his legs are rubbed down with linament and wrapped comfortably for the night. Competing three days in a row at this level is a lot for a horse.

The final day of the event, I'm in the top ten in the standings—which means if I can have a double-clear round today, I have as good a chance as anyone to place in the ribbons. Leo and I warm up minimally—I'm trying to save his legs, a potentially risky move. But when we pass under the dark blue Longines arch into the arena, it feels like we're hyperfocused. We know exactly what to do.

I let Leo have a look at a funky red fence, but these are all jumps we've seen the first two days. We're ready for this.

When the buzzer goes off, I barely have to push him into a canter as I steer him to the first line. We gallop up and over the Just World fence and on to the red oxer. We hit our strides perfectly, turning carefully to a skinny plank fence. Leo gives it a wide berth, and we rollback to a broken line with a liverpool and a sprawling oxer. After the oxer, I collect Leo for the triple combination—a row of blue and white Longines fences with the classic Longines timepiece beside each standard. We fly through the triple with precision, hitting our strides exactly the way we should.

We canter past the sideline, with beach spectators gathered right on the fence. But Leo barely gives them a glance as we charge through a line of water-inspired fences, then turn to fly over the water. The final line of the course, I sit back, collecting him so that we give the last jumps the respect they need. We soar over an oxer then four strides to an airy vertical. Leo jumps it with every ounce of power he has, and we get several long moments of air time before hitting the ground and zooming through the timers—clear. The crowd erupts in cheers, and I lean down to pat Leo's neck, both of us breathing hard.

"That's a clear round, ladies and gentlemen, for Trina Powers and Leonidas. They'll be back to join us for the jump-off."

I give Leo his reins as we pass the VIP lounge area—where I swear I see Gisele Bund-chen. Tripp told me she was here, and I didn't quite believe him. She smiles, waving at me, and I'm so out of sorts, I don't even wave back.

Grayson's waiting for us at the in-gate, his smile drawing me in with a magnetism for the ages. "Amazing!" he cheers, quickly taking Leo's drop noseband off and giving him a treat as we walk around the warm-up ring. We pause on the edge of the arena and I hop down. Grayson envelopes me in a surprising hug. "Great ride," he says.

I try not to linger too long and pull away before Grayson does. "Thanks," I say as I roll my stirrups.

"What can I do?" he asks.

"Could you walk him around while I get some water? We'll be going back in once all the first rounds are done."

"Sure thing," he says with a little salute, taking Leo's reins from me. I watch them walk away, feeling something I can't quite put my finger on as the two of them circle the arena.

Before I know it, we're back in the ring for the jump-off. There are only five of us that made it to the second round of this final day, and I'm third in the line up. We get a good pace to the first fence, angling it so that we can get the rollback to the skinny plank fence. We gallop seven long strides to the Swedish oxer, hitting it right in the middle before a quick turn to the brick obstacle. The final line is an in-and-out. I press him to the base of the jump before sitting back at the last second, balancing him as we soar over the combination.

Then we're through the timers. Clean.

I move my reins to one hand, holding my other hand up, fist raised in victory. Through the applause of the crowd, I search out Grayson's face. He's cheering like I just won—and maybe I did—with wild abandon, his hands above his head and his head thrown back in a whooping scream. I smile as Leo and I walk to him. He wraps his hands around Leo's neck, not caring in the least for all the sweat on the horse.

I dismount and Grayson pulls me into a crushing hug—something I'm getting very familiar with, and I don't hate it.

We watch the next two riders—one with a rail and one goes clear, with a time that's just barely faster than mine. But my ride is still good for second place, so when it's time for the winners to take the center stage, I'm on the second-place podium. I find that I'm still searching for Grayson's face, even here. I forget about the traditional champagne spray—the other two riders have beat me to it, and I have to scramble to grab my bottle to spray them with it. We laugh, sipping the champagne straight out of the bottle once the bubbles die down. And for some reason, all I can think of is the bottle of champagne

I shared with Grayson at the Polo club on the golf course. As the champagne fizzes down my throat, I'm grateful yet again that I didn't sell Leo that day.

It feels like we're exactly where we need to be.

On the way home, Grayson claims it's his turn to pick the music. We're both giddy with the win, riding the wave of champagne bubbles and silver medals. I don't even care that his music is slightly more hardcore than mine—he opts for bands like Rise Against and The Used whereas I'm a little more mellow with my love of Death Cab and The Postal Service. But all in all we enjoy the same music. Which is surprising: Grayson and I could not be more opposite.

Grayson: billionaire.

Me: decidedly *not* a billionaire.

Grayson: super smart, highly educated, enjoys reading. A world-renowned *doctor*.

Me: uhhh, not even a little.

Grayson: handsome, put together, and suave. Designer clothes.

Me: whatever the opposite of 'suave' is. Literally not a stitch of designer clothes in my closet.

But we connect over music, for which I'm grateful. It gives us something to talk about on these long drives we keep taking together.

"Hey, Chevy," Grayson says, and I bite my lip to keep from smiling at his nickname for me. "Rocket Summer: too whiney or totally into it?"

"Hmm...a little whiney, yes. But I still jam to them when I'm in a peppy mood."

Grayson's eyebrow raises. "When are you in a peppy mood?"

I smack his arm. "Hey! I'm sometimes peppy."

He shrugs, but there's a mischievous smile on his face. "You're a lot of things, but I don't think peppy is one of them."

"That's why it's a *mood*."

He nods, but the laugh he's biting back tells me he's not convinced. "Whatever," I say. "I'm peppy. Sometimes."

"I'll believe it when I see it."

I bob my head in time with the music to show him just how peppy I can be, but then I give up because, well...I'm not really peppy.

A few minutes later, Sugarcults "Pretty Girl (The Way)" comes on. I recognize it from the first few guitar riffs, and before the lyrics can start, I change the song.

"Not a fan of Sugarcult?" Grayson asks.

"Just not a fan of that song," I say as I turn my attention out the window. We're chugging down the Turnpike with approximately a hundred million other people going twenty-five over the speed limit. *Welcome to Miami*, I think. Not that Palm Beach is much better.

Grayson leans into the middle console. He glances at me briefly before putting his eyes back on the road. "It seems like there's a story behind that..."

I sigh, not wanting to say anything, but Grayson did share vulnerably with me before, so it feels like it's my turn. "It was my breakup song. With Victor."

I brace myself for Grayson to ask more questions, to do surgery on my heart, uprooting the gory details of my past dating life. Instead, he says, "Ah."

"Don't act like you don't have a breakup song," I say. "And not 'Artist in the Ambulance,' that's not a breakup song."

"Oh I agree. And I definitely do."

"What is it then?"

"Wanna guess?" He glances my way, eyebrows raised in a challenge.

"Hmm...Death Cab's 'Title and Registration'?"

"Good guess, but no."

It's my turn to lean on the center console, and now I can feel the heat radiating off of Grayson. It's not entirely unpleasant. "Is it something surprising, like Adele? Or maybe like Kelly Clarkson's 'Since U Been Gone'?"

Grayson laughs. "It might be surprising, but it's not a female singer."

"You sure it's not Taylor Swift? I could see you rocking out to "All Too Well," the ten-minute version."

"She does have a plethora of good breakup songs to choose from, but no."

I keep throwing out songs, but I don't strike gold. "Heartless" by Kanye West. "Somebody I Used to Know" by Gotye. Nope, nope.

"Oh! Oh! I know, it's Bon Iver. Are you a sad, mopey Bon Iver guy?" I narrow my eyes at him. "Please tell me you're not."

Grayson gives me a playful side-eye. "I'm really not."

"I give up." I nudge him with my elbow across the console. "What's your break up song?"

"I'll tell you but you can't make fun of me."

"I absolutely will not promise that."

Grayson laughs, a clear, full laugh that fills the cab of the truck. "Fine, fine. It's All American Rejects 'Gives You Hell.'"

"No. Way." I cackle before covering my mouth with my hands, trying unsuccessfully to smother my laughter. "That's the greatest thing I've ever heard. I can totally picture you strutting around your house, bottle of beer in one hand, scream-singing that song. Please tell me you did that."

"I did not do that. Not exactly, anyway."

"Oh c'mon, don't mess up my visual I've got going. I like what I'm picturing in my head, I'm not willing to part with it."

"I'm a little afraid to ask, but what's going on in that pretty little head of yours?"

I flush at Grayson's words, reminding myself that it's probably a phrase he says to his daughter and he accidentally used it on me. There's no way someone like Grayson thinks I'm pretty.

"I'm waiting," Grayson says, drumming his fingers on the steering wheel. "Look, I told you my embarrassing breakup song, the least you can do is tell me what you're picturing in your head."

"Okay, okay." I sit up straighter. "So, you're jumping around in your tighty-whities—"

"I do *not* wear tighty-whities—"

"Shh, don't ruin it. You've got like a dirty white undershirt and for some reason, a tie around your head."

"Like a headband?"

"Exactly, like a headband."

"At some point you grab a broom and you're just rockin' out, yelling into your broom-mic. It's pretty epic."

"Well, I have to disappoint, but what actually happened was I listened to this song as I ran. It was a workout/motivational song."

"That's lame. My version is way better."

"Yes, but my version's *true*."

"Eh, semantics. We'll go with my version."

Grayson laughs again, and it feels like the sound is filling not only the truck, but my heart as well. "You're a cheeky little one, aren't you?"

The truth is: I'm almost never 'cheeky,' but I shrug, a smile tugging on my lips when I say, "Sometimes."

34

Santa Monica

Mila

Matthew's planning to propose this week, which means he's been texting me nonstop—for someone who barely talks, the guy sure can text a lot. But I'm having a hard time keeping it all straight—between trying to train him for his new position as barn manager, overseeing a new wave of volunteers, preparing for the World Cup Qualifier in San Juan Capistrano next week, and Alex's licensure exam...I'm surprised I remembered to brush my teeth this morning.

But, now that I think of it, I'm not even certain I remembered to do that.

I'm in the Cottage, on the phone with Luna—arranging for Cyrus to ship out to California with their barn—when Alex peeks his head into the room. "Time to go," he tells me.

I grab my purse, following Alex out to our car, as I finish up coordinating a drop-off of Cyrus with Luna. I'm just relieved that Trina and Luna are taking the horses there so that I can stick around for Alex's exam, and then fly out to San Juan Capistrano.

We're pulling into Good Hope Farm—the Craig family ranch in Davie—when I realize something. "I forgot the sign!"

"What sign?"

"Matthew made a sign for the proposal and he had it shipped to us so that Monica wouldn't find it. It's, like, a key part of this proposal. We have to go back."

Alex glances at the time. "Babe, we don't have time. We're barely going to be there on time as it is."

I drop my head to my knees, silently berating myself—how could I possibly screw up my best friend's engagement? If I hadn't been so distracted talking on the phone or if

I'd given myself more time to get ready or just been a better friend this wouldn't have happened. Tears sting the corners of my eyes, and I blink them back.

"What can I do, Alex?" My voice sounds pitiful, even to me. Alex pulls up to the Craig's main house, shifting into park.

"How about I drop you off and go get the sign? At the very least, we can hold it up when he proposes instead of it dropping down like he originally planned."

"Okay." I nod, a single tear spilling out. I swipe it away. "Thanks," I say, but thanks doesn't seem to really cover it—*you're saving my tail, you're way better than me, I don't deserve you* all seem like better options. Instead, I press my lips together, holding back my thoughts, and give him a quick kiss before exiting the car.

I hurry to the back of the house, where Matthew's siblings—Katie Jo, Luke, Mikey, and John—are all working on our snowball fight scene for the proposal. Two massive snow machines have created a small patch of rapidly melting snow in the Craig's backyard. The siblings are attempting to create as many snowballs as possible and storing them in two Yeti coolers.

Katie Jo wraps me up in a swift hug, the hot pink tips of her blonde hair blowing into my face when John starts the snow machine back up. "What'd ya think?" she asks me with her thick Southern accent.

I glance around at what is essentially a slab of ice over the grass and laugh. "I think maybe we should've brought ice skates instead."

Katie Jo laughs and then starts singing Taylor Swift's "Welcome to New York" in her sweet Southern twang. Matthew's intention with this scene is to recreate the epic Christmas Eve snowball fight we had in New York. In retrospect, the idea of recreating the scene is more grandiose than the reality. I hope Monica appreciates the effort anyway.

I greet all of the Craig siblings—Luke gives me a cheerful nod from his wheelchair (I saw him earlier today at the Center), John gives a polite but distant wave, and Mikey almost throws out my back in a bone-crushing hug. That's essentially the Craig siblings in a nutshell. If Matthew were here, he'd probably tip his hat at me silently.

When Katie Jo reveals the engagement ring, an awed hush falls over the group. A round brilliant diamond holds the center of the yellow gold band, with two smaller rubies on either side of the center stone. Dainty filigree decorates the side of the bands, wrapping around the side stones. It's lovely and unique—something very befitting of Monica.

"Didn't know bull riding paid so well," Luke says.

"You wouldn't know, would you?" says Mikey, who is also a bull rider.

"And neither would you, Michael," John mumbles. Mikey responds by punching John in the shoulder, and in a split second the two are going at it, albeit in an affectionate way. I shake my head—having grown up with only one sister, I'm always a little amazed by the Craig brothers.

"It's Granny's ring, you goose," Katie Jo says, yanking Mikey away from John by his t-shirt. "Now let's focus so we can finish this up." Katie Jo digs into the cooler, pulling out a clear plastic orb that opens in the middle. It makes me think of one of those Christmas ornaments you can fill yourself. She pops it open, placing the ring box in the center, and then closes it up, handing it to John, who starts to pack snow around it. When he's done, Katie Jo sprinkles gold glitter all over the snowball to differentiate it from the others.

Before I know it, the rest of the Craig family, along with Anya, have descended on the ice block. I know that Luke told Anya what was happening today, and I'm surprised by how serene she looks, and I wonder if it's just for show. When Monica and Matthew arrive, we're all in our positions, and the second Mikey snipes Monica with a snowball, it's on.

Pure pandemonium breaks out as we all start throwing snowballs at each other. Alex shows up a few minutes into the fight, tucking the sign under one of the coolers and joining the chaos. This time there's no teams, it's every man for himself, and we're having a blast. Katie Jo jumps on Mikey's back, throwing snowballs at all of us as he runs around the snow patch.

Even Anya and Mrs. Craig, who are typically very buttoned-up, seem to have loosened up and are having fun.

When we run out of snowballs, we're all tingling from the cold, laughing, and breathing hard. Matthew takes the golden snowball from the hiding spot Katie Jo put it in and hands it to Monica. "Open it," Matthew says, his voice barely above a whisper, but we're all holding our collective breath—we could hear a piece of straw fall to the ground right now.

Monica crunches the snowball between her gloved fingers, revealing the plastic orb below. She gasps when she finds the ring box hidden inside. Matthew smiles and drops to one knee. Alex and I shuffle to get the sign, unraveling it between us.

"Monica Perez," Matthew says. "I can't imagine living any longer without making you mine. Will you marry me?"

Monica squeals and says yes, and Matthew picks her up, twirling her around. When he puts her down, she squints at me and Alex and the sign. That's when I glance down and realize...the sign is upside down.

Of course.

After Matthew's proposal, we all head inside the Craig's house for a little party. Monica's parents and brother show up, along with a couple of our friends from undergrad. We celebrate with Mrs. Craig's famous hummingbird cupcakes and fruity punch in glass cups. Monica's drinking out of a glass that says "Future Mrs. Craig." It has a hand with an engagement ring on it—with only the ring finger lifted so that when you first glance at the glass, it looks like the hand is flicking you off.

"Who got this for you, my dear?" Mrs. Craig asks. Her tone is restrained, but anyone who's met Mrs. Craig knows she scandalized. "Mila?"

"Don't look at me," I say, eyes wide in panic. "I'm not that edgy."

Monica laughs. "She's really not," she says, as if this were an insult instead of a compliment. She turns the glass to admire the front. "I actually got it for myself."

Mrs. Craig looks like she's about to pass out from Monica's confession. In just a moment, she'll be fanning herself and asking for smelling salts. "Did you know you were getting engaged?" I ask, afraid someone somewhere spilled the tea.

"Not specifically," Monica says with a shrug. "But it popped up on Etsy with a discount, so, score!" She smiles like this is the most normal thing in the world—to buy yourself an engagement present...before you're engaged. "It's just been sitting in a box in my car."

"That's...confident," Mrs. Craig says.

"What can I say?" Monica says. "It's good vibes only up in here." She waves at her chest, and Mrs. Craig frowns.

"She means she's an optimist," I translate.

"Ah. That's lovely," Mrs. Craig says with a shaky smile. I press my lips together to hold back a laugh. Matthew, and his whole family, have done so much for Monica—but Monica is certainly going to help them all loosen up in the best way possible.

Katie Jo gifts Monica an oversized sweatshirt that says "In My Engaged Era" with "I Said Yes!" on the sleeve. I didn't realize this was a gifting type of situation—but Katie Jo's thoughtful like that.

After about an hour, I notice that Anya's missing from the group. I find her in the sunroom at the front of the house, her wheelchair angled toward the windows.

"Hey, you doing okay?"

She shrugs, keeping her gaze out of the window. "Just thinking."

"Penny for your thoughts?"

She sighs, flipping her dark hair over her shoulder. "I guess sometimes I wonder how well I belong in the Craig family. They're so perfect...and happy." She glances down at her nails, fidgeting with her cuticles. "I'll never be like Mrs. Craig, baking and jolly."

I take her hand in mine, squeezing it. "Hey, do you need the *you-are-enough* pep talk you gave me the other day?"

"No." She groans. "Yes."

"Luke Craig pursued you relentlessly—despite you being low-key mean to him for months. He loves you, Anya. If he wanted to be with someone like his mom, he totally could have. But he didn't. He chose you. And he keeps choosing you every day."

"That's true enough," she says with a dainty sniff.

"Look, if and when you guys get married, you'll belong in this family because you belong with Luke. Besides, his family loves you. You balance him out so well."

Anya nods, more convinced this time. "Now *that* is true. The man needs balancing, desperately."

I laugh, squeezing her hand again. "Come out whenever you're ready. Just because the Craig family is wonderful doesn't mean they aren't overwhelming. It's okay to take breaks."

I leave my sister in the sunroom, my heart stuttering just a little at our interaction—because if Anya doesn't feel like she's enough, then there's no hope for the rest of us.

And yet, we're getting through it.

35

Friends With You

Irina

In May, we head out to California for the Nations Cup Qualifier—including Mila, Alex, Grayson, and DeDe. Grayson rents us a massive house right on the water that can only be described as *baller*. Luna and I arrive a few days early to get the horses settled, with Grayson, DeDe, and the others to follow in a few days. Before everyone else arrives, I fall into an easy routine of green tea in the mornings on the balcony overlooking the water, and then dinners on the pool patio watching the sunset. Despite the beauty of it all, it feels like something's missing. I refuse to let my brain—or heart—acknowledge that it's Grayson.

So that leaves me feeling surprised at the butterflies stirring within me on Thursday as I wait for Grayson and the others to arrive. All day long, I've felt keenly aware of the time—counting down in my mind to when their flight will land. I made sure to flat the horses early so I could get back to the rental in time to shower and change. It's *possible* I dabbed on a teeny tiny amount of blush and tinted lip balm. And a few swipes of mascara. Hey, even a tomboy like me can want to look pretty sometimes, right? That's my prerogative as a strong, independent woman.

I'm pacing the living room when DeDe comes barreling through the front door. Despite my affection for her—and Mila and Alex, who are right behind her with their new dog-child, Chance—my eyes are searching for her dad. And when he walks in, looking like he emerged from a Nike catalogue in his joggers and fitted workout shirt, the butterflies break free. They are throwing a rager of a party—not just in my stomach, but my chest, my heart, even my throat. Heck, they're probably taking up space in my brain too. Because why not?

When Grayson's eyes meet mine, I have to press my hand against my stomach to calm it. Has he always been this handsome? Did I somehow forget how good he looks in the four days I spent apart from him?

And despite all of the emotions swirling with me, I have no idea what to do right now. Do I wave at him? Go hug him? Lay a smacker on him? Grayson and I have known each other for about nine months now, but we've never hugged in greeting. Sure, we had a couple of celebratory hugs at the Longines Global Champions Tour in Miami, but I would've hugged a gorilla if he'd been standing beside me after my ride. But friends hug when they haven't seen each other in a while, right?

While I'm contemplating this, DeDe runs right into me, wrapping her arms around me. "Trina!" she shouts. Alex and Mila take turns hugging me as well before DeDe pulls them away to check out the pool.

Their warmth and affection emboldens me.

I'm going to hug Grayson.

When everyone's out on the patio, Grayson and I walk toward each other. And I swear it all happens in slow motion—the way his eyes track my movement, how he runs a hand through his hair. But when I'm one foot away from Grayson, I completely chicken out. To make matters way worse, my hands go rogue in a weird greeting choreography. I wave, then salute him, and then, for the pièce de résistance: finger guns.

What in the name of Margie Engle did I just do?

Grayson, whose arm is now outstretched for a hug, soaks up my awkwardness and ends up patting me on my back. If I were a normal person with normal impulses, I would've leaned into the outstretched arm, making it a side hug. Normal. Right?

But, my friends, normal is not what we're working with today.

And my lack of normalcy is clearly contagious, because after Grayson thumps me hesitantly on the back, he raises his hand for a high five.

A high five.

As in: the typical greeting of ten-year-old boys. Not the warm reception of two friends who haven't seen each other for several days. I've left him hanging for far too long as I contemplate the disaster that is this interaction with Grayson, so when I raise my hand to high five him, he's already lowering his outstretched hand.

We both fumble—I shove my hands into pockets as he scratches his neck.

Awkward turtle's got nothing on us. More like awkward brachiosaurus. So painfully awkward he had to die off.

"I was, uh, going to—" I start as Grayson says, "I'll just go find—"

We don't even bother finishing our sentences and shoot off in opposite directions as fast as humanly possible.

With the rest of our crew in San Juan Capistrano, the house swells with energy and excitement. Somehow, Grayson and I manage to get past our initial weird interaction without saying a word about it. Because he can, Grayson hires a chef to cook for us. We enjoy sprawling dinners on the patio and jumping into the pool or hot tub after we eat.

My typical day-to-day life is filled with a lot of people—primarily barn people—but I go home by myself every night. Having a house so full of people I love is bittersweet—I'm having a blast here, but it makes me realize how lonely I am. I want this all the time, not just for a week. It makes me wonder what it would've been like growing up with a big, loud, loving family instead of two parents too overworked to pay me much mind and just one sibling.

The horse show is a different kind of show than we normally experience—it's a five-day event, with one warm-up course ride and then three official days of competition. It's akin to a single-elimination sporting event, where about half of the riders are eliminated after each day of competition. It's a team competition, where the scores of one rider counts for the whole team. So even if only one of us advances to the end of the competition, we still have a chance to make it to the Nation's Cup Final in Barcelona in October.

These types of events are important for proving our ability to compete with a team, and the USEF Olympic committee will weigh this kind of competition more heavily.

On the first day of warm-up rides, Anne Kursinski is coaching us in the warm-up ring, which is a nice change of pace for me. I get to show up as a competitor and not a trainer for once. The whole scene would be perfect if Evangeline Rutherford weren't here, making snide comments at my expense whenever she can. But even with her present, the trip is idyllic in many ways, from the company (Eva not withstanding) to the weather to the show itself.

I take my time with Leo in the arena, letting him get used to the massive grass ring. We check out as many individual fences as we can before the buzzer sounds, and I treat the course like we're at home and it's just another Saturday with Ellie setting fences for me.

The next day, our first round of rides is exhilarating as we don our Olympic-caliber coats with the USA flag on the sleeve. Leo and I are focused and deliberate as we navigate the course. We keep all the fences up but incur three time faults. Since it's such a big arena, I'll have to press Leo to pick up the pace even more tomorrow. But our ride should be enough to carry us through to the second day.

I get to hang back in the spectator area to watch Mila—a rare treat for me, since I'm usually at the in-gate with her. Mila and Cyrus radiate passion as they speed around the course. Whereas I'm typically more reserved in my rides, Mila's always searching for the angles, where she can cut turns tighter, leave out strides, or gallop like a maniac. I smile as I watch my friend whipping around the arena—no risk of time faults here, ladies and gentlemen.

Sometimes I wonder if you could combine Mila and I, we would make the perfect show jumper. Not that it could happen, it's just something I'd love to see.

36

She Rides Wild Horses

Mila

Trina and I both get through the first round of the Nations Cup Qualifier. It's a unique experience for me to be part of a team and to be training with the Chef D'Equipe, Anne Kursinski, for the event instead of Trina. The venue is gorgeous, with the Santa Ana mountains in the background and the sea breeze not too far off. The sprawling grass arena is even bigger than the International Arena—meaning that Cyrus wants to let loose and it's easy to get strung out as we ride.

On the second day of competition, our team walks the course with Anne—I can't believe I'm on a first-name basis with Anne Kursinski! Trina and I linger in the arena with Trina giving me extra pointers, and then she heads back to the barn while Alex and I walk the show grounds with Chance. Of course, the pup gets tired after about five minutes which leaves Alex carrying him. He is *so* whipped. I'd be jealous of Chance if I didn't know how much Alex loved me.

Before we left for California, Alex took his licensure exam. Right after the exam, he received an unofficial passing score, but we'll get confirmation in a few weeks. I'm planning a celebration for when we get back, but last night Grayson had the chef make Alex's favorite meal and we toasted him with Jacques Selosse champagne.

Alex seems much less stressed since the exam. The trip is well-timed for him to get a little vacation.

We're looking around at a vendor with funny shirts and stickers when we run into Eva Rutherford and her boyfriend and trainer Pierre. Alex and Pierre have been acquaintances for a while—Alex used to work at his barn before he started working at Trina's. They start talking, leaving Eva and I to stare awkwardly at each other. I wouldn't even consider us acquaintances, and I know she's got a weird thing against Trina.

"I'm surprised to see you still with Trina," Eva says, as we continue casually perusing shirts. "I thought you were training with Jimmy Torano now."

"Well I just moved my horse to Jimmy's barn so I could have him closer to home, but Trina's still training me at the shows."

Eva and I chat for a few more minutes, pointing out our favorite shirts. A part of me feels like I'm being unfaithful to Trina, even though I'm just being polite to Eva. She's nice enough to me, but I know she's said some really mean things to Trina.

I laugh at a shirt that says, *My Therapist Eats Hay*. I consider getting one for Anya, and I wonder if they have a matching sticker for Luke's wheelchair. I think even Anya would approve of this one.

Pierre comes up behind Eva, saying, "You ready?"

Eva sets down a mug she was looking at and turns to me, "When you're ready to graduate from an amateur, let me know. Pierre would love to train you." I glance at Pierre, wondering if he set her up to say that, but his look is blank.

"I'm good, thanks," I say, keeping my tone just barely polite.

"What was that about?" Alex asks after Eva and Pierre are gone. Chance wriggles out of Alex's arms, and Alex sets him on the ground where he quickly wraps us up in his leash.

"I don't really know," I say, stepping around Chance as I try to untangle myself. "I don't know what that lady has against Trina."

"Me either." Alex shrugs. "Maybe we should keep our distance."

"Good idea."

We walk back to the barn to check on Cyrus. I grab a bag of treats out of my tack trunk, and after checking his legs, I work through a series of stretches with him—coaxing him into the stretch naturally with the treat.

Alex and Chance go out to grab us lunch and it's just Trina and me in the barn together. She's clearly tense, her shoulders bunched almost to her ears. The way she's moving around the barn, opening and closing her tack trunk with frustrated little snaps, I'm worried that maybe Eva said something to her. "You doing okay?" I ask.

"Fine." She shrugs, not even stopping what she's doing to look me in the eye.

Something erupts in me at Trina's blatant lie, and I snap, "What is up with you lately? You're not giving me *anything*." I wasn't planning on confronting Trina, but the question spills out of me.

Finally, she stops and looks at me. Her jaw clenches, but she doesn't say anything. Of course she doesn't—why would I expect her to?

"If you keep treating your friends like this, one day you'll find you don't have any."

She throws her hands up, as if I'm being ridiculous—and maybe I am, but I'm tired of this version of Trina, and I'm not walking around on eggshells anymore. "What are you talking about?"

"You're distracted, out of it, not responsive when I ask you what's up. You left my birthday party early without even a word, you've ended lessons early—which has *never* happened before—you left me hanging at the course back in November. But what's worse is that you're not being honest with me, Trina."

"I'm not *lying* about anything," she says.

"You're obviously not fine, but you keep insisting that you are. It's a lie by omission, but it's a lie nonetheless."

Trina sighs, running a hand down her face. She looks like she's on the edge of breaking, so I push it a little farther, "Look, Trina, you don't *have* to be my friend, but if we are going to be friends, it's got to look different than this."

"You're the one who left me!"

I rear back, surprised at the vehemence in her tone. "When I went to Jimmy's?"

"Yeah, but even before that—you left me for the Center, for Alex, for your perfect little happy life that's perfectly full without me."

"Oh." I collapse on the tack trunk. "I didn't realize I'd done that."

"Because you're happy and fulfilled and things are just peachy—"

"But they're not all peachy. And I've missed you."

"I've missed you too." She sits down next to me. "I'm sorry I've been so distracted lately. This whole thing with Grayson has been hard for me." She sighs, leaning her head back against the stall wall. "I told myself I wouldn't let a man get between me and my horse ever again, and here I am."

"It seems like you guys are working through it though," I say. "I mean, he hasn't taken off Leo's shoes this week, right?"

She laughs, shaking her head. "No, that's true. It's gotten...better."

"Look, I'm sorry if you felt like Alex and I abandoned you or something. We have missed you, terribly. There's a Trina-shaped hole in our lives." I nudge her shoulder with mine, and she gives a small smile. "How about this: why don't we decide to be more intentional with our friendship? We can take turns going back and forth between

Wellington and Davie. Even with all the competing, we both need to take breaks and have friend time."

"Yeah, I could definitely use that."

"Let's do it."

I wrap an arm around Trina, pulling her into a hug, and surprisingly, she melts into the gesture.

During our second ride, Cyrus is pulling me around the arena like a bulldozer. I'm standing on my toes, fighting him with every ounce of energy that I have. We plow through jump five, a lovely oxer with golden horse head standards. After that, Cyrus seems to understand that he probably needs to listen to me a little more. I take a long turn in order to get him collected and on the bit, so that we're composed for the triple combination. We charge through the three-fence obstacle, a rousing staccato, landing hard but clean on the other side.

I can hardly catch my breath as we rollback to a skinny brick fence that we barely clear. By the time we round the corner to a broken line of Longines fences, we're finally in a good rhythm. The rest of our ride is uneventful, if not completely smooth, and we only end with the four faults. It's enough to keep us in the event, and we'll proceed to the final event on Friday.

I stick around for Trina's course, watching with our other teammates and Alex. She and Leo are a sight to behold, and I can feel the entire sideline held in rapture as they expertly navigate the round. It's as if we're watching a Masterclass in show jumping—each fence is ridden with perfect balance, each stride so intentional, every turn is crisp, and each jump seems effortless.

At the end of her ride, Trina slows Leo to a walk, throwing her arms around him and kissing his neck. My heart squeezes at the sight of Grayson greeting them at the entrance. I'm over the moon to see the two of them finally working as a team—and I can't help but hope they'll become something more.

37

Soft Place to Fall

Trina

On Wednesday afternoon when we're done showing for the day, Grayson flags me down in the hallway of our rental house. "Hey can you help me with something?" He's wearing a pair of slacks with a white undershirt, and it takes all of my self-control to not trace the lines of his chest through his shirt. *Focus, Trina.*

"Sure."

He leads me into his bedroom, where several shirts are laid out on his bed. "I'm meeting up with an old friend from college, and I don't know which shirt matches."

I snort. "Grayson, if you're asking me for fashion advice, you're barking up the wrong tree." My closet is filled with outfits mostly in black, since that's the easiest thing to throw on without thinking too hard.

He shrugs and says, "I like your sense of style. It's understated and classic."

I tuck my hair behind my ear, not quite meeting Grayson's eyes. "Um, thanks."

"But I'm colorblind and I can't tell what shirt goes with these pants. Are they tan or brown? I can't really tell."

I stare at Grayson, a little dumbfounded, because Grayson is usually dressed impeccably, like he walked straight out of a photo shoot.

"Wait, so, how do you normally pick out your clothes?"

He fiddles with the button of a blue and white checkered shirt. "Cate bought all my clothes for me. She used to pair outfits for me, but…" he grimaces, rubbing the back of his neck. "I've been having my housekeeper do it for me lately, or sometimes DeDe. I'd ask her, but Mila and Alex took her out, so…" he looks up at me expectantly, looking vulnerable in a way that has my heart melting into a puddle of goo.

Something about this whole thing is so endearing, I want to wrap Grayson up in a hug. He's *colorblind*? His ex-wife picked out his whole wardrobe—that I've relentlessly judged him for—and now he needs his housekeeper or daughter to match his clothes for him?

I'm dying.

I'm dead.

"You should wear this one," I tell him, pointing to a light blue button down that I'm certain will bring out the blue undertones in his gray eyes. And then I skedaddle out of there faster than Secretariat at the Belmont because I'm not sure how much more my heart can take of Grayson J. Sterling.

That evening, I'm sitting in the hot tub. I assume everyone has drifted off to bed, and I'm allowing myself a moment to sink in and enjoy the alone time. I lean my head back against the edge of the hot tub, letting the jets hit me. The hot water pounds into my aching shoulders and I let out a groan.

"Sounds like you need a massage," Grayson's voice cuts through my reverie, and I jerk up, inadvertently splashing myself in the face. "Sorry, didn't mean to startle you." He chuckles, and that's when I notice Grayson is shirtless.

I repeat: *Grayson is shirtless*. And he is actively climbing into the hot tub with me. Alone.

I glance around, looking for a backup—anyone, even DeDe, would suffice. But there are no heroes today.

Grayson, clearly not aware of the frantic thoughts roiling through me, sighs into the water. "Took forever to get DeDe to bed. With the time change, you think she'd be exhausted. But it's like a reverse psychology thing and she's wired."

"How'd you get her to sleep?" I ask, if only to fill the space in my brain with something other than the visual of Grayson's physique. He's not buff or tall—if I had to guess, he's probably a 5'8" to my 5'2"—but he's lean and toned in a way that has me sitting on my hands so as not to do anything rash.

Not that I ever would. It's just...a precautionary measure.

"I used to tell her stories, but she'd just engage too much with that. So now if she has a hard time sleeping, I go through anatomy."

"Anatomy?" My brain is stuck on that term, only picturing Grayson's body in my mind, even though I know that isn't what he's talking about.

"I usually start with bones, going head to toe. Frontal bone, temporal, parietal, occipital—that sort of thing. She's usually out by the time I get to the vertebrae."

"I can't imagine why," I say dryly.

He laughs, his lips tipping into a half smile. "She'll either have every bone memorized by the time she's twelve, or—"

"Or she'll never want to have anything to do with science, ever."

"I suppose that's an option."

"She'll be dating someone in her twenties and the moment he mentions he's a physical therapist, she'll be gone. It'll be her red flag." Grayson laughs, his eyes twinkling from the patio lights. "'Oh, you're into human biology? Deal breaker,'" I say in twenty-year-old DeDe's voice.

We both laugh, leaning our heads back against the edge of the hot tub. After being apart from Grayson for a few days, this conversation is a reminder of what he is to me—a good friend. Someone I can laugh with. Someone I can—

"What are your deal breakers, Chevy?" he asks, slicing through my thoughts.

"What?"

"Your red flags, what are they?" He says it so casually, like this is a normal conversation we have. How can he be so *chill*? Meanwhile, I'm over here with my heart rate at 130 bpm, sweat beading all over my scalp at the mention of romance.

"Oh, um, I don't know," I lie. "What are yours?"

"I want someone who is genuine and not materialistic," he says immediately, like he's given this a lot of thought. "It's okay to like nice things, but that can't define your personality."

"Makes sense."

There's silence, like he's waiting for me to reciprocate—he *did* share, and now it's my turn. It's the only reason I blurt out, "I just want to be someone's most important person, that's all." I say it so low, I'm not even sure Grayson heard me. But after the confession, I'm pretty sure my heart rate jumped to 150. Why did I say that? I sound so pathetic.

There's a swish of water, and suddenly Grayson's right beside me. I force myself to keep my eyes on his face and not on the bare skin of his chest floating above the water.

"You know you deserve that and so much more," he says, his voice gravelly. And the way he says it, it's so believable. I find myself hoping—hoping it's true, hoping someone is out there for me like that. I glance over at Grayson, wondering…but no, that would be crazy. A guy like Grayson would never go for someone like me. Not only is he ridiculously gorgeous, impossibly rich, but he's also the smartest person I know. If he had any idea about my disability…

"You don't believe me?" he asks, genuine concern in his eyes.

"It's not that…" *It's totally that.*

"Don't let how one guy treated you determine your worth. He's an idiot if he made you feel any less than amazing."

I search his eyes, still filled with concern. Like he actually believes I'm worth something more than I really am. The problem is, it wasn't just Victor. It was every other person in my life—except for Tripp—from my parents to my guidance counselor to every teacher I ever had. No one with authority in my life has given me any reason to believe that what Grayson is saying is true.

He runs a wet hand through his hair, and a little piece of hair falls in his eyes, making him look that much more attractive. He's sitting so close to me—why is he sitting so close?—and I'm really having a hard time with this whole shirtless thing. It should be illegal for Grayson to be shirtless around me.

The sliding glass door opens and Mila and Alex emerge from the house in their swimsuits. My heart sinks, which is not a good sign, and I tell myself it's not because I want to be alone with Grayson.

"One day," Grayson says, lowering his voice so that Alex and Mila can't hear him as they cross the patio to the hot tub. "Some guy will sweep you off your feet, just you wait."

Aaand, there it is. Proof that Grayson would never in a million zillion years consider me as a romantic prospect. *Some guy* doesn't exactly equate to *this guy*. I feel nauseous with embarrassment that I let myself even consider the fact that he might like me. And that I *want* him to.

"Thanks, Grayson," I say, trying to withhold the disappointment in my voice. A few minutes later I excuse myself, heading to bed with a heavy, and very confused, heart.

Don't Stop Believing

Mila

"You like her," I say once Trina is safely on the other side of the sliding glass door. I lean back against the hot tub jet, laying my arms over the edge, feeling like a boss babe because I'm totally shipping these two.

Grayson gives me a sheepish smile while Alex chides, "Babe, you can't just go around accusing people of having romantic feelings."

"I am right though." I lean forward. "Aren't I right, Grayson?"

He sighs, shrugging his shoulders in and out of the water. "You're not wrong."

"See?" I turn to Alex, smiling. "I told you."

"It's the principle of the thing," Alex says.

"It's fine," Grayson says good naturedly. "Besides, I could use your advice. Trina's not exactly an open book, although we have been getting closer."

I'm practically vibrating with excitement—I can't believe my luck. A thoughtful, good-looking billionaire doctor is totally into Trina. All of my dreams (for Trina) are coming true. Trina just needs to get in line. "Look," I say as I tuck my legs underneath me. It takes everything within me not to bounce on my knees or clap my hands. But I can't scare away Grayson. *Play it cool, Mila.* "This is a classic slow burn situation."

Grayson's brow furrows, and I suppose he's not up on all the romance tropes out there.

"That means if you guys were in a romance novel, it would take the whole novel for one or both of you to realize your feelings," I explain. "Or, if it were a series, it might take a few books."

Grayson nods slowly and I'm starting to worry I've freaked him out, until he says, "I'm fine with slow burn. That's what's best for me anyway. I've got DeDe to think about."

"Exactly," I say, as if that's what I was thinking of when I said 'slow burn.'

"Trina's one of the most loyal people on this planet," Alex says, and I know he's speaking from experience—Trina was there for him when his dad died, despite how things had gone down between Trina and Alex's cousin, Victor. She's gone out of her way to rescue Alex from a variety of bad situations—from false accusations to testifying at his Immigration hearing. And, of course, she's worked with me through my crippling fears and helped me to become the Grand Prix rider that I am today. "But you'll have to earn that loyalty."

"From what I can tell, you're doing a good job so far," I say. "I mean, aside from the ShoeGate thing."

"ShoeGate?" Grayson laughs. "I hadn't heard that one."

"Oops." I chuckle nervously. "All is forgiven though, I'm sure."

"Maybe. Either that, or Trina will make sure it gets engraved on my headstone: 'He was a nice guy, but he took all the shoes off of my horse before a Grand Prix.'"

We all laugh. "I don't think she'd put it on your headstone," I say. "Mention it in your eulogy? Absolutely. Headstone? Probably not."

"Well that's a relief," Grayson says. "So, how can I take this from a slooooowwww burn, to a slow-ish burn situation?"

I think for a moment. "Trina's got her walls up, that's for sure. I think to break them down, it would be a good idea to get her out of her comfort zone a little more. Someplace where she's a little less prepared. At the barn and at the show, she's in control. But I've seen how she's loosened up a bit being here, out of the norm."

Grayson is nodding, like he agrees with my assessment. "So I shouldn't just ask her on a date?"

Alex and I shake our heads. "I mean, can you take her on a date without it being a *date*?" Alex suggests.

"Like a sneak-a-date!" I say.

"A what?"

"A sneak-a-date," I say, like it's the most normal term in the world. "In high school, when my parents wouldn't let us date, that's what Anya and I would call it. Like, *oh we're going to the movies with a whole group of friends*, but once we were there, we would pair off with whatever guy we were into."

Alex frowns. "I'm not a fan of this story."

I nuzzle his cheek, pressing a kiss against his scruff. "If I knew you in high school, you'd be my sneak-a-date."

"It would probably take more than four years to rustle up the courage to talk to you," Alex says.

"It worked out in the end though, didn't it?"

"True enough." He places a quick kiss on my lips and turns back to Grayson. "Alright, man, you gotta work on the sneak-a-date, ideally in a place where Trina's outside of her comfort zone."

"Right, but not too far out of her comfort zone, or she won't agree to it."

"Got it." Grayson pulls himself out of the hot tub, sitting on the edge. "Mission: sneak-a-date, coming soon."

And, I can't help it, this time I clap my hands.

Trina's walls are going to come crashing down.

Alex and I are in the kitchen making lunch the next day when I overhear Grayson telling Trina about a charity event he's attending in Palm Beach next week. My knife hovers above the mayo jar as I listen.

"I paid for a table, but now I have to fill it," I hear Grayson's muffled voice say. I'll give him a B- for his delivery—he's beating around the bush more than he needs to be. "I was hoping some people at the barn would want to come."

"I'm sure Ellie and Ryan would like to go," Trina says, and I cringe, setting down my knife. Grayson needs help, STAT. I tug Alex out into the living room, where Trina and Grayson are sitting with Chance curled up in the crook of Trina's legs.

"Where are we going?" I ask casually. Or at least I *hope* I sound casual.

"Grayson's got a charity event he's trying to get people to go to." Trina's scrolling through Instagram, not even looking at Grayson. Uh oh.

"That's so nice," I say, my voice sounding unnaturally high. "What's the charity?"

"Sumatran rhinos," Grayson says, and the lack of confidence in his delivery is starting to make sense. He couldn't find a charity for kids with cancer or wild mustangs?

"How fun!" Okay, now I sound like I'm trying too hard. *Sumatran rhinos, really*?? No wonder Trina doesn't want to go. Snoozefest.

"They're endangered," Grayson says, almost defensively. "There's only sixty-five left in the world."

"What a shame," I say as genuinely as I can muster. "That's amazing that you're helping that cause, isn't it, Trin?"

"Yeah," she says noncommittally. Hmm...maybe Trina's not feeling Grayson? Could I have read the situation wrong?

"Apparently, rhinos are the closest living relatives to horses," Grayson says, trying to regain ground.

At this, Trina's eyebrows raise. "Really?"

"Oh my gosh then we totally need to support this cause," I say, and I can practically feel Alex rolling his eyes. I'm trying *way* too hard right now. "Is there room for us at the table? Trina, you're going, right?"

Trina shrugs. "I don't have anything to wear to some fancy dinner."

"That's a fixable problem," I say, glancing at Grayson to encourage him.

"I can get you something," Grayson says, and I frown. *That* is not the encouragement I meant to give him. He sees the look on my face and quickly remedies, "How about you girls go on a shopping trip, my treat?"

Everyone in the room gives Grayson skeptical looks. "Hey, if I don't get to spend money on my friends, it's completely pointless being this rich!" he says, throwing out his hands.

This gets a small smile out of Trina, and I internally squeal. She totally likes him, too!

"Look, bring DeDe with you, you'll be doing me a favor," Grayson says, gaining steam. "She needs some girl time, anyway. Her mom's out of the country for a while."

Trina nods. "Sure," she says. "We'll do it for DeDe."

"And the charity event?" Grayson asks, and I literally cross my fingers.

"Sure," she says with a sigh. "For the horse cousins."

Later, when Trina's gone to bed, Chance and I corner Grayson in the kitchen. "Sumatran rhinos, Grayson, *really*?"

"They're an endangered species!"

"But rhinos?! That's the best you could come up with?"

"Have you seen a baby rhino? They're cute."

I scrunch my nose, but Grayson's busy on his phone, pulling up a picture of a baby rhino. Alex saunters into the kitchen to make some tea, giving me a side eye that says, *Don't give him a hard time*. Well, too late for that. When Grayson shows me a picture of a baby rhino, I change my tune. "Okay, that *is* cute." I grab Grayson's phone to show to Alex. "Babe, look at this. I think we need a baby rhino. Can't you see it at the Center? It would be a huge hit."

"Uhh..." He raises an eyebrow at me, as if to say, *Haven't we had enough of a bad experience with animal purchases lately?*

"They're so cute, though."

"Maybe they're cute?" he says skeptically. "In a really ugly sort of way."

"Whatever," I say, handing the phone back to Grayson. "I'm fully supportive of this save-the-rhinos thing now. But you should've led with this picture."

"I think it was the horse-relative thing that got her," Alex says.

"Shocker," Grayson says, voice dripping in playful sarcasm.

"Hey, she's single-minded. If you got a problem with that, there's the door," I say with enough humor in my tone to show I'm joking. Sort of.

But Grayson smiles, sticking his hands in his pockets. "I like that about her," he says simply. "We're kindred spirits."

I smile back at Grayson, doing a little happy dance—internally, of course—while I pray that this save-the-rhinos event works on Trina's walls.

All we can do is hope.

For the final day of the FEI Longines Nations Cup Qualifier, we all wake up early, clearly too excited to sleep. Even DeDe, with a penchant for sleeping late, is bright-eyed and bushy-tailed at six AM.

Cyrus and I are one of the first to go, with Trina being one of the last since she's ranked higher. Cyrus and I have a very solid ride—only one rail down and a good time. We'll be one of the best four-faulters.

Leo and Trina, however, are in perfect sync. Leonidas's bay coat shimmers in the sunshine, looking regal with his button braids dotting his long neck. Trina's in the bright red coat with blue lining that all the American participants—myself included—are wearing, with her pristine white breeches underneath. They look Olympic-worthy, and my heart flutters with anticipation for them. It's true that I want this for myself, but even more so, I want this for Trina. There's no one more deserving than she is.

They glide over the course like they were made for this. My breath catches when Leo gets too deep to a fence, but he shifts his front end to miraculously avoid the rails. They coast over the water jump, Leo's body stretched out like he's a dancer. He drifts wide as they come into the triple combination, but Trina expertly navigates him through it despite the drift, and they get through clean.

By the end of the course, I have tears in my eyes because this is one of the most beautiful rides I've ever seen in my life. When they sail over the last vertical, flying through the timers, the whole crowd erupts in cheers. It's as if we all know how glorious of a spectacle Trina and Leo are—and even her competitors are on their feet, clapping.

Her ride alone seems like enough to qualify us for the Nations Cup Final in October, but the announcer makes it official as our team heads to the center stage, taking third place for the event. I hug Trina, who's still glowing from her ride. "You did amazing!" I say, jostling her with my hug. Even Eva Rutherford's sour face—she got disqualified in the second round—isn't enough to dampen our enthusiasm.

Trina's proven beyond a shadow of a doubt that she's capable of holding her own in a team victory like this, and Cyrus and I didn't do too shabby either. As they place our medals over us and we take pictures, waving and cheering with our teammates, I soak it all in. We're one step closer to our Olympic dream.

39

The Great Escape

Trina

I should feel like Cinderella right now—with this gorgeous dress that Grayson's heavy black AMEX purchased for me—but instead I feel like a piece of meat being squished into sausage casing. After the super fancy department store's tailor adjusted my dress to perfectly fit me, I'm forced to wear a pair of off-brand Spanx to make it look right. I gaze in the mirror, running my hands over the black satin fabric that clings to my hips. I've never been in a dress this formfitting before. It's a simple black dress, but when I turn around, the back plunges almost all the way to my butt.

I don't know why I let Mila and DeDe convince me this was a good idea. I even had to buy a pair of weird sticky boob cups since I can't wear a bra with this dress. I glance down at the time on my phone. Grayson will be here in five minutes—and the man is never late. My heart rate speeds up because for some reason this feels like a date. Even though it's definitely not a date—there's nothing inherently sexy about a Save the Sumatran Rhino charity event. Except that I'm in this gorgeous, restrictive dress, waiting for a man that I'm very much attracted to, who is rapidly becoming one of my closest friends.

It's not a date, but it *is* complicated. My stupid heart has made it complicated.

I try chastising my poor heart—reminding it that we don't do men, we do Olympic medals. Plus, even if we were open to the idea, someone of Grayson's caliber would never, ever look twice my way.

This little piece of instruction doesn't seem to make a difference to my silly little heart when a knock sounds at my door. I wobble to the front of my apartment, my legs shaking more from nerves than from the heels Mila forced me to wear. My palms are sweating as I open the door.

When I see Grayson, my heart falls to the floor, crashing down three stories into the Florida limestone where it will forever be buried. Because Grayson is the definition of drop-dead gorgeous. His hair is slicked back, his custom suit tailored to perfection—no Spanx needed. He looks like he could be the next James Bond, with his mission to break my heart in two.

"Hi," I say, but it comes out strangled. I clear my throat, trying again. "Hi, Grayson."

"Trina," he says. "You look..." he trails off, and I hold my breath, waiting for whatever adjective he's going to use. Serviceable? Stuffed like a sausage? "Beautiful."

"Oh." I wasn't expecting *that*. "Thank you."

Grayson briskly pulls on the ends of his sleeves, adjusting his cuffs. And oh my Muse, why is that so attractive? Have I ever, in the span of my existence, noticed a man doing that? "You ready?" he asks, as if he didn't just do the hottest thing since the Red Hot Chili Peppers came on the scene. "Want me to carry anything?"

I frown. "Uh..."

"There's not, like, a hair dryer or full-length mirror you need to bring with you?" He's got a playful glint in his eye as he makes a show of looking around the door behind me. "It seems as though women always have lots of *stuff* they're trying to bring with them to things like this."

I tilt my head up, steadying myself against the door frame. "Guess I'm not like most other women."

Grayson smiles, and something about it makes my knees weak. "No," he says, holding out his arm for me to take. "You're not."

Grayson leads me to a massive limousine, which makes me feel like this is prom or some other school dance I never went to. I press my hand to my stomach, trying to still the swooping that's happening in there. As we get closer, I realize that the limo isn't an ordinary limousine—it's a stretch Chevrolet Tahoe. "They didn't have any Toyota limos available, huh?" I tease, nudging Grayson's side.

He laughs, leaning closer to me. "I thought you'd prefer the Chevy."

I glance over at his gray eyes. Our faces are so close, especially with the height I've gained in these heels, and my breath sticks in my throat. He got the Chevy limo...for me? As, like, a joke? Or is he being sweet and thoughtful? It's hard to tell, but the look in his eyes is making me think it's the latter. Though I'm not sure my heart can accept that.

I school my face into a smirk and say, "Smart man. A Toyota limo would've been a total bore."

"They don't call you Chevy for nothing." His lips tilt into the sexiest smile that ever lived. Be still, stupid heart.

I roll my eyes—when really what I want to do is melt into a puddle at Grayson's feet. "No one calls me Chevy except you."

"Doesn't that make me special?"

Yes. "It makes you *something*."

The limo driver appears out of seemingly nowhere, opening the door for us. Grayson's hand goes to my lower back to usher me in—which means that his fingers graze my bare skin. I suck in my breath at the electricity pulsing from his hand into my skin. I scramble into the limo, flush from the brief touch, and I'm grateful for the darkness so Grayson can't see how intensely I'm blushing. Adrenaline pumps through me as if I'm in the middle of a Grand Prix course, instead of sitting in a limousine with Grayson Sterling.

Grayson slides in next to me, a mischievous look on his face. "I've never been in a limo before," he says.

I'm actually a little surprised—it seems like if you're a billionaire, you'd be driving around in them all the time. "Not even for prom?" I ask.

"I didn't go to prom," he says with a shrug.

"Me either," I confess, feeling like this similarity ties us together more than it probably should. So what? Lots of kids don't go to prom. It doesn't mean Grayson and I are suddenly soulmates. The limo starts rolling down the road, making my stomach lurch. Or maybe that's just Grayson's affect on me.

"We should probably take advantage of this, then," Grayson says, and I'm having trouble not reading into what he's saying. Does he want to make out back here or what? "I hooked up my phone to the speakers, so we can play whatever we want."

Obviously Grayson was referring to blasting music...not making out. Because why would he?

Also, what is wrong with me? I think this stupid black dress has weird mojo in it that's making me want to kiss Grayson.

(Let's not mention the other zillion times I've thought of kissing Grayson. We're blaming it on the *dress*, people!)

"I made us a playlist," Grayson says, and BOYS LIKE GIRLS "The Great Escape" starts to play. I can't help the smile that's taking over my face because I love this song. It's such a classic rock-out-in-the-car song. "Want to stick your head out the sunroof? Or will that mess up your hair?"

I lean into Grayson, the song making me feel more daring. "I'm not like other women, remember?"

Grayson smiles as he opens the sunroof, his eyes not leaving mine the entire time. I kick my heels off and step onto the seat so I can get through the sunroof. Wind whips around me, tossing my hair all around. From inside the limo, Grayson turns the music up right when the lead singer says, "We'll scream loud at the top of our lungs." I smile, lifting my hands into the air and let out a whoop.

Then Grayson's behind me, his chest grazing my bare back as we both squeeze through the sunroof. He laughs, the vibrations from his chest zipping through my body. I shift so that he's not touching my bare skin, but this is much worse because now I can see Grayson up close in all his glory. He tilts his head back and starts scream-singing the chorus. The wind is making a complete mess of his hair, but he doesn't seem to care.

For a moment, it feels like we really are back in high school. I imagine what it would be like if I knew Grayson back then—not that he'd *ever* hang out with someone as dumb and lame as me—but I let that go for now. Grayson and I are just two wild and free kids with nothing to lose and the whole world to gain. It's like we really are making a great escape, back to a time that never existed for me, and I get to be a person I want to be but have no hope of ever becoming—someone carefree, fun, relaxed. Someone who is loved, who knows there's another person out there who has her back. Someone like Grayson.

The song changes to Jet's "Are You Gonna Be My Girl" and I laugh when Grayson knows *all* of the words. He's singing them at me with all of the zeal and swagger of lead singer Nic Cester.

When the limo turns a corner, Grayson and I aren't ready for it, and we collide into each other. Grayson's hands go to my hips, steadying me as I wrap my fingers around his shoulders. For a moment I can't think. There are no words, no thoughts forming in my head. There is only Grayson and his body pressed flush against mine. Some strange, almost primal urge wants to take over—I feel it, like a devil on my shoulder, tempting me to pull Grayson down into a kiss.

Then reality comes roaring back into the forefront of my mind. I press away from Grayson, glancing down. "I'm just going to..." I trail off, not sure what it is I need to do, except get some distance from Grayson. I slip down from the sunroof and settle into the corner of the limo, running my fingers through the myriad of tangles in my hair. A minute later, Grayson sits down beside me as we pull into Ellie's neighborhood. Honestly, I'd been so wrapped up in this time with Grayson that I'd forgotten we were picking up Ellie.

"Guess we should act like adults when the kids get here, huh?" Grayson says, as if that's why I'm not singing in the sunroof anymore.

"Yep." I don't even look at him, I find that I can't.

"Could you, uh, help me?"

I force myself to look casually over at Grayson—but with one glance, I erupt into laughter. His hair is sticking up in all different directions from the wind. And, of course, because he had some kind of strong-hold product in his hair, it's now stuck that way. "I don't know, Gray, I think you're rocking that mad scientist look."

"I always did think that Einstein was a sexy guy." He scoots next to me, so that his thigh is pressed against mine. I reach up, running my fingers through his hair, trying to flatten it back to his head.

"Einstein was the sexiest," I say because I need to say something right now—my face is inches from Grayson's, I can feel his breath skittering across my face, and my hands are in his hair. This is exactly like all of the times I've thought about kissing Grayson—the only thing that's missing is his lips on mine.

"Oh yeah? Is that your type?" Grayson says, his gray-green eyes fixed on mine. I'm afraid he can see my desire etched on every inch of my face, so I keep my gaze on his hair. I'm taking my task very seriously, smoothing it down far more than I really need to. But who knows when I'll have an opportunity like this again. The limo pulls to a stop in front of Ellie's house. I run my hand once more through Grayson's hair, letting my fingers linger down his neck, just a smidge. I'm just getting it out of my system, and then when I'm done I won't feel the need to be close to Grayson anymore.

Ha. Joke's on me because the moment I pull away, I want more. "There," I say. "All better."

"Darn," Grayson's breathes out. "No more sexy Einstein vibes. Guess I won't be scoring with you tonight, huh, Chevy?" He winks at me, which only serves to make me feel like I've just tumbled down into Alice's Wonderland. Is Grayson *flirting* with me? There's no way.

The limo door opens, and I jump away from Grayson, not wanting Ellie to see me so close to him. Though I'm pretty sure my feelings are written on my face, clear for the whole world to see.

The rest of the evening is (mostly) uneventful. Mila and Alex meet us at the Chateau Iorio—a fancy house right on the water. Inside, there's Blackjack, poker, and roulette tables scattered throughout the space. Waiters circle with hors d'oeuvres in black jackets and white gloves. Part of me feels like I'm a pony who accidentally stumbled into a Grand Prix, but Grayson doesn't leave my side and for some reason having him next to me makes me feel more like I belong.

There's a silent auction, which I'd normally never pay attention to, but Grayson says, "I'll bid on something for you, if you'd like."

When I give him a skeptical look, he shrugs and says, "It's for the rhinos."

"Right. The rhinos." I look through the options: a natural pearl necklace and earrings, a therapeutic massage, a yoga bundle.

"How about swimming with the orcas in Norway?" Grayson says, reading the other silent auction items. He tilts his head down so he's right next to my ear, his breath on my neck as he speaks. "Or a Zoom date with Bachelor star Blake Moynes." He raises his eyebrows. "Would you like that? A date with Blake?"

I press my lips together, shaking my head. Why does it feel like Grayson is fishing for something? "How about the equine sprouted barley grass & supercharged Omega oil by Equigreens?" I ask.

"You want me to bid on something...for Leo?"

"Well, yeah." *Obviously.*

Grayson chuckles, leaning down over the silent auction paper. My eyes go wide when I see his bid—way higher than anyone else's, but also about a thousand times more than the Omega oil is worth. "Grayson," I whisper. "That's way too much."

"It's for the rhinos." He gives me a cheeky grin. "And Leo." He puts his hand on my back, leading me down toward the other silent auction items. "Now, let's pick something for you."

"You just did!"

"No...that was for Leo. Pick something for *you*."

I hesitate, my eyes sweeping over the options.

"What do you want?" Chills shiver down my back as Grayson sweeps my hair behind my shoulder. Is that something friends do? Because I'm feeling very *un*friendly right now. "Chevy?"

I look up at Grayson. "The flying lesson," I blurt before I can stop myself.

Grayson smiles, his eyes crinkling in a way I'm starting to adore. "It's yours."

He leans down, writing a number that makes my eyes just about fall out of my head. "Grayson." I grab his arm. "That's too much." We've already been through this song and dance, yet it still feels like too much. 'It's for the rhinos' doesn't quite feel like it can cover what's going on here.

Grayson stands up, putting his hands in his pockets. "If I can't spend my money on things like this, what's even the point?"

"Right. What else would a billionaire do except save the rhinos?"

Grayson shakes his head. "No, Chevy. That—" He nods his head at the equine Omega oil. "That was for the rhinos. This, this is for you."

"Why?"

"Why not?" When he can tell I'm not convinced, he changes tactics. "Look, who would you rather win this thing, you? Or..." he looks around and nods at a woman in a red dress. She's got more makeup on than I've ever worn in my entire life, her ear sagging with the weight of the massive gems dangling on them. "Her?"

I scoff, rolling my eyes. "We don't even know her, Grayson. She could be a very nice person."

He raises his eyebrows, giving me a look that says, *Do you really believe that*? He leans down, his mouth brushing against my ear as he whispers, "No one here deserves this more than you."

With that, he puts down the bidding pen, leaving his exorbitant price for the flying lesson and walks away. I'm left feeling shaken, like something just shifted inside of me that I'll never be able to get back into place.

And I'm not sure I want it to.

40

Provider

Mila

In the weeks after we get back from San Juan Capistrano, we find out that Alex officially passed his licensure exam. It's not surprising, but it is wonderful news. I organize a small get together to celebrate with both of our families and Luke in attendance in a private room at Casa D'Angelo Ristorante.

After appetizers but before the entrees come out, we all go around and say a few encouraging words about Alex. Luke tells of a few humorous situations at the Center where Alex handled himself with all of the integrity and gentleness we've all come to know and love about my husband. Mrs. Caballero's tearful sharing brings me to tears as she talks about how hardworking Alex is, how he stepped up to take care of her after his dad died, and the incredible man he's become—a man his father would be so proud of.

Even my dad manages to say a few nice things about Alex, until he ends by saying, "Someone give this man a raise."

We all chuckle, some of us a little more nervously than others.

And then, for the pièce de résistance, my lovely father adds: "Maybe if we give him a raise, my daughter will stop using my credit card so often. I already pay for her horse and all those shows."

I wish the ground would open up and swallow me alive right now. Because not only is everyone in the room looking at me like the spoiled brat that I am, but Alex's tightening hand on my knee tells me that my husband is mortified.

And now we have the rest of our dinner to sit on eggshells.

Wonderful.

After an hour-long dinner, and then a twenty-minute drive to drop Mrs. Caballero off at her house, I'm finally alone with Alex. The moment his mom is safely tucked inside her house, he says to me, "Tell me about the credit card." His voice is low yet firm—and for some reason, this is so much worse than if he were yelling at me.

"My dad gave me an emergency credit card, which I may or may not have been using for more than emergencies."

"I see." It's silent as Alex navigates the car from Stirling to Griffin Road. "And when did he give you this credit card?"

"When I went to college."

"And I'm guessing you used this credit card to buy the dog and the music course and equipment?"

I nod, even though I'm not sure if he can see me in the dark. When we finally pull into the Center and drive all the way back to the Cottage, Alex puts his car in park and turns to look at me. I can barely meet his eyes. I feel like I'm an inch tall—and just as capable of being married as a toddler is.

"Look, Mila, I appreciate you getting those things for me and thinking of me in that way. But that moment with your dad in the restaurant back there—" He cuts off, shaking his head, and I'm inwardly melting of shame. "That was really awful for me. I never, ever want your dad to view me as incapable of taking care of you."

"I'm sorry, Alex. I really wish that hadn't happened. I didn't think anything of using the credit card. It's just that, you know, my dad has all this money and we don't, so it felt harmless."

"Maybe it felt harmless when you were swiping that card, but it really undermines me as your husband. As your provider."

"I'm sorry," I repeat, feeling at a complete loss for words. I know I messed up, but I don't know what else to say to fix this. Tears blur my vision, and I press my lips together to try to keep them from coming.

Alex's dark eyes pierce mine as he gazes at me, letting me see the hurt still whirling there. "When we said 'for richer or poorer,' I meant that, Mila. I'd just like to know that you did too."

And then he gets out of the car, leaving me alone to cry.

Bridle Buzz ✓ · Follow
Southampton, NY

392 likes

Bridle Buzz Tuning in from the Hamptons this week! Alicia Monet swept the five-star Grand Prix on Sunday with a double clear for the ages. She also looked stylish in a mauve Klein Equestrian helmet.
Sadly, Trina Powers and her steed Leonidas had several rails in the final Grand Prix of the weekend. It seems like her luck after the Longines event in CA has gone downhill. Maybe she needs that billionaire of hers to buy her a new horse.
Five-time Olympian Oscar Sigaro was seen on the show grounds in a rare appearance with Evangeline Rutherford. Evangeline was wearing a custom DiLoren jacket in a lovely gray-blue as she competed in the Hamptons.
Tune in next week for more horse show gossip at the Hamptons! Let me know in the comments: what did you think of Alicia's helmet? Would you sport a mauve helmet? …
more

View all 12 comments

Prius Equine Not sure I could sport the mauve! But the blue coat is cool. Too bad for Trina.
Richard Trulo Not sure why this account mixes horse show news with fashion...just tell it to us straight.
Diane Witts LOVE the helmet!!!!!! And the jacket!!! Where can I get them????

 Add a comment...

5 hours ago

41

One Good Horse

Trina

August finds us in the Hamptons—which sounds far more glamorous than it actually is. There's no lounging in a sailboat happening around here, people. No, we're sweating and grunting as we tear around a Grand Prix course at the Hampton Classic horse show. Despite the temperature creeping up on ninety degrees, they haven't waived coats for this show, so I've sweated through my jacket by the time Leo and I finish our ride.

After I've handed off Leo to Grayson so he can cool him off and get him settled back at the barn, I turn my attention to Mila. I set a practice fence and she warms up. I move the rail higher and higher until we're both satisfied that Cyrus is ready to go in the ring.

At the in-gate, I give Mila a few final thoughts as we watch the rider in front of her. "Have him check out the lighthouse fence when you get in there," I say, pointing to an oxer with towering lighthouses as the jump standards.

Mila trots into the ring and as she shows Cyrus the lighthouses, I hear a couple pairs of boots navigating the seating area behind me. I recognize Eva Rutherford's voice as she talks with another person I can't quite hear. They're discussing the Instagram account, Bridle Buzz.

"Did you see what they wrote about Trina?" the other person says. "Scathing."

Eva titters. "Honestly, she deserves it. She thinks she's so much better than us because she hasn't been riding ready-made horses but look where she is now. The sad thing is, she actually thinks she's Olympic material."

"She did really well with that one horse years ago."

"One decent horse does not an Olympian make," Eva says. A part of me wants to stomp up there and ask her, *Does five ready-made horses make you an Olympian?*

The thing is: Eva's wrong. All you need is one good horse—it's not like you can compete in the Olympics with five different horses.

It only takes one.

But whether or not that's true for me remains to be seen. Eva and her annoying friend could be right: I could be fooling myself to think I'm Olympic material. And that thought stays with me, like a nagging injury, all throughout the horse show weekend.

42

August Slipped Away

Mila

I'm still feeling on edge with Alex about the credit card fiasco by the time we arrive in New York for the Hamptons Classic. Despite Alex and Anya's attempts to convince me otherwise, it's like I have a gaping hole in my center that needs to be filled by Cyrus and winning.

I pour myself into this weekend, focusing every ounce of energy on Cyrus and the course. For the Grand Prix on Sunday, I walk the course twice—once with Trina and then another time on my own, planning each stride, each turn. During our warm up, I cut our rollbacks tighter than ever before, pushing Cyrus to his limit.

At the in-gate, I give Alex a perfunctory kiss before walking into the grass arena. I trot Cyrus to the lighthouse fence, letting him take a good look at it as I mentally go over the course once more.

Our ride is a disaster from the start. We chip in at the very first fence and knock the rail down. I get a bad angle after a rollback, and Cyrus breezes right past the fence, not even realizing we were supposed to jump it. I circle, and we try again, clearing the fence this time. We have another rail at the in-and-out, and when Cyrus stumbles under the dropped rail at his feet, we miss the next fence in the broken line. It counts as a refusal, and we're disqualified.

I've never been disqualified before in a Grand Prix. Trina has some thoughts for me at the in-gate, but I can hardly comprehend what she's saying. Alex walks silently beside me as we head to the barns.

"I'll go grab us some food," he says when we get back, somehow sensing that I need space.

After I untack Cyrus and settle into a corner of his stall to cry, I'm still reeling from the course. If I'm not good at this, what am I even good at? And why does it feel like no matter what I do, I'm letting someone down, worst of all Alex.

I want to go to the Olympics—I want to be at the very top of this sport—but I'm not even sure the process is worth it.

And worse, I wonder if I've lost myself so much on this journey that I don't even know who I am anymore.

way after forever

Mila

We're back home for a few weeks and I've just broken our toaster oven for the umpteenth time while attempting to reheat leftovers for dinner. Alex comes into the kitchen to witness my utter failure at life, hair still wet from his shower. Without warning, tears spring to my eyes, and I hunch over the kitchen counter, sobbing.

"*Mi amor*," Alex says, wrapping his arms around me. "Come here." He turns me gently so I can cry into his chest.

"I break everything," I cry. "*I'm* broken."

"You're not broken," Alex says, taking my face in his hands so I can gaze up at him. There's so much warmth and love in his eyes that it settles my crying. "But I do have a theory. Can I share it with you?"

"Yes," I sniffle.

"Come sit with me." Alex leads me to the couch, settling me onto his lap. "Let me ask you this: if your phone runs out of battery, do you throw it out? Get a new phone?"

"No?" This feels like a trick question, and for some reason my brain jumps to my dad's emergency credit card. I did *not* get a new phone on the credit card. I've got *some* boundaries.

"If your car runs out of gas, do you ditch it? Leave it on the side of the road and find a new one?"

"Uh, no?"

"They're not broken, they just need filling up." He gently kisses my temple. "And you, *mi tesoro*, are badly in need of a filling up. You've run yourself ragged with everything you're trying to do. Of course you're having a hard time staying fully charged—anyone would be."

"Okay, but what can I do? I can't really off-load anything I have."

"Maybe, maybe not. But I think what we need to start with is making sure that your tank is filled. We gotta make sure you slow down and do things that you enjoy, that make you feel filled up."

"Hmm." I nod. "I can try that."

"How about tonight we take a break from the social media stuff and we can order dinner." Alex takes my phone, putting it onto the coffee table. "On our debit card though."

I groan. "But—"

"No buts, Mila. Let me take care of you, okay? I want to take care of you." He shifts me so that I'm sitting beside him on the couch instead of in his lap, and says, "Hold on." He jogs back to our room, grabbing his phone and putting a song on. "Dance with me?"

He holds out his hand, and I take it, smiling. The soft guitar notes of "way after forever" by the indie artist vaultboy fills our living room. Alex tenderly presses me against his chest, swaying me in his arms as vaultboy sings, "I'm gonna love you way after forever."

Alex shifts me so that I can see his face as he sings along to the song—telling me he's going to love me through all the good times and all the mistakes, over and over again.

I know I don't deserve this, but I allow myself to sink into it, to enjoy the feel of his arms around me, his love wrapping around me in the best possible way.

Trina and I stick to our new friendship resolution and this week I sleepover at Trina's, like old times. After my talk with Alex, we decided that one way I could get re-filled is by hanging out with my friends. Plus, Alex told me he was bro-ing out with some guys to work on music together. Those weren't exactly the words he used, but that's what I heard.

Trina shows me her cold plunge barrel from Grayson and asks if I want to use it. "It's actually been really helpful for muscle recovery. I don't feel nearly as sore as I used to."

I try—and fail—to keep my face from looking like an alien just sprouted out of Trina's blonde head. "Trina, I want to go to the Olympics, but not *that* bad."

She laughs as we settle onto her couch to watch some kind of old school Western with Russell Crowe and Leonardo DiCaprio. "I never knew Russell Crowe was such a looker," I say as we burrow under blankets on Trina's couch.

"Are you kidding? He's a babe."

I grimace. "Maybe he *used* to be, but he looks more like he's searching for a role as Santa Claus these days."

Trina laughs, shoveling a scoop of almond butter onto an apple slice. Our sleepover fare is rough compared to normal standards—there's no Jeni's ice cream up in this joint—but since we're both focused on our training, we've got apples and almond butter along with a spread of hummus and sliced veggies. The only nod to something yummy are the chocolate-covered almonds in a tiny bowl on her coffee table.

"Russell's cute in this film," Trina says. "But I'm more of a Leo DiCaprio fan myself."

I roll over onto my stomach so that I'm practically in Trina's lap. "You know who looks an awful lot like Leo?" I waggle my brows.

She points an apple slice at me. "Don't say it, Mila."

I stand up and prance around the room like I'm a fancy billionaire. "Oh look, I own your horse now," I say in a deep voice. "With my fancy watch and my Ferrari—"

"Maserati."

"I'm a billionaire, baby. Everyone, buy dresses on me!" I pretend like I'm throwing money around the room, shaking my hips, while Trina cackles.

"That's the worst impression of Grayson ever."

"Oh so you can do a better one then?"

Trina stands up, grabbing her sunglasses from the kitchen counter and putting them on with a swagger. "Grayson J. Sterling," she says, her voice low. She sticks her hand out, shaking my hand. "I invented the atom and I run Ironmans in my spare time." She lowers her sunglasses. "*Backward.*"

We take turns doing Grayson impressions that are increasingly wacky until we collapse with laughter on Trina's couch. We both jump when there's a knock on the door. "Amazon package?" I ask, but I don't think even Amazon delivers packages this late.

Trina tiptoes to her door, peeking out of the peephole. She gasps, stepping back from the door. "It's him!" she whisper-yells.

"Him who?"

"*Grayson.*"

"Trina?" Grayson's voice comes from the other side of the door.

"What do I do?" Trina whispers.

"Open the door!"

"I look like a bum!" She gestures down at her sweatpants.

"I, uh, can hear you guys," Grayson says.

Trina stares at me wide-eyed and mouths, "Oh my gosh!" Then she takes a deep breath, squares her shoulders, and opens the door. "Oh, hey Grayson," she says casually. I bite my lip to keep from laughing.

"I brought this for you," Grayson says, holding up a vitamin bottle. "You mentioned you were out."

Trina takes the bottle from him, fingers lingering over Grayson's. "Thanks."

"I know it helps with your knees." Grayson rubs the back of his neck, and it takes everything within me to not do a happy dance right here in front of them. Because these two are obviously *so* into each other.

"It really does," Trina says.

They're clearly stalling, wanting to talk with each other more. But of course, I'm here, ruining the moment. So I grab my keys and say, "I was just getting ready to head out, good to see you, Grayson."

"Oh. Hey, Mila," Grayson says, as if he didn't even realize I was behind Trina.

"What are you doing?" Trina says, grabbing my elbow as I'm about to walk out. "You're supposed to spend the night."

"Ha, that's right." I twist my keys around my fingers. "Girl time."

"Well, sorry to interfere with girl time."

"You could join us," I say. "We were just talking about Trina's obsession with Leonardo DiCaprio, who, some might say is your—"

"Okay," Trina says, drawing out the word loudly. "Better get back to our movie night, see you later, Grayson!" She waves quickly, closing the door in Grayson's surprised face. "What are you doing?" she hisses at me.

I shrug innocently. "Just chatting with Grayson, what are *you* doing?"

She holds up the supplements. "Taking vitamins, obviously."

"So necessary to take your vitamins at ten o'clock at night," I tease.

Trina rolls her eyes, but internally, I'm way past the happy dance—there's a conga line forming inside of me, because Trina is falling in love.

44

Relaaaaax

Trina

We're at the World Equestrian Center in Ocala. It's a Friday morning, and I'm downstairs in The Equestrian Hotel at Emma's Patisserie, searching for a breakfast option that won't add ten pounds to my hips just by looking at it. I'm about to give in and order a chocolate croissant when Grayson stumbles in. He looks like our horse transporter ran over him—and then the horses unloaded on top of him. His hair—which is typically without a strand out of place—is sticking up in all different directions, his clothes are dirty and rumpled, and his eyes are bloodshot with dark circles under them.

"What happened to you?" I ask after ordering his go-to coffee order with an added two shots of espresso for good measure.

"That bad, huh?" He runs a hand over his face, his hair flopping in his eyes. "Coco was on colic watch, so I stayed up with her," he says, referring to one of the horses in our barn who was having a hard time after the drive to Ocala—the vet heard abnormal gut sounds and put her on colic watch, which meant someone had to stay with her all night.

"Grayson. We have people we *pay* to do that."

"I know, but Rondo was falling asleep so I relieved him." When he catches my look—incredulous—he gives me a tired half-smile. "I sold my business so I could do whatever I needed to do for DeDe."

"It's not even DeDe's horse! Do you even know who she belongs to?"

He shrugs, like it doesn't matter.

"Where is DeDe, anyway?"

"She's asleep in the room, Luna's with her."

"Let me get this straight: you left your daughter—who's the reason you came here—with Luna so you could take care of someone else's horse?"

"Well, when you put it like that, it sounds..." he trails off, rubbing the back of his neck.

"Grayson, you traded in your business for-for, well, this," I wave my hands around, trying to encompass the horse world. "I bet you're working just as many hours as ever before."

"Might I remind you, I went to medical school, where they take the idea of forced labor and make it a sport."

I laugh, thinking that being a student-groom sounds similar. Except you make way less money than a doctor once you're on your own. "Do you have shavings in your hair?" I lean forward, plucking the undeniable curl of light wood pieces from his brown hair. "Did you lay down in the stall?"

At this, Grayson gives me a sheepish grin. "The vet said she shouldn't roll, but Coco likes to lay down in the stall. So I just laid behind her so she wouldn't roll." He stuffs his hands in his pockets, seeming bashful about the fact that he practically spooned with a horse all night.

I gape at him, trying to rein in my incredulity...and my attraction. Despite how disheveled Grayson looks at the moment, he snuggled a colicking horse all night. That gets at least twenty thousand extra attraction points in my book.

I glance away from Grayson as I try to remember what it was we were talking about. But all I can see in my mind is the visual of Grayson lying beside Coco, and the image does something to my heart that it has no business doing.

Lock it down, Trina.

I clear my throat, forcing myself to put on my no-nonsense trainer voice. "Grayson, the point is: you don't relax. Go, take a break. Do something fun—something *you* actually want to do."

"Hey, I *want* to be here."

Our orders are ready, so we grab them and head to a table outside the cafe. I take a sip of my green tea, wishing I had caloric room for honey—but Emma's Patisserie has been a formidable opponent in the calorie department. I need all the help I can get.

"You know what I mean. *Relax*, Grayson."

He crosses his arms, leaning across the table to fix me with a stare. "I will, *but*, I feel it necessary to point something out first."

"What's that?"

He cocks his head to the side, cupping his ear with one hand. "Hey, kettle, kettle," he says in a sing-song voice that reminds me of someone calling out 'hey, batter, batter,' when someone's up to bat in baseball. "Hey, kettle, kettle," he repeats.

"What are you doing?" I laugh.

He straightens, his crooked smile making my stomach dip. "Kettle, pot," he says, pointing at himself, then me.

"Aha. So?"

"So you need to relax too." He takes a long sip of his white chocolate mocha and then says, "And I have just the idea."

I back my chair away from the table, throwing my hands up. "Oh no, no you don't." Grayson is giving off happy puppy vibes right now—and that can't be good. I have no idea what he's thinking, but I know whatever it is, it's going to require a lot more from me than simply relaxing. I point my finger at him. "Grayson Sterling, don't you dare."

"Trust me, Trina. Give me twenty minutes and then meet me right back here, okay?" He gives me a wink—a *wink*—and then darts off, not waiting for my response.

"You're being a panda!" I call after him. He's halfway down the hall, but he still hears me, because he turns around, walking backwards, and gives me a massive smile.

And I just know: I'm in trouble.

Against my better judgment, I'm still at Emma's twenty minutes later, when Grayson strolls back in, looking smug.

I sigh. "What did you do?" I ask warily. I stress-drank all my green tea, and now my heart is skipping dangerously.

He sits at the table, putting his forearms on the granite, and leaning forward he says, "You're gonna love it."

"I'm going to hate it." I press my palms flat on the table between his forearms and ask through gritted teeth, "What. Did. You. Do?"

He smiles so mischievously, so sweetly, that I'm about to hightail it out of here when he says, "I booked you a massage."

My stomach drops. "No you didn't."

He nods magnanimously. "I did indeed. A ninety-minute massage at the spa here."

I put my head in my hands and groan. "Ninety minutes? Grayson, what am I going to do for ninety minutes? I could barely take a bath for *two* minutes."

"You're going to *relax*, to enjoy yourself."

"While I lay completely naked and vulnerable as a complete stranger touches me? Uh, no thank you."

A look flickers across his face that I can't quite read. He clears his throat and then says, "If you're uncomfortable with it, I can cancel."

"Or...you could take it yourself."

He considers this for a moment before he says, "How about a compromise? We both get one."

I think for a second. I've never gotten a massage before—could never afford one. I suppose if I hate it, I could just...leave. "Fine," I say with a sigh. "But if I don't like it, what do I get as payback?"

Grayson drums his fingers on the table. "Hm. How about you get to pick what I do for my relaxation?"

I bite my lip to hold back a smile. "Deal."

I go to stand up, but Grayson stops me with a hand to my arm. "One more thing."

"Hm?"

"If you *do* like it, then I get something."

"What's that?"

"You crash this wedding with me." He juts his chin out at the hallway, where we passed workers bustling around preparing for an event.

I roll my eyes. "Are you serious? How old are we, nineteen?"

He shrugs. "Make the deal or don't."

"Fine," I say. "But you're just doubly ensuring that I won't like the massage."

He grins his playful smile at me. "I'll take the bet either way."

We both stand, and with a flourish, Grayson waves a hand. "After you," he says, waggling his brows. "Towards relaxation."

I poke a teasing finger to his chest. "Hey, it's your money to waste." He captures my hand with his, and my smile falters, dipping along with my stomach. Grayson leans over my hand, and for a second I think he's going to kiss my hand. But then he makes this ridiculous production of bowing over my hand, and I laugh.

He grins up at me from his still-bowed position over my hand, his green-gray eyes twinkling with glee. "Indeed it is, m'lady."

45

Dancing in the Moonlight

Trina

The massage starts out as a massive fail. I feel five thousand percent uncomfortable underneath this thin sheet, waiting for this perfect stranger to come in and rub me with smelly oils. I'm tense when the massage therapist starts, and I'm literally cursing Grayson in my head.

Who does this? Who voluntarily allows this to happen? Better yet, who *pays* for this?

That is, until the massage therapist starts working on my very sore right shoulder.

Oh, that's nice. Some might even say it feels good. "Take a deep breath," the massage therapist instructs. I comply, breathing out as she pushes into a particularly tight knot. After a few more deep breaths and magic fingers on my muscles, my shoulder feels better than it's felt since, well, *ever*.

Okay, so I *might* understand why people do this.

Thirty minutes into the massage, I drift off into the sweetest nap I've ever taken. When the massage ends, I'm relaxed, well-rested, and annoyed that I have to face Grayson and tell him I enjoyed this.

I consider pretending I hated it, but when I run into Grayson in the hallway after my massage, I can tell that one look at my face tells him everything he needs to know. He nudges my robe-clad shoulder with his and leans down to say, "I'm not going to say I told you so."

I roll my eyes, but a traitorous smile breaks across my face before I can stop it.

"You're welcome," he says with his own smile.

"Thanks, Gray," I say genuinely.

We part ways at the end of the hallway, heading into our respective restrooms, but the moment I'm away from him, my stomach drops. Because I'm pretty sure Grayson's going to make me crash this wedding with him. Public declarations of love, decadent cake, and dancing with Grayson by my side? I have no idea how my heart is going to walk away from that unscathed.

Later that evening, after the show, I come back to my room to shower and change. I don't have anything wedding-guest appropriate, but Grayson said he would take care of it. Which makes me infinitely uncomfortable. A few minutes after I'm out of the shower, there's a knock at my door. A woman with a blonde topknot and dark rimmed glasses holding a garment bag and a shoe box.

"Trina Powers?" she asks.

"Yes?"

"These are for you." She holds out the dress and shoes. "From Mr. Sterling. Enjoy."

I'm left gaping at the door, holding a dress and shoes that apparently Grayson bought for me. When I get back inside, I find a lacy black semi-formal dress and a matching pair of heels—in just the right size. I immediately text Mila: *Did you tell Grayson my size??*

All I get back from her is a string of angel emojis.

Great.

But when I put on the dress and heels, I feel like a million bucks. Or maybe a billion. I'm grateful Grayson didn't send me something outrageous or outside of my comfort zone. It's like he really knows me, which makes me feel equal parts fluttery and...terrified.

Turns out, crashing the wedding is pretty fun. Sure, it starts out a bit awkward—what if someone realizes we aren't supposed to be here? What if, despite Grayson's best efforts,

I'm not dressed quite right? But Grayson's quiet confidence is infectious, and soon we're eating multiple slices of cake and dancing like we belong there.

All the classic wedding dance songs are out in full number, and to our credit, Grayson and I are committed to having fun. He's shaking his hips in typical white boy fashion as we dance the Macarena, we're in perfect sync with the Cupid Shuffle, and jumping up and down with the best of them when "Shout!" comes on.

We're laughing and breathing hard when the DJ takes a break. The bride's brother comes up to the mic holding a guitar. "We're going to slow it down a bit here," he says, holding a guitar pick between his fingers. "This is one of Tara and Jim's favorite songs, so I thought I'd surprise them with a little rendition tonight."

When he begins strumming his guitar, I immediately recognize Death Cab for Cutie's "I Will Follow You into the Dark." A brilliant smile breaks across Grayson's face. *Of course* he loves this song too.

I should take a break and get water, but when Grayson reaches out his hand to me, I do something almost unthinkable: I take it.

Then, I'm being pulled into Grayson's arms, my palm on his chest as my other hand nestles into his grip. We fit perfectly together, like he's my missing puzzle piece to a one-thousand-piece puzzle that you find lost under the table.

It's wonderful and horrible at the same time.

Despite myself, I let my body sink into Grayson's. I feel every single place where we're touching. His fingers softly grazing my back. His chin resting against my temple. Our legs brush against each other's as we sway slowly. Despite the pace of the song, Grayson's heart is hammering underneath my hand, the beat vibrating my palm. I wonder if he can feel my heart beating just as wildly against his chest.

The lyrics are strumming up something within me I haven't faced since Victor left: I don't want to face this life alone. I want someone by my side as I stare down the terrifying maw of life and death. And as much as I love Leo, there's a hole in my heart that even he can't fill. I haven't let myself think that thought—I'm not even sure I'm allowing it now. And yet, there it is. With startling clarity, I realize I want Grayson. Not just as a friend or business partner but as a life partner.

I have no idea if that's even a possibility—he just got divorced, who knows if he actually wants to try love again. But something about the way his heart is beating below my fingers, and the way he's holding me so gently, it has a terrifying hope fluttering in my chest.

And then, a series of really unfortunate events takes place.

I move my head to glance up at Grayson at the exact same time he moves his head to look at me. Our faces collide—first our noses brush, then our lips are touching but not in an intentional way.

And instead of leaning into it—either fully kissing him or laughing it off as the accident it was—I freak out. I jump back like I just got electrocuted. I look at Grayson and I'm sure my stare is akin to a wild, feral animal. I don't even give myself a moment to take in his surprised face—or is that disappointment? I'll never know because I bolt.

Yes, ladies and gents, I *run* out of the ballroom like the grown adult woman that I am. If my life had a soundtrack, this moment would be punctuated by New Found Glory's "All Downhill From Here."

Because I accidentally just sort-of kissed Grayson Sterling, and as much progress as we've made in our working relationship, I'm not sure how we'll ever recover from this.

46

Pucker Up

Mila

Alex and I are lounging on the couch when there's a pounding at our hotel room door. I rise to get it, but Alex puts a hand on my shoulder and says, "Let me." I don't know if he's being chivalrous because I'm tired from competing or because he thinks the big bad wolf is at our door. Either way, I'll take it.

When Alex opens the door, Trina rushes into the room. "I kissed him—well, I almost did. I mean, not almost. I did. Except it wasn't all the way—" she groans as she paces back and forth in front of the hotel room couch. "I shouldn't have—I don't even like it—oh my gosh—"

Trina's dressed elegantly in a black lace dress that hits just below her knees along with a pair of heels. *Heels.* I repeat: Trina is in high heels.

I've never heard Trina talk like this before. Not once have I heard her say anything about her seemingly nonexistent dating life, but it's more than that. She's frantic, oversharing. Trina *never* overshares. She's the epitome of calm, cool, and collected. Except for right now, where her eyes are wide and frenzied, looking all around the room as she talks as if whoever she kissed is going to hop out from behind a door.

"Whoa, there," I tell her as I stand, holding up my hands and slowly placing them on her shoulders. "Take a deep breath and start again. But from the beginning so we can understand you."

Surprisingly, Trina obeys, closing her eyes and taking a deep breath. When she exhales, I'm met with a slightly floral scent. "Okay, there we go. Now, sit and tell us what's going on."

Alex hovers, clearly making Trina nervous, so I wave him into a chair. He sits, looking as unsure as Trina about the girl talk about to commence.

Painfully, haltingly, Trina tells us about her interactions with Grayson—from his first day at the barn until today. Some of it we already know, some of it we've pieced together on our own, but we listen intently as she dishes. We cringe when she tells us about Ellie and Ryan keying Grayson's Maserati, and cheer as she recounts the interaction with Antonio. She hesitates to tell us about them driving around, listening to music and talking—and I can tell that that meant more to her than she's letting on. "It's been complicated since then. We have...boundaries, I guess. But we sure like to cross them. And tonight..." she cuts off, shaking her head.

I glance over at Alex, who's covering a smile with his hand. For all his quiet confidence, there's a hidden hopeless romantic under all that tall, dark, and handsome.

"What happened tonight?" I press gently.

Trina's looking down at the ground, like she's too embarrassed to look us in the eye. Which is probably for the best because I'm sure both of us look like kids on Christmas waiting for our parents to wake up.

"It's...complicated," Trina repeats.

"Yeah, you mentioned that."

"No, I mean, what happened tonight is complicated."

"You, uh, want to spell it out for us?"

"I wish I could re-enact it," she says, shaking her head. "I don't know how to explain it."

"We could re-enact it," I tell her, and she blanches.

"I'm not going to kiss you, Mila."

"No, I mean me and Alex could do it. You position us and stuff."

She's quiet, looking back and forth between us, evaluating. Alex nods, telling her he's game. "Fine," she sighs. "But you're not allowed to make fun of me."

I cross my heart. "I would never."

A moment later, Alex and I are swaying in the middle of the room. Trina has positioned and prodded us—quite thoroughly and seemingly unnecessarily I might add. "So then, I went like this," she takes my head and shifts it toward Alex, while at the same time turning Alex's head toward me. "Wait, except our faces were closer. Ugh, you're so tall, Alex. Can you crouch a little? No, not like that. Yes, fine, okay."

I'm really starting to feel like a puppet on a string—with a vengeful toddler pulling the strings—when Trina turns our heads again toward each other. Our faces are so close, our noses and lips collide and we kiss. "No—" Trina groans. "No puckering. Do it again but without the pucker."

At this, Alex lets out a pent-up laugh.

"Alex!" I chide him.

"I'm sorry," he says, trying to compose himself. "Pucker is such a weird word."

I giggle a little, thinking of how strange it sounds. "Pucker," I repeat, moving my lips in an exaggerated way. "You kind of have to pucker when you say it too. Pucker, pucker. Yeah, see that 'er' part makes you pucker."

"Pucker, pucker," Alex is doing it now too, his lips puckering in an exaggerated way. Trina is staring at us in a wide-eyed way, as if she's not sure whether we've lost our minds or she's the one who's lost it.

"Okay, babe, let's focus," I say, patting Alex's back. He straightens up, pulling me flush against him, but then remembers that he's supposed to be shorter and crouches again. Something about the whole thing makes me start giggling again, and then Alex is laughing too, whispering, "Pucker," in my ear until I'm howling with laughter.

"Okay, that's it," Trina says, throwing her hands up.

"No, no, sorry Trin," Alex says, wiping tears from the corners of his eyes. "We'll behave, I promise." He gives me a stern look, as if this is all my fault.

Alex leans down, our faces together, and then we turn—without Trina's help this time—our noses and lips brushing against each other, but there's absolutely no puckering this time.

"Yes!" Trina shouts, a little too loudly in our ears. "That's exactly what happened! Except it was an accident—I looked up at him at the same time he was turning to look at me, and our lips kind of...met."

"Huh," Alex says. "You explained it really well just now. Using words."

Trina scowls at him, but her features turn desperate soon after. "What do you think? Is it a kiss?"

"Hmm." I look up at Alex and say, "Can we do it again?"

Alex gathers me to him, brushing his face against mine. "No, it didn't look so intentional," Trina says, standing very close to us. I give her a back off look.

"We're trying to figure it out," I tell her.

"Okay." She holds up her hands, but continues to stay very close to us, watching. Which isn't uncomfortable, like, at all.

"So, is it a kiss if you don't pucker?" Alex muses after we've brushed lips several times.

"Hm. Kiss me," I tell him, he leans in and presses his mouth against mine, but I don't move my lips at all. "Did that feel like a kiss?"

He squints his eyes, thinking, then shakes his head. "You try." I do the same to him and shake my head.

"Nah, that's not a kiss."

"Intention seems important," Alex says.

"And the puckering is pretty vital," I say with a small smile at my husband.

We turn to Trina and I put a hand on her shoulder. "So I'm confident you didn't kiss Grayson."

At this, Trina groans and covers her face with her hands.

"Wait, I thought you'd be happy to hear that? Did you *want* it to be a kiss?"

Her hands fall to her sides, and she looks utterly defeated. "It just means that I ran away for no reason. If it wasn't a kiss, I didn't need to hightail it out of there."

Alex and I sigh simultaneously, and we pull Trina into a hug, patting her back. She sighs into the hug, letting us comfort her, which shows me just how desperate she's feeling. "You could, uh, always go back down and tell him you needed to, I don't know, go to the bathroom?"

Trina extricates herself from the hug, checking her watch. "For forty-five minutes?"

"Okay, so not that..."

"What about telling him the truth?" Alex says. When Trina and I both look at him with eyebrows raised, he shrugs and says, "What? It's not a bad idea."

"And what is the truth, Alex?" Trina snips at him.

"That you're attracted to him, you like being around him, but it's complicated because he's the owner of your horse and you both have ruined relationships behind you that makes you feel afraid."

It's deathly silent as Trina stares at Alex as if he'd just announced he's a house elf going off to Hogwarts. After about a minute too long, Trina smacks her lips together and says, "Well, thanks for this. It's been real...enlightening."

And before we can stop her, Trina leaves the room. "Trin!" I call after her, rushing into the hallway.

"Thanks for your help," Trina says, all of a sudden with her professional walls up. "I'll see you tomorrow." She gives a quick wave and darts down the hall, leaving Alex and me speechless.

Back inside our hotel room, Alex says, "That was interesting."

"I know, I've never seen her like that before."

"She must really like Grayson."

"I know, she's terrified."

"She'll figure it out."

"Will she?"

"I hope so." Alex reaches out for me and pulls me against him, grazing my nose with his. "Now," he says, "Pucker up, wife." And we collapse into laughter, our lips so tight with smiles that we find we can't actually pucker.

47

Almost Doesn't Count...Right?

Trina

Since I'm a mature adult, I avoid Grayson like he's a bad case of distemper. He's called and texted multiple times, so I shut off my phone, kick off my heels and climb into bed fully clothed. I'm not thinking about how we'll face this tomorrow. No, all I can think of is the here and now: I'm hiding in this bed and I'll never get out.

My mind flicks back—repeatedly—to the wedding. Dancing with Grayson felt so natural, so wonderful. I even gave in to the thought of being with him. Not that he'd ever want to be with someone like me. Grayson's so suave, so put-together, so intelligent. I'm the frumpy kid who sat at the back of the class.

I groan when I think about our almost-kiss. Of course I'd be klutzy enough to *kind of* kiss Grayson. I couldn't even be good enough to do the deed all the way.

There's a thumping at my door, and my heart leaps into my throat. What if it's Grayson? I pad over to the door on tiptoe to look through the peephole. It *is* Grayson.

"Trina, c'mon," he calls through the door. "Can we just talk?"

Against my better judgment, I open the door just a crack. "There's nothing to talk about, Grayson."

"You kissing me and then running from the room and not answering my calls tells me there's lots to talk about."

I fling the door open. "I didn't kiss you! There was no puckering. No pucker, no kiss. It was an accident."

Grayson's eyebrows raise skeptically. "Ah. I didn't know about the puckering rule."

"It's not a rule, it's just—" I groan. "It's not about the puckering. I didn't kiss you, Grayson."

He takes a step closer, crowding me at the door. "Then why did you run away?"

"Because-because," I throw my hands up. "Because I'm an idiot, I don't know. I got freaked out."

Someone across the hall opens their door and calls out, "Some people are trying to sleep! Can you keep it down?"

"Sorry," Grayson says, hand raised in apology. "Can we continue this conversation inside?" he asks me, his voice low.

"Fine." I step back, allowing him entrance into my room. When the latch closes, it feels like the lock clicking on a prison door. My heart flies into overdrive.

Grayson, ever cool-headed, leans against the door frame, arms crossed.

"Why did you get freaked out, Trina?"

"Can we stop with the twenty questions?" I groan. "It was an accident, I didn't mean for that-that—whatever that was. I would never kiss you, okay?" I say defensively. I need Grayson to believe me, even though I don't believe myself.

Something flashes in Grayson's eyes. He unfurls from the wall, pushing closer to me so that we're practically toe-to-toe. I swallow, trying—and failing—to steady my breathing as Grayson's warmth radiates over me.

"Am I that repulsive that it would be so horrendous to kiss me?" There's a touch of anger in his voice that I don't understand. I gape at him, trying to wrap my head around what he's saying: is he implying he wouldn't mind kissing me? But no, that can't be right.

Part of me wants to respond honestly: *You're not the horrendous one, I am. Who would want to kiss* me?

But I don't say that. Instead, I take a step back and say, "Yes." Because *yes* it would be horrendous, for my heart, if I kissed Grayson. I'd never recover.

The moment the word is out of my mouth, Grayson visibly recoils. Hurt flickers across his face, and I realize how awful my 'yes' was. In an attempt to cover up my attraction, to protect my heart, I offended Grayson. I try to backtrack. "Grayson, I—"

He raises a hand to stop me. "No, it's okay, I get it." His voice is low, resigned. He turns to leave and I reach out a hand to grab his arm, but at the last moment, I pull away.

I'm trying to think of something—anything—to say to fix this, but my mind is a complete jumble of stupidity. No coherent words are coming to me as Grayson says, "I'll leave you alone, then," as he opens the door.

"It's not you," I start, but before I can finish, Grayson has left the hotel room. And I'm left feeling worse than ever.

48

Isn't It Ironic?

Trina

After the almost-kiss disaster in Ocala, Grayson maintains his distance. He comes to the barn with DeDe for her lessons, but he's distant and barely polite with me. The irony of all of this is that *this* is what I wanted from the beginning—for Grayson to keep his distance. And now that it's happening, I'm gutted.

I feel like someone has sliced open my heart and I'm bleeding all over the place.

Worse yet, losing Grayson's friendship is like I've lost a vital organ. I'm walking around as a shell of a person.

I alternate between berating myself for letting myself get so close to Grayson, and mourning the relationship as if it were a breakup.

We've never even kissed—not really—so why does this hurt so much?

In September there's two more shows in Traverse City, Michigan and we're high point champion at the second show. Grayson and DeDe didn't come since they went on a—last minute, seemingly unplanned—vacation to the Keys.

Then we're in Barcelona in October for the Nations Cup Final. When we qualified back in May, I envisioned going out and doing fun things with Grayson around Spain. Instead, we stick mostly to our hotel rooms. Team USA places second in the event, which is enough to land our country a spot in the 2024 Olympics. When we get home, I'm just relieved that Leo traveled internationally without any major illness or injury. But the whole endeavor has left me feeling depleted.

And I'm left to wonder if there's anything—or anyone—out there that can fill this gaping hole in my chest.

49

Let Me Love You

Mila

I'm in my office, where I should be working on the volunteer schedule for the week, but all I'm thinking about is Trina and Grayson and why they won't quit this slow burn thing and finally just...burn. The past several weeks as we've bounced from show to show, Grayson's been missing in action and Trina's been back to her old ways of sky-high walls and brusque responses. I'm really tired of it. So I give in, putting the schedule aside to text Grayson.

Mila: *Hey Grayson, just wanted to check in and see how things are going with Trina since we last spoke.*

I send the text and then watch as the three dots appear and disappear several times. Eventually, Grayson responds with: *It's complicated.*

Mila: *Let me guess...one step forward and two steps back?*

Grayson: *More like ten steps back.*

Mila:

Grayson: *I really like her, but I don't want to force myself on her if she doesn't feel the same way.*

Mila: *Don't give up Grayson.*

Grayson: *Are you sure that's the right move? She hasn't so much as looked at me since Ocala.*

I send him a GIF of a girl yelling "Mama didn't raise no quitter!"

Mila: *I've never seen Trina look at a guy the way she looks at you.*

Mila: *I mean, to be completely honest, I've never seen her look at a guy, ever. But that has to count for something right?*

Grayson responds with the GIF of Jim Carrey in Dumb and Dumber saying "So you're telling me there's a chance?"

Mila: *Alex says that once her walls fall, she'll be all in. She's the most loyal person we know. She's just scared.*

Grayson, who's clearly moved past text, responds with a GIF of a man in Vikings horns singing "I won't give up."

I laugh, leaning back in my chair, gazing at Alex at his desk. "I'm just saying, in a million years, would you have paired Trina with an eccentric billionaire?"

Alex swivels his chair so that we're facing each other. "I wouldn't call Grayson eccentric per se."

I show him the GIF Grayson just sent me, and he laughs. "Okay, so he has his odd moments." He reaches out, pulling me into his lap. "What I always hoped for, for Trina, is someone who loves her the way she deserves." He traces my face with his fingers before cupping my cheek in his palm, tugging me in for a kiss. The sweetness and security behind his kiss is intoxicating and, for a moment, I forget we're at work. I press against his chest, leaning my forehead against his. I smile, thinking how amazing it is that I get to work with my husband like this.

"I hope she'll let him love her," Alex says.

"Me too." I press one more quick kiss to his lips. "Speaking of which, I have something for you." I get up and rummage through my desk until I find a Ziplock bag. I present it to Alex with a flourish.

"What's this?" he holds up the bag, examining the plastic pieces inside of it.

"My dad's credit card."

Alex's eyes widen. "You really did a number on this thing." The card is in teeny tiny pieces, thanks to the super sharp Cutco knife someone gifted us for our wedding. I haven't used it to cut anything in the kitchen, so I figured I'd put it to good use with Tato's emergency card.

"I was going to put it in the trash, but then I thought it was kind of like a vow of sorts." I settle back onto his lap, my arms going around his neck. "For richer or for poorer, Alex."

Alex smiles up at me. "For better or worse," he says before kissing me.

50

Phone Down

Trina

I'm hoping and praying some of the awkwardness between us will drop away when we see each other again. When Tuesday rolls around and DeDe and Grayson show up at the barn for her lesson after we're all back from our travels, it's clear that, although some of the chill has thawed, our interactions remain stilted.

Grayson hangs on the railing as DeDe takes her lesson, offering a few encouraging remarks to DeDe, but he never once addresses me. We let DeDe fill in the silence as we walk back to the barn after her lesson. I sigh in relief when Grayson gets a phone call and heads to his truck to take it.

DeDe watches him go. "He's been sad lately," she says.

My heart plummets to the ground. Why is DeDe saying this to *me*? Does she know I'm part of that sadness? "Oh," I say eloquently. "Did something happen?"

She shrugs and then dismounts outside the barn. "I don't know," she says. "He's just been weird for a while." She looks up at me as she holds Persephone's reins, and something about the look in her eyes makes me feel even more guilty. It's as if she's asking me, *Don't you know why my dad is sad?*

I clear my throat, and then offer a really lame response: "Sometimes, grown-ups are sad, but eventually we find a way to be happy again."

She raises a quizzical eyebrow at me before turning to walk into the barn. I sigh, running my hands through my hair. Kids make things so complicated.

After Grayson's phone call, he finds me in the breezeway and gestures for me to meet him in my office. My heart is beating erratically as I walk into the office.

"I just had a...strange phone call," he says, leaning against my desk to face me. The stilted way he's been talking to me lately has dropped away, and I should be grateful for that, except that Grayson looks upset. His brows are furrowed, his jaw tense.

"Okay?" I cross my arms, propping myself against the door jamb—as far away from Grayson as I can get without colliding with the tack in the corner.

"Do you know who Keenan Wilder is?"

"I'm not sure." I frown, trying to place the name. "He's a USEF guy?"

Grayson sighs. "He's on the USEF Olympic committee. He's one of the politicos who decide who makes it onto the Olympic show jumping team."

"And he just called you?"

Grayson nods, scratching his jaw thoughtfully. He opens his mouth to say something, and then closes it, shaking his head.

"Grayson, what did he say?"

"Well, he seemed to imply that you could make it on the team..."

"That's good news," I say, almost questioningly, because Grayson still doesn't seem happy.

"*If* we pay him."

Shock rolls through me, slight at first until it's at an eleven on the Richter scale. If the door jamb wasn't holding me up, I would've fallen. "He's asking us to, what, pay him off? Is it a bribe thing? I don't understand."

"He seemed to think you'd be...open-minded to this arrangement."

My jaw drops. The way Grayson's looking at me, with narrow skeptical eyes, it hits me: Grayson thinks I want this. That I somehow set this into motion with this scammer. "Are you freaking kidding me? Grayson this is insanity. I want to *earn* my way on to the Olympic team—not because of your fat pockets, but because of my talent and hard work."

He gazes at me for a long time, his eyes roving over my face, seemingly taking in what I just said. In those few seconds, it feels like a Salem Witch Trial and he's about to hang me or set me on fire.

But then, he sighs, pushing himself off the desk. "I believe you."

I slump against the door, relieved.

"I'm not sure what we should do from here, though," he says.

"What do you mean you're not sure what to do from here? We never talk to him again. Block his number, forget his name." There are three other people on the Olympic selection committee—I'm certain that they're not *all* corrupt. We still have a chance at this, even without Keenan Wilder in our pockets.

"But don't you think we should report him?"

"It's just your word against his—from a phone call. There's no evidence." What I don't say is: *what if this messes up my Olympic dream? What if reporting Keenan blows up in my face?* I groan, pressing the heels of my palms into my eyes. How in the world did we get stuck in this situation?

Also, are people in the habit of *paying* their way onto the Olympic team? Is that a thing I've been too naive to know about?

Grayson starts pacing around my office. He's a fidgeter if I've ever met one: whenever he's thinking deeply, he has to *move*. He probably burns an average of 300 extra calories a day from fidgeting.

"We could create evidence," he says, almost to himself.

"How would we do that without implicating ourselves?"

"We have to get someone on board with us from the start, someone who can corroborate our story."

"Mila and Alex?"

He shakes his head. "Has to be an impartial party."

I'm hesitant to give any suggestions, because at this point I'd like to just bury my head in the sand and pretend this isn't a problem. But Grayson seems determined to fix this, so I say, "What about a journalist?"

Grayson looks up at me, eyes alight. "Yes. A reporter. That's perfect." He thinks for a second and then says, "I think I know just the person."

51

Falling Slowly

Trina

A few days later, we're sitting with Miami Herald reporter, June Baldwin. She's a middle-aged woman with not a stitch of makeup on—something that makes me like her more for some reason. If she didn't even have time to put makeup on this morning, it must mean she's deadly serious about her job. She lets her words speak for themselves, instead of her looks.

We're huddled around her desk, about to call Keenan on speakerphone so that Grayson can arrange a meeting place with him. Over the past few days, Grayson has assured me that he will make sure I won't get tangled up in this mess. He'll be the one to talk with Keenan and to meet with him if need be, but my name won't be associated with it all. I came today for two reasons: intrigue and to support Grayson. It doesn't hurt that it's an excuse to be around Grayson again. After the Keenan phone call, it feels like we're getting back to normal, slowly but surely.

"Alright, let's do this, then," Grayson says, taking his phone out. June unlocks her phone and starts a voice recording.

"This is June Baldwin, recording on October 27, 2023 a phone conversation between Grayson J. Sterling and USEF Olympic selection committee member, Keenan Wilder." She nods at Grayson to call Keenan.

I hold my breath as the phone rings, waiting for Keenan to pick up. On the third ring, I'm afraid he won't and all of this will be for naught. But finally, he answers. "Keenan Wilder," he says in a smooth voice.

"Hi, Mr. Wilder. This is Grayson Sterling. We spoke the other day?"

"Yes, hi, Mr. Sterling. How can I help you?"

"I was hoping there was still an opportunity for my horse to be considered for a spot on the Olympic team." When Keenan doesn't respond, Grayson glances up at June, who rolls her hand as if to say, *Keep going.* "You, ah, mentioned the other day that a financial exchange could help raise their chances?"

"Well, I can't guarantee anything," Keenan says in his honeyed voice. The guy would make an amazing announcer, if he weren't a crook. "But your donation could ensure that your horse's name is brought up."

"I see. What's the going rate for that these days?"

"Two fifty," Keenan says breezily.

"Two hundred and fifty thousand dollars?" Grayson says it with a fair amount of incredulity in his voice—and I'm not sure if it's for the sake of the recording or if he's actually in disbelief.

"It's an honor to even be discussed at our selection meetings."

Grayson rolls his eyes but then says, "That's very true, Mr. Wilder."

Once they set a meeting time and place, Grayson hangs up.

"Will that be enough?" I ask June.

"It's a start," she says, poking a pencil in front of her messy bun to scratch her scalp. "It's going to take me some time to dig around and get more information on this guy. The editor wants what he calls a 'full dig.' Not just a passing interest piece, but an exposition. Honestly, if we could get more than one instance of bribery, it would make the case even stronger, but it's still pretty condemning if you meet up and he accepts money from you."

"Wait." I gape at June and then Grayson. "Not, like, real money, right?" I say, sounding like the idiot that I am.

June gestures toward Grayson, who says, "I've got a plan for how to pay him." Apparently, I still look unconvinced, and Grayson reaches between our chairs to put a comforting hand on my back. "It'll be okay, Trina." His gaze is steady, and his tone is soft in a way that makes me wish we weren't sitting right in front of June Baldwin. "I've got you."

And for some reason, those three words are the most reassuring and terrifying words I've heard from Grayson's mouth. Because I believe him—I trust that he's got my best interests at heart, that he'll protect me and take care of me. And it scares me to the very core of my being.

Because, despite all of my attempts, I think I'm falling for Grayson J. Sterling.

52

Electric Slide

Trina

As we leave the Miami Herald offices, the breeze whips around us as we walk past palm trees to Grayson's truck. My hair is going in all different directions, and I'm certain I look like a kid who stuck her finger in an electrical outlet. Grayson, on the other hand, is perfectly poised—not one hair out of place. Which is some kind of modern-day miracle because his hair also doesn't look like it's plastered to his head. It still looks soft and touchable. Not that I'm thinking of running my fingers through it or anything, I'm just making an observation.

Grayson reaches out and puts his hand on my back, leaning in to say, "I think we need to do something fun. It's been all business lately." It's as if Grayson's palm is a nuclear power reactor, with all the energy flowing from him into me. I can feel his touch, not only on my back, but flowing all through my body.

"Riding *is* fun," I say, almost defensively as I try to ignore the sparks pulsing through me.

"I know, but I'm thinking of a different kind of fun."

Did Grayson just waggle his eyebrows? What's gotten into him today? It seems as though the aftermath of our encounter in Ocala has been replaced by a new dynamic. Something almost...flirty.

I've finally wrangled my hair into a hair tie, so I can give him sufficient side-eye. "The last time we did something 'fun,' it ended in disaster."

Grayson gets even closer to me, his fingers inching toward my waist. "I wouldn't call it a disaster," he says with a glint in his eyes. "Although I wouldn't mind a happier ending this time around." Then he winks at me.

I repeat: Grayson *winked* at me.

My jaw drops and my feet literally freeze to the sidewalk. Grayson keeps walking toward his truck, so casual and calm it's like he doesn't even know about the fireworks he just set off inside of me. Did he just say what I think he said? I shake my head. No, I must be reading into his words...*and* his actions. He just means that he would prefer for us to not have fought.

And the wink? And the hand on my back? That was just...well, that part is confusing. I don't know what to make of that.

I manage to scrape my jaw off the ground and catch up to Grayson, who's already at his truck, holding my door open. "Uh, thanks," I mumble oh-so-eloquently.

I climb into the truck, but Grayson's still there beside me. Except now he's propped himself against the inside of the door, looking coy—mischievous, almost. "So, what say you? Something fun on Monday?"

I lock myself into my seatbelt so I don't do anything crazy—like cross the distance between us and kiss Grayson. And it won't be a sort-of kiss this time. *Oh, no.*

"Trina?"

I realize he's been waiting for my response while I'm lost in my thoughts about what Grayson's lips would feel like on mine. "Something fun, sure. With other people? Maybe Mila and Alex?"

A look flickers briefly across his face—maybe disappointment? Or am I reading into that too?—but Grayson quickly recovers. "Yeah, whoever you want." He closes the door and gets in on his side, and I don't know why my heart is racing about doing 'something fun' with Grayson. I lean back in my seat, closing my eyes, as I remind myself: Grayson is my *friend*. That's it.

Moments flash through my mind, contradicting my thoughts. Grayson winking at me. Grayson showing up at my door with vitamins at ten o'clock at night. Grayson dancing with me at the wedding in Ocala, the way I fit perfectly into his arms. Grayson with the Chevy limo, pressed against me as we sang at the top of our lungs in the sunroof. Grayson in his tuxedo, whispering in my ear at the silent auction. "No one here deserves this more than you." That's what he'd said.

Friends do those things, right? But even as I try to convince myself of it, a dangerous desire for *more* with Grayson blooms in my chest.

I shake my head, reprimanding myself.

Hoping for anything else is insanity.

Bridle Buzz ✔ · Follow
Wellington, FL

1,407 likes

Bridle Buzz Congrats to the equestrians who made USEF's long list for the 2024 Olympics yesterday! The list includes Wellington locals Evangeline Rutherford (pictured in a fetching red coat - so very Olympic of her!), Trina Powers and Mila Caballero.
Who do you think will represent the good ole U S of A in the 2024 Olympics?! Comment below and let me know! ... more

View all 34 comments

Parker Lowes I think Melanie Lorenzo will be on the Olympic team.

Renea Ceras @Parker Lowes - she's not even on the long list. You have to be on the long list to make it onto the short list.........

Lucky Equestrian Farm Congrats, ladies!!! 

 Add a comment...

2 hours ago

53

The List

Trina

I get a phone call from Mila the next morning. "Did you see it?" she shrieks into the phone. "The long list! Trina, it's out!"

My brain is scrambling for a foothold, trying to comprehend what Mila's saying. It takes me a moment to realize she's talking about the USEF Olympic committee's selections. They release a 'long list' several months before shortening it later in the season. "The long list? From USEF?"

"Yes! And Trin, *we're on it.*" I glance at the phone, not even sure I'm hearing her right.

"Are you sure? They just released it?"

"I'll send it to you. Trina, this is it. The first step to going to the Olympics!"

Mila's voice is practically hysterical with excitement, and for some reason, I can't match her enthusiasm right now. "Let me look and I'll call you back."

A moment later, Mila's text pops up with a link to USEF's list of twenty-three competitors who are being considered for the Olympic show jumping team. I find Mila's name first, and when I scroll further, there's my name.

Trina Powers.

My stomach churns, wishing I could be certain that I'd earned my way onto that list—and not because of the fiasco with Keenan Wilder. I look back up at Mila's name. Emotions roll through me uncomfortably. I am happy Mila's got a chance to go to the Olympics—she's my student, I've trained her for years, she's worked her butt off to get here. But it's also a hard reality that we might be competing for the same spot.

My scrolling stutters at another name: Eva Rutherford.

One thing is for certain: I'd much rather Mila make the team than Eva. But the fact that Mila and I both made the long list should give me reason to hope. Maybe it'll work out with Keenan Wilder. Maybe I'll earn my way there alongside Mila.

My fingers hover over my phone, wanting to call Grayson, to tell him the news. Instead, I tuck my phone back into my pocket and head out to the barn.

54

Hanging Out

Mila

It's a Friday night with no horse show this weekend, so I invited Trina down to go out to a celebratory dinner with us after we found out that we both made the long list. We head to Baires Grill in Las Olas—an Argentinian steakhouse with live music. One of Alex's new music buddies is currently performing what Alex called 'synthpop.' The guy's name is Matt but his stage name is Slade.

"Are you going to have a stage name?" Trina asks.

Alex shakes his head vigorously, as if Trina just asked him if he planned to run around the restaurant naked. "I'm just having fun with it right now," he says, even though I know it's more than that for Alex. But he'll talk about it when he's ready.

Trina and I order the skirt steak with salad, Alex orders the burger—I don't think he'll ever break the habit of purchasing the cheapest thing on the menu, no matter who's paying—and then we settle in to chat while we wait for our food.

"What's new with you, Trina? Besides going to the Olympics," Alex says, wagging his eyebrows.

Trina looks down at her drink, twisting it on its coaster, and I notice the slightest dusting of pink along her cheekbones that wasn't there a moment ago. Is Trina *blushing*?

"Anything you care to share with the class?" I tease, assuming her blush has to do with Grayson.

She sighs, running her hand through her hair. "I didn't actually qualify for the long list," she tells us, finally meeting my gaze. Then, she goes on to tell us all about Keenan Wilder and the investigative journalist they're teaming up with at the Miami Herald.

"So you think you made the long list because of that?" Alex asks.

"Well, obviously," Trina says, fidgeting with her silverware. I reach out, taking her hand.

"Not *obviously*, Trin. You've worked hard and you deserve a place up there, as much if not more than anyone else on there."

Trina shrugs, swirling her straw in her drink. It hurts my heart to see her struggling to see her worth—especially in this context. Trina's the most focused, hardworking horse-woman I know.

"What's Grayson think?" Alex asks.

"We haven't talked much about it. He called me but..." she sighs, not finishing her sentence.

"But you've been avoiding him since your almost-kiss?" I raise my eyebrow. I also assume that Grayson has been avoiding Trina—judging by his sudden absences at the recent horse shows. But it's been so chaotic I haven't been able to pin either of them down to shake them. I mean...*talk* to them about it.

"No? Sort of. Yeah, I guess. Except for a visit to the Miami Herald office."

"I thought you guys were getting close," I say, feigning an innocence I don't possess. "You seemed to have a good thing going."

"Yeah, I mean, we did. But I guess I'm not able to be friends with an attractive guy." She throws her hands up as if to say, *What can you do*?

"So you think he's attractive?"

"In an objective sort of way, yeah."

Alex and I stare at her expectantly for a long moment. She groans, running her hands over her face. "Fine, I think he's insanely beautiful. Infuriatingly gorgeous. I can't get his stupidly handsome face out of my head. Are you happy?"

I roll my lips together to hold back a smile, but Alex doesn't even try to hide his. "Yes," he says.

"What am I supposed to do?"

"That's easy," Alex says. "If he makes a move, accept it. Sink into it."

Trina snorts. "Like Grayson would ever make a move on *me*."

I lean onto my elbows, propping my chin on my hands. "You sure about that, Trin? Grayson hasn't made *any* moves?"

Trina's mouth opens, then closes. Her eyes are staring off into the distance and she's clearly thinking. Considering the things Grayson has done. "Maybe? He's just a really nice guy."

"He's not *that* nice, Trina. Not to me anyway," Alex says. "Not that he's mean, but he's certainly not picking me up in custom limousines or buying me dresses."

"Thank God for that," I laugh.

"Hey, I'd look good in satin," Alex jokes, running his hands down the side of his torso.

We all crack up as the waiter delivers our meals. The steak is tender and flavorful; the salad is solid but can't really compare to the French fries on Alex's plate. I sneak a few to my plate and then add a couple to Trina's plate too.

After our meal, when the waiter comes to clear our plates and offer dessert, Trina makes a show of rejecting dessert, but Alex says, "I think you guys can take a break from your diet to celebrate tonight." He gives us both an unyielding look.

"Fine, fine," I say, throwing up my hands in surrender. "If I have to get dessert, I'll take the molten lava cake."

"Churros for me," Trina says quickly.

"I'll take the panqueques," Alex says. "And two decaf cappuccinos."

He raises a questioning eyebrow at me, and I nod smiling. "You know me so well."

"It's not hard when you literally have a sign in our kitchen that says, 'Feed me coffee and pastries and tell me I'm pretty.'"

"What can I say? I'm not a complicated woman."

Alex laughs, tilting his head back and forth, "Hmm, let's not go *that* far."

"Hey!" I poke him in the side, and he quickly grabs my hand, wrapping it in his.

When our dessert comes out, Alex holds up his cappuccino in a *cheers*. "To half of the 2024 Olympic team."

"From your lips to God's ears," Trina says as she clinks her water cup with our cappuccino mugs.

"He's got an inside track to the Big Guy," I fake-whisper to Trina behind my hand.

Alex rolls his eyes, but he doesn't fight me on it, which is proof enough for me.

"I do want to say one more thing," Alex says.

"Advice from the inside man? I'm all ears."

Alex shakes his head, smiling in that bashful way of his. "It's just, it's always scary to jump into the deep end. Even if you tiptoe from the shallow side, eventually the ground drops from below your feet and you'll have to swim."

Trina sobers, her fork hovering over her dessert. "What if I'm not sure I want to swim?"

"I guess that depends on whether or not you can turn away from the person waiting for you in the deep end." Alex reaches across the table to grab my hand, twining his fingers through mine. "Falling in love is an act of faith, for anyone. The bottom line is: do you believe in Grayson?"

through mine. "Falling in love is an act of faith, for anyone. The bottom line is: do you believe in Grayson?"

55

The Magic Kiss

Trina

Grayson arranges for a 'fun' yet mysterious outing on the following Monday on our day off. He's included Ellie, DeDe, Mila, and Alex in our plans, which doesn't seem like nearly enough people to protect me from Grayson's increasingly magnetic presence. It's true that I'm falling for him, but it doesn't mean I have to *like* it.

No, I'm going down kicking and screaming.

We're driving in Grayson's truck—which is growing on me, despite being a Toyota "truck"—with DeDe and Ellie in the backseat. Mila and Alex will meet us wherever we're going. Grayson told me to bring along several contradictory outfits—warm weather clothes with gloves, a hat and scarf; a bathing suit and shorts; a dress and heels; something to get messy in. There's no way we could be using all of those things in one afternoon, so I have to assume the other outfits are a decoy for whatever it is we're really doing.

When we pull up to the beach, I'll admit I'm a little disappointed. I'm not really a beach gal—laying around in the sun while reading isn't exactly my jam. But maybe I'll busy myself with building sand castles with DeDe and do my best to ignore Grayson in his swim trunks. Easy peasy, right?

But when we get out to the sand, there's a line of horses waiting for us near the water. A woman with deeply tanned skin and sporty sunglasses calls out, "Mr. Sterling?"

Grayson waves and DeDe squeals, clapping her hands as she shuffles across the sand. "We're going to ride on the beach, Trina!"

And I can't help it, I smile too. If I were six years old like DeDe, I might be squealing and clapping too. Grayson chats with the woman in charge as DeDe and I head to the bathroom to change. Ellie must've known the plan because she's dressed for the occasion in shorts and a t-shirt with her bathing suit underneath. We'll ride bareback—at least I assume we will based on the lack of saddles on the horses—and it hits me: when was the last time I've ridden bareback? I didn't realize I've missed it until this moment.

Maybe Grayson was right, I did need some fun.

Once we're changed, the woman holding the horses hands us a clipboard with waivers to sign and then pairs us up with our mounts. Alex and Mila show up a few minutes later as I'm mounting a paint Quarter Horse named Ty. The gelding's face is half-brown, half-white and he has one brown eye and one blue eye. I love that there's so much variation in horse's coloring and characteristics—and I think, not for the first time, that humans aren't half as interesting as their equine counterparts.

Once we're all mounted bareback, the woman in charge, Lisa, leads the way down the beach.

"Can we swim?" DeDe asks, enthusiasm painting every syllable.

"Sure, honey," Lisa says.

"I didn't think you could swim horses in the ocean here," Mila says behind me, her question pointed at Grayson, who's riding beside me.

Grayson shrugs. "I worked it out with Lisa," he says.

"You mean Benjamin Franklin worked it out with Lisa?" Ellie snickers ahead of us.

Grayson smiles but doesn't say anything about Franklin's influence on the situation. I heel my horse closer to Grayson's, a palomino mare with a buzzed mane named Ginger. "Thank you for this," I tell him. "I agree, we could all use some fun."

Grayson nods, his eyes crinkling as he smiles. "You're welcome."

"Y'all ready to pick up the pace?" Lisa calls back to us. A cheer goes through our group as we press our horses into a canter.

I've ridden a lot of horses in a lot of different places, but I've never ridden on the beach. Galloping across the sand and splashing through the edge of the ocean is surreal. It's as if I'm fulfilling a recurring dream I never knew I had. My legs close around Ty, the warmth of his sides soaking into me so that it's hard to tell where I end and he begins. Right now, we are one. Floating across the sand, it's conceivable that we might sprout wings and take to the heavens. As his neck elongates with his gait, I give him the reins and he gains speed. Water and sand are flicked up by the horses' hooves, splattering all of us, but we don't care—each and every one of us is smiling and whooping with delight. It's a horse person's dream come true and we're all soaking up every moment of it.

Trusting that Ty will follow the horse in front of him, I knot the reins at his withers and splay my hands on either side of me, feeling the rush of the wind around me. I am flying.

In this moment, I don't have a care in the world. I'm not thinking about the Olympics or Keenan Wilder or even about Grayson and my complicated feelings for him. I am simply existing in the world. Not as a horse trainer or a dyslexic woman or anything else. I am simply *me*, nothing more, nothing less.

And, for the first time in a long time, I feel free.

We spend the rest of the afternoon riding along the coast, splashing in the water and swimming the horses around a hidden inlet off the beach. Someone from Lisa's outfit brings a picnic, which we eat on a secluded stretch of beach, before we gallop back to our starting point. We're all giddy yet exhausted from the sun and exercise. So much so that when I dismount, I lose my footing, stumbling sideways so that my feet are right under Ty's belly. Sensing my imbalance, Ty steps backward with me—only to land right on my bare foot.

I cry out as his hoof digs into the top of my foot. I shove his side and he quickly moves over, but the pain of him stepping on me leaves me feeling lightheaded. Stars spark on the edge of my vision as I fight for consciousness. I'm gasping for air, tears streaming unbidden down my face as I crumple to the ground, clutching my foot.

"Trina," Grayson's at my side, assessing the situation. Without another word, he picks me up, cradling me to his chest. "Take her horse," he tells someone over his shoulder as he walks across the sand, holding me gently, like precious cargo.

Away from the horses and the others, safe in Grayson's arms, I let myself cry. Pain is pounding through my foot, and I'm certain I can feel every single nerve ending at the top of my foot—it feels as though Ty's hoof sliced through each and every one. The ache is all-encompassing, and I hold tightly to Grayson's neck to keep myself grounded.

At his truck, Grayson flings the back door open and sets me gently onto the seat. His hands go to my face, cupping my cheek. "Are you okay?"

I nod, but the tears are giving me away. Grayson's thumbs wipe at my tears, and I take a shuddering breath. "I'm going to examine your foot," he says, and I nod again, though

I'm sad his hands are leaving my face. They could stay there forever, if they wanted to. I wouldn't mind.

But then they're on my foot, fingertips gentle around my ankle and the bottom of my foot. I close my eyes, relaxing into his hold. I feel as his finger traces, ever so lightly, the semi-circle of Ty's hoof shape now tattooed on my foot in a growing bruise. "How's this feel?"

I suck in my breath as his finger presses into my foot. "Why do doctors do that?" I grind out through gritted teeth. "Yes, it hurts, man! It freaking hurts!"

"I'm sorry," he says genuinely. His fingers trace the large bone in my foot, and despite the pain pulsating through it, Grayson's touch feels like heaven. I don't want him to stop. And then, he does. He sets my foot down carefully and says, "We should get it X-rayed."

"No, it's okay, it's not that bad," I lie.

"Trina, *a fifteen-hundred-pound* animal just stepped on your bare foot." He leans into me, his stomach pressed against my knees. And my breath hitches in my throat. Friends do this, right? They stand this close to each other…right? "We are getting it X-rayed, even if I have to Baker Act you to do it."

I put my hands on Grayson's shoulders, telling myself that I need to do that to steady myself, even if that's only partially true. Friends totally do this. "That feels like a very panda bear thing to do."

Grayson scoffs, rolling his eyes. "You with the panda bears," he says, his hands going to my hips.

There's a siren blaring in my head at this—there's no real *friend*ly reason for Grayson to be touching my hips. Unless he just *wants* to touch me. The realization that Grayson is voluntarily touching me in a not-even-a-little-bit platonic way, it's like someone just threw a stick of dynamite into my chest. His fingertips pull me to the edge of the truck seat, and I can't breathe. In fact, I don't think I'll ever breathe again. I'll die right here in Grayson's arms.

I just hope he kisses me first.

But Grayson doesn't seem to be concerned about my near-death status. He's taking his sweet time as he brushes my hair back from my shoulder, his fingers lingering on my shoulder, then tracing a line down my back. I shiver at his touch, but it doesn't stop him from inching closer. His lips graze my collar bone, and then the sensitive spot on my neck just below my ear. His breath fans out across my skin, tickling my neck in the most magical sensation I've ever experienced.

His hand goes to the back of my neck, his fingers splaying through my hair. And I brace myself—Grayson is going to kiss me. And I'm going to take Alex's advice and lean into it. Accept it. Maybe even utterly lose myself in it.

"Is she okay?" DeDe calls out from the other side of the truck. Grayson jerks back from me, miraculously avoiding my hurt foot. Then, the opposite back door opens and DeDe's climbing into the backseat. "Did you kiss her already?"

"Uh, excuse me?" Grayson says, clearly flustered. He's leaning against the truck door, trying to look casual, but even I can see he's rattled. *By me.* Grayson J. Sterling is rattled by *me*. It takes all of my self-control not to throw up my hands and whoop. Because, seriously, who saw *that* coming? I'm busy doing an internal happy dance while Grayson is repeatedly clearing his throat. "Kiss...her?"

"Yeah, like, did you kiss her foot to make it better?"

"Ah, yes, right," Grayson says with a nervous chuckle. And let me tell you: calm and collected Grayson is handsome as heck, but flustered Grayson is dead sexy.

"Did he kiss it?" DeDe asks me, clearly not willing to let it go.

"I have not yet been kissed," I say, and then I have to bite the edge of my lip to keep from smiling. Because I'm pretty sure DeDe is going to force her dad to kiss my foot.

"Right, well," Grayson says backing up. "Best remedy that then." He wipes his hands on his shorts nervously, and then lifts my foot, his head leaning down to plant a kiss on the top of my foot. Just as his lips connect with my skin, Grayson's eyes flick up toward mine, and now I know I need to go to the hospital. Not for an X-ray, but because I'm pretty sure my heart just stopped at the sight of this man kissing my foot.

Holy Evanescence. I'm definitely going to be repeating this memory in my mind for a long, long time.

"Good job, Daddy," DeDe says. "That'll make it feel better," she reassures me. "Oh, I forgot my helmet," she says before jumping back out of the truck.

Grayson heaves out a sigh, laughing as he runs his hand through his hair nervously. "That was...interesting." And somehow, the distance between us has closed again. "Did that kiss make you feel better?" he asks, his voice barely above a whisper, right beside my ear. Electricity shimmers down my neck, dancing down my spine.

"Surprisingly, yes," I say. "I think I'm all healed."

"Well, there's more where that came from." The tip of his nose trails up my neck, across my jaw, so that we're practically nose to nose. "Later," he says, before placing a tiny kiss on the tip of my nose and pulling away.

I shudder, feeling suddenly cold by his absence. As if by magic, the pain in my foot is gone, and in its place is an overwhelming longing for Grayson's lips on mine.

56

New Job

Trina

The drive back from the beach is pure torture. All I can think of is the feel of Grayson's breath on my neck, his nose tracing my jawline, his face hovering millimeters from mine.

Oh my gosh.

Grayson wants to kiss me.

I'm giddy with the thought—completely, utterly, unabashedly delighted with this realization. I feel like a kid on Christmas with a surprise trip to Disney World about to get her first pony.

But we have a forty-minute drive ahead of us to drop Ellie back at the barn—and then...I don't know what. We can't exactly make out with DeDe around. That's kind of a no-no, right?

As we drive, DeDe chattering in the backseat about the beach experience, the metal straw in my now-empty water bottle starts rattling in the bottle. I put a hand over the bottle, holding the straw in place so it doesn't make that annoying sound anymore. Also, it doesn't hurt that I'm slightly closer to Grayson, with my hand on the middle console, facing his side.

A moment later, Grayson casually lays his arm on the middle console beside my water bottle so that our hands graze each other. I press my lips together to hold back my smile. And then Grayson's pinky reaches up and tangles with mine.

The giddy girl inside of me forces a massive smile out of me—and it stays put all the way back to Wellington.

At the barn, Grayson drops Ellie and then says, "If you come with me to drop DeDe at her mom's, I can take you to get an X-ray."

"Oh, sure," I say, even though I don't want an X-ray. All I want is to be alone with Grayson.

So we drive another torturous twenty minutes to Cate's house, dropping off DeDe. I'm a little disappointed when Grayson doesn't immediately kiss me the moment we're alone, but I *suppose* making out in your ex's driveway is a little weird.

We're driving toward Wellington Regional, when Grayson makes a sudden turn into a local park. He skids to a stop, triple parking across several parking spots. He throws the truck into park, climbs out, and jogs around the front of the truck. I don't even have to ask what he's doing. I unbuckle my seatbelt and turn toward him the moment he opens my door.

It all happens in an instant: my arms go around his neck, his around my waist pulling me to him. His lips crash against mine in an achingly satisfying explosion of all of the tension that has built up between us. My legs go around his waist, and he picks me up so that I'm crushed against him. My fingers tangle in his hair as I tilt my head to deepen our kiss.

This, right here, is the kiss to end all kisses. No kiss has ever existed like this one.

It's as if we're pouring into this kiss all of the things we've felt but never said aloud—the attraction, yes, but more than that, the deep friendship and understanding we've built over the past year. I'm finally telling Grayson just how much he means to me—that I miss him when he's gone, that I dream about him, that he's the person I've always wanted and never found. Until now.

And, amazingly, with every brush of his lips, he's saying the same things back to me.

This kiss, this man, this moment, has completely ruined me for every other kiss, every other man. And I wouldn't have it any other way.

"I need to tell you something," I say breathlessly as we pause between kisses.

"Can you tell me while I do this?" Grayson says trailing kisses down my neck.

"I'm dyslexic," I blurt.

Grayson pulls back, setting me gently onto the truck seat. "Oh," he says. "Cool?" he says it questioningly, like he doesn't know what to say or what I'm expecting of him.

"I just wanted to tell you before we got too far. I don't know, I feel like I've been lying to you about me."

His brows furrow, and I want to reach out and smooth the line between them. "Why do you feel that way?"

"Because this is who I am, and you don't even know about it." I push myself back in the seat, creating distance between us. "You're so, y'know, smart and educated and I'm just really...not."

Grayson reaches out, tracing my hair line with his fingers before pushing my hair behind my ear. "Are you afraid your dyslexia would change something between us?" he asks ever-so-gently.

I shrug, biting my lip. "Trina," he says, nudging my chin up to look him in the eye. "I appreciate you telling me, but this isn't 'who you are.' Your dyslexia doesn't define you any more than you having blonde hair or brown eyes. It's a part of you, sure, but it's a small piece of the whole. And, on the whole, you are incredible. Dyslexia and all."

My eyes scan his, looking for any hint that he's just saying what I want to hear—but Grayson is all genuine. One hundred percent real. I could cry with the realization. "I just don't see what you see in me. Why do you even want to, you know—" I gesture a hand between us, because I'm not really sure what to call this. We just kissed. Like, a lot. But does that mean we're dating? In a relationship? I don't know.

"Trina Powers, you are a force to be reckoned with. I love your ambition, how hard-working you are, and yet you don't look down on people who aren't on your level. You bring people up with you instead of trying to push others down. You are real."

I laugh caustically. "Yeah, a real disaster."

"We're all disasters, Trina." Grayson leans back, and the look in his eyes makes emotion well within me. Has he always looked at me like this? How did I miss it? "But if you're up for it, I'd like for you to be *my* disaster." He takes my hand, kissing my knuckles. "My gorgeous, fierce, hilarious disaster."

I gaze across at him hesitantly, as if to say, *Are you really sure*? But Grayson just laughs and says, "You really don't know how amazing you are, do you?"

I bite my cheek, unsure of what to say. The obvious answer being a clear *no*.

"How about this?" he says, pulling me closer to him again. "My new job will be to tell you all the ways you blow me away."

I shake my head, a smile cropping up at his words. "And my job?"

"Your job will be to believe me."

57

Picasso

Trina

Grayson and I make kissing a sport. It becomes our personal challenge to find a time and place to kiss no matter where we are. We kiss in the corner of the ER while I wait for my X-ray. We kiss at red lights and stop signs. We kiss goodbye at least fifteen times.

Over the next week at the barn, we kiss in my office, the tack room, and my personal favorite, with me propped on a few bales of hay in the feed room.

By the time the weekend rolls around, I haven't tired one bit of kissing Grayson J. Sterling. In fact, I'm craving him even more than ever before. Because now that I've tasted him, I realize exactly what I was missing out on this whole time.

Every single time that Grayson reaches down to kiss me, I feel like I've hit the jackpot. Why am I the subject of his affection? I can't even believe it. Despite the fact that Grayson has been doing a very good job of telling me all the things he likes about me.

The tender way you treat DeDe.

The way you encourage others and lift them up. You always have a kind word for your students and friends.

You're the hardest worker I know.

You don't make excuses for yourself.

You fill out those riding pants in the best way possible.

The way you bite your lip drives me crazy.

With each compliment, my confidence in Grayson's affection for me is growing.

That is, until Caterina shows up at the barn.

It's a Tuesday afternoon, DeDe's usual time for lessons. Caterina pulls up in her Audi and she gets out dressed in head-to-toe white—a very risky move at a barn. She's pristine and drop-dead gorgeous. Her blonde hair is slicked back in a ponytail that's way too fancy to be called 'ponytail' but I don't know what else to call it. The hairdo accentuates her sky-high cheekbones. Perfectly applied winged liner make her brown eyes look huge and alluring.

"Trina," she calls, walking down the barn aisle in her heels. I don't know if anyone has ever been to this barn in heels, and yet here she is. She reaches down to air-kiss my cheek and says, "I know, I look ridiculous. Not dressed for the barn at all. But I had an appointment and realized I have some time to see some of DeDe's lesson. It's been so long since I've seen her ride." She looks genuinely pained by this fact, and I feel a sliver of sadness for her.

But then I remember I'm dating her ex-husband, and it's as if I just got hit by a bulldozer of shame and embarrassment. Sure, it's not my fault Caterina and Grayson split up, plus Caterina's the one who moved on and has been dating someone for a full year. But it still makes my insides lurch uncomfortably.

"Hey, Cate," Grayson says, coming out of my office. He walks up behind where I'm standing, putting a hand on my lower back as he approaches us. Cate's eyes latch on to Grayson's hand placement, widening just enough to show disbelief.

And I don't blame her.

Because if you look at Caterina and then at me, there's a clear winner in basically every department. It's true that we both have blonde hair and brown eyes, with similar coloring and builds. Grayson definitely has a type. But Caterina's supermodel beautiful with an advanced degree in some subject I can't even spell. Meanwhile, I look like a bizarre Picasso version of Caterina. Like all the pieces are there, just put together wrong.

"You want to come out to the ring? We're just about to head out there," I say to Caterina as I subtly step away from Grayson's hand, which has stayed put despite Caterina's questioning look. Just outside the barn, Luna is holding Persephone as DeDe mounts her horse. The four of us head out to the arena for DeDe's lesson, the blinding sun makes me squint. An unsettling tension is swirling between the three adults, and it's the first time since Grayson kissed me that I've wondered if it was a good idea.

58

In My World

Trina

Friday rolls around and Grayson finds me in Leo's stall, running my hands over his legs like I usually do at the end of the day. "Hey," he says, arms casually tossed over the stall door. Today, his hair isn't slicked back, and it's a little sweaty, falling in his eyes in a boyish way. My heart squeezes at the sight. I'm not sure I've ever seen anyone so handsome.

I can't believe I get to kiss this man.

I stand, pressing up on tiptoe to brush my lips against his to prove to myself that I do, in fact, get to kiss this man still.

Yep, still true.

"I'm taking you on a date," he tells me. I notice that he doesn't say, *I'd like to take you on a date.* Or *Where do you want to go?* He's taking charge, and normally I'd call him a panda, but right now I am *all* about this.

"You don't have to do that."

"Yes I do, Trina. You deserve a hundred thousand fancy dates, plus a million other things."

I respond by kissing him again. "Thank you."

"You're quite welcome."

Over the next few weeks, Grayson takes me on a myriad of dates—every single one insanely thoughtful and special. We're still waiting for the Miami Herald article on Keenan

Wilder to be released. June has informed Grayson that she's digging deep for this one. I'm grateful, but some days I wish she'd dig a little less deep and just get it over with already. It's left me anxious and tense, but in the meantime it's as if Grayson has made it his personal mission to distract me with extravagant dates.

A paddle boarding adventure through the mangroves in Lake Worth.

A spa day at the Breakers Resort that made me permanently rethink my position on massages.

A polo game with Sunday brunch at The Pavilion.

One thing is for certain: Grayson knows how to spoil a girl.

It's a Wednesday evening and Grayson surprised me with a yacht ride and a chef-made meal right on the boat. Sometimes, I forget Grayson is a billionaire, with his down-to-earth persona—and let's be real—the way he cleans a stall. It's just not very billionaire-like. But tonight, when we showed up to his yacht, I said, "I didn't know you owned a yacht."

He shrugged and said, "Sometimes I forget I have it."

So, yeah, there's my daily reminder that Grayson J. Sterling is a billionaire with a capital-B.

We're on the deck of the boat, seated at a little table shimmering with candles. For an appetizer, we're eating seared scallops with some kind of citrus sauce, decorated with flowers that Grayson *says* are edible, but that I won't be brave enough to try. "Tell me about Victor," Grayson says in that brusque way of his. I almost laugh—Grayson's certainly thawed around me, but he's still Grayson.

"Why?" I keep my eyes fixed on my plate, cutting through a scallop.

"He's part of your story, which means he's part of you."

I almost shudder at his words—I don't want to think of Victor as being a part of me. "We met when I was trying out a horse. He wasn't really a horse person, more like horse-adjacent. But it was his buddy who owned the horse and he was considering buying it as an investment of sorts. So he watched while I rode the horse and then my student, who was looking to buy the horse too." I put my fork down, wiping my hands on my pants. "He was charming. In retrospect, too charming. Like he saw that I was an easy target or something—someone he could boss around."

Grayson's silent as I talk, but I'm afraid to look at his face. I don't want to see what he thinks about how pathetic I am.

"That's what Victor was all about, being in control. He had multiple businesses that he was running, and as far as I know, they were all sketchy. Not that I knew at the time—I was young and dumb. He bought me my first Grand Prix horse, Blue Thunder. Blue was something else." I smile, shaking my head. Even though Victor messed everything up with Blue, I can't help but think of that horse with nothing but love and fond memories. As if Victor couldn't taint that. "Anyway, Victor was always into this outside-the-box stuff—like he always had 'insider knowledge.' I just trusted him—I assumed he knew more than me. He was doing this gene therapy on Blue, and I had no real idea of what was going on. I was just so naive. It ended up crippling Blue—he's out in a pasture in Micanopy now. I've made a bit of money breeding him, but nothing to make up for losing him as a Grand Prix horse."

Grayson reaches across the table, taking my hand. "I'm sorry, Trina."

I shrug, finally meeting his gaze. Instead of the pity or judgment I expected, there was only compassion. I want to tell him it's okay, but honestly, I'm not sure the hole in my heart left from Blue getting injured will ever heal.

"Where's Victor now?" Grayson asks as if he's afraid Victor will pop up any minute.

"He got arrested—something with one of his businesses, like a Ponzi-type scheme he was running..." I shake my head, still not completely sure what exactly happened. "I had no idea until the Feds showed up to search my apartment. He wasn't a citizen, so they deported him."

"Sounds like he deserved it."

"I offered to marry him, to keep him from getting deported." Tears fill my eyes as I think about how pathetic I was to lay my life down for the likes of someone like Victor. "He wouldn't even take me up on it. I wasn't even enough to keep a crook like him—"

Grayson's chair scrapes backward, and he's on his feet. He rounds the table with intentional strides until he's standing in front of me. He shifts my chair so I'm facing him, then he bends in front of me. "Trina," he says, his voice deathly serious but his eyes soft as the glowing twilight behind him. "I'm sorry that Victor was such a tool he didn't know what he had. But no man should define you, no man should make you feel like you're enough or not enough." He cups my face in his hand, running his thumb across my cheekbone. "You *are* enough, not because someone makes you feel that way, but because of your inherent worth as a human being." He sighs, dropping his hand so that it falls into my lap. "I know that doesn't fix anything or make what you feel disappear...but you have to know that the problem is with *Victor*, not with *you*."

"It's not just Victor, though. My whole life is a montage of being worthless."

There's fire in Grayson's eyes when he pulls me out of my seat, wrapping me in his arms. "Not anymore," he says. "That ends today." Then he kisses me like I really am worth something.

After dinner and a dessert of key lime pie, Grayson and I lean on the railing of his boat, watching as the stars start to come out, covering the night sky in tiny pinpricks of light. "I can't do anything like this for you," I tell him.

"Hmm." He nuzzles into my neck, kissing along my collarbone—a favorite spot for him. "Well, that's where you're wrong."

I lean back so I can see his face. "What could I possibly do for you that's anywhere close to this?"

"You could do this," he says, leaning forward to kiss me.

I laugh, catching his face in my hands, kissing him back. "In what world is me kissing you on par with a yacht ride?"

He smiles, rubbing his nose against mine. "In my world, Trina."

59

Double Trouble

Mila

As much as I've been rooting for Trina and Grayson, it's still surreal to be on a double date with them. It's a Friday evening and we're heading to Konro, a fancy Japanese restaurant in Palm Beach. When Trina told me we'd be at the chef's table, I didn't realize there was only one table at Konro—it's more of a U-shaped bar top—with the chef himself serving us. There are only eight of us at the table for ten, with Trina, Grayson, Alex, and me taking up one side of the table. On the menu are twelve courses tonight—*twelve*—with the chef's sommelier wife overseeing the wine pairings.

I've never seen Trina looking so beautiful and free—there's a glow about her I've never seen before. And the way that Grayson handles her, with gentle touches and adoring looks, makes me giddy. Alex, too, has been smiling the whole time.

Everything is going so well until none other than Eva Rutherford waltzes into the restaurant alongside her boyfriend Pierre, twenty minutes after the start time of our seating. I feel Trina tense beside me.

"Look who it is," Eva calls from the other side of the table, as if we're her long-lost friends. We give a polite wave, but Eva insists on practically shouting to us across the restaurant. "I saw that you two made the long list as well. Congratulations!" She holds up a wine glass in a *cheers*. "Maybe we'll be teammates."

Trina mutters something under her breath that sounds like *Let's hope not*. And unfortunately I share her sentiment. Eva is just...a lot. Even I feel like I'm being judged around her, though she's technically only been polite to me.

When Eva continues to try to talk to us, despite the chef's obviously annoyed looks, Alex leans in and says, "I volunteer as tribute." He stands from his chair, stretching. "Come rescue me with the next course."

I kiss his cheek. "Thanks, babe."

Trina visibly relaxes once Eva's attentions are turned away from her. I go to reassure her when I notice that Grayson's arm is around her, and I smile, happy Trina's got another person looking out for her.

On our way home, Alex and I are listening to music in the car. "Thanks for saving us from Eva during dinner," I tell him. "It looks like you and Pierre get along well."

"Apparently he's been into making music lately too. We're going to get together next week to work on some stuff."

I raise my brows. "Keeping enemies close, huh?"

Alex scoffs. "Pierre's not the enemy—and honestly, Eva isn't either. Just because she's got mean girl vibes doesn't mean she's Trina's enemy."

"Just make sure you know whose side you're on, Mr. Caballero," I chide.

60

Quoi?

Trina

June Baldwin's in-depth article about Keenan Wilder's bribery and coercion finally comes out the day before we leave for France. Grayson reads it aloud to me as I pace around my office. It turns out, Keenan was deeply in debt. June uncovered all kinds of hidden tidbits about the USEF Olympic committee member—he was originally thrown into debt after a bulging disc surgery went wrong that cost him tens of thousands in extra medical bills, then went through a messy divorce that cleaned out whatever was left. You almost start to feel bad for the guy until June reveals that he's a chronic gambler, and—oh yeah—he bribed lots of people to get their names thrown into the ring for the Olympic team. And not just this year either. Apparently Keenan Wilder has been at this game for quite a while.

I'll hand it to June, she certainly did her job. She's thorough and precise while maintaining the journalistic distance that shows her integrity. She recounts the way Grayson came forward and baited Keenan, without using any names. Both of us are kept anonymous, which was the deal in the first place, but I'm still relieved she followed through with it.

After reading the article and discussing it, we call Mila and Alex and recount it with them, since they've been anxiously waiting as well. Then, we decide to turn off our phones and watch a movie at Grayson's. DeDe is with her mom for the week so it's just the two of us at his home. We leave tomorrow for the Saut Hermès in France, and we've had enough drama for one day, between the article coming out and getting Leo ready for his international flight. He left today with Luna, upon Grayson's insistence that I should rest up before my own international flight.

So we snuggle up on Grayson's couch and watch *The Horse Whisperer*. "Would you like me more if I wore a cowboy hat?" Grayson asks with a cheeky smile when Robert Redford comes on the screen.

What I want to say is, *If I liked you even an ounce more, we wouldn't be able to call it 'like' anymore.* "I like you plenty without a cowboy hat," I tell him instead.

"Okay, but like, what about every once in a while? Special occasions? That wouldn't make you—what's the word they use these days—*swoon*?"

I laugh, snuggling deeper into him as we talk. "You want to know what makes me swoon?" I say, feeling suddenly very vulnerable with him. It's crazy what a person will say when their walls are falling.

"I'm dying to know."

"When your hair falls in your eyes." I run my fingers through his hair. "When you show up at the barn with your boots and jeans. When you're sweaty after working all day."

"So what you're saying, Miss Powers," he says, pulling me into his lap. "Is that you're swooning over me every day?"

I laugh, nuzzling against him. "Pretty much."

"You're a blessed woman, then," he jokes.

"Yes, I am," I reply, without one ounce of humor.

SOAR

Bridle Buzz ✓ · Follow
Wellington, FL

523 likes

Bridle Buzz Grayson Sterling was spotted in a mysterious meeting with USEF Olympic committee member, Keenan Wilder, in November. A source says that the two men shook hands and exchanged a briefcase. which likely contained a lot of cash, according to our insider. Could Mr. Sterling be trying to pay for a spot on the Olympic team for his rider and apparent new mistress, Trina Powers?? Wilder's misdeeds were recently uncovered in the Miami Herald, but who knew Sterling and Powers were involved in it too?! It's clear both Powers and Sterling have met with Keenan on multiple occasions. Hmm…what do you think? Innocent or guilty?? …
more

View all 16 comments

Lauren Morton She's always acted too good for everyone. Glad she's finally getting her due.
Victory Equestrian Center Guilty. 💯 💯

 Add a comment…

3 hours ago

61

Everything is Not Okay

Trina

I fall asleep on Grayson's couch, and sometime in the night he carries me to his guest bed like the gentleman that he is. I wake the next morning in a panic. I slept way later than I ever have, and I still have to pack for France. I gather my things and race out the door, leaving Grayson with a quick kiss and hurried goodbye.

A couple hours later, when Grayson picks me up at my apartment, I realize I haven't checked my phone since last night. As we drive to the airport, I'm scrolling through my notifications. I have missed calls and dozens of texts from almost everyone I know, including my parents.

Tripp: *Just calling to check in with you. Everything OK?*

Mom: *Please tell me you're not involved in this funny business with the USEF crook.*

Mila: *Call me when you can. Don't check IG.*

A couple other trainers and riders that I know have texted me things like, *Is it true??* and *I know you're not in with this Keenan guy.*

"Oh no," I say as I connect the dots about why everyone is texting me.

"What is it?" Grayson asks.

I open my Instagram account and head to the latest Bridle Buzz post. There's a picture of Grayson and Keenan meeting in the park. Another shot shows Keenan opening Grayson's briefcase, clearly counting bills. There's another two pictures of Grayson and me—one at a horse show, and then another of us at Konro, cozied up together. Two more photos show me with Keenan—one photo is at the International Arena at Wellington International and then another at what looks like a coffee shop.

Except, I've never met with Keenan in my life. The photos are clearly photoshopped, but who would want to frame me? That's a lot of hoops to jump through just to point the finger at me.

At a red light, I hand Grayson the phone, letting him read the caption: *Grayson Sterling was spotted in a mysterious meeting with USEF Olympic committee member, Keenan Wilder, in November. A source says that the two men shook hands and exchanged a briefcase. which likely contained a lot of cash, according to our insider. Could Mr. Sterling be trying to pay for a spot on the Olympic team for his rider and apparent new mistress, Trina Powers?? Wilder's misdeeds were recently uncovered in the Miami Herald, but who knew Sterling and Powers were involved in it too?! It's clear both Powers and Sterling have met with Keenan on multiple occasions. Hmm...what do you think? Innocent or guilty??*

"Mistress?" I scoff. "You're not even married, I can't be your mistress."

"That's what you're concerned about with this?" Grayson says, eyebrows raised.

"No, of course not. I've got my entire family texting me, thinking I'm involved in some sort of scheme." I take my phone from Grayson, wanting to chuck it out the window.

People's comments are scathing—they think Grayson and I are really involved in this mess, and they are not being gracious about it.

When I think this can't get any worse, I get an email from USEF. I re-read it several times before it computes what they're saying. Even with my Open-Dyslexia extension to make reading easier on my phone, the words jumble and become useless the first few times I attempt to read the email. "They're suspending me," I say.

"Who?"

"USEF." I hand him my phone so he can read the email himself. "They're suspending me while they conduct an investigation into these allegations with Keenan Wilder."

"We'll find a way to fix this, Trina," Grayson says calmly, as if this didn't just detonate all my social capital, ever.

"That's easy for you to say, Grayson."

"What's that supposed to mean?" Grayson eyes me as we pull into the parking garage at the airport, looking for a spot.

"It means you can move on from this, you have a whole life and reputation outside of the horse world. Your closest friends and family don't know or care about this, you're above all this."

"Hey, I'm the one in the pictures—"

"But I'm the one who's going to be ruined by this."

"I'm not going to let this ruin you, Trina. We'll fix it." Grayson pulls into an empty spot, throwing the truck into park.

"There shouldn't be anything to fix! If you'd kept your word, I wouldn't be in this situation in the first place."

Grayson shifts his body toward me, his eyes wild with anger. He takes a deep breath, closes his eyes, and then opens them, saying, "I'm going to give you a minute to calm down while I get our bags out."

Then he gets out of the truck, making me feel like a child who just got chastened by the last person who was on my side.

Grayson and I go through security in a tense silence. I haven't apologized to him, though I know I probably should. It's not really Grayson's fault that I'm getting raked over the coals by the entire show jumping community. It wouldn't have happened if he hadn't reported Keenan, but Grayson protected me the best he could. It wasn't good enough, but he tried.

And he's probably right, that this can be rectified to some extent—June will vouch for us, but to what measure will our reputations be salvaged? I'm just not sure. There might always be a group of people who will think we're guilty, like McClain Ward with the horse murders scandal.

Once we're near our gate with plenty of time to board, Grayson pulls me into the first-class lounge. "Can we talk?"

I exhale deeply, nodding.

"I know you're freaked out by this, but can we be on the same side?" He runs his hands down my arms, taking my hands in his. "We're in this together."

"I know." I shake my head. "I'm sorry, I am freaked out. But I shouldn't take that out on you."

"We'll figure this out, okay?"

I nod, letting Grayson pull me into a hug. I try to let him comfort me, but it feels like nothing will be okay until this is fixed.

62

Nausea

Mila

Alex, Chance, and I are on our way to Paris. I know, it's a tiny bit ridiculous that we're bringing our dog with us all the way to France—we certainly had to jump through a few thousand hoops to make it happen—but the little Jack Russell has wormed his way into our hearts and refuses to give us any relief from the adoration we're compelled to pile on him.

But as we're driving to the airport in Luke's fancy truck with Anya in the passenger seat, I can't help the nausea that's welling within me. "I need to throw up," I say.

"Pull over, Luke, she means business," Anya says.

Luke pulls over on the side of Weston Road and I throw myself out of the door and empty the contents of my stomach on the grass. When I'm done, Alex offers me water and helps me back into the truck. "I've never seen you get nervous this early before a horse show," he says.

"Maybe because it's international?" Luke offers.

"It's probably just all this stuff with Trina stressing me out."

They all nod, and we drive quietly to the airport. Well, as quietly as we can with Chance running between us all, licking us to death.

When we get to the airport, the guys hop out of the truck—or, in Luke's case, rolls down the specialized ramp—Anya turns around, reaching a hand out to me. "Hey, *sestra?*"

"Yeah?"

"There are other reasons for nausea, you know."

"I don't feel sick."

"That's not what I'm talking about."

"Oh." I glance over at the airport employee who's telling cars to keep moving in the drop-off zone.

"Just, you know," Anya says, her blue eyes piercing right through me. "Think about it before you compete."

She squeezes my hand and I get out of the truck, my stomach roiling with more than just nausea.

63

Boulevard of Broken Dreams

Trina

After a long flight where Grayson dozed most of the time while I seethed, we're finally in Paris. I'm hesitant to check my notifications after the morning we had, but when I see a text from Luna that says to call her immediately, my heart drops. We're standing up, waiting to deboard the plane as I call her with shaking hands. What else could go wrong?

"Trina?" Luna's voice is tense, and my heart drops.

"What's wrong?"

Grayson turns from in front of me, his brows furrowed in concern.

"It's Leo. He had an accident getting off the plane."

I close my eyes, wishing this were a nightmare I could wake up from. "Is he okay?"

"He can't walk. The vet is with him now, but it looks like he has a sprain in his right hock and a deep laceration in his gaskin. They're stitching him up now but he lost a lot of blood."

"Oh my gosh," I say. Grayson takes my hand, squeezing it as he pulls me forward off the plane. He knows something is wrong. We pass the cockpit and head up the ramp toward the airport.

"Trina, I hate to be the one to tell you this, but they don't think he'll be able to compete for at least a couple months. I'm so sorry."

"Okay...I've got to go. Keep me updated."

I hang up with Luna and put my phone in my bag. Grayson guides me through the airport, and he seems to get that I'm not ready to talk about the phone call with Luna. In silence, we go through immigration, then collect our baggage and clear customs. With every step, I feel like my life is unraveling more and more. Like by the time we make it to our hotel, I'll just be an unspooled thread, barren and useless.

We're waiting just inside the doors of the airport for a car service when Grayson finally turns to me. "Do you want to tell me what happened?"

"Leo got hurt getting off the plane. He won't be able to compete."

Grayson pulls me against his chest. "I'm so sorry," he says, but I'm stiff as a board. I don't want his comfort right now. I want someone to blame, a place to put my anger.

"You should be," I say, pressing against his chest.

He rears back. "What's that supposed to mean?"

"It means, if you hadn't pushed us to travel internationally, this wouldn't have happened!"

"You act like I forced you into this." He holds out his hands.

"You've been pushy every step of the way, Dr. Sterling," I say, tone dripping with disdain. I know that a long, sleepless flight and all of the trauma of the day has me not thinking clearly, but I don't even care right now. I'm angry, and I need to let it out.

"Unbelievable." Grayson shoves his hands through his hair. He turns away from me, and for a moment I think he's going to walk away. But then he pivots so that he's right in my face. "You know what I think? You *want* this to be my fault."

I scoff. "Why would I want that?"

"Because you're scared. Too scared to fall in love because you let Victor mess up your heart."

"I didn't *let* him—"

"Yes you did, Trina. Don't lie to yourself about that, you're too good for that. *You* decide if a person gets to ruin you or not. You can't control anyone else's actions except for your own. Victor was a jerk, but you've allowed yourself to be a victim. That's not like the Trina I know to allow herself to be a victim."

Tears threaten to fall, and I suck in a breath. "Well, maybe you don't know me that well after all."

"You and I both know that's not true." His eyes are so dark with anger, they might as well be black. I've never seen him like this before. "So stop trying to make me out to be Victor. I'm not him, but you're too injured to accept that."

I step back, his words like a slap to my face. "Maybe you're right," I choke out before the tears take over. "I *am* too injured for the mighty Grayson Sterling, who could walk away from his eight-year marriage without so much as a chip on his shoulder."

I turn on my heel and hurry away from Grayson as the tears finally come, blurring my vision as I slip through the airport crowds.

I hopped on a shuttle that said 'Paris—Opera' and paid with my credit card. An hour later, I've ridden the shuttle until it looped back to the airport and then returned to Paris—Opera, wherever that is. There's no other way to put this: I'm sulking. I watch Paris fly by the window, not really seeing anything except my dreams go up in flames. I finally decide to get off the shuttle at a stop that doesn't look like I'm going to get trafficked. I collapse onto a bench, setting my purse down beside me as I cradle my head in my hands.

I have been royally screwed, but also, I royally screwed up.

Grayson's words may have been harsh, but I think he's right: I allowed Victor to mess up my heart. I allowed my heart to not heal. And it's my lack of trust that has led me to this point: where I'm looking for something to be Grayson's fault, so I can be proven right, instead of falling into the terrifying black hole that love is.

After Victor, I covered my heart in scar tissue so that no one could worm their way through ever again. But now that I have the choice of entrusting my heart with someone, I'm looking for a way out. Because it's scary to make that jump, to allow myself to fall in love. I want my heart to soar, to be completely free, but it can't unless I let go of my old hurts and bruises.

When I finally glance up, ready to catch a cab—if not completely resolved about my next move—I reach for my purse. And it's not there.

I jump up, looking under and behind the bench, then down the sidewalk to see if I can find anyone sprinting away with my purse. But it's nowhere to be found.

I rake my hands through my hair, groaning. "Oh my gosh." My heart begins to stutter, panic closing in as I realize I'm in a strange city, where I don't speak the language, without a phone, a wallet, or any form of identification. "Oh my gosh."

I'm walking around Paris at night, alone, purse stolen, horse injured, suspended from competing, possibly ruined things with my boyfriend, and all I can think about is that I'm an idiot.

I've pushed against Grayson, not wanting him to distract me from my goal, but when all that I've worked for is ripped away, what do I have left? Because that's the thing: horses get injured, purses get stolen, bodies get broken. But like Grayson said, *I* get to decide. I get to decide how I face this: if I'll face those hardships alone, or with someone by my side. If I'll handle this as a victim or as a warrior. Wounded or resilient.

I mean, sure, Grayson could leave me and screw me over just like Victor did—but Alex was right, love is an act of faith. Faith that the other person will keep loving you, keep sticking with you, all the way till the end. And it's my choice whether I'll have faith or not.

If you'd asked me if I'd have faith in love six months ago or a year ago, I would've laughed in your face. But today, despite everything that's happened...I choose faith. I choose love.

First things first: I need to apologize to Grayson.

If only I can find a way to the hotel.

64

Mila in Paris

Mila

When Trina took off at the airport, Alex and I convinced Grayson she'd be okay—she's an adult, she can take care of herself. But now that it's been a couple hours and we haven't heard from her, we're all starting to get a little worried. While we wait for word from Trina, we're trying to figure out how to fix the USEF suspension problem.

"Who has a vendetta against Trina? Who would want to do this to her?" Grayson asks, pacing around his hotel suite. He obviously has the nicest suite in the hotel—with amazing views of Paris out of every window, multiple bedrooms and bathrooms, an ample sitting room with a fruit, meat, and cheese board and champagne on ice waiting when we got here. It's more like an apartment than a hotel room. Alex and I are sitting on one of the couches, picking at the charcuterie board. Chance—the lucky dog—is curled between us, getting bits of cheese and meat from us.

Alex and I make eye contact. "What about Amber?"

"Who's that?" Grayson asks.

Alex gives a slight nod. "A couple years ago, she accused Alex of poisoning the horses at Zen. He got arrested and got into trouble with ICE. Turns out she was just being vindictive, so Trina kicked her out of the barn. I haven't seen her since then, though."

"Can we look her up?" Grayson asks. We all pull out our phones to search for her. Turns out she's blocked both Alex and me on Instagram, but Grayson is able to see her profile. "Looks like she lives in Virginia now."

"Hmm. I think whoever is behind Bridle Buzz has to be a Wellington local, they have too much insider info."

"Good point."

Grayson continues his pacing while Alex and I settle on his couch, scrolling our feeds for leads. "Hey, what about that guy, Louis? Trina sold him that Ammy Owner mare who ended up lame a month later. He was pissed at her and told everyone within a thirty-mile radius about it, even though it wasn't her fault." Alex says.

"Huh, I didn't know about that. Must've been before my time."

Alex's dark brows knit together as he thinks. "Hm, maybe that's too long ago to be relevant. It's been maybe six, seven years then?"

"Surely the statute of limitations on that guy's anger has run out by now," Grayson says. "Besides, I get the sense that this Bridle Buzz person is a woman."

I nod. "That feels accurate." I keep scrolling until I come across a post from Eva Rutherford—a shot of her beside one of her horses modeling a pair of Vogel boots. "Hey, what about Eva?" I tilt the phone toward Alex, showing him the photo, which just so happened to be posted a few minutes after the Bridle Buzz post this morning.

"Not this again, babe."

"She really doesn't like Trina, though."

"Can I see?" Grayson leans over the couch looking at the phone. "Oh yeah, that lady really doesn't like Trina."

I give Alex a raised brow look that says, *See?*

"Okay, but just to play devil's advocate: what has ever happened between her and Trina to precipitate her faking photos of Trina and throwing her under the bus like this?"

"Wasn't that the lady at Konro? She could've been the one to take that picture of us that's on Bridle Buzz."

"You're right! She was there and the picture is at the perfect angle from where she was sitting." I snap my fingers. "Wait a minute. I might be on to something. Can you pull out the photo of Trina on Bridle Buzz with Wilder?" I smack Alex's leg repeatedly to hurry him up.

"Okay, okay, one sec." When he finds the picture, I hold up the photo of Eva beside Alex's phone.

"See the boots?" I point at Eva's boots on her account and then at the boots in the fake picture of Trina. "Those are custom made Vogel boots. Trina doesn't own those. But, apparently, Eva does." I zoom in on the rose gold spur rests on Eva's boots, then the same color spur rests on the fake Trina shot. "How many people in the *world* have rose gold spur rests? I mean, come on."

"Wow." Grayson scratches his day-old scruff.

"So, what now?" Alex says. "I believe Eva is behind Bridle Buzz, but how do we clear Trina's name?"

"I think first," Grayson says. "We need to find Trina." He glances down at his watch, then at us, concern etching over his features. "It's been almost two hours since I last saw her at the airport. I know she's a grown woman and can take care of herself, but also, we're in a foreign city..." he trails off, clearly unable to put words to his worst nightmare.

We all take turns calling and texting Trina, but after another fifteen minutes, we still haven't heard from her.

"What if Mila and I head back toward the airport? We can drive around that area and see if we spot her."

Grayson nods. "I'll post up in the lobby and will call the minute she gets here. I'm also going to give June Baldwin a call. She can help us."

As we leave, Alex says, "We'll find her, man. It's going to work out." Then he gives Grayson one of those bro-hugs that I always tease him about, but as he pats Grayson's back, my heart squeezes. Grayson looks haggard, drenched in sadness. Even Chance licks the air in Grayson's direction, like he knows Grayson needs love. And seeing Alex—and our sweet dog— comfort him, even a little, makes me grateful for my husband.

We leave the hotel, but vindicating Trina's name seems like a far easier task than locating her in the massive city of Paris.

65

Warrior

Trina

By some Parisian miracle, I find a cab driver who kind of, sort of speaks English. "Purse stolen," I say as I mime to him, gesturing to where my purse should be, and then thumbing behind me, like it's gone. "My boyfriend is very rich," at least, I hope he's still my boyfriend, "he'll pay you for helping me."

"Call boyfriend," he says. "Evidence." He hands me his cell phone, but I don't know Grayson's number by heart. The only phone number I do have memorized is my brother's, so I dial him.

"Dr. Powers," he answers.

"Tripp! Thank God you picked up."

"Trina? Are you okay? I've been reading all kinds—"

"Yes, I'm okay, I'll explain later but right now I'm in Paris and my purse got stolen. I have a cab driver willing to take me to our hotel, but he needs proof that my very rich boyfriend will pay him *very well* once he brings me to the hotel."

"Okay," he says dragging out the word. "Do you need me to—"

"Tripp," I say, my voice syrupy sweet. "My darling *boyfriend,* can you meet me outside the hotel in twenty minutes to pay for the cab?"

"Ah, yes, right." He clears his throat. "Sure thing, *sweetheart.*"

The cabbie leans into the phone speaker. "You pay cab fee? And time for phone?"

"Yes, of course, anything for my sugarcakes. I am very rich, so rich you can't believe it."

I roll my eyes, but the cabbie seems convinced because he gestures for me to get in the cab.

"Thanks, Tripp." I drop my voice a little, leaning into the corner of the backseat. "Can you call Dr. Sterling to let him know about our arrangement? He, uh, won't be happy."

"Okay, but why—"

"Thanks, baby, see you soon." I hang up on my brother and hope against all hope that Grayson doesn't kick me to the curb once we get to the hotel.

When we pull up to the hotel, Grayson's waiting outside. He opens my cab door, and pulls me out, crushing me against his body. "Thank God you're okay." He runs his hands over my hair, then leans back to inspect my face, as if he can't believe it's really me. "We've been so worried about you." He squeezes me against his chest again and I sag with relief into his body.

"Hey, rich boyfriend," the cabbie calls from the window. "You pay now?"

Keeping an arm around me, Grayson reaches into his wallet and throws a couple bills at the cabbie who exclaims: "*Very* rich, very good!"

I laugh through tears, as I wave thanks to the man. Grayson leads me into the hotel, but as soon as we're in the lobby, I stop him. "I just want to say something before we get too far. I'm sorry, Grayson. You were right, about everything. I've been—"

"No, I'm sorry, I was needlessly harsh with you. I'm hurting too, Trina. But that doesn't mean—"

I shake my head. "No, I don't think so. You were right on. I've allowed myself to be a victim, but not anymore. I've decided, well, that I'm going to be..." My face heats with embarrassment as I think about what it is I want to say. But saying it out loud all of a sudden seems almost silly.

"What is it?" Grayson asks, cupping my cheek with his palm. "You can tell me."

His eyes are soft and welcoming, but even with his encouragement, I gaze at the ground when I mumble, "I'mgonnabeawarrior."

Grayson leans in closer. "What's that?"

I take a deep breath, facing Grayson. "I'm going to be a warrior." I still whisper it, just a little clearer this time.

Grayson smiles his heartbreaking smile, which quickly turns coy when he says, "A little louder for the people in the back?"

"I'm going to be a warrior," I say firmly this time.

"You *are* a warrior, Trina."

And the way he says it, I believe it. "I am a warrior."

He tilts his head back, calling out through the lobby, "She's a warrior!"

I laugh, cheeks heating with embarrassment, but it doesn't stop me from cupping my hands around my mouth, and shout: "I'm a warrior!"

"Yes you are," Grayson cheers.

"Sir? Ma'am?" the front desk clerk raises an eyebrow at us.

"Sorry," Grayson says. Then, he gestures at me, still tucked under his arm. "She's going to the Olympics."

This seems to mollify the clerk, and as we turn toward the elevators I feel the need to remind Grayson of how far we are from that. "You do remember—"

Grayson silences me with a finger to my lips. "What are you?"

"A warrior."

"That's right." He takes my hand, lacing his fingers through mine. "Now let's go fight for this."

66

We Need a Resolution

Mila

After driving around Paris for an hour, we get the call that Trina made it to the hotel. We head back to Grayson's super fancy suite, with an incredible view of the Eiffel Tower lit up in all its glory at night. When we get there, Alex and I pull Trina into a chest-crushing hug while Grayson orders us some food.

"We're glad you're okay," Alex says.

"Oh, you know, it's a favorite pastime of mine," Trina says. "Pouting around Paris."

"Sounds like the name of a bad emo cover band, Pouting Around Paris," Grayson says.

"Speaking of emo cover bands," Alex says. "I'm going to call Pierre."

"Pierre, as in, Eva's boyfriend?" Trina asks.

"Yeah, Pierre and Alex are BFFs," I say with a teasing eyeroll.

Alex grimaces, and I know he feels guilty—like by being friends with Pierre, he somehow betrayed Trina. "We make music."

Trina and Grayson gape at Alex. "I'm sorry, you do what now?" Trina says.

"Is that a euphemism? Something you need to tell us, Alex?" Grayson teases, with a wink in my direction.

Alex reddens adorably and tries to backtrack. "No, I mean, we lay down beats."

Trina covers her mouth with her hand, giggling. Grayson's gray eyes are dancing with humor.

"Babe, not helping," I tell him. "Pierre and Alex do this techno-music thing—you know what? That *is* a hard thing to explain in a way that doesn't sound...you know..." I shrug apologetically.

"We get what you're saying," Trina says. "Just giving you a hard time, Alex."

"I'm just going to go now," Alex says. "I'll let you know what Pierre says."

While Alex is on the phone with Pierre, and Trina and Grayson get a call back from June Baldwin, I head downstairs to the little convenience store to see if they have anything for nausea. As I search the aisles, I come across something that reminds me of my conversation with Anya earlier today. So much has happened, I'd forgotten all about it.

"Well, what the heck," I say as I pick up the item and head to the cash register.

When we all gather back in Grayson's suite, both Alex and Grayson have updates. "June will provide an affidavit to USEF explaining our involvement with bringing down Keenan Wilder," Grayson says.

"Pierre was genuinely disturbed by the way Eva's gone about all of this, I'm not sure he'll help us, but I'll follow up with him in a couple days. I think he'd at least be willing to tell someone at USEF that those pictures aren't of Trina."

"Thank you, Alex," Trina says, pulling Alex into a hug. "I'm grateful for you all. Even if nothing gets fixed, I've hit the jackpot with the three of you."

Grayson wraps his arms around Trina, pressing a kiss to the top of her head. "We'll get it fixed, Trina. We're fighting this to the end."

I throw my arms around Grayson and Trina, tugging Alex and Chance with me. Chance grunts, wiggling his little body to get more space. Trina laughs tearfully, and just when I think she's going to push us all away, her hands reach out and pull us closer.

That night, as I climb into bed with Alex, he opens his arms to me. I snuggle into him, settling my head against his chest to listen to the steady beating of his heart. Of all the music Alex has created this year, this beat is my favorite sound.

Chance, of course, has to squirrel his way in between us. Alex laughs, kisses my head, then pulls Chance up to kiss him too. "I love my little family."

I prop myself up on an elbow. "I love our little family too." I smile down at him, tracing his cheekbone with my fingertips. "But there's one more kiss to give."

Alex leans in to kiss me again, and I let his lips brush against mine before saying, "I appreciate the extra kiss but...the one more kiss isn't for me."

He frowns, not understanding. Until I pull back the covers, stretching back to lift my pajama shirt to reveal my stomach. "One more kiss, right here," I say, patting my lower abdomen.

Alex's eyes follow the motion of my hand, then swing back up to my face, eyes wide. "*Qué*?" He reaches a tentative hand over my stomach, fingers splaying across my skin. "Are you serious?"

"*Si, mi amor.*"

Alex's eyes fill with tears as he lets out a little laugh of disbelief. Then, as if the news has really hit him, he pulls me against him, kissing me. His tears mingle with mine as we meld into each other. He trails kisses all across my belly, his tears soaking my skin. He's murmuring soft words in Spanish to my stomach and I smile. Chance army crawls up to my chest, and I pull him into my arms. "I think we lost him," I tell Chance. "He might never acknowledge us again."

Alex laughs, finally leaving the tiny child forming within me, to wrap his arms around Chance and me. "How can you love someone you've never even met before?" he asks, wiping tears from the corners of his eyes.

I cup his face in my palm. "I think it has something to do with loving the one who helped create them."

His hand skims over my hair, cupping the back of my neck. "Just when I thought I couldn't love you more, you go and do this," Alex says, kissing me.

I laugh, kissing him back. "Okay, but I'm pretty sure you did this to me," I tease.

"*We* did this," he says, tugging me against his chest. "Together."

The next morning, we all head to the barn where our horses are being kept. I check on Cyrus, feeling his legs for any inflammation then checking his water and feed to make sure he's been eating and drinking. Of course, Luna will have made sure he was doing well, but it feels right to check for myself too.

Trina's meeting with the vet to discuss Leo's leg, but when I find her in the tack stall with a tearstained face, I know the news isn't good. I pull her into a hug, knowing that there are no words that could make up for the crushing disappointment she's experiencing right now. "I'm so sorry, Trina."

She steps back, wiping her face with her sleeves. "What can you do? That's life. One step forward, two steps back."

"What did the vet say?"

She shrugs. "He's hopeful he'll fully heal, but we definitely won't be competing anytime soon. At least two, maybe three months to be on the safe side. We'll get a second opinion once we're back stateside but needless to say, this blows my Olympic dream."

"Well, I wanted to talk to you about that…"

Trina gives me a skeptical look, unsure how I could possibly rectify her situation at this point. "Okay?"

"I'm pregnant."

It takes Trina a moment to react, but once the news hits her, she wraps her arms around me. "Oh my gosh! Congratulations, Mila!"

"Thanks," I say with a queasy smile. All the jostling from the hugging is making me feel nauseous. "But I can't compete anymore."

"Oh." Trina's brows crease, like she didn't realize the repercussions of my pregnancy. "Dang."

"It's okay, truly." I place my hands on my belly, glancing down. I half-expected this morning to see a baby bump, but my stomach was just as flat as ever. "This is exactly what's supposed to happen." I look back up at Trina. "Besides, this means you have a horse to ride to the Olympics."

"Wait, what?" Shock flickers over Trina's brown eyes. "No, Mila, I can't—"

"That's the thing, Trina, you can. You've ridden Cy almost as much as me. And I can't ride him. If you don't compete with him, no one will. He'll just be the most amazing Grand Prix horse ever, sitting in a stall during the 2024 Olympics…" I raise my eyebrows and give her a pointed stare.

"Oh my gosh, who am I kidding, *of course* I'll ride Cyrus." She places her hands on either sides of her cheeks, a parentheses on either side of her brilliant smile. "Thank you, Mila."

I smile back at her, grateful I could give this gift to one of my dearest friends. "You deserve it, Trina."

67

Dance, Dance

Mila

When Trina rides Cyrus, it's as if she's coming home. If I thought Cyrus and I made a good team, Cyrus and Trina are like the married couple that's been together so long they can read each other's minds. You know the ones, where they can communicate with a brief look? Yeah, that's Trina and Cy. Maybe I should be jealous, but right now, I just feel amazed. And content.

I sit back in the stands at the Saut Hermes, watching my trainer and one of my dearest friends ride my horse. Since USEF doesn't have jurisdiction here in Europe, Trina can still ride and compete here. Alex is beside me, his hand on my stomach—I'm not sure it's left its spot there since I broke the news to him about my pregnancy. It's amazing how I can feel insanely productive just sitting here. I mean, my body is putting together another human. I could literally do nothing else for nine months and I would be far more productive than any other nonpregnant human around. It's a freeing feeling.

It also makes me realize that I really am enough just as I am—I don't have to be anything to be worthwhile, I can just be...me. That's enough for me. And it's enough for Alex, too.

As we watch Trina's round with Cyrus, it makes me think of a pas de deux—a pair of ballerinas floating through a routine together. Cyrus, lifting her over fence after fence. Trina balancing delicately atop his powerful body. The two of them in this beautiful dance, twining through not only time and space but cementing themselves as a work of art.

I look over at Alex, taking in his quiet yet proud smile as he gazes down at my still-flat belly. And then I glance back as Trina and Cyrus gallop through the timers, a perfect and clean round behind them, and it feels like this is exactly how it's supposed to be.

When Trina finishes her ride for the day and we're all back in Grayson's hotel suite, Alex is scrolling his phone when he says, "Have you looked at Instagram?"

Trina sighs. "I don't think I'm ever going on Instagram ever again."

"No, look." Alex hands her his phone. "Pierre whistle-blew on Eva."

We all huddle around Alex's phone, where Pierre's Instagram post details how Eva altered incriminating photos of herself to throw Trina under the bus and potentially save her own neck. He exposes her as the gossiper behind the Bridle Buzz account and claims that she paid Keenan Wilder for a spot on the Olympic team.

Various commenters are saying that they never believed Trina could be guilty. The internet is a fickle world.

"Wow," Trina says, exhaling loudly. She tilts her head back against the couch, gazing up at the ceiling. "That's pretty vindicating. I almost feel bad for Eva."

Grayson raises his eyebrows, and Trina says, "I said *almost*." After Grayson reads the post aloud, they pass the phone to me.

"Whoa," I say, scrolling the unedited picture of Eva with Keenan and then screenshots of conversations between Eva and Keenan about paying for a spot on the Olympic team. "Seems like he's got a bit of a chip on his shoulder, huh?"

"If the music he creates is any indication, things have been rough between him and Eva for a while," Alex says quietly. Knowing Alex, he'll be there to support Pierre through this. "He mentioned some things to me yesterday that were really...concerning." Leave it to my therapist husband to be discreet about whatever Pierre confided in him. But based on the way Pierre's blasting Eva in this post, it couldn't have been good. "I'm going to text him."

"You're a good man, *mi amor*," I say as I lean in to kiss him.

"Have I told you before how much I love it when you speak Spanish?" he murmurs against my lips.

Beside us Trina groans like we're grossing her out. Chance jumps into her lap at the sound, planting his feet on her chest to lick her face. We all laugh as Grayson says, "Aww, he thought you felt left out."

Grayson pulls Trina and Chance into his lap, wrapping his arms around them. "It's going to work out, Chevy," he says, planting a kiss on her head.

I try not to stare, because I've never seen Trina cuddling with a guy before—but the giddy girl inside of me is doing her happy dance because Trina is going to get her happily-ever-after after all.

68

Two Months Later

Trina

Between June Baldwin's affidavit and Pierre's public testimony against Eva, my USEF suspension was lifted while we were in France. Mila was right: Cyrus and I do make a great team. We swept the Saut Hermès like a force of nature, only to return to Wellington and storm the show world there.

The USEF Olympic selection committee did something unprecedented: they added us to the long list retrospectively. I mean, sure, we were both on the list before—just not together.

Tonight is when the committee will release their official selections for the 2024 Olympic team. Grayson, Mila, Alex, and I are all huddled around Grayson's computer at his dining table, refreshing the website obsessively as we wait for the release.

"Oh! Oh! There it is!" Mila shrieks, pointing at the screen, as if we're not all staring at it.

"I can't look," I say, covering my eyes with my hands. "Just read it to me."

"The 2024 Olympic team will consist of McLain Ward, Laura Kraut, Todd Minikus, and…Trina Powers."

"What!? What?!" I drop my hands to look at the screen, but I've been caught up in a crushing hug from all sides—Grayson, with his arms around my waist, Mila with her shoulder against my face, and Alex with his long arms capturing us all together. My arms are caught in front of me, unable to return the hug, so I just accept it.

"We did it, we did it," Mila starts chanting as Grayson jostles us back and forth in time with the chant. I'm laughing and crying, overwhelmed by the moment. Pure exhilaration washes over me, and I let it consume me.

I'm going to the Olympics.

I finally find a way to wiggle my arms free so I can wrap them around my friends and Grayson. We did it. And as much as I wanted to be a strong, independent woman making it to the top of my sport by myself, I never would've made it here without these three. They made it happen for me.

So, maybe Kelly Clarkson was on to something with "Miss Independent."

What *did* happen to Miss Independent?

Oh, she fell in love.

And it was the best thing that could've ever happened to her.

69

Epic-Logue - 3 years later

Mila

The early morning chill seeps through my jacket as I walk to the Center's barn. The scent of hay and shavings carries through the air—my favorite smell.

I smile as I reach the feed room, the horses whinnying low as they wait for their breakfast. Our barn manager, Matthew, is on vacation with his wife, my best friend Monica, so I'm feeding the horses today. I don't mind—being away from my two kids under two years old is essentially like being on a vacation myself. I left them curled up in Alex's arms in our bed. Try as we might, that's where they always seem to end up, along with Chance, who wouldn't deign to sleep in something as unseemly as a dog bed.

We're still in the Cottage, though we've expanded it since our firstborn, Diego—named after Alex's dad—was born. We debated finding a bigger house, moving off of the Center's grounds, but we belong here. This is our home, in more ways than one.

And, as an added benefit, Alex now has a soundproofed music studio in the new addition to our house.

Every day, I'm learning more and more to soak up the tiny moments, to be present in my life and enjoy whatever comes my way.

I still have goals of course. But I don't let those goals fill in the holes of my life anymore. They're more like the cherry on top.

After I feed the horses, I head back to the Cottage to wrangle my own brood. When I get inside, Alex is cooking eggs while our oldest plays with the pots and pans on the floor and our daughter, Liliya, sits in her highchair, playing with Cheerios. It's an absolute mess in our house—with Tupperware and cookware scattered across the kitchen. Below our daughter's highchair is a variety of food I don't recognize anymore and that Chance won't even eat. Under the table is a smattering of sensory play items from kinetic sand to rice dyed in multiple shades—an activity that took far too much prep and not enough payoff in my opinion.

It's funny that I used to think *I* was a mess. Our kids are way beyond that. Although, Alex might argue that it's a combination of me *and* our kids that's really disastrous. But he'd say it with love in his eyes...as he sweeps up the mess beneath the table.

I kiss Alex as he scrambles eggs—which makes Diego jealous. He quickly toddles over, hands raised for me to lift him up. I laugh, pulling him into my arms. *"Gordito,"* I call him as I kiss his chubby cheeks. The moment Lils sees me, she starts shrieking, her tiny hands making the sign for milk.

"I'm coming, I'm coming," I say as I attempt to put Diego down. He doesn't oblige me, so I pick up both kids and head to the couch, where I nurse Liliya as my little *gordito* attempts to rearrange my hair with his spit.

After I feed Lils, we all sit at the table to eat breakfast. Typically, Alex is an incredible chef—Michelin star level, at least in this kitchen. But today the eggs leave a bad taste in my mouth and I feel queasy as I push them around my plate. Everyone at the table devours theirs, but I can't find it in me to finish mine. Even my normal cream-with-coffee sits uncomfortably in my stomach.

An hour later, we get the kids in the car and I shuttle them to the Craig family compound. Mrs. Craig generously watches our kids while we work—she says it's a gift to her since she doesn't have her own grandkids (yet). The woman is a saint of the highest order, and she loves our kids as if they're her own.

Once she takes Diego and Liliya to swing in the backyard, I'm tempted to find a back bedroom and take a nap instead of heading back to the Center, but the horses are calling my name, and I must answer.

We're having our morning meeting in the tranquility garden—we used to have it in the lounge, but we've outgrown that. Even the garden is packed with our therapists, volunteers, and a full-time stable hand, along with Anya, Luke, Alex, and me.

Alex leads the group in a short meditation, reminding us of our purpose here. We all take a moment to get centered—pun totally intended—and then I run through the schedule for today. We have multiple support groups, individual counseling sessions, and a field trip from a school for children with autism. I assign our volunteers to various roles and then Anya gives her typical safety briefing. It's more like a safety grumping, but she takes her role as safety officer very seriously—as she should.

As the group disperses, Alex comes up behind me, his arms around my waist, his nose nuzzling my neck. I sink into his warmth, my hands on his.

"Can you two be professional for once in your life?" Anya teases.

"Hey, I don't have to share her here so I have to take advantage," Alex says, pressing kisses along my neck and into my hair. "The *ninos* own her the second she's home, but she's all mine here."

Anya rolls her eyes, but she's got a small smile on her porcelain face. "Just knock it off when the clients show up," she says.

Alex responds with, "Sure thing, boss," at the exact same time as I say, "You're not the boss of me." Mature, I know. But, what can I say? She's my sister.

When our first client of the day shows up, we're all business—much to Anya's relief, I'm sure.

Later that day, we gather around Mrs. Caballero's food truck, Mama C's. She serves lunch at the Center and occasionally heads to food truck rallies and other special events to rave reviews. I've ordered her arroz con grandules, but something about the scent of the meat is off today. We're sitting in the office, eating lunch with Luke and Anya. "Does this taste right to you?" I ask Alex, shoving a spoonful into his face. He takes a bite, closing his eyes.

"Tastes amazing," he says. But when I test out another bite, my mouth starts to water. And not in a I-can't-wait-to-taste-this way. Nope, this is a I'm-going-to-hurl mouthwatering. I toss the container onto my desk and run out of the office into the bathroom, heaving over the toilet.

When I get back, Luke and Anya are looking at me expectantly. Alex holds out his arms, and I curl into his lap. "Are you late?" he asks quietly.

"I have no idea," I confess. Who has time to track something as mundane as a period?

"She totally is," my sister says, as if *she* keeps track of my cycles. I press my face into Alex's neck, laughing pathetically through tears.

Yep, definitely pregnant.

After Alex and I have hugged, and I've leaked out all of my tears, I straighten up. "Three under three, that's...wow." Alex has a happy but dazed look on his face.

"You do know how this keeps happening, right?" Luke says with a wicked grin. "Or do we need a biology lesson?"

"You'd think after all these years you guys would figure out how it's done," Anya says with her signature eye roll.

Alex gives a sheepish grin, but I tell them, "I think we've figured it out just fine, thank you very much. Some might even say we've *mastered* the process." But then I'm running back to the bathroom, which really hurts my delivery, and my ribs. Throwing up is not for the faint of stomach.

Later that day, after the kids are down and Mrs. Caballero is settled in to watch the monitors, Alex and I head out for a wild night on the town—well, not exactly. Once a month, we meet up with Trina and Grayson, Luke and Anya, and when they're in town, Matthew and Monica, for something fun. We used to do things like go dancing or karaoke or go to concerts. Now we mostly meet up for a meal and sometimes, if we're not too tired, we'll play a board game. Tonight the six of us gather at Luke and Anya's home in the Craig family compound. We sit outside on the patio, twinkle lights strung overhead, as we eat dessert from Mrs. Craig's kitchen and play Settlers of Catan.

"How are you feeling?" I ask Trina, my hand going to her rapidly growing belly bump.

"I'm finally over the morning sickness, but now I'm just exhausted all of the time. Grayson's getting buff carrying me from the couch to the bed every night."

I laugh, my gaze finding Grayson, who's watching his wife with so much love and protection in his eyes. She hadn't planned to have kids—Trina was actually relieved that Grayson already had a daughter when they got married. But being with Grayson has softened Trina in so many ways, rounding her out to be the person she was always meant to be.

"They call it a geriatric pregnancy because I'm so old," Trina says with an eye roll. "I should be offended, but I'm just too tired to care."

"What matters," Anya says, with a touch of bitterness in her tone, "is that your *body* doesn't think you're too old."

"That's true," I say, steering the conversation away from pregnancy for my sister's sake. "These are amazing," I say, taking a bite of one of Mrs. Craig's elaborate sourdough pastries. Honestly, I'm just so relieved that something I ate today tastes good to my pregnant palate. "I don't understand how she can bake while she has the kids. I barely have the ability to form an independent thought when they're with me."

"I mean, she had five kids," Grayson says. "Two probably feels like a vacation."

"Your mom is impressive," I say to Luke.

"Yeah, but can she ride a Grand Prix horse?" Trina says, tilting her mug of tea at me as if to say, *Don't sell yourself short.*

"Get on a horse with a 'pancake saddle'?" Luke says. "Mama wouldn't be caught dead."

"We're well on our way to five," Alex says, with a twinkle in his dark eyes.

"Do you mind?" I ask as my hand finds his, our fingers twining together.

"Creating little replicas of the most beautiful person in my life? How could I mind that?"

"Well...they're messy."

Alex laughs. "I won't fight you on that point." He tugs me closer, kissing my temple. "But I'd rather my life be filled with all these beautiful messes than not. If I lived my life a thousand times, a thousand times I'd want to end up right here."

I kiss him then, in the middle of our friends, hoping to convey to him every ounce of love I have for this incredible man.

When Anya chides, "Get a room," I laugh, breaking free from our kiss. I glance around the patio at some of my favorite people in the world. People I've laughed with, cried with, competed with, and would easily jump in front of a bullet for. We've been through so much, and I know our journeys aren't over. It's just the beginning.

I hold my sister's gaze across the table—my strong, sweet, smart *sestra*. Whose life was crushed, and yet she came through like the fighter that she is. I'm so proud to live my life beside her, through the rise and fall and crazy turns that is our life.

I smile at Trina, thinking of how she's opened up and let her walls fall. She's soaring higher than she'd ever dreamed she would. All because of Grayson.

I glance around at the men in our life. Alex, Luke, Grayson. Good men, faithful men. Men who broke down our walls and mended our hearts. Who have loved us through our most unlovable moments, and somehow keep coming back for more.

...And they love our four-legged children as much as we do.

We are blessed.

In the years to come, Trina and Grayson will go on to have two kids, and Trina will compete in the Olympic games three more times, once with Leo. She will train several other Grand Prix show jumpers—including Demetria Sterling—and continue to become USA Show Jumping's Chef D'Equipe for many years. Grayson stayed true to his word and groomed for her—and DeDe—all the days of his long life.

After his Grand Prix days were over, Cyrus retired at the ViaTech Center for Equine-Assisted Therapy, where our clients fed him a steady supply of mints and groomed him until long after his dappled gray coat turned fleabitten.

As for me, I never did go to the Olympics—but all my dreams came true. Together, Alex and I built the ViaTech Center into a nationwide franchise, helping people all over the country to find hope and healing in these incredible animals. Alex went on to produce music for many, many up and coming indie artists, building a name for himself as someone who brings out the absolute best in each artists he works with.

Oh, and we surpassed the Craig family in their number of kids—six in total. Diego, Liliya, Joseph, Daniel, Sofia, and our final surprise baby born the summer after my sweet gray gelding passed: Cyrus.

And now, even though we're worn down and our joints are creaking with age, we still find a way to dance. Every now and then, Alex will find me in the kitchen—I'm still not there very often—or in the barn. He'll put on a song, place my hand in his, and we'll sway to the music that, for us, has never stopped playing.

And Anya and Luke? Well, that's their story to tell.

THE END

WANT MORE LUKE & ANYA?

Scan the QR code or go to the link below to sign up to be the first to find out about Luke & Anya's story.

http://tinyurl.com/TurnAnya

TRINA & GRAYSON BONUS SCENE

Scan the QR code or go to the link below to read about Trina and Grayson at the Olympics, plus an engagement.

http://tinyurl.com/TrinaGrayson

Author's Note

Wow. It's hard to believe this series is done. What a joy and privilege it's been to pen these books. When I first sat down to write JUMP, I didn't know if I had a horse book in me—I'd only written sci-fi prior to writing JUMP! I had one little idea for an inciting incident—something that had actually happened at WEF one year: an ICE raid. I had this vision of a girl "saving" a handsome groom with a kiss. And, well, the rest is history.

That story flew out of me like nothing else had before and I knew that this was the book I was meant to write. I didn't even intend to make it into a series, but these characters and stories were begging to be written! So much of this series is about characters who need to heal from their wounds, and in many ways I wrote this to myself. Because I needed (and still need) healing. We all do. And yet we're all still worthy of love. I hope that resonates with you, dear reader. You are loved and you are worthy of love—no matter how much life has beat you up.

A few practical notes: the path to being on the US Show Jumping Olympic team is very convoluted. It's hard to capture that in a book like this. I did my best, please forgive the rest.

It's estimated that 1 in 10 people have dyslexia though many are never formally diagnosed. I know that dyslexia is something that presents differently for each person and it won't always manifest like it did in Trina's case. I hope and pray that no one experiences the neglect that Trina experienced, but it's a reality. 62% of people who drop out of high school have difficulty reading. Many feel what Trina felt—unintelligent and inadequate. But the reality is that dyslexia is a form of neurodivergence that can be challenging yet it opens up a whole new way of thinking that neuronormative people can't experience. Some companies these days are seeking out individuals with dyslexia. Did you know Albert Einstein had dyslexia? Struggling to read is **not** a reflection of intelligence. If you, your child or someone you know has difficulty reading, get informed about dyslexia through the International Dyslexia Association at dyslexiaida.org.

My husband and I married very young (at the ripe age of 20), not too far off from Alex and Mila. I mined a few scenes from our own early days of marriage for this story. If any of you think that Mila was a hot mess in this book, I promise you that I was far worse as a young married woman! But God got me through and thankfully my wonderful husband loved me through it. (Don't worry, he had his own moments that I had to forgive him for, too!) We've been married almost fifteen years now and even though I adore writing these love stories, ours is still my favorite.

I absolutely love connecting with readers, so please reach out! You can find me on Instagram, Facebook and TikTok @tiffanynoellechacon. I have a Facebook reader group where I give updates, let you vote on things like character names and book cover designs, and post teasers and bonus content! Join here:

Acknowledgements

Thank you, God, for books, for horses, and for love.

To my husband, who sacrificed a lot of time, energy and sanity in order for this series to be written. Thank you. Thank you for believing in me even when I didn't believe in myself and for letting me borrow your faith in me. I thank God every day that he gave me you.

My boys, Finn and Justus, who bring me so much joy. I love you so much. Thank you for sharing me so I could write this series.

My parents have supported me in every way a daughter could be supported and I'm endlessly grateful. You guys make it difficult to write dysfunctional families (which I thankfully did less of in this book) because of how, well, functional you are. I love you both so much, 'individually and collectively' as Dad likes to say.

Endless thanks to both the Stearns and Chacon families. My in-laws, Jeff and Lisa, are parents to me in their own right. I'm grateful to go through life right beside you guys. (Literally *right beside*—they are my next door neighbors!) In order of importance (just kidding, in order of age): many thanks to Dorothy and Scotty, Joey and Philippa, Kyle and Amanda, Ryan and Andrea, and Daniel.

My brother, Daniel, is an incredible filmmaker and he created a book trailer for my first novel, JUMP, that is amazing. Thank you, thank you, thank you. Many thanks to Nora Pantoja and Gabriel Jose Bonilla who played Mila and Alex. Y'all are so talented and I'm blessed to have worked with you. (Also, if you haven't seen the trailer, check it out in the QR code below. And follow Daniel's filmmaking projects on Instagram @daniel.filmmaking. You won't regret it.)

Many, many thanks to Joyce Bloemker who edited this novel. I gave her the roughest draft I've ever given anybody, and she still managed to help it shine. (For the record, she would have deleted that comma in the middle of the last sentence!) She gave me many ideas for making this story the best it could be (including the idea of Mila cutting up her dad's credit card and adding more Monica into the story!) She endured many late night texts from me about the story (bet you regret giving me your phone number, don't you, Joyce?!) and encouraged me when I felt unsure about this book. Thank you, Joyce, for loving this story as if it were your own.

Many thanks to Tamara Shanaman for all your insight into working at an equine-assisted therapy center!

Kristi Carlo, my dear friend who has been so supportive, helped me make sure the specifics of Alex's licensure exam and internship were on point. Thank you, my friend!

Jesi Colston has been a wonderful friend who has supported me in multiple ways, including bringing copies of my books on vacation with her to put in little free libraries around the world!

Thanks to my friend Olivia who shared her experience with dyslexia with me.

I'm so grateful for everyone on my launch team who helped promote this book! You ladies are awesome. Special thanks to my social media team who made graphics and reels for the book!

Infinite thanks to Lauren, our babysitter, without whom this book would not have been written. I love and appreciate your enthusiasm for my boys.

To all of the bloggers, podcasters, bookstagrammers, BookTokers and others who helped spread the word about this series, thank you thank you thank you!! You are the lifeblood of this industry and I'm grateful for you.

To all who left reviews and spread the word about this series, you have no idea how much that means to me. You are helping my books to find their way into the hands and devices of its ideal readers. Thank you!!!

And thank you, dear reader, for continuing this journey with me and making this dream a reality. Before I wrote JUMP, I was disheartened and thought I might not write again. The fact that this book has turned into a series—all because people are actually reading it and loving it—is truly surreal for me. Thank you so much for your support and enthusiasm for these books.

VIEW THE JUMP TRAILER HERE:

Scan the QR code or go to
the link below to see the
JUMP trailer:

https://tinyurl.com/jumptrailer

About Tiffany

Tiffany was riding horses before she could walk. She's a five-time IAHA national champion and competed regularly at the Winter Equestrian Festival with her gentle giant, Obi-Wan. She received her Masters of Fine Arts in Creative Writing from the University of Tampa. Her writing is an outpouring of her love for horses, and her love for love. She lives in Tampa with her middle-school sweetheart and her two wild and crazy sons.